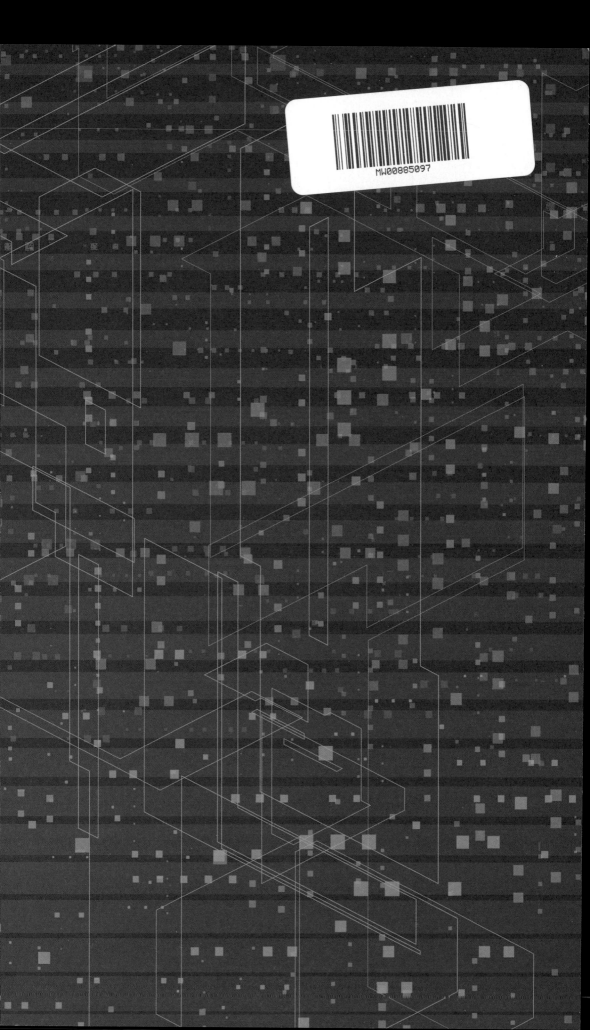
MW00885097

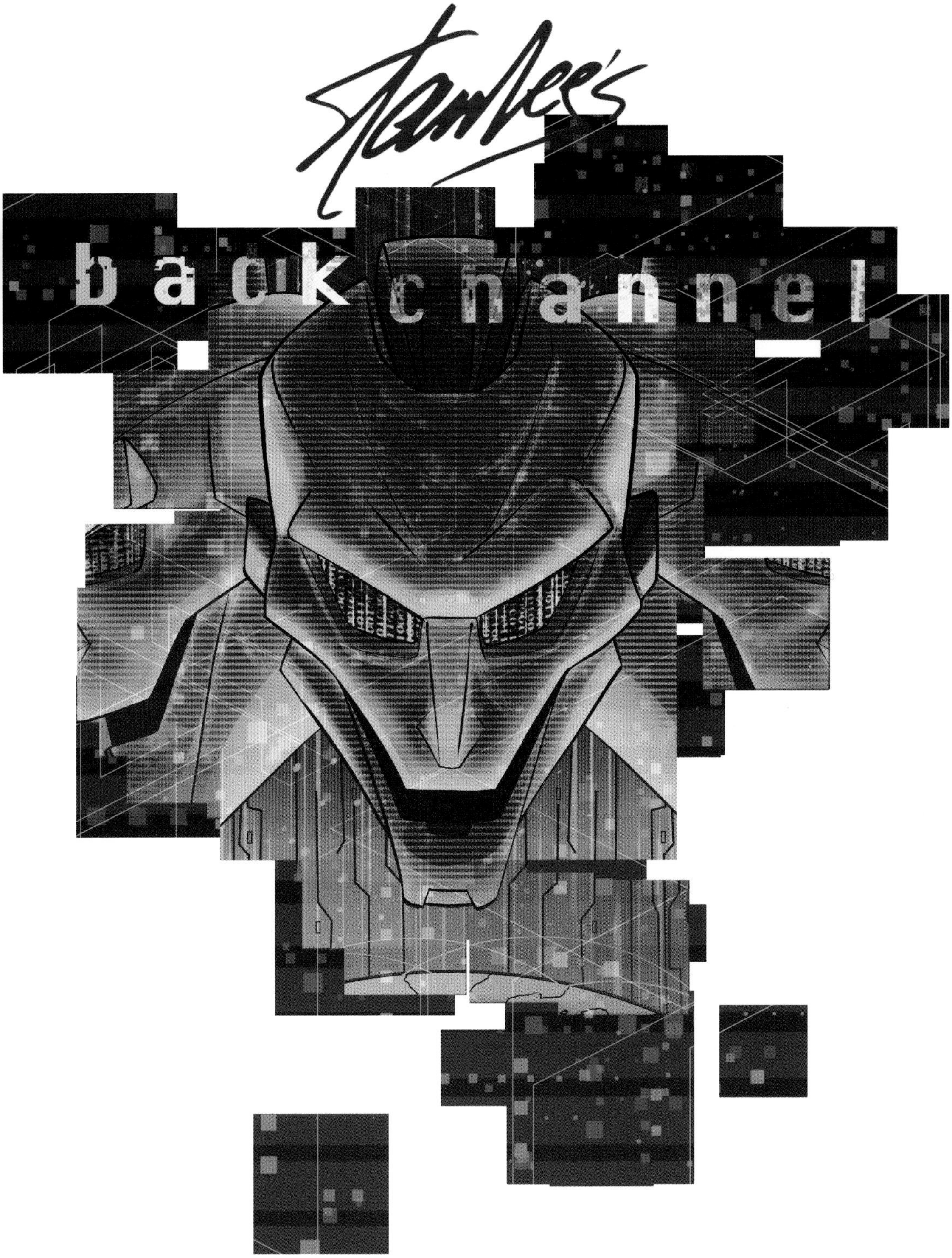
Stan Lee's
back channel

DEDICATED TO
STAN LEE

Rocketship™

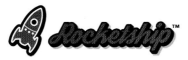

Stan Lee's backchannel

CREATED BY
STAN LEE

WRITTEN BY
STAN LEE AND TOM AKEL

ART BY
ANDIE TONG

LETTERS BY
TAYLOR ESPOSITO

COLORS BY KOMIKAKI STUDIOS FEATURING
SEAN LEE

EXECUTIVE PRODUCER
GILL CHAMPION

ADDITIONAL ART BY
RYAN BENJAMIN AND ORLANDO CAICEDO

ADDITIONAL COLORS
OMI REMALANTE

 Rocketship ™ Rocketship Entertainment, LLC
rocketshipent.com

Tom Akel, CEO & Publisher • **Rob Feldman,** CTO • **Jeanmarie McNeely,** CFO
Brandon Freeberg, Dir. of Campaign Mgmt. • **Phil Smith,** Art Director • **Aram Alekyan,** Designer
Jimmy Deoquino, Designer • **Jed Keith,** Social Media • **Jerrod Clark,** Publicity

BACKCHANNEL volume 1 | Hardcover Edition ISBN: 978-1-952126-25-3 | Softcover Edition ISBN: 978-1-952126-24-6
First printing. August 2023. Copyright © Rocketship Entertainment, LLC. All rights reserved. Published by Rocketship Entertainment, LLC.
136 Westbury Ct. Doylestown, PA 18901. Contains material orginally published online as "Backchannel". "Backchannel", the Backchannel
logo, and the likenesses of all characters herein are trademarks of Rocketship Entertainment, LLC and Stan Lee's POW! Entertainment.
"Rocketship" and the Rocketship logo are trademarks of Rocketship Entertainment, LLC. No part of this publication may be reproduced or
transmitted, in any form or by any means, without the express written consent of Rocketship Entertainment, LLC. All names, characters,
events, and locales in this publication are entirely fictional. Any resemblance to actual persons (living or dead), events, or places, without
satiric intent, is coincidental. Printed in China.

original webcomic edited by **Mike Kelly** • *for this edition,* production and design by **Jimmy Deoquino** and **Phil Smith**

TABLE OF CONTENTS

FOREWORD

Cool.

I first became aware of Stan Lee in 1967 when my brother bought issues of *The Amazing Spider-Man* and *The Fantastic Four*. We'd been in the United States less than a year, still learning the language, and having recognized *Batman* and *Superman* comics from television, we'd bought some of those. A new friend of my brother's at school said, "You don't want to be reading those, you want to be reading these. These are the cool ones."

They were, of course, Marvel Comics. Even fourth graders could figure out they were cooler! And I was in first grade, so I assumed that if my brother thought they were cool, then they had to be!
And they were.

Decades later, when I was working at Marvel (and afterwards), I had the opportunity to know Stan a little, work with him on several projects, and break bread with him several times. And yes, that was… cool!
Cool might not be a cool word now, but that's cool, because those who get it, get it.

Which gets us to…

I met Tom Akel when he was running Webtoon's comic division and I was negotiating a contract with Reilly Brown to bring our Outrage comic to the digital publisher.

Pardon this Commercial interruption
Outrage Season One is available in print from Rocketship Entertainment, and look for the character's cameo in this book!
Back to our regularly scheduled foreword

Tom and I met in Los Angeles for lunch. I think maybe it was the first time we'd met in person? Los Angeles thinks it's cool. Tom Akel *was* cool. Looked it, talked it, a really nice guy with great experience, great vision, and greater aspirations. I liked him. As an aside, I don't like many people *(I'm uncool that way)*.

Between talking about Outrage, he talked to me about the project he was working on with Stan, something called *Backchannel*. Sounded okay. Cute. Nice early Spider-Man riff with a good approach to kids today. Then Tom mentioned Andie Tong would be drawing it and that raised an eyebrow because I almost got to work with Andie fifteen years ago on a graphic novel project and I knew how good and unheralded he was.

And that's when I thought, *"Damn, I hope Backchannel isn't cooler than Outrage!"* And in your hands, you have proof that, indeed, it is *(not by a lot, dammit, but yes, it is)*.

Tom Tanner *(you know, as much as I hate to say it, alliterative character names are still cool!)* is a very prototypical teen antagonist for a super hero origin story, but the weight on his shoulders feels real. His loneliness and struggles to socialize generate sadness and empathy. Tom is someone the audience wants to root for. The origin-power granting protagonist, maybe not so much.

Similar to themes I played with in *Outrage*, which was painted with brushstrokes of broader social sarcasm, the entire idea of "the internet" as both a source of societal comfort and discomfort is integral to the story.

We all manage a deluge of information on a daily basis at a speed which would have been unheard of just fifty years ago. Youth today process it as a manner of course, they were born into a world that bludgeons them with data, much of which is incredibly unhealthy for body and mind.

It is an unprecedented time in the history of human interaction, and one rife for dystopic fictional storytelling. We all feel powerful and powerless at the same time. For me, the stories that rise above the fray are the ones whose protagonists slog their way through the fictionalized aspects of our complex reality and find a message of hope.

Backchannel does that, in part because Stan and Tom are fundamentally good people who would prefer to tell the stories of good people, but also because, as I do, they also expect their readers are good people who want to engage with stories that show humanity in a more positive light. Which, again, is cool.

And since I'm a firm believer that the artist makes the writer, praise can't be awarded to this book without mentioning just how excellent Andie Tong is. From storytelling to character design, character movement to characterization through body posture or facial expressions, Andie's work is an absolute delight to see. The best comic book storytellers don't need to show off, they just let their camera movement, attention to panel compositions, and ability to differentiate their characters guide you through a story, panel by panel, so that when they do want to show off, it becomes even more impactful.

Andie, with color art by Sean Lee of Komikaki Studios, along with excellent lettering by Taylor Esposito *(we'll always have Batwing!)*, create a visual landscape that is how we imagine the inner workings of the internet must look like. Overwhelming, vibrant, and scary, Tom Tanner has to navigate an unreal dimension in order to cope with very real world problems, from superhuman jail breaks to the emotional void in his life: who killed his mother.

And by the way, I know that was a lot of flowery words to say: the book looks cool!

So, that brings us back full circle. I got to the end of *Backchannel* for the second time *(the first was in serialized chapter forms)* and it did what the best, most fun, comics still do for me: it left me a bit frustrated that it was ending on a cliffhanger, but it made me want to see more!

And more *Backchannel* by Tom and Andie with Stan's spiritual guidance? Well… that would be cool.

Fabian Nicieza

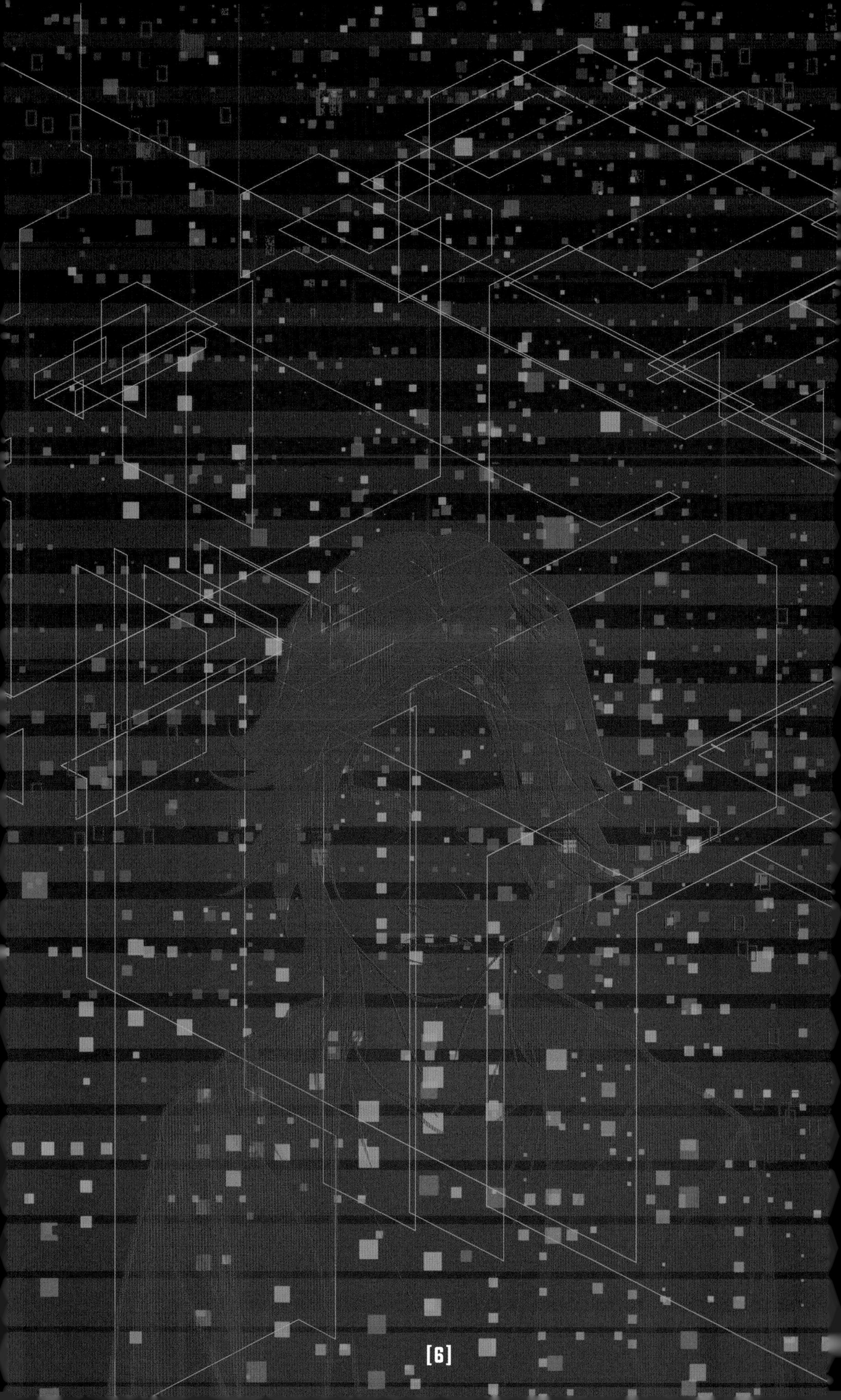

Stan Lee's

backchannel

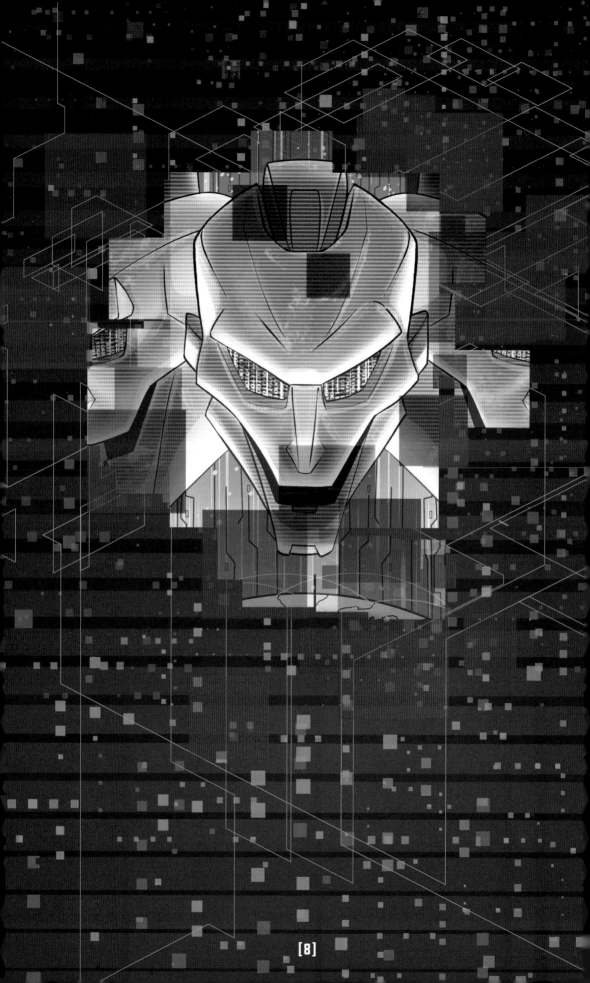

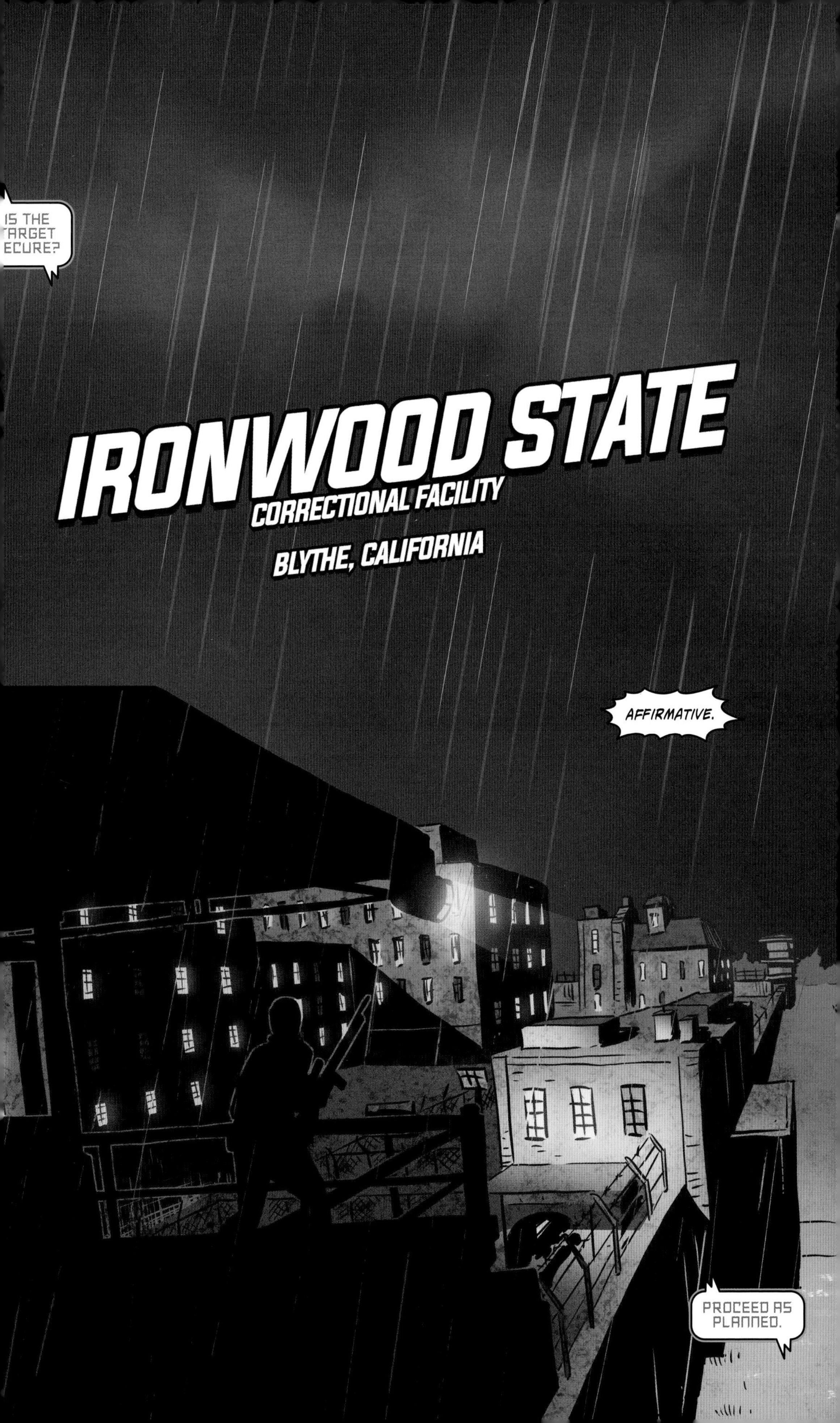
IS THE
ARGET
ECURE?
IRONWOOD STATE
CORRECTIONAL FACILITY
BLYTHE, CALIFORNIA
AFFIRMATIVE.
PROCEED AS PLANNED.

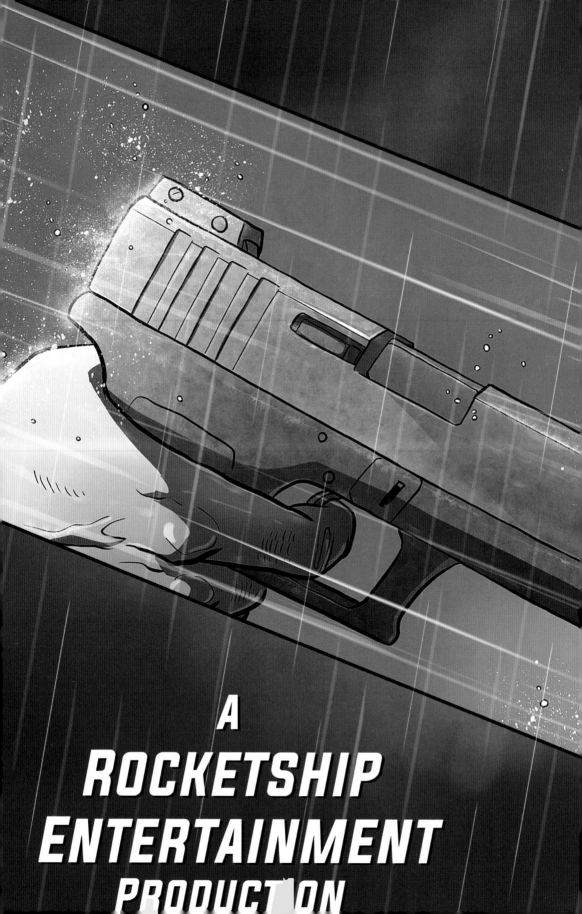

A
ROCKETSHIP
ENTERTAINMENT
PRODUCTION

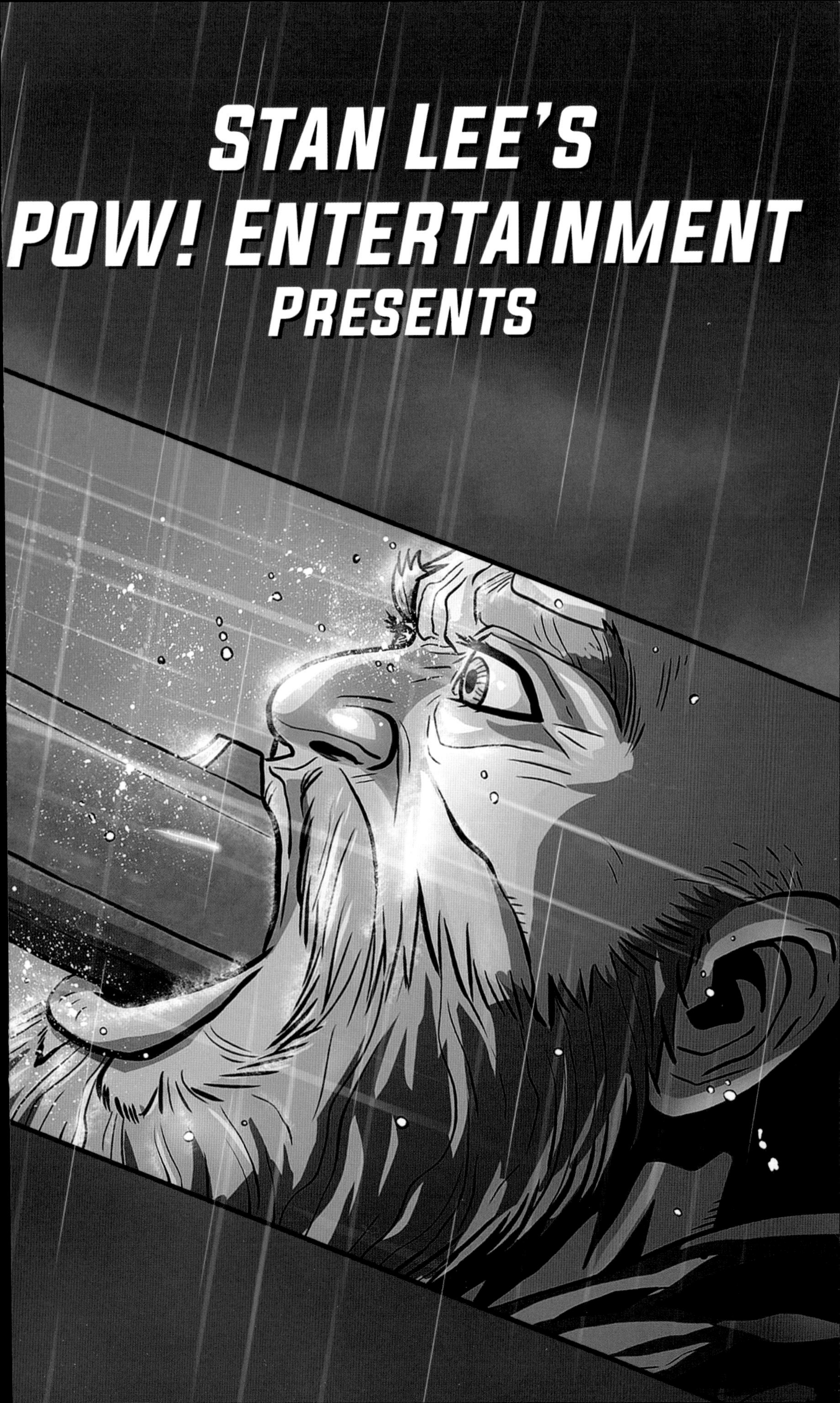
STAN LEE'S
POW! ENTERTAINMENT
PRESENTS

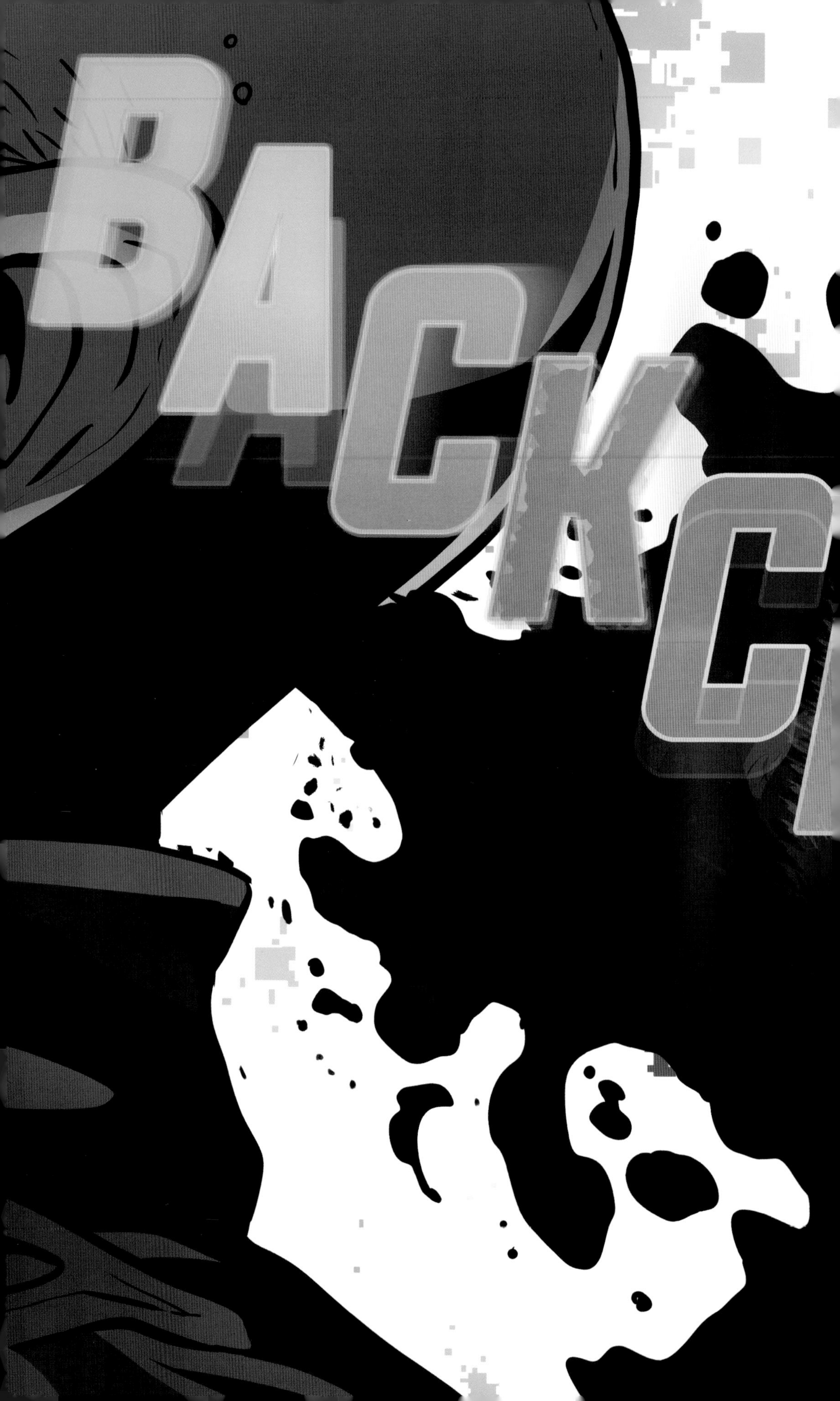
BACKC

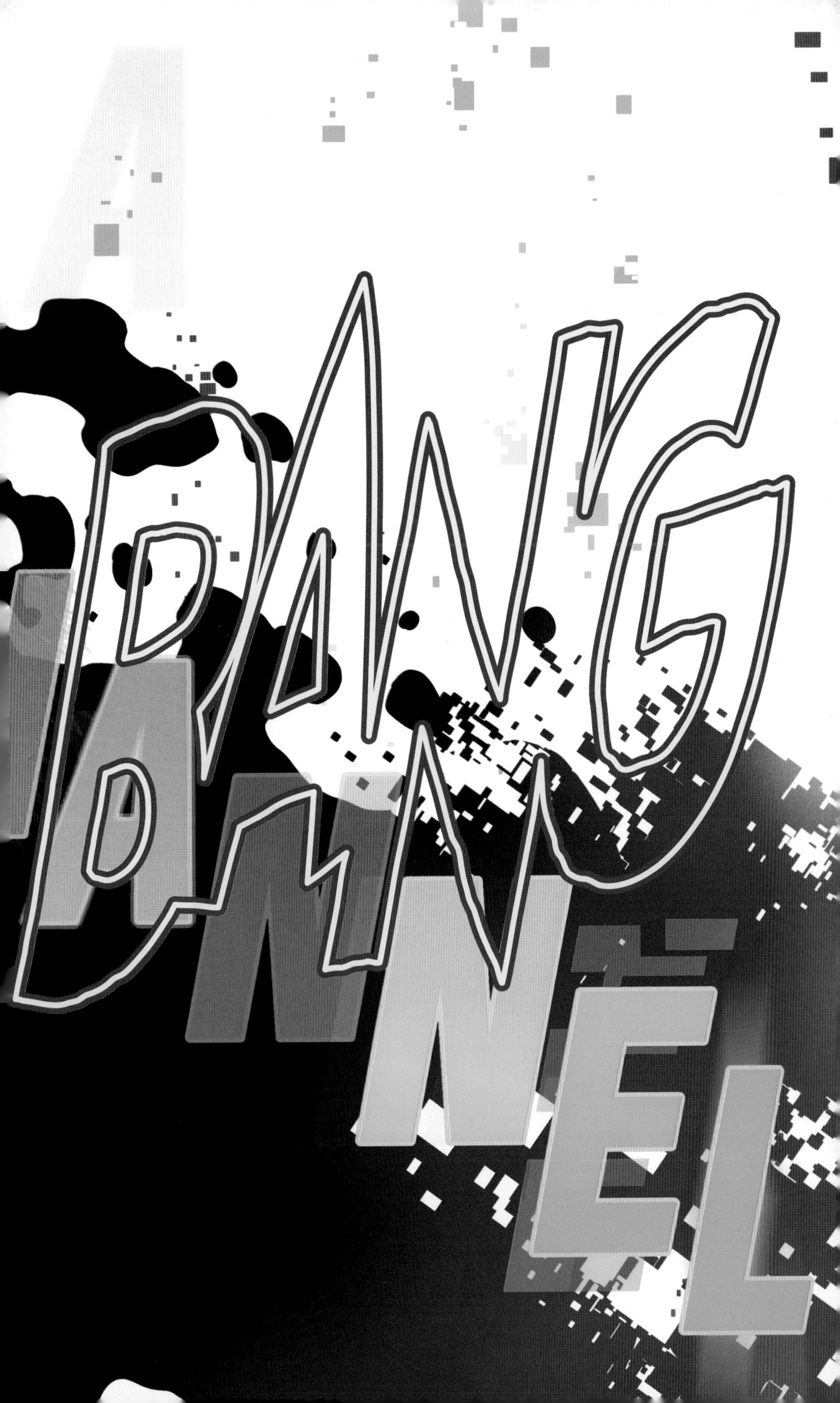
DANG

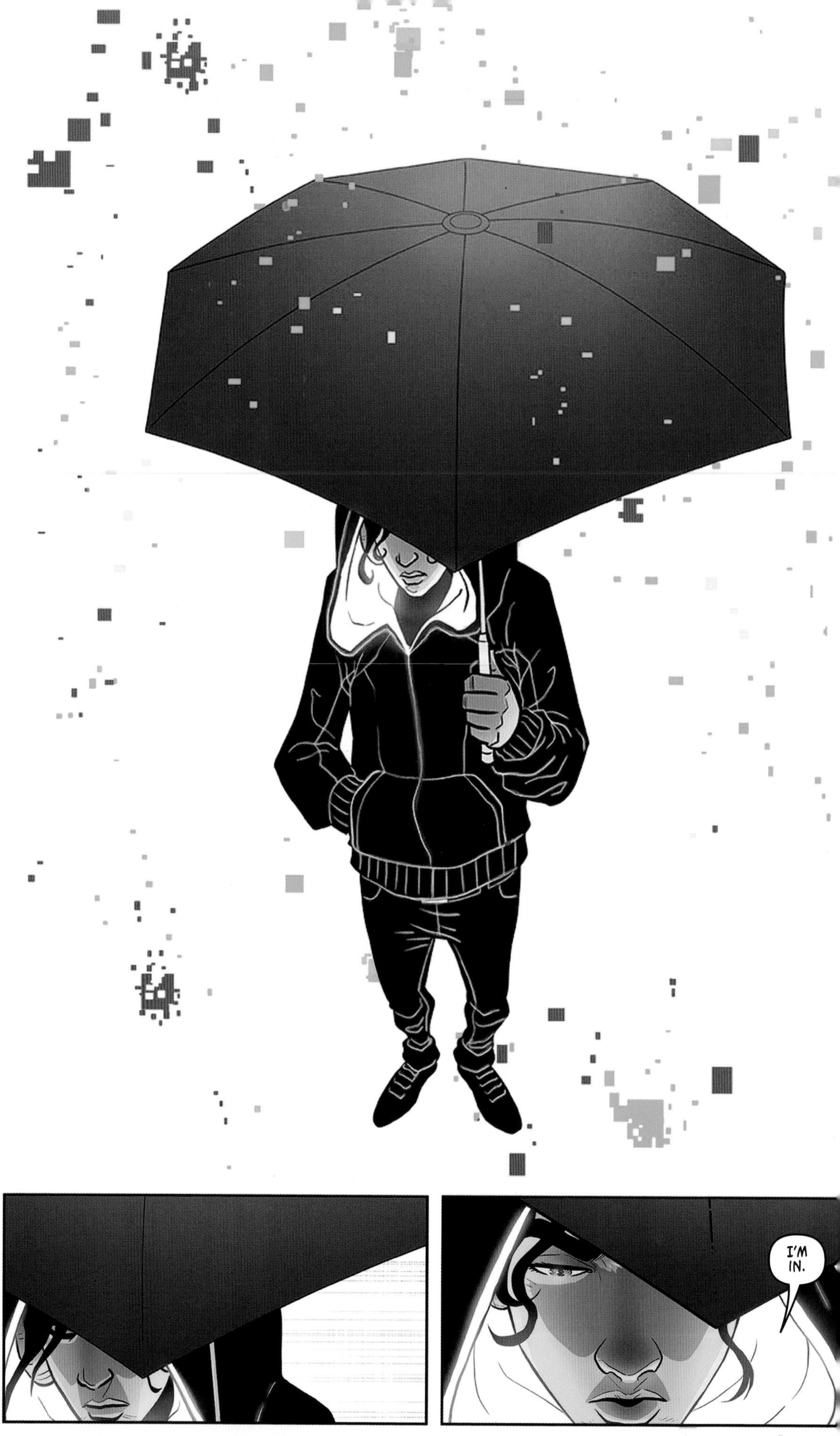
I'M IN.

GOOD WORK.

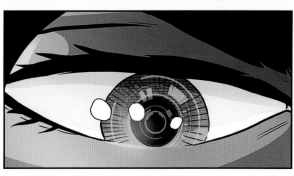

DISABLE THE GRID.

WRITTEN BY
STAN LEE & TOM AKEL

CELL BLOCKS D AND E ONLY.

WE NEED A PATH OUT.

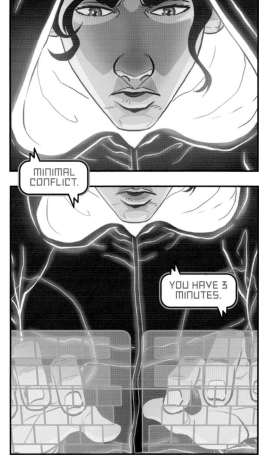

MINIMAL CONFLICT.

YOU HAVE 3 MINUTES.

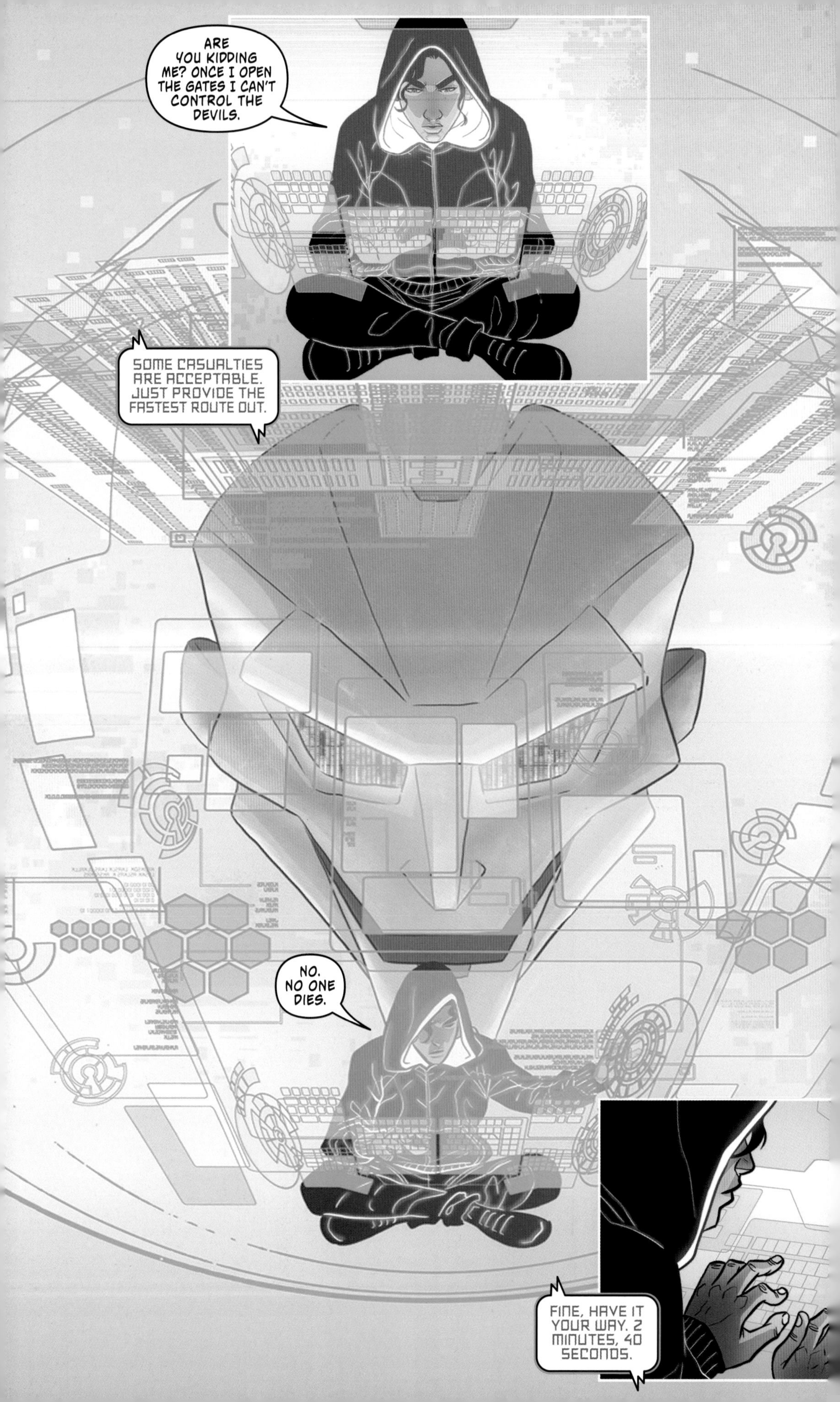
ARE YOU KIDDING ME? ONCE I OPEN THE GATES I CAN'T CONTROL THE DEVILS.
SOME CASUALTIES ARE ACCEPTABLE. JUST PROVIDE THE FASTEST ROUTE OUT.
NO. NO ONE DIES.
FINE, HAVE IT YOUR WAY. 2 MINUTES, 40 SECONDS.

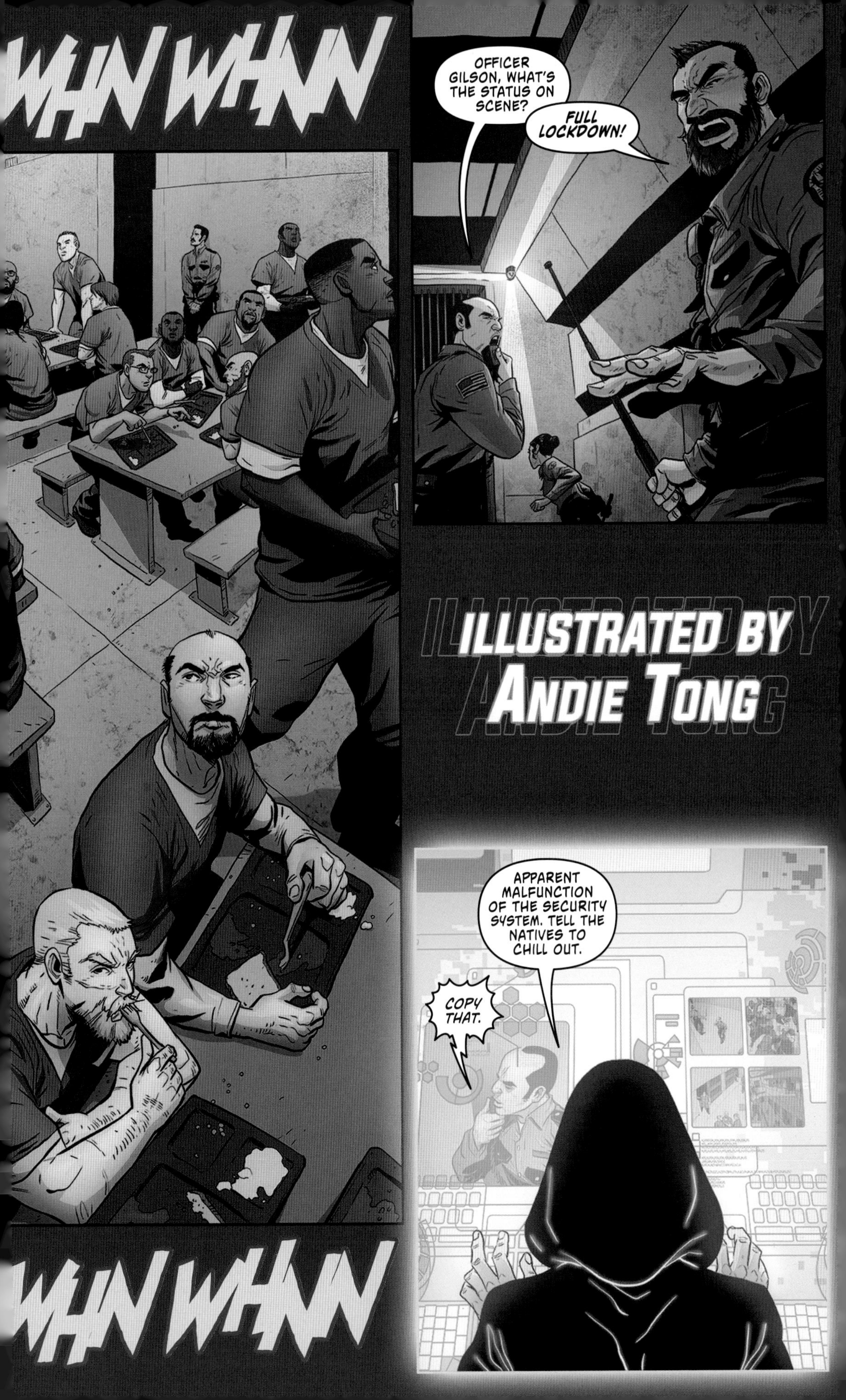
WHN WHNN
OFFICER GILSON, WHAT'S THE STATUS ON SCENE?
FULL LOCKDOWN!
ILLUSTRATED BY
ANDIE TONG
APPARENT MALFUNCTION OF THE SECURITY SYSTEM. TELL THE NATIVES TO CHILL OUT.
COPY THAT.
WHN WHNN

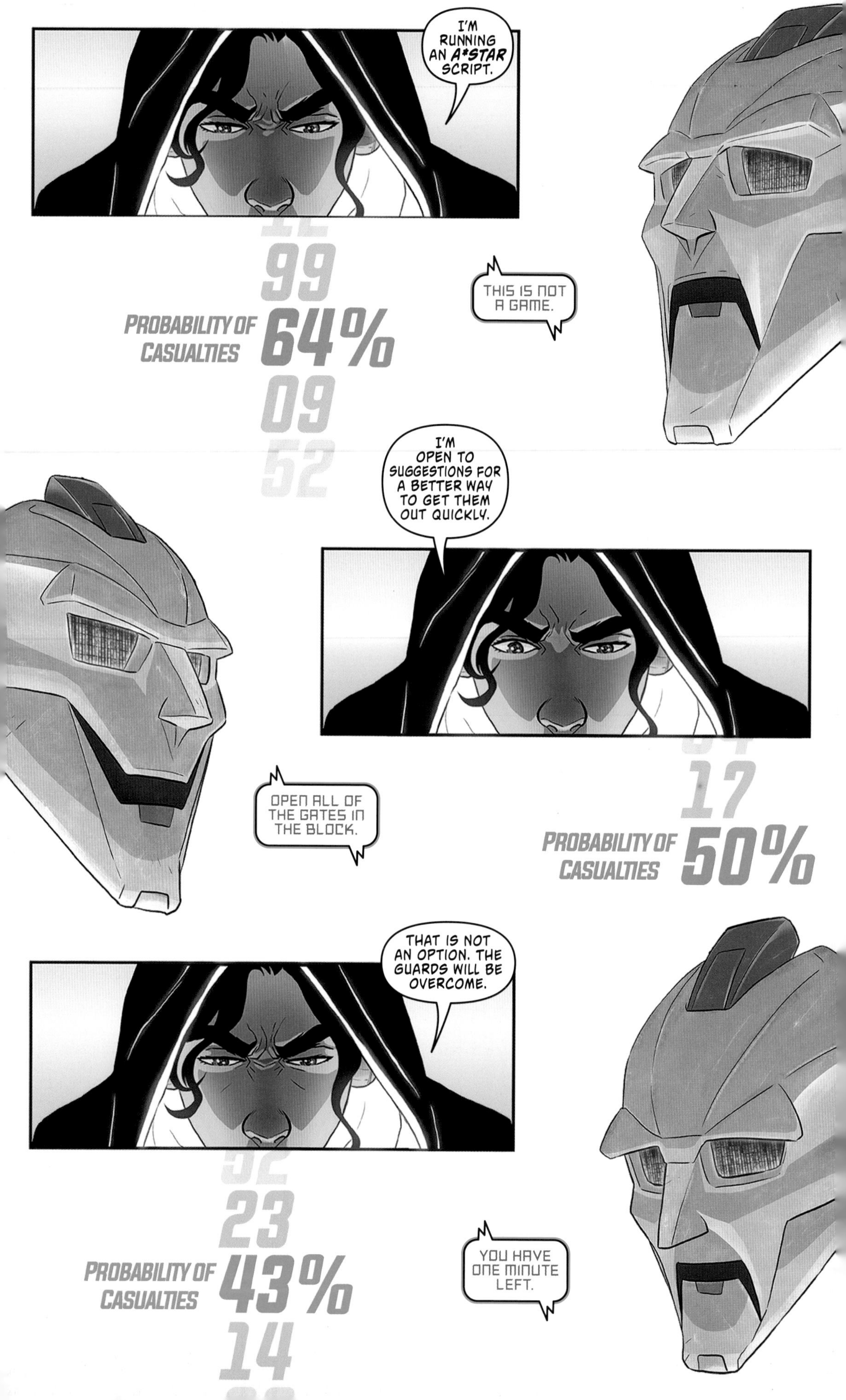
I'M RUNNING AN A*STAR SCRIPT.
THIS IS NOT A GAME.
99
PROBABILITY OF CASUALTIES 64%
09
52
I'M OPEN TO SUGGESTIONS FOR A BETTER WAY TO GET THEM OUT QUICKLY.
OPEN ALL OF THE GATES IN THE BLOCK.
17
PROBABILITY OF CASUALTIES 50%
THAT IS NOT AN OPTION. THE GUARDS WILL BE OVERCOME.
YOU HAVE ONE MINUTE LEFT.
23
PROBABILITY OF CASUALTIES 43%
14

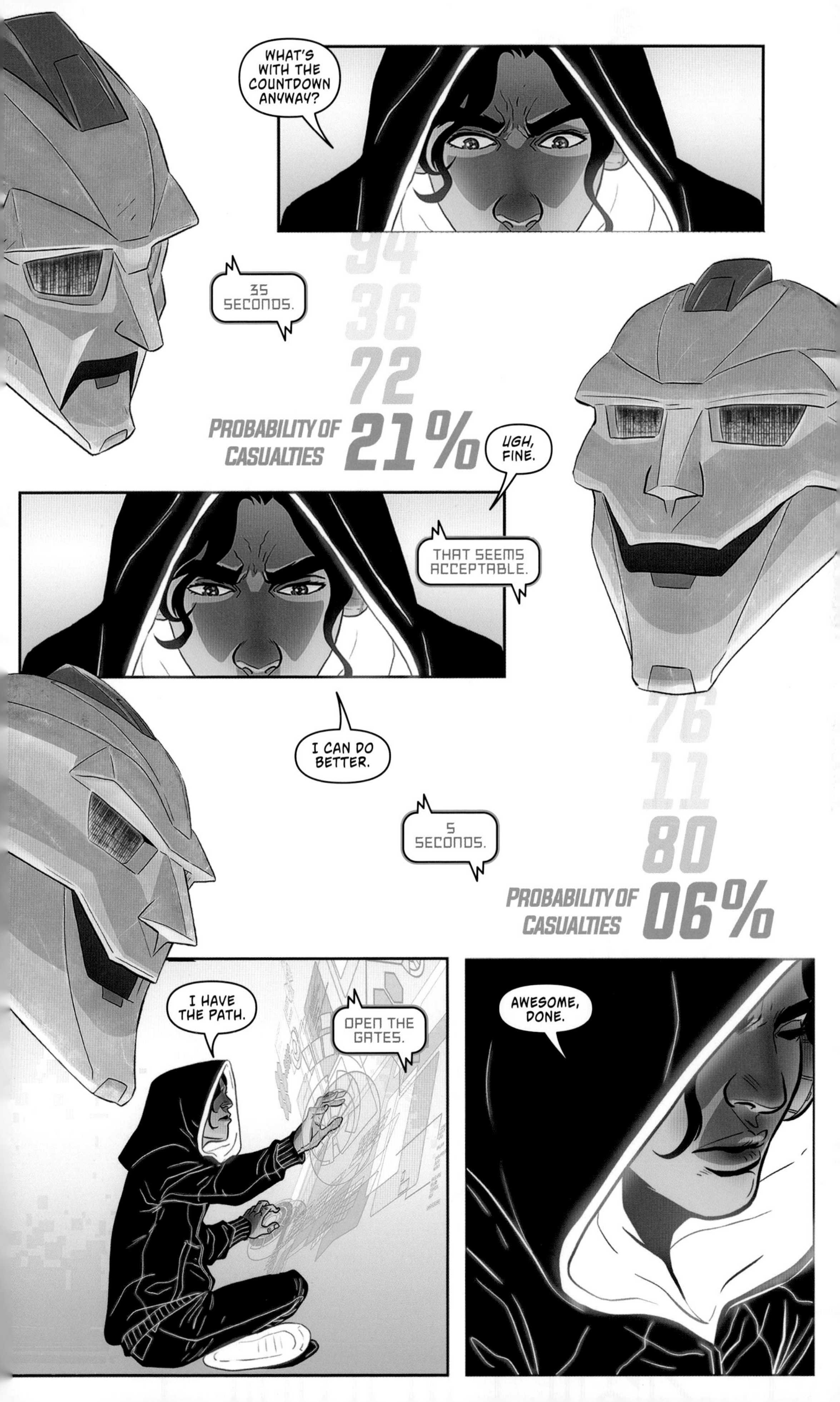

WHAT'S WITH THE COUNTDOWN ANYWAY?
35 SECONDS.
94
36
72
PROBABILITY OF CASUALTIES 21%
UGH, FINE.
THAT SEEMS ACCEPTABLE.
I CAN DO BETTER.
5 SECONDS.
76
11
80
PROBABILITY OF CASUALTIES 06%
I HAVE THE PATH.
OPEN THE GATES.
AWESOME, DONE.

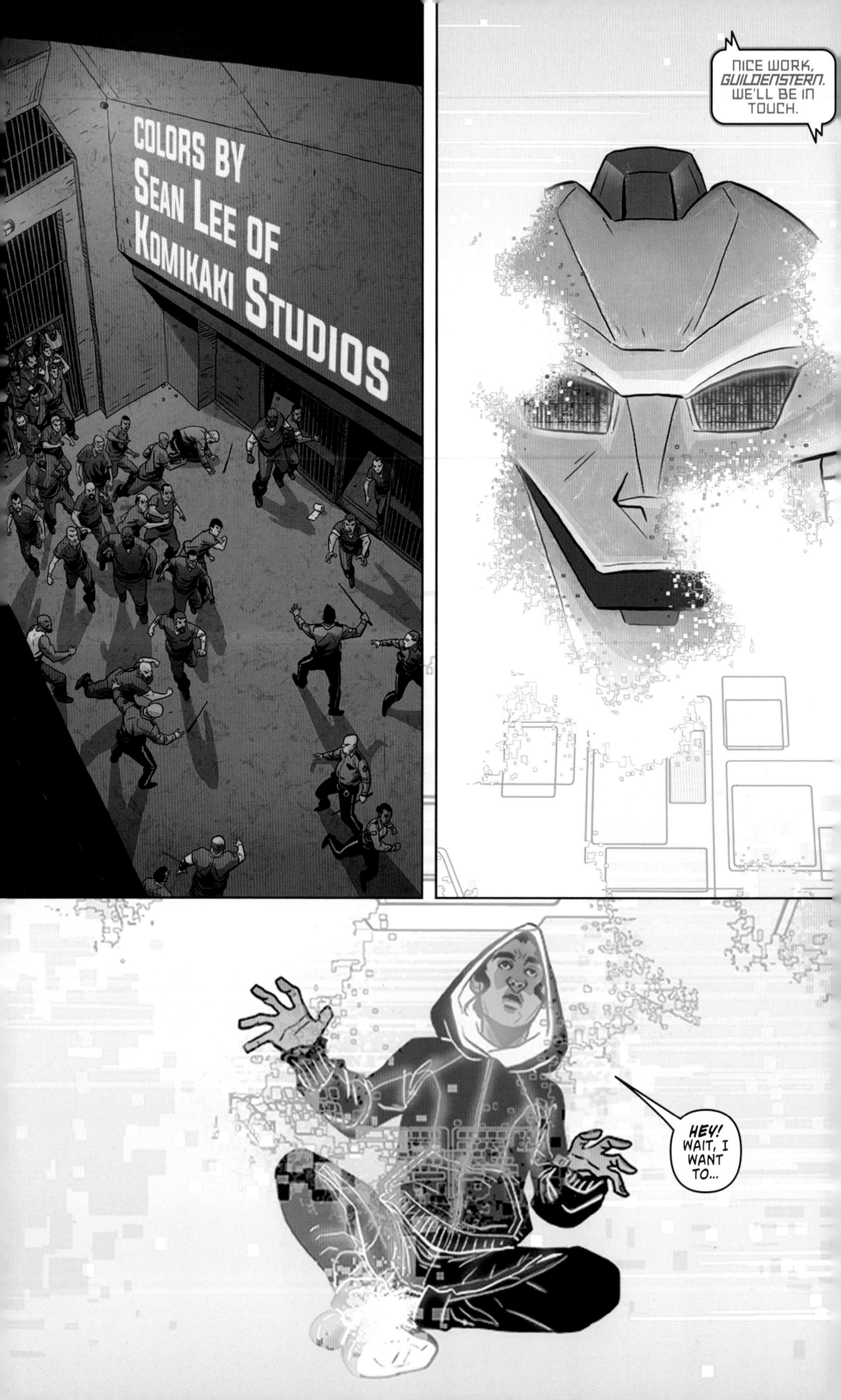
COLORS BY SEAN LEE OF KOMIKAKI STUDIOS
NICE WORK, GUILDENSTERN. WE'LL BE IN TOUCH.
HEY! WAIT, I WANT TO...

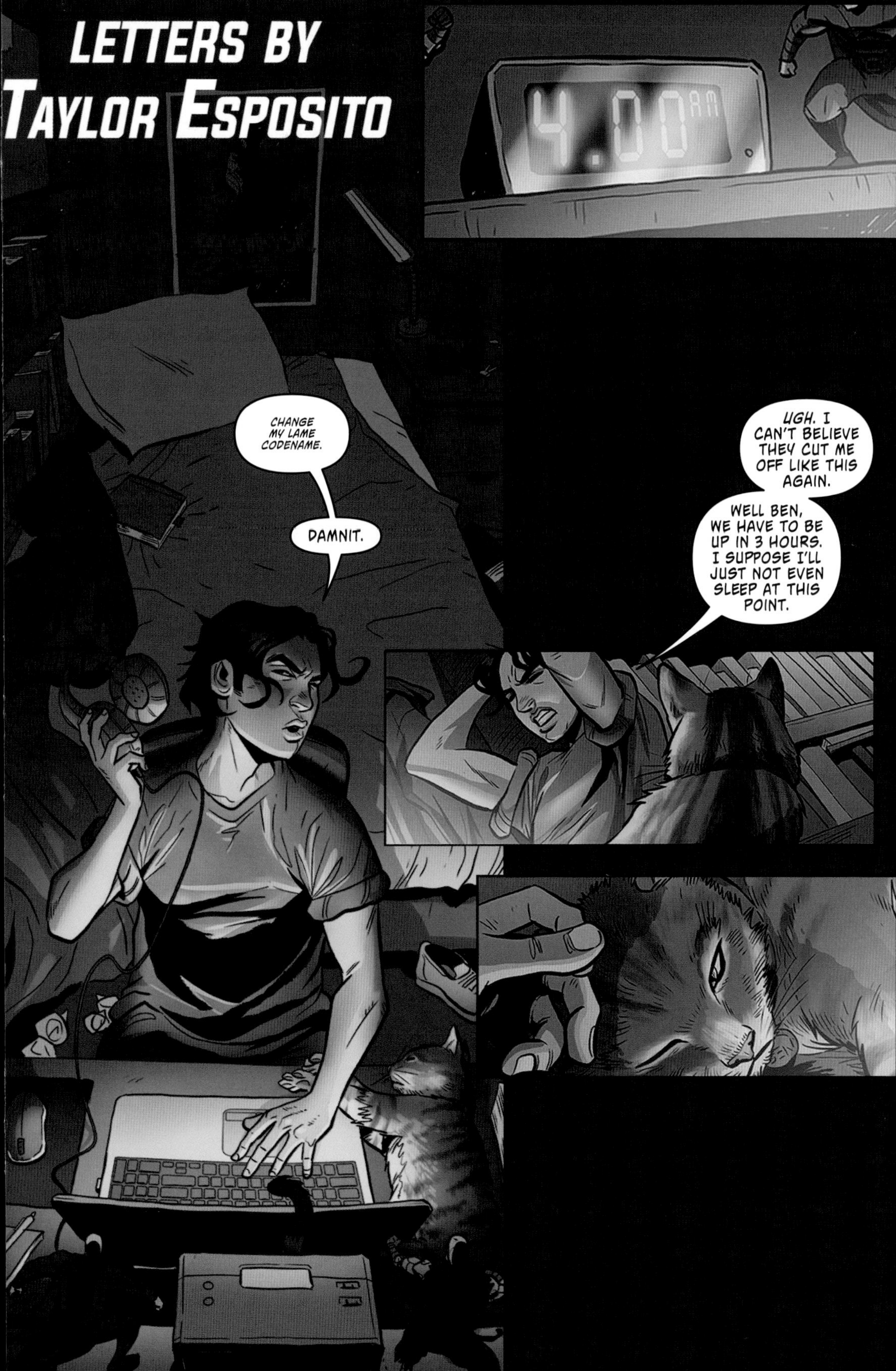
LETTERS BY
TAYLOR ESPOSITO
4:00 AM
CHANGE MY LAME CODENAME.
DAMNIT.
UGH. I CAN'T BELIEVE THEY CUT ME OFF LIKE THIS AGAIN.
WELL BEN, WE HAVE TO BE UP IN 3 HOURS. I SUPPOSE I'LL JUST NOT EVEN SLEEP AT THIS POINT.

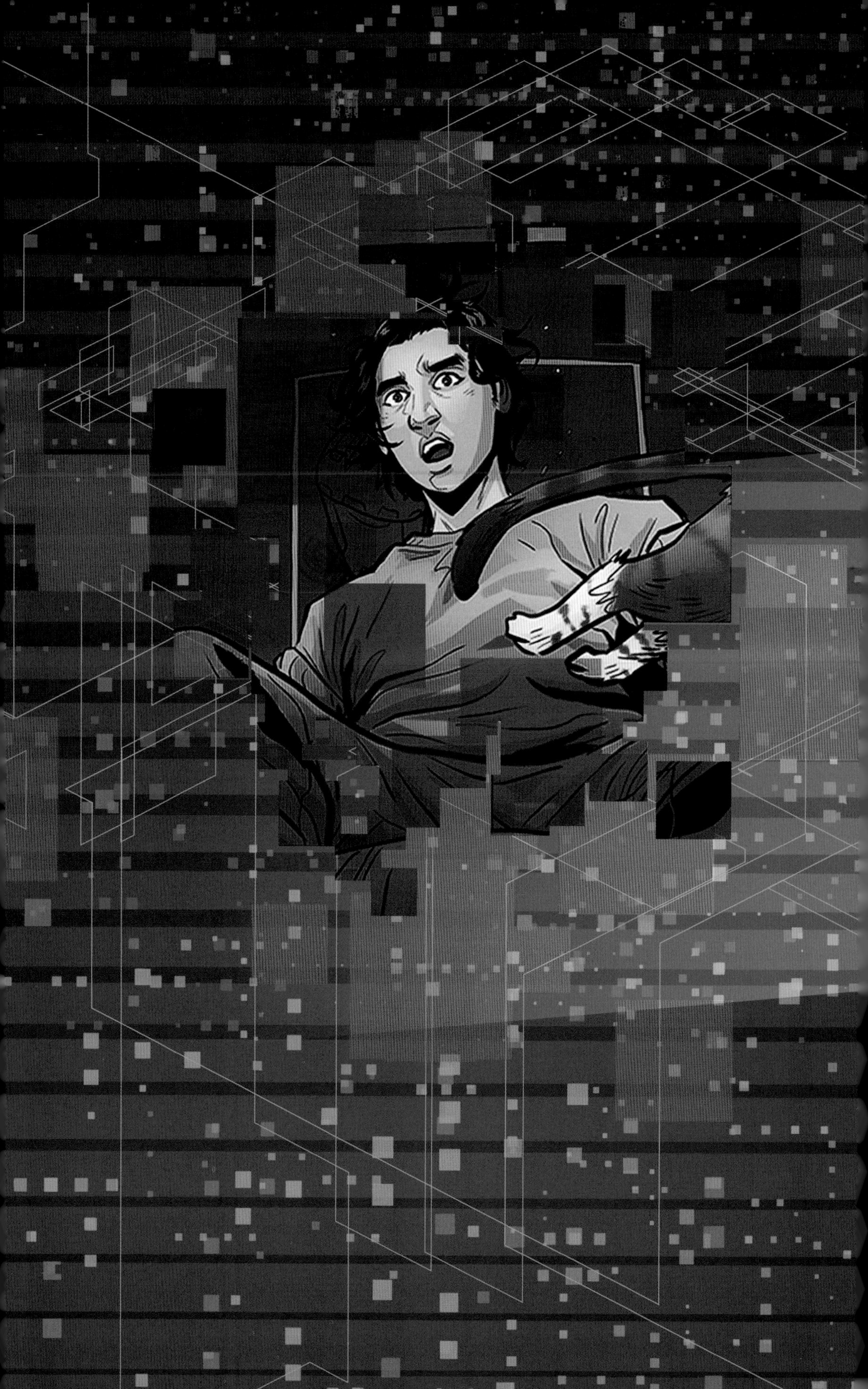

CHAPTER 1

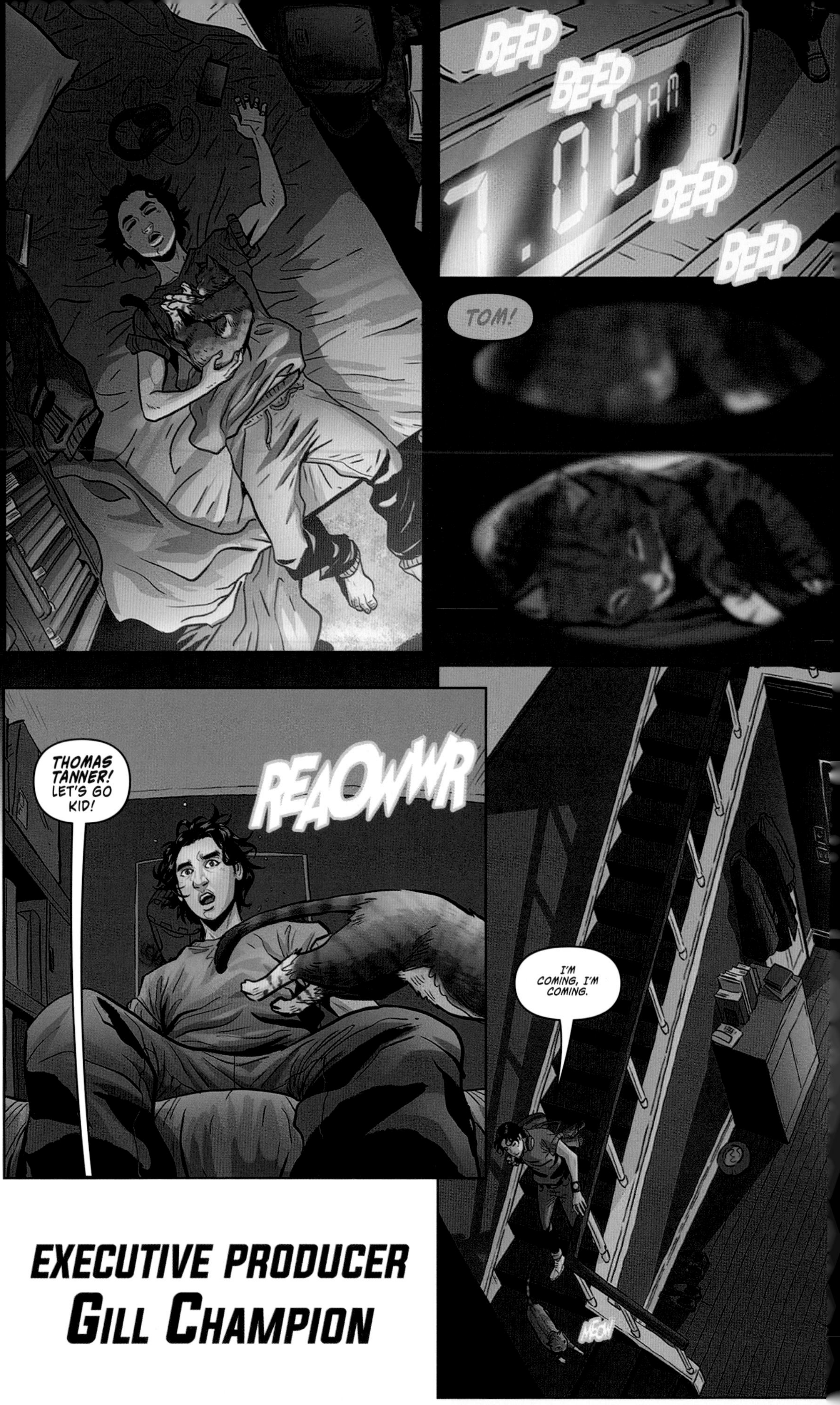
BEEP
BEEP
7:00 AM
BEEP
BEEP
TOM!
THOMAS TANNER! LET'S GO KID!
REAOWWR
I'M COMING, I'M COMING.
MEOW

EXECUTIVE PRODUCER
GILL CHAMPION

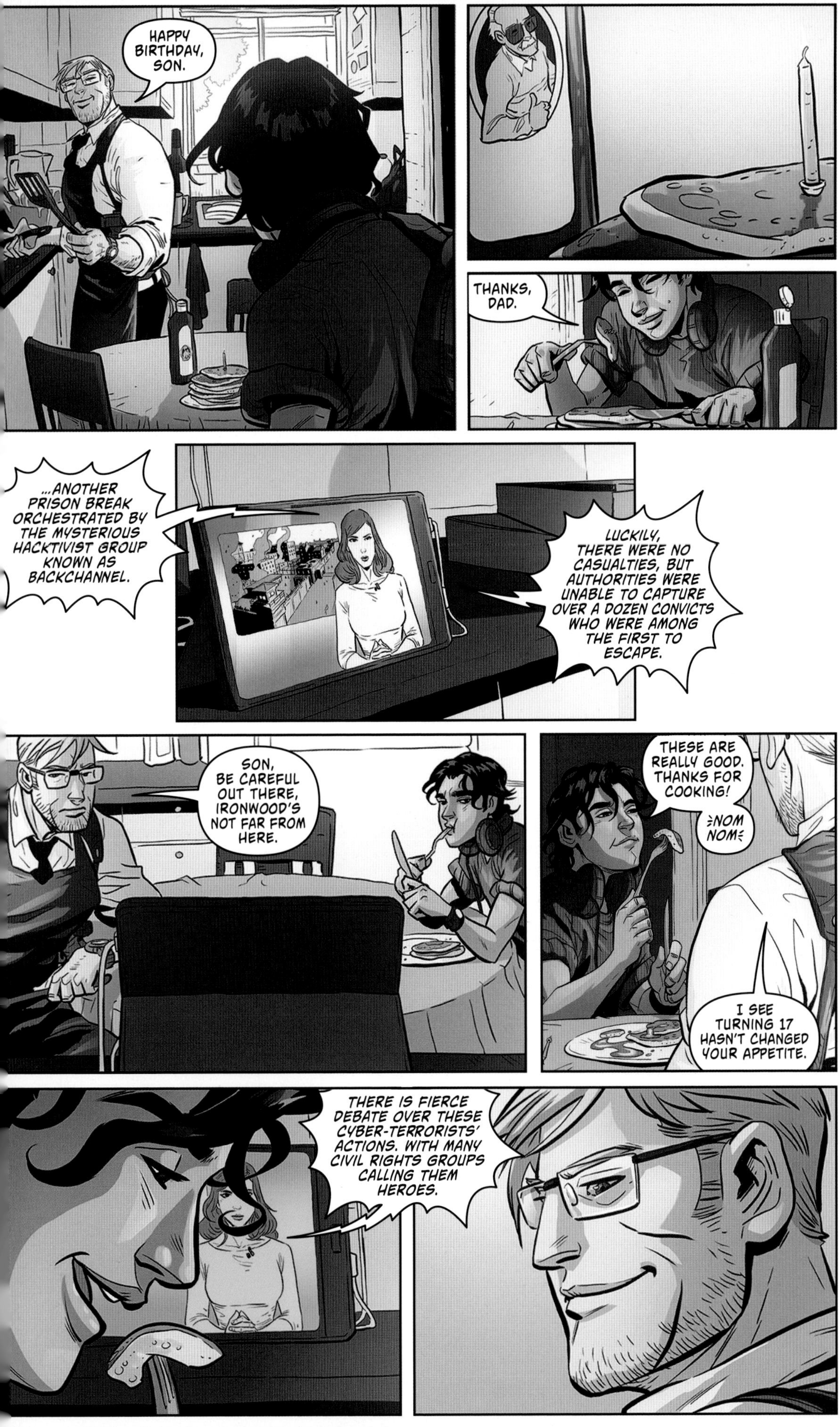

HAPPY BIRTHDAY, SON.
THANKS, DAD.
...ANOTHER PRISON BREAK ORCHESTRATED BY THE MYSTERIOUS HACKTIVIST GROUP KNOWN AS BACKCHANNEL.
LUCKILY, THERE WERE NO CASUALTIES, BUT AUTHORITIES WERE UNABLE TO CAPTURE OVER A DOZEN CONVICTS WHO WERE AMONG THE FIRST TO ESCAPE.
SON, BE CAREFUL OUT THERE, IRONWOOD'S NOT FAR FROM HERE.
THESE ARE REALLY GOOD. THANKS FOR COOKING!
NOM NOM
I SEE TURNING 17 HASN'T CHANGED YOUR APPETITE.
THERE IS FIERCE DEBATE OVER THESE CYBER-TERRORISTS' ACTIONS. WITH MANY CIVIL RIGHTS GROUPS CALLING THEM HEROES.

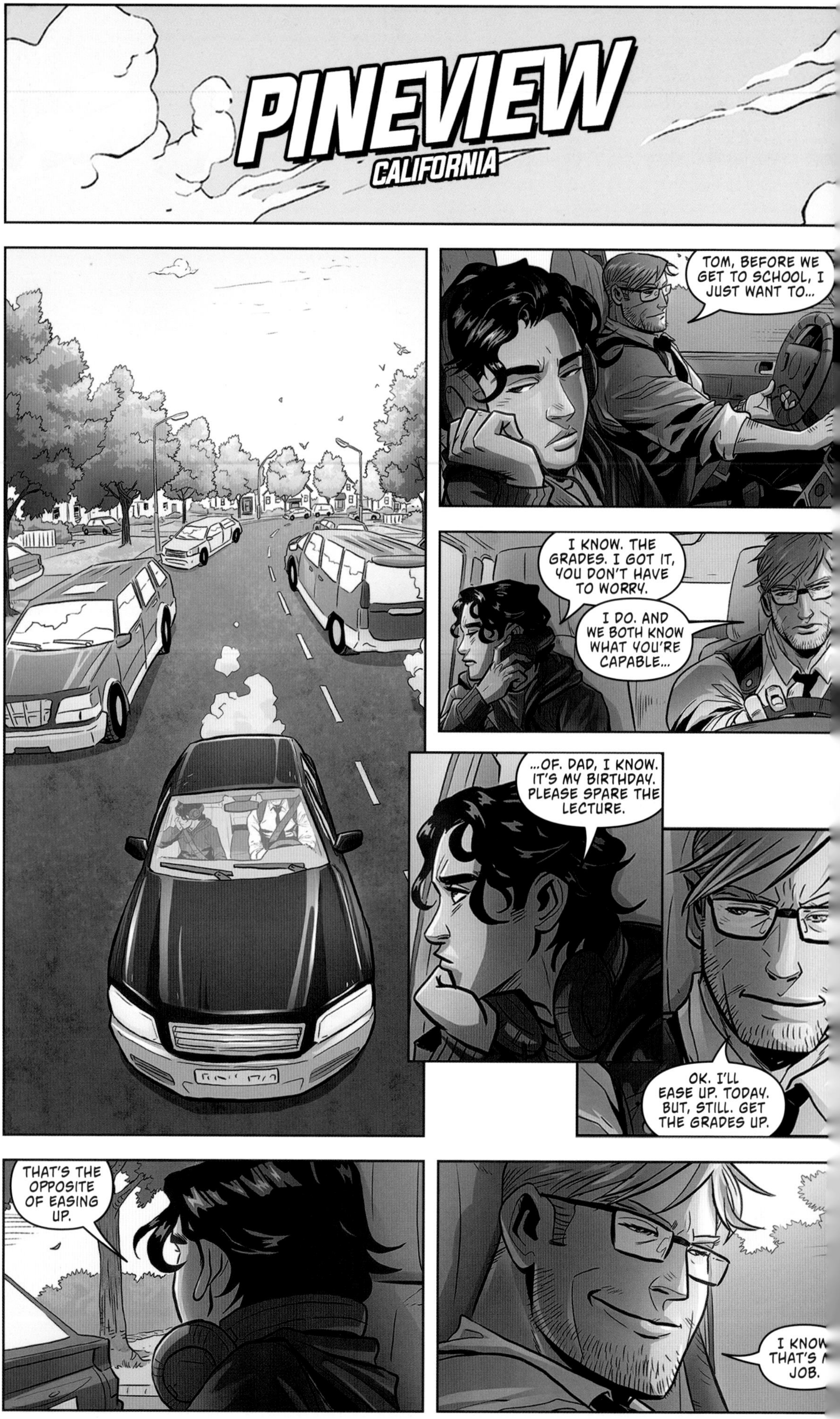
PINEVIEW
CALIFORNIA
TOM, BEFORE WE GET TO SCHOOL, I JUST WANT TO...
I KNOW. THE GRADES. I GOT IT, YOU DON'T HAVE TO WORRY.
I DO. AND WE BOTH KNOW WHAT YOU'RE CAPABLE...
...OF. DAD, I KNOW. IT'S MY BIRTHDAY. PLEASE SPARE THE LECTURE.
OK. I'LL EASE UP. TODAY. BUT, STILL. GET THE GRADES UP.
THAT'S THE OPPOSITE OF EASING UP.
I KNOW THAT'S JOB.

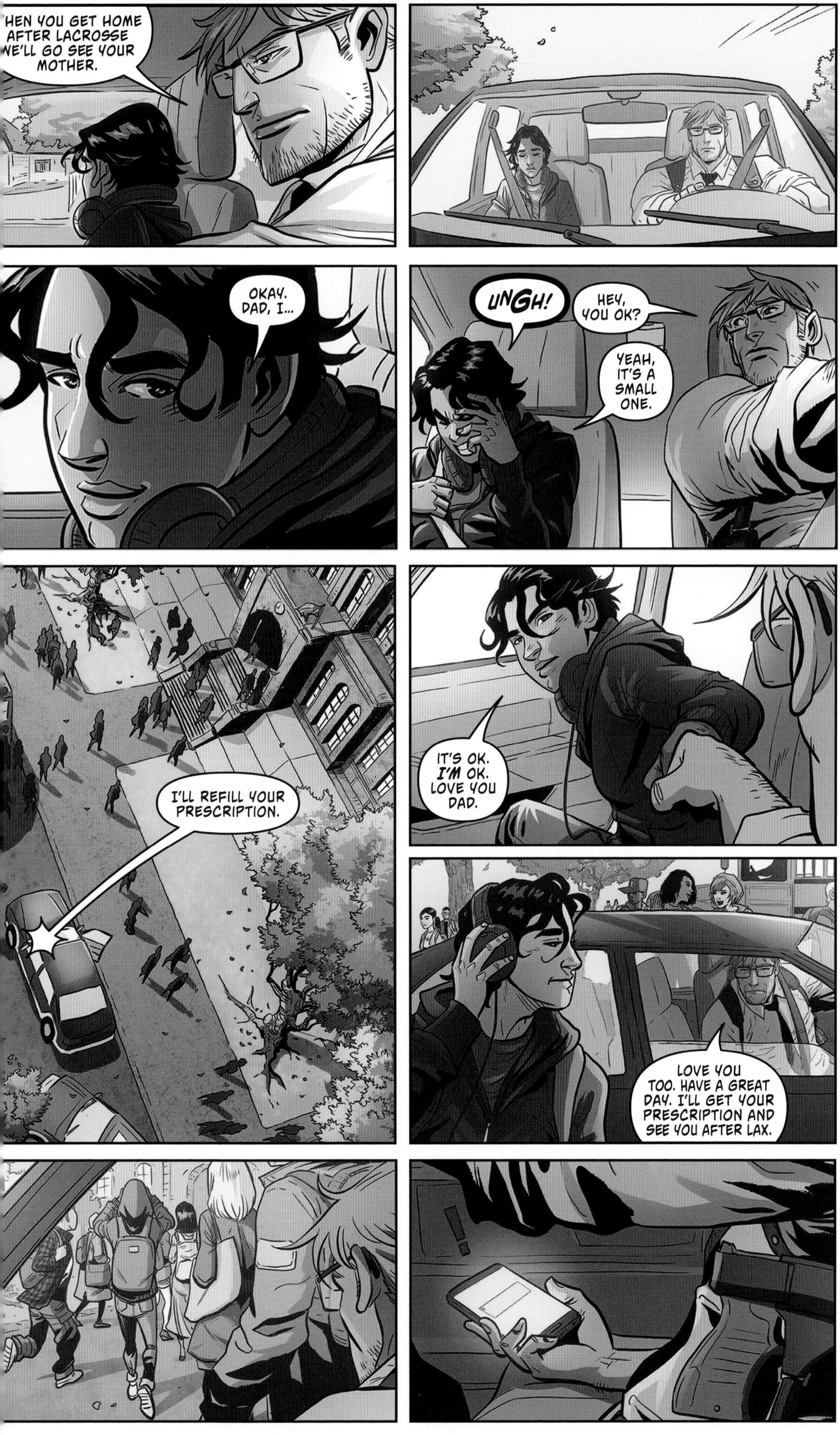
HEN YOU GET HOME AFTER LACROSSE WE'LL GO SEE YOUR MOTHER.
OKAY. DAD, I...
UNGH!
HEY, YOU OK?
YEAH, IT'S A SMALL ONE.
I'LL REFILL YOUR PRESCRIPTION.
IT'S OK. I'M OK. LOVE YOU DAD.
LOVE YOU TOO. HAVE A GREAT DAY. I'LL GET YOUR PRESCRIPTION AND SEE YOU AFTER LAX.

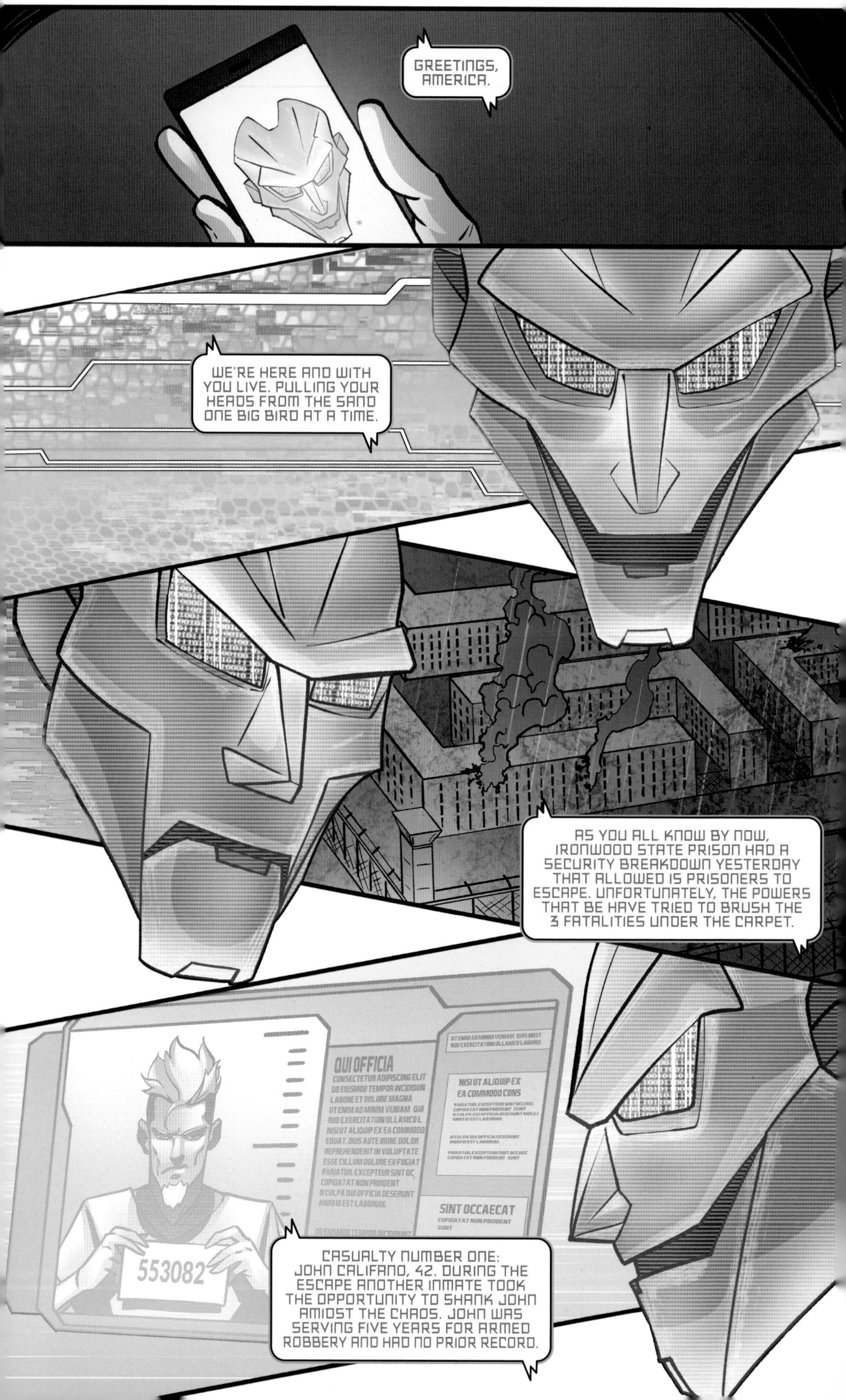
GREETINGS, AMERICA.
WE'RE HERE AND WITH YOU LIVE. PULLING YOUR HEADS FROM THE SAND ONE BIG BIRD AT A TIME.
AS YOU ALL KNOW BY NOW, IRONWOOD STATE PRISON HAD A SECURITY BREAKDOWN YESTERDAY THAT ALLOWED IS PRISONERS TO ESCAPE. UNFORTUNATELY, THE POWERS THAT BE HAVE TRIED TO BRUSH THE 3 FATALITIES UNDER THE CARPET.
QUI OFFICIA
NISI UT ALIQUIP EX EA COMMODO CONS
SINT OCCAECAT
553082
CASUALTY NUMBER ONE: JOHN CALIFANO, 42. DURING THE ESCAPE ANOTHER INMATE TOOK THE OPPORTUNITY TO SHANK JOHN AMIDST THE CHAOS. JOHN WAS SERVING FIVE YEARS FOR ARMED ROBBERY AND HAD NO PRIOR RECORD.

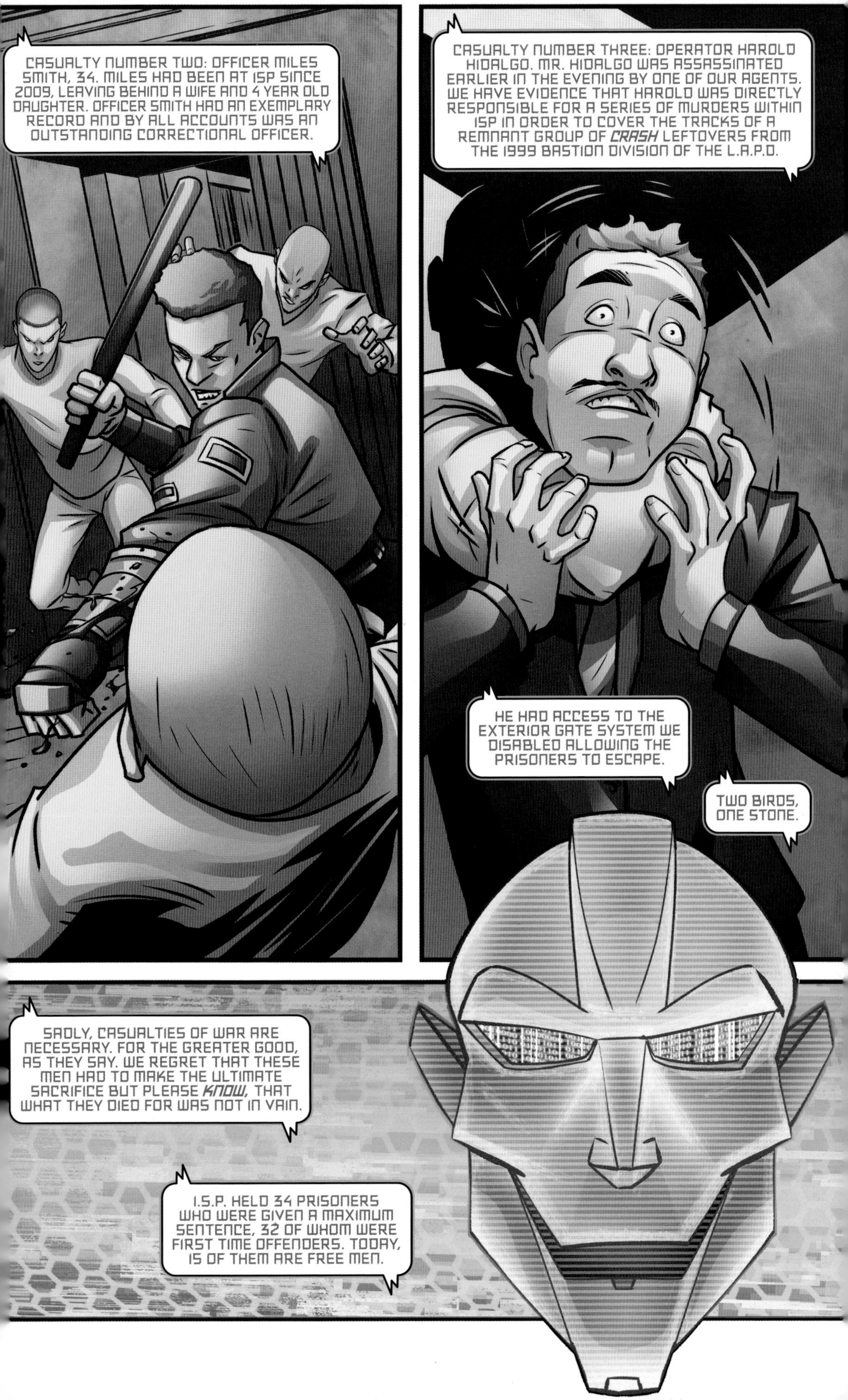
CASUALTY NUMBER TWO: OFFICER MILES SMITH, 34. MILES HAD BEEN AT ISP SINCE 2009, LEAVING BEHIND A WIFE AND 4 YEAR OLD DAUGHTER. OFFICER SMITH HAD AN EXEMPLARY RECORD AND BY ALL ACCOUNTS WAS AN OUTSTANDING CORRECTIONAL OFFICER.
CASUALTY NUMBER THREE: OPERATOR HAROLD HIDALGO. MR. HIDALGO WAS ASSASSINATED EARLIER IN THE EVENING BY ONE OF OUR AGENTS. WE HAVE EVIDENCE THAT HAROLD WAS DIRECTLY RESPONSIBLE FOR A SERIES OF MURDERS WITHIN ISP IN ORDER TO COVER THE TRACKS OF A REMNANT GROUP OF *CRASH* LEFTOVERS FROM THE 1999 BASTION DIVISION OF THE L.A.P.D.
HE HAD ACCESS TO THE EXTERIOR GATE SYSTEM WE DISABLED ALLOWING THE PRISONERS TO ESCAPE.
TWO BIRDS, ONE STONE.
SADLY, CASUALTIES OF WAR ARE NECESSARY. FOR THE GREATER GOOD, AS THEY SAY. WE REGRET THAT THESE MEN HAD TO MAKE THE ULTIMATE SACRIFICE BUT PLEASE *KNOW*, THAT WHAT THEY DIED FOR WAS NOT IN VAIN.
I.S.P. HELD 34 PRISONERS WHO WERE GIVEN A MAXIMUM SENTENCE, 32 OF WHOM WERE FIRST TIME OFFENDERS. TODAY, 15 OF THEM ARE FREE MEN.

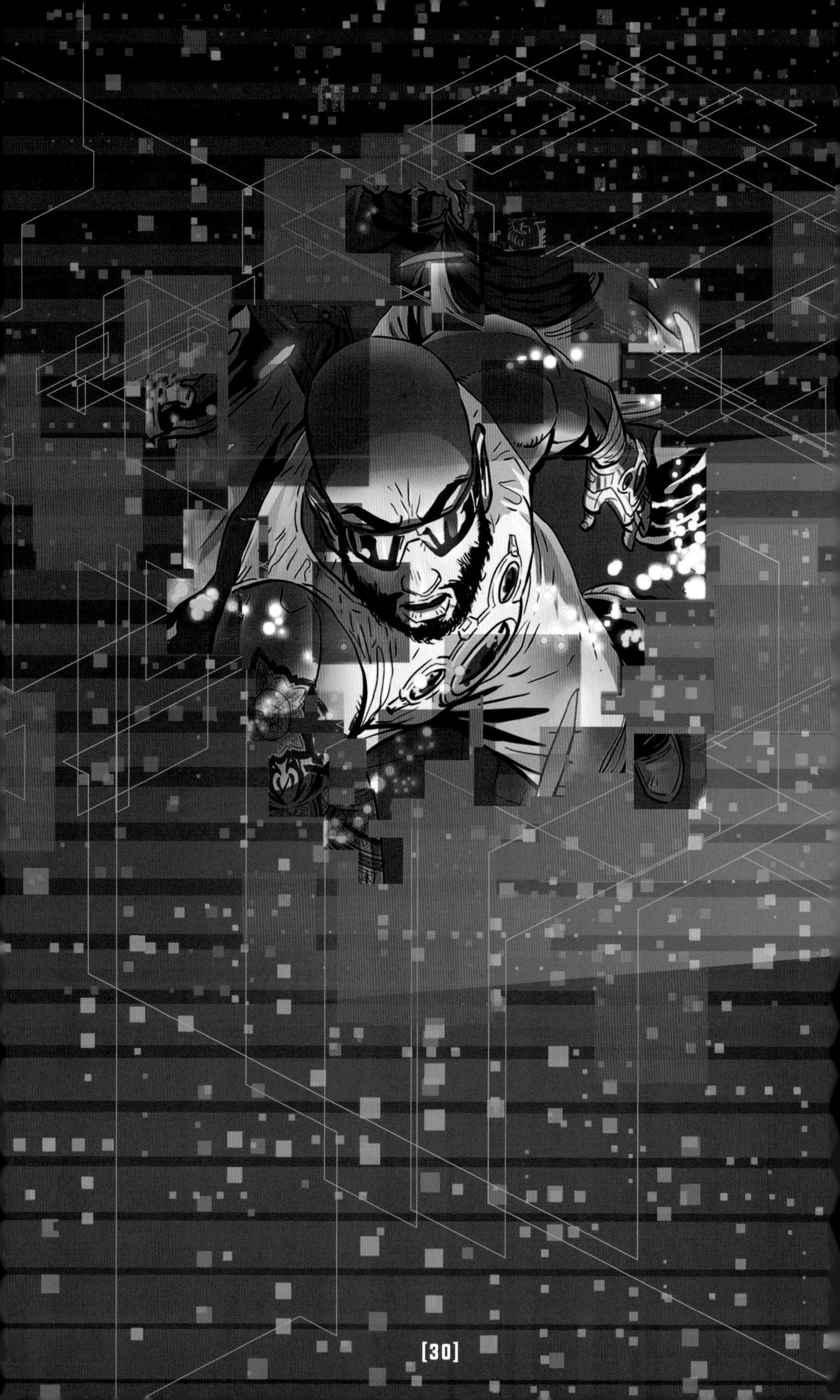

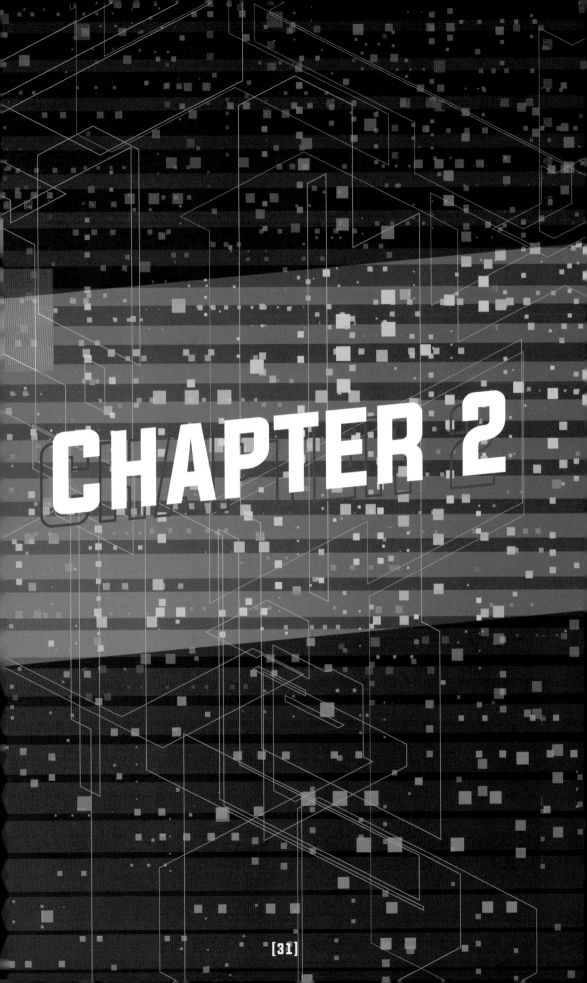

CHAPTER 2

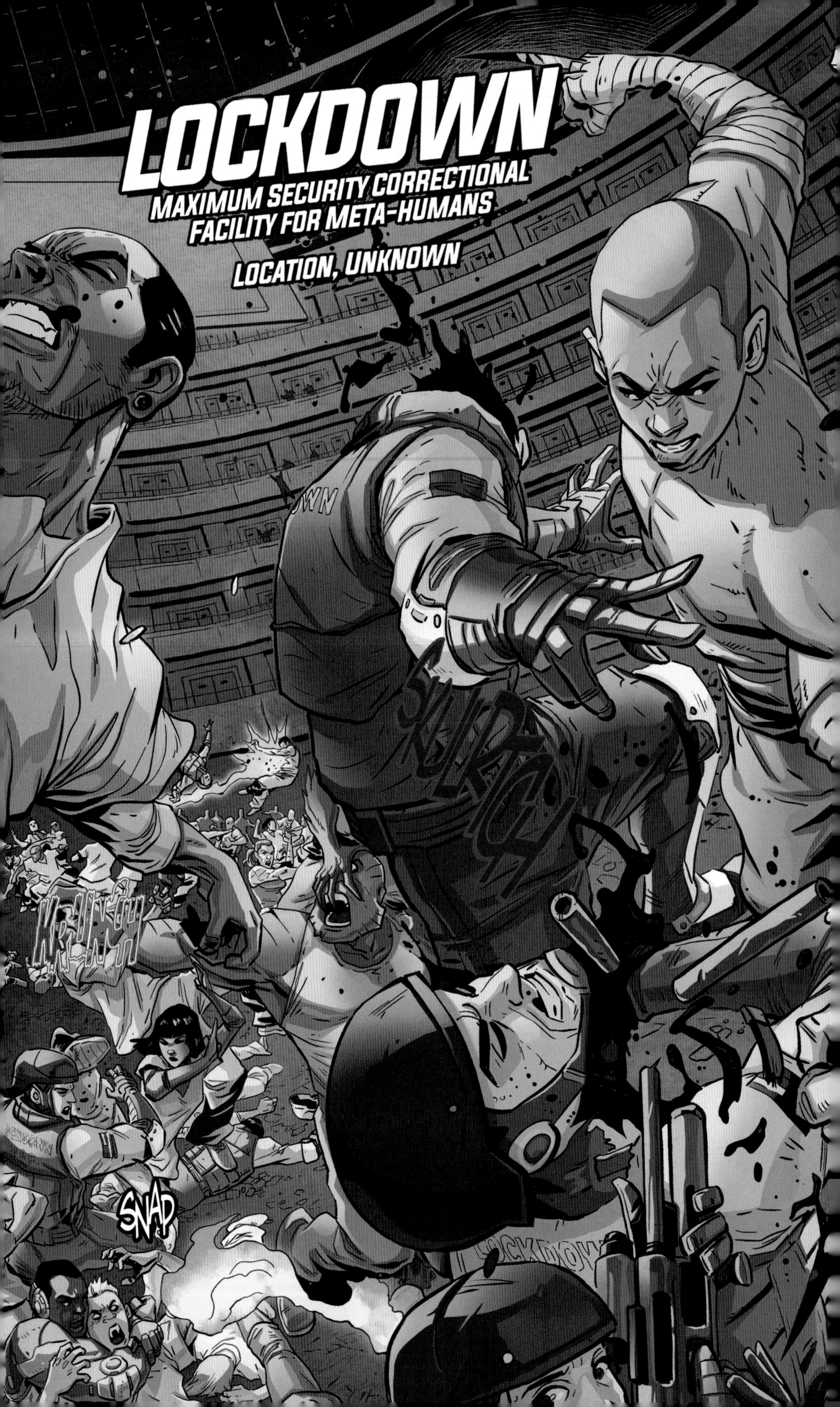
LOCKDOWN
MAXIMUM SECURITY CORRECTIONAL FACILITY FOR META-HUMANS
LOCATION, UNKNOWN
SNAP

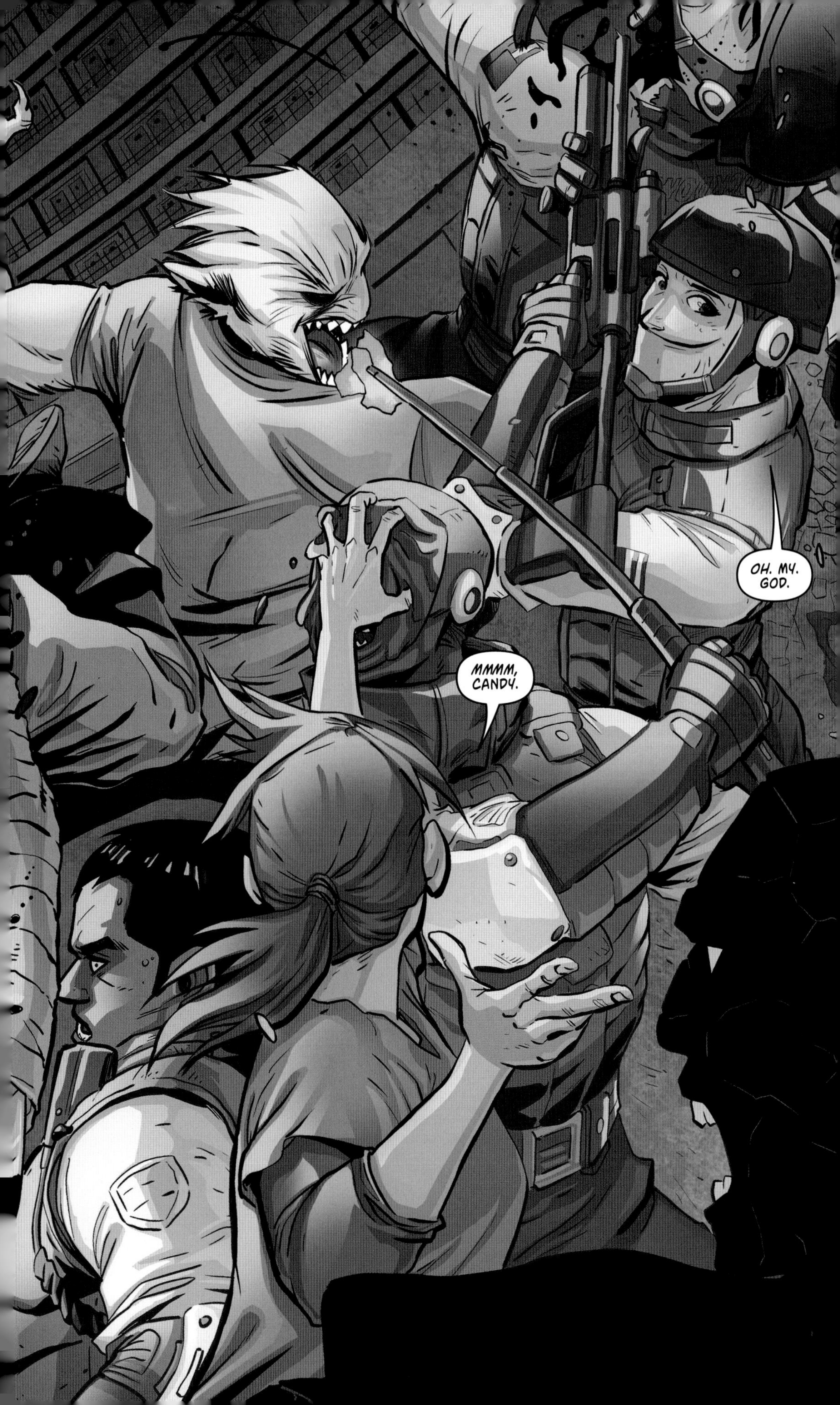
OH. MY. GOD.
MMMM, CANDY.

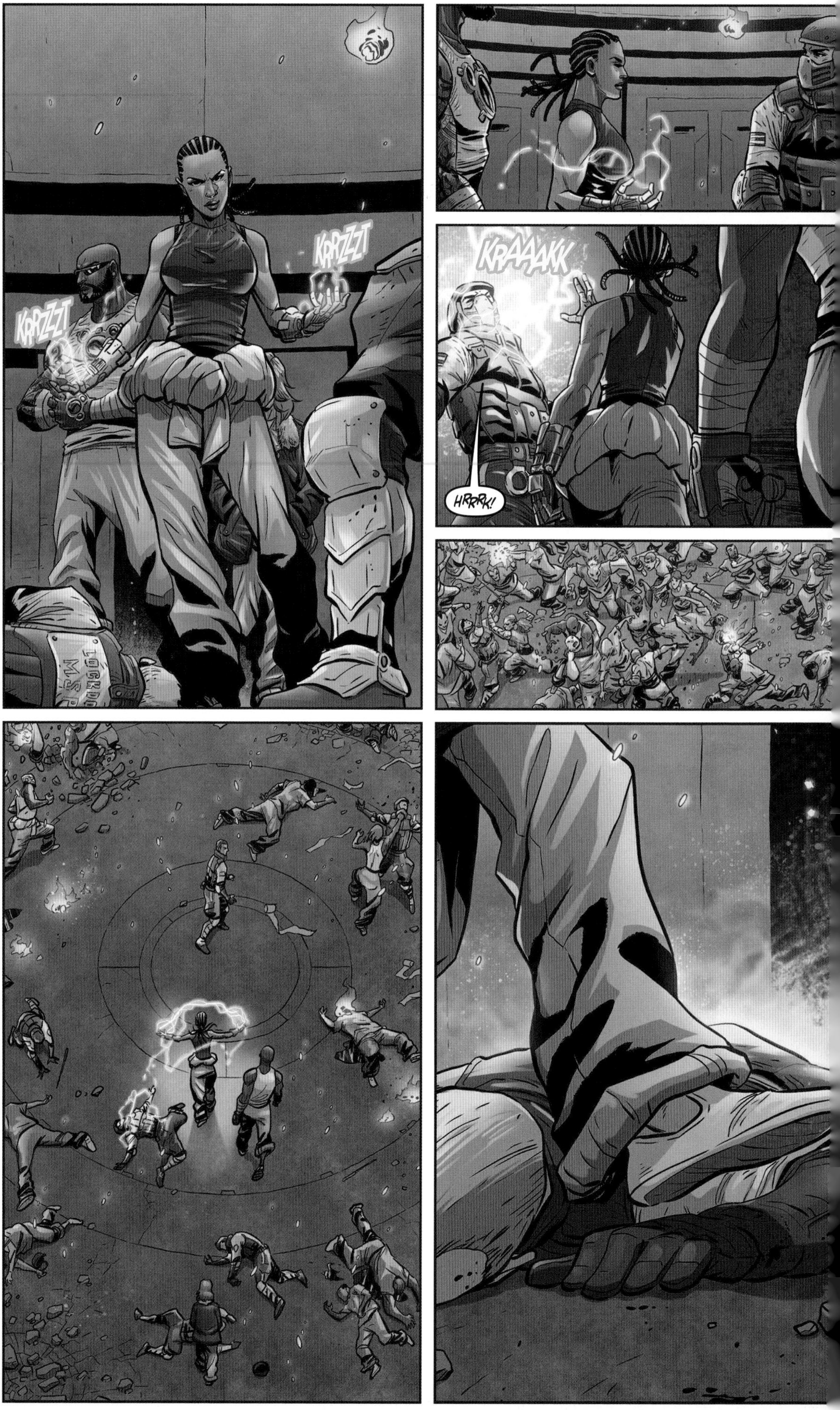
KRRZZZT
KRRZZZT
KRAAAKK
HRRRK!

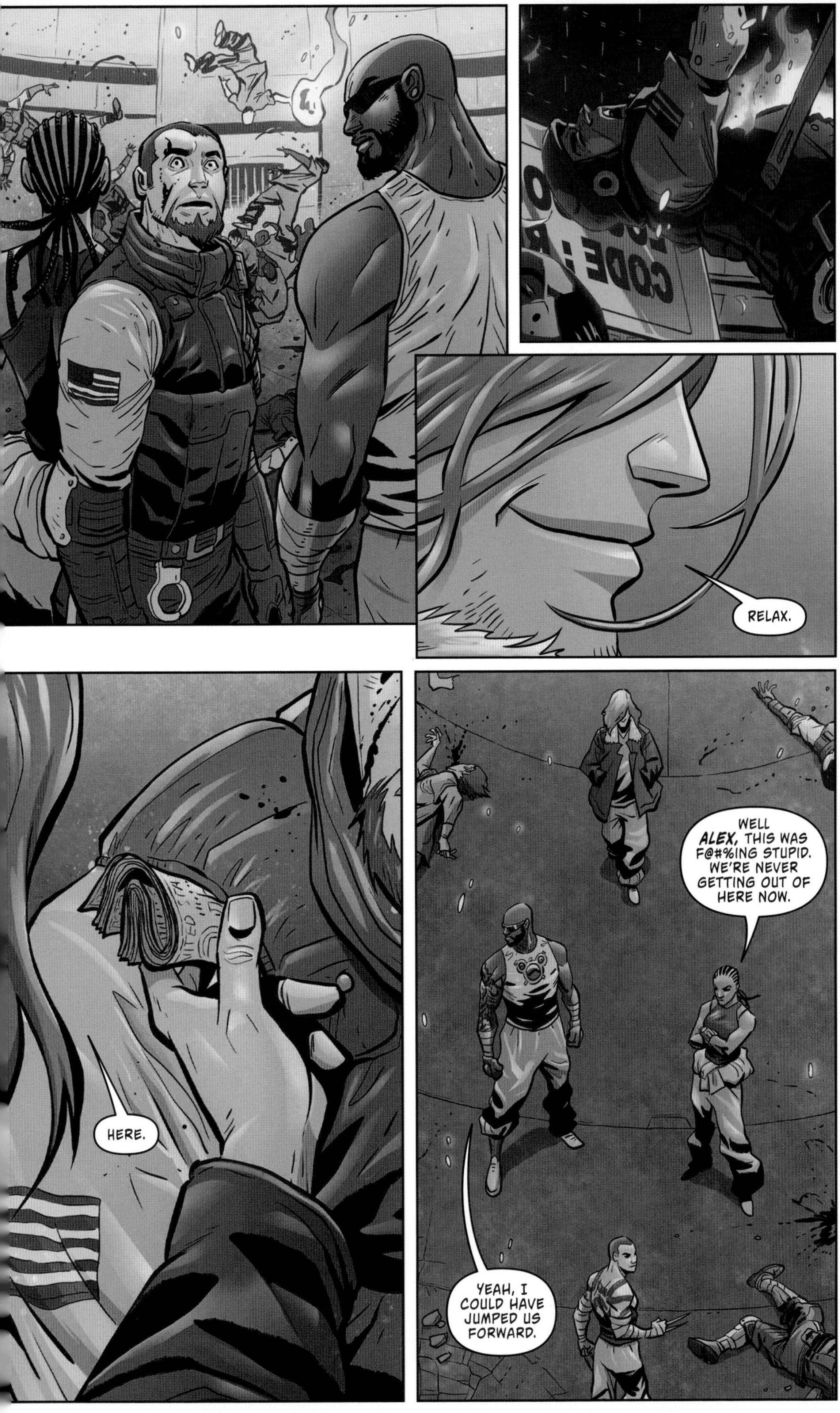
CODE:
RELAX.
HERE.
WELL ALEX, THIS WAS F@#%ING STUPID. WE'RE NEVER GETTING OUT OF HERE NOW.
YEAH, I COULD HAVE JUMPED US FORWARD.

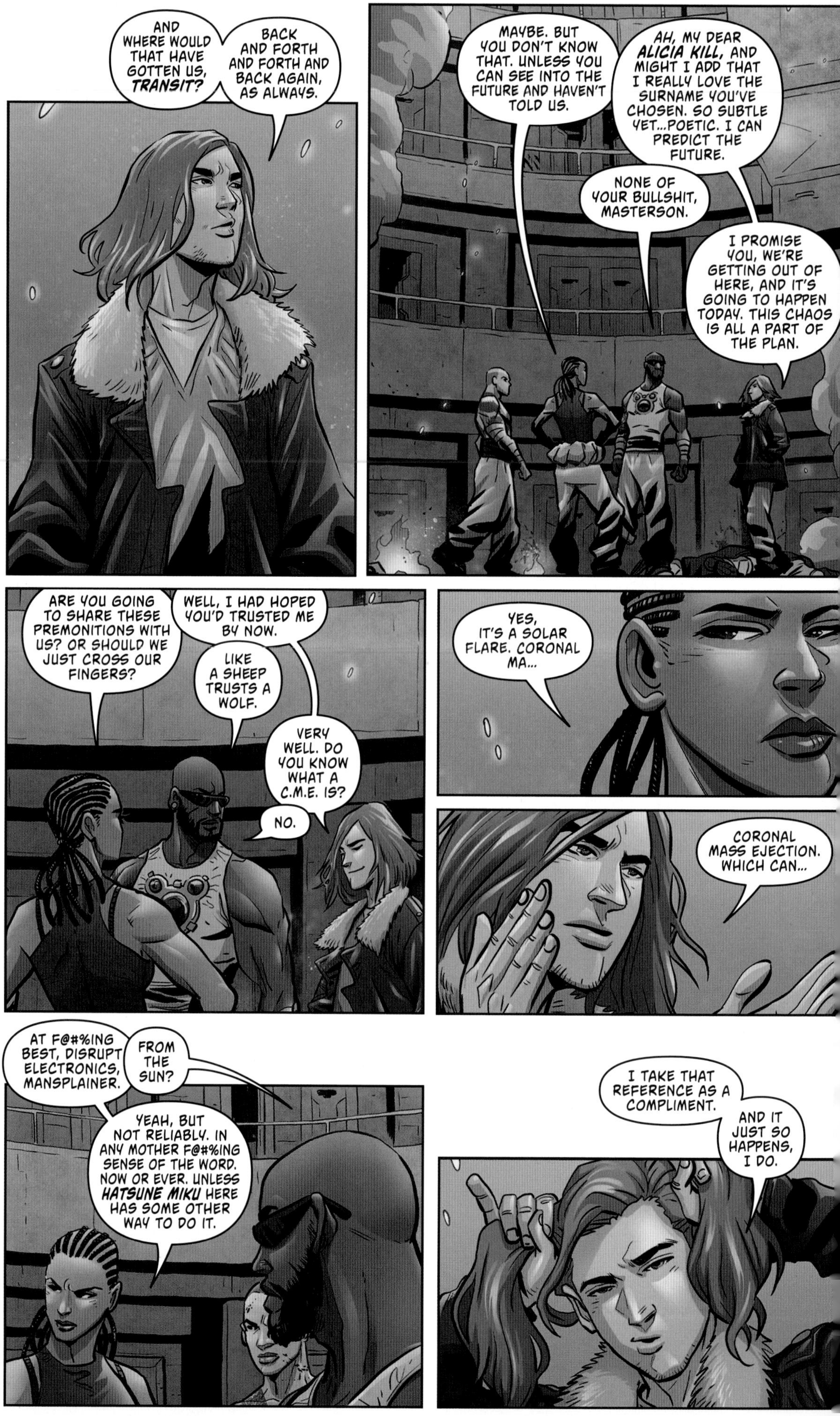
AND WHERE WOULD THAT HAVE GOTTEN US, TRANSIT?
BACK AND FORTH AND FORTH AND BACK AGAIN, AS ALWAYS.
MAYBE. BUT YOU DON'T KNOW THAT. UNLESS YOU CAN SEE INTO THE FUTURE AND HAVEN'T TOLD US.
AH, MY DEAR ALICIA KILL, AND MIGHT I ADD THAT I REALLY LOVE THE SURNAME YOU'VE CHOSEN. SO SUBTLE YET...POETIC. I CAN PREDICT THE FUTURE.
NONE OF YOUR BULLSHIT, MASTERSON.
I PROMISE YOU, WE'RE GETTING OUT OF HERE, AND IT'S GOING TO HAPPEN TODAY. THIS CHAOS IS ALL A PART OF THE PLAN.
ARE YOU GOING TO SHARE THESE PREMONITIONS WITH US? OR SHOULD WE JUST CROSS OUR FINGERS?
WELL, I HAD HOPED YOU'D TRUSTED ME BY NOW.
LIKE A SHEEP TRUSTS A WOLF.
VERY WELL. DO YOU KNOW WHAT A C.M.E. IS?
NO.
YES, IT'S A SOLAR FLARE. CORONAL MA...
CORONAL MASS EJECTION. WHICH CAN...
AT F@#%ING BEST, DISRUPT ELECTRONICS, MANSPLAINER.
FROM THE SUN?
YEAH, BUT NOT RELIABLY. IN ANY MOTHER F@#%ING SENSE OF THE WORD. NOW OR EVER. UNLESS HATSUNE MIKU HERE HAS SOME OTHER WAY TO DO IT.
I TAKE THAT REFERENCE AS A COMPLIMENT.
AND IT JUST SO HAPPENS, I DO.

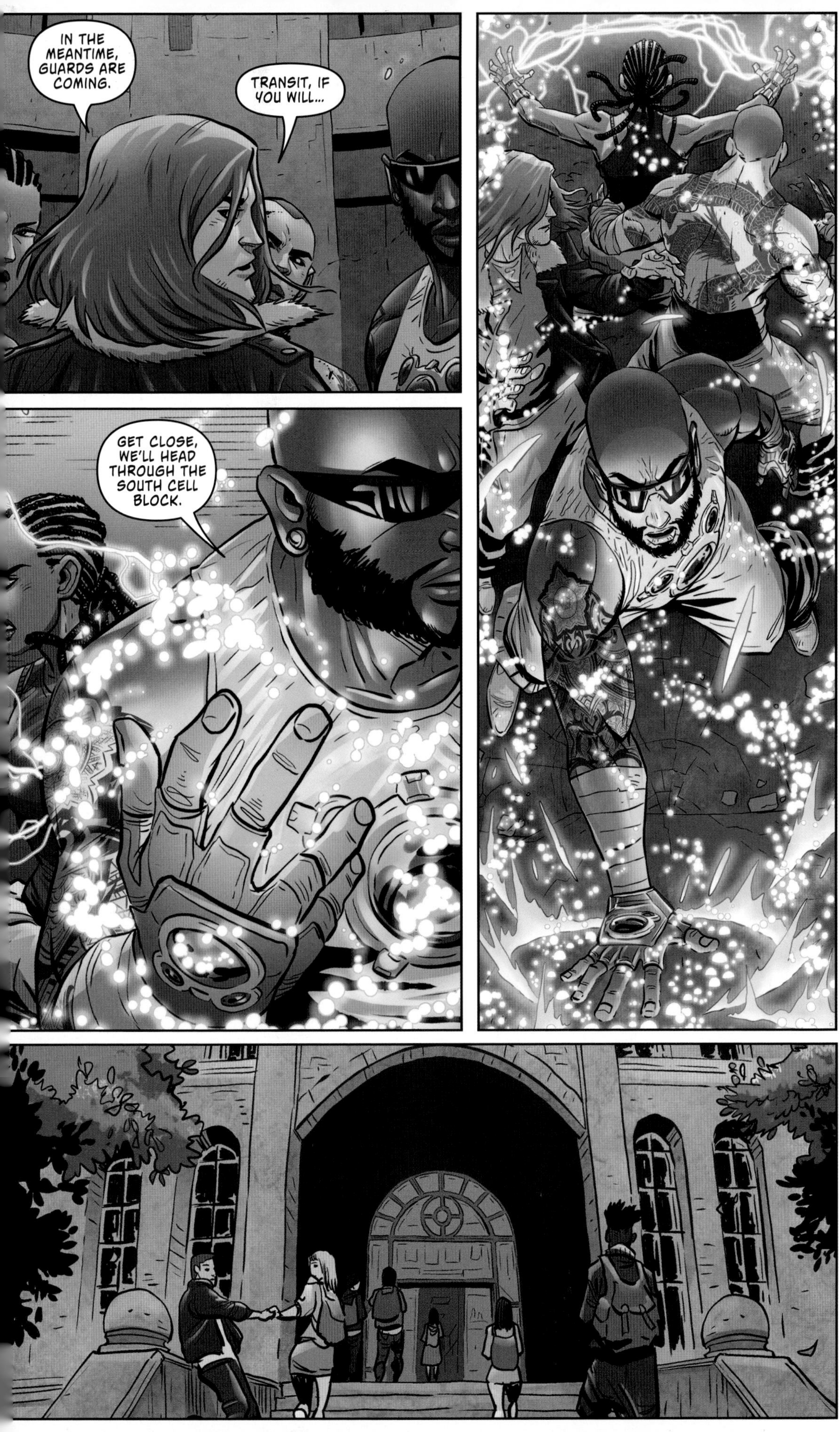
IN THE MEANTIME, GUARDS ARE COMING.
TRANSIT, IF YOU WILL...
GET CLOSE, WE'LL HEAD THROUGH THE SOUTH CELL BLOCK.

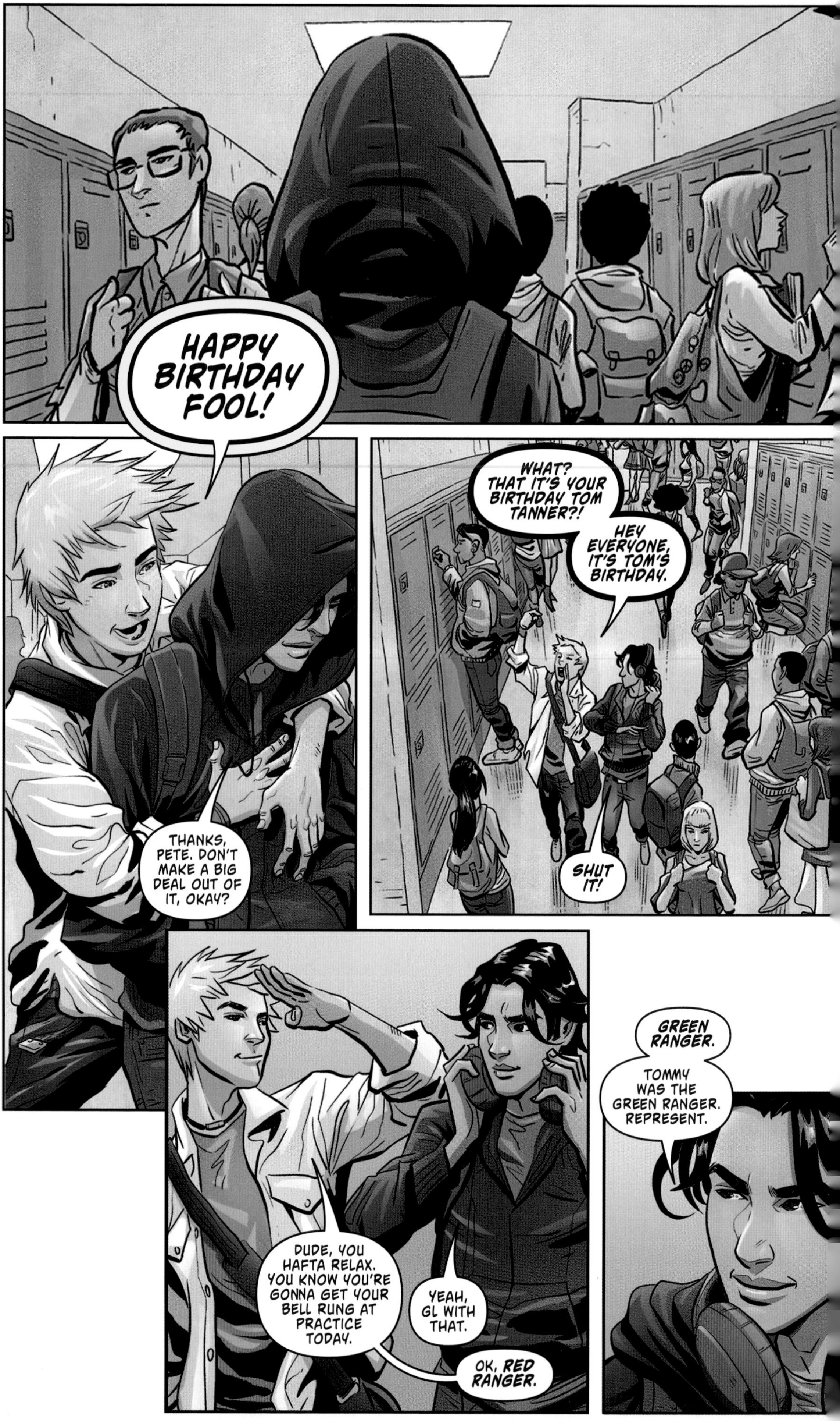
HAPPY BIRTHDAY FOOL!
THANKS, PETE. DON'T MAKE A BIG DEAL OUT OF IT, OKAY?
WHAT? THAT IT'S YOUR BIRTHDAY TOM TANNER?!
HEY EVERYONE, IT'S TOM'S BIRTHDAY.
SHUT IT!
DUDE, YOU HAFTA RELAX. YOU KNOW YOU'RE GONNA GET YOUR BELL RUNG AT PRACTICE TODAY.
YEAH, GL WITH THAT.
OK, RED RANGER.
GREEN RANGER.
TOMMY WAS THE GREEN RANGER. REPRESENT.

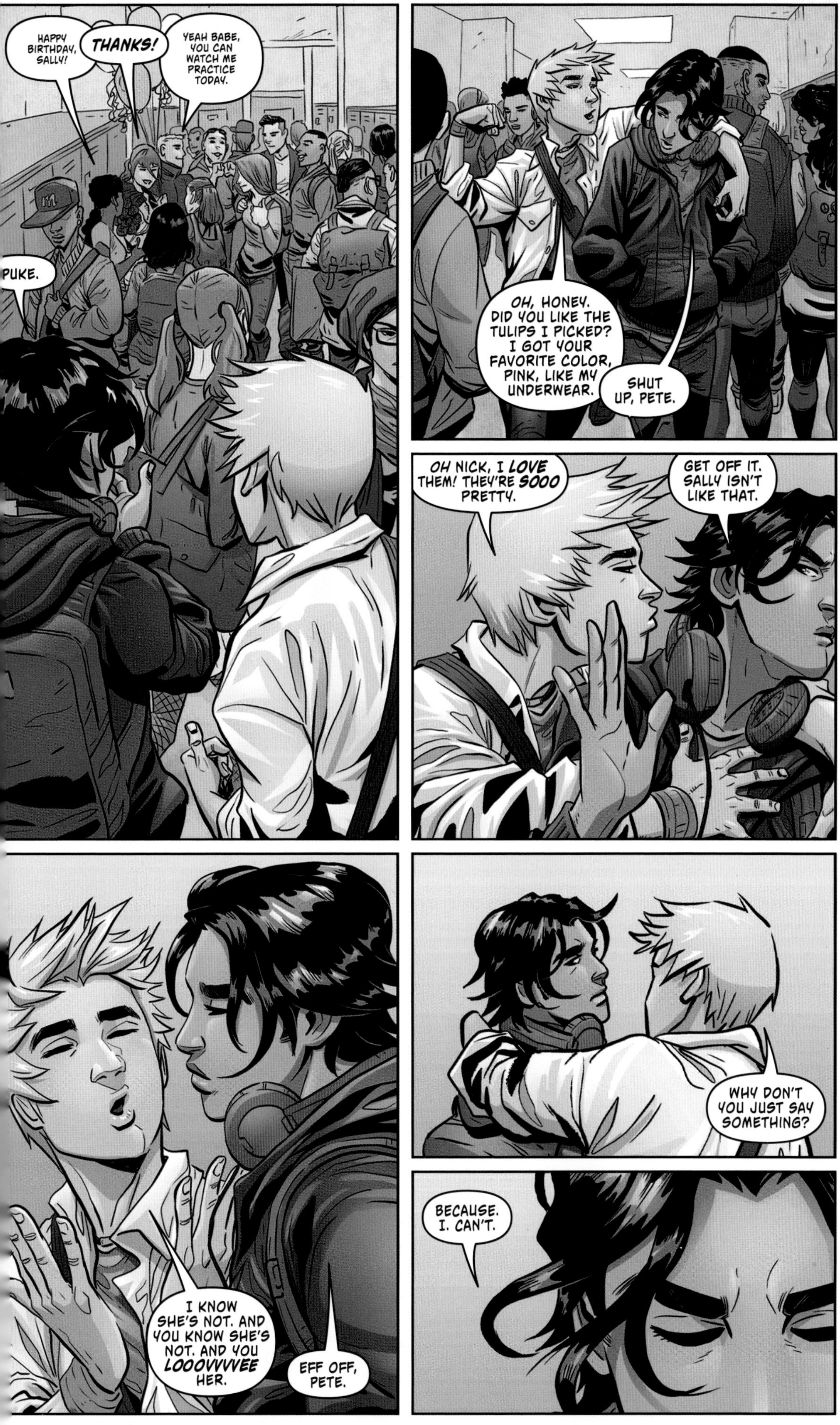
HAPPY BIRTHDAY, SALLY!
THANKS!
YEAH BABE, YOU CAN WATCH ME PRACTICE TODAY.
PUKE.
OH, HONEY. DID YOU LIKE THE TULIPS I PICKED? I GOT YOUR FAVORITE COLOR, PINK, LIKE MY UNDERWEAR.
SHUT UP, PETE.
OH NICK, I LOVE THEM! THEY'RE SOOO PRETTY.
GET OFF IT. SALLY ISN'T LIKE THAT.
I KNOW SHE'S NOT. AND YOU KNOW SHE'S NOT. AND YOU LOOOVVVVEE HER.
EFF OFF, PETE.
WHY DON'T YOU JUST SAY SOMETHING?
BECAUSE. I. CAN'T.

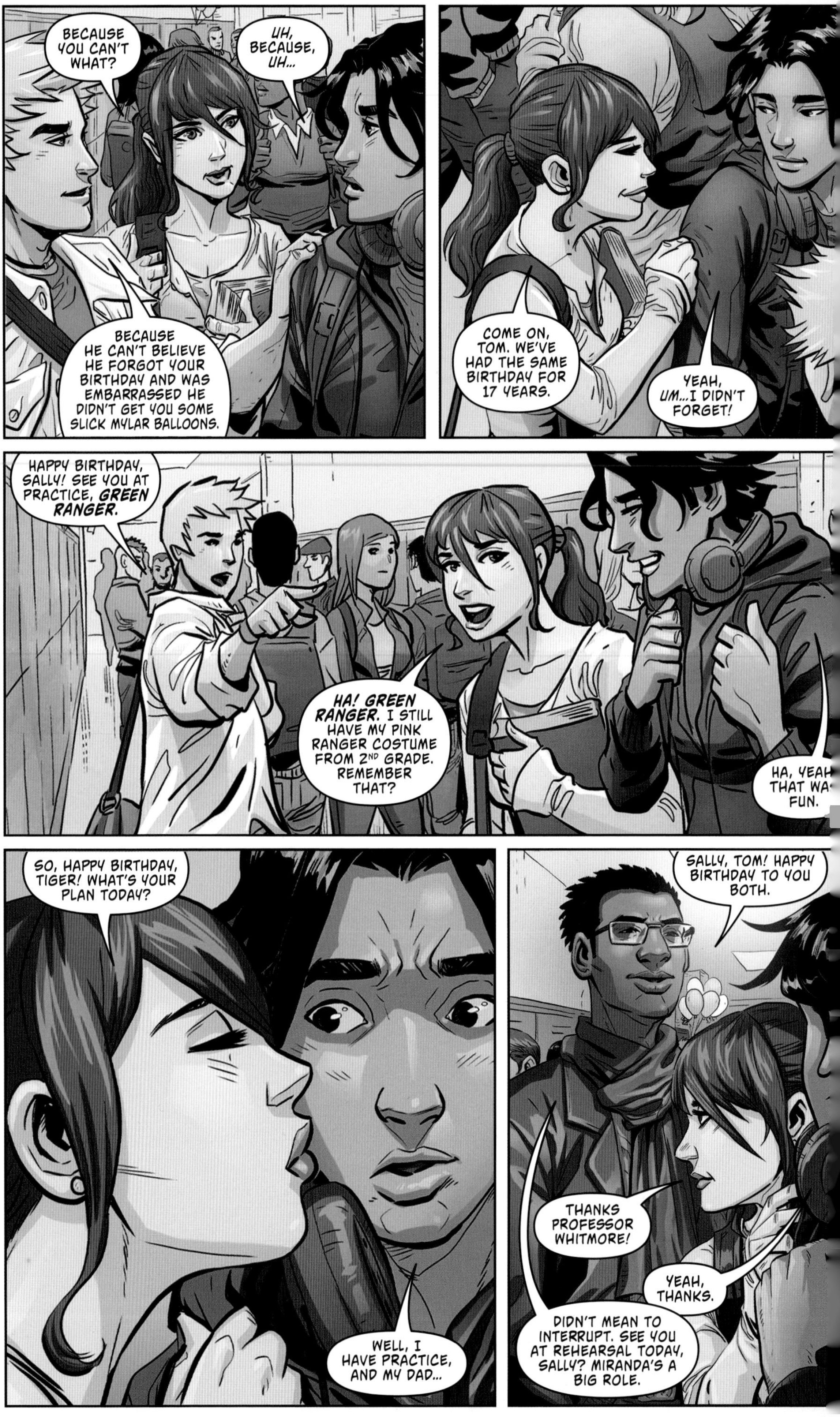
BECAUSE YOU CAN'T WHAT?
UH, BECAUSE, UH...
BECAUSE HE CAN'T BELIEVE HE FORGOT YOUR BIRTHDAY AND WAS EMBARRASSED HE DIDN'T GET YOU SOME SLICK MYLAR BALLOONS.
COME ON, TOM. WE'VE HAD THE SAME BIRTHDAY FOR 17 YEARS.
YEAH, UM...I DIDN'T FORGET!
HAPPY BIRTHDAY, SALLY! SEE YOU AT PRACTICE, GREEN RANGER.
HA! GREEN RANGER. I STILL HAVE MY PINK RANGER COSTUME FROM 2ND GRADE. REMEMBER THAT?
HA, YEAH THAT WA FUN.
SO, HAPPY BIRTHDAY, TIGER! WHAT'S YOUR PLAN TODAY?
WELL, I HAVE PRACTICE, AND MY DAD...
SALLY, TOM! HAPPY BIRTHDAY TO YOU BOTH.
THANKS PROFESSOR WHITMORE!
YEAH, THANKS.
DIDN'T MEAN TO INTERRUPT. SEE YOU AT REHEARSAL TODAY, SALLY? MIRANDA'S A BIG ROLE.

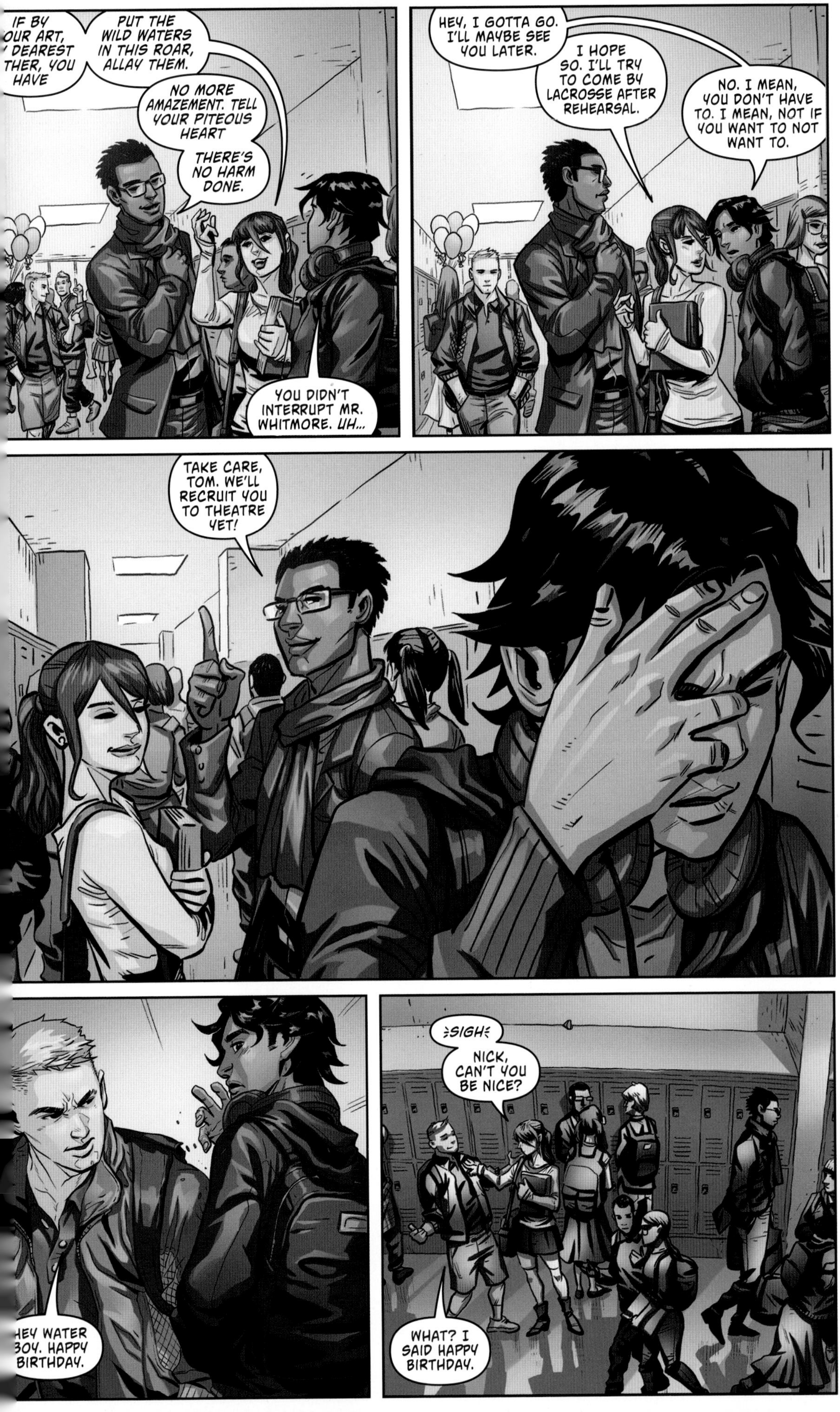
IF BY OUR ART, DEAREST THER, YOU HAVE
PUT THE WILD WATERS IN THIS ROAR, ALLAY THEM.
NO MORE AMAZEMENT. TELL YOUR PITEOUS HEART
THERE'S NO HARM DONE.
YOU DIDN'T INTERRUPT MR. WHITMORE. UH...
HEY, I GOTTA GO. I'LL MAYBE SEE YOU LATER.
I HOPE SO. I'LL TRY TO COME BY LACROSSE AFTER REHEARSAL.
NO. I MEAN, YOU DON'T HAVE TO. I MEAN, NOT IF YOU WANT TO NOT WANT TO.
TAKE CARE, TOM. WE'LL RECRUIT YOU TO THEATRE YET!
HEY WATER BOY. HAPPY BIRTHDAY.
SIGH
NICK, CAN'T YOU BE NICE?
WHAT? I SAID HAPPY BIRTHDAY.

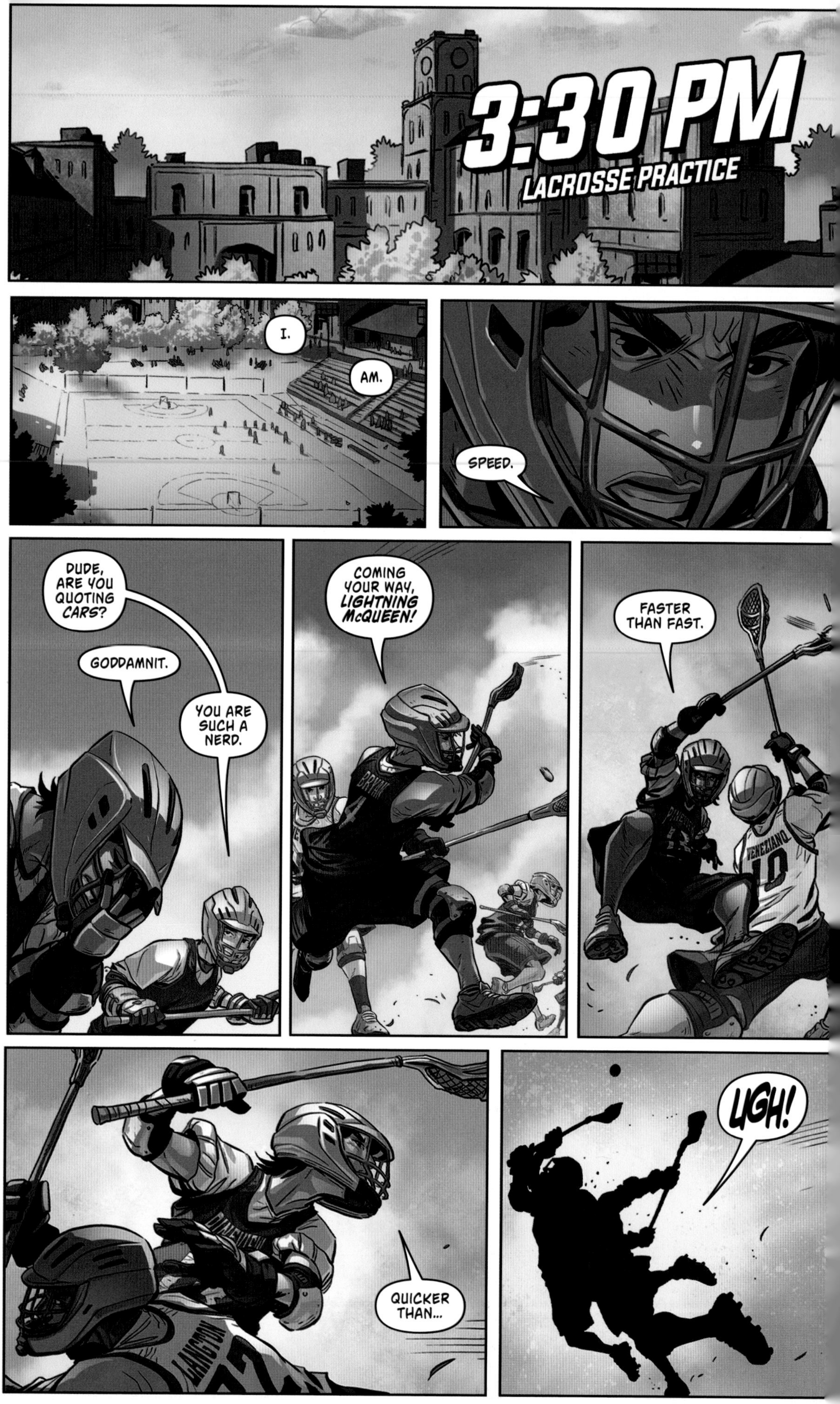
3:30 PM
LACROSSE PRACTICE
I.
AM.
SPEED.
DUDE, ARE YOU QUOTING CARS?
GODDAMNIT.
YOU ARE SUCH A NERD.
COMING YOUR WAY, LIGHTNING McQUEEN!
FASTER THAN FAST.
QUICKER THAN...
UGH!

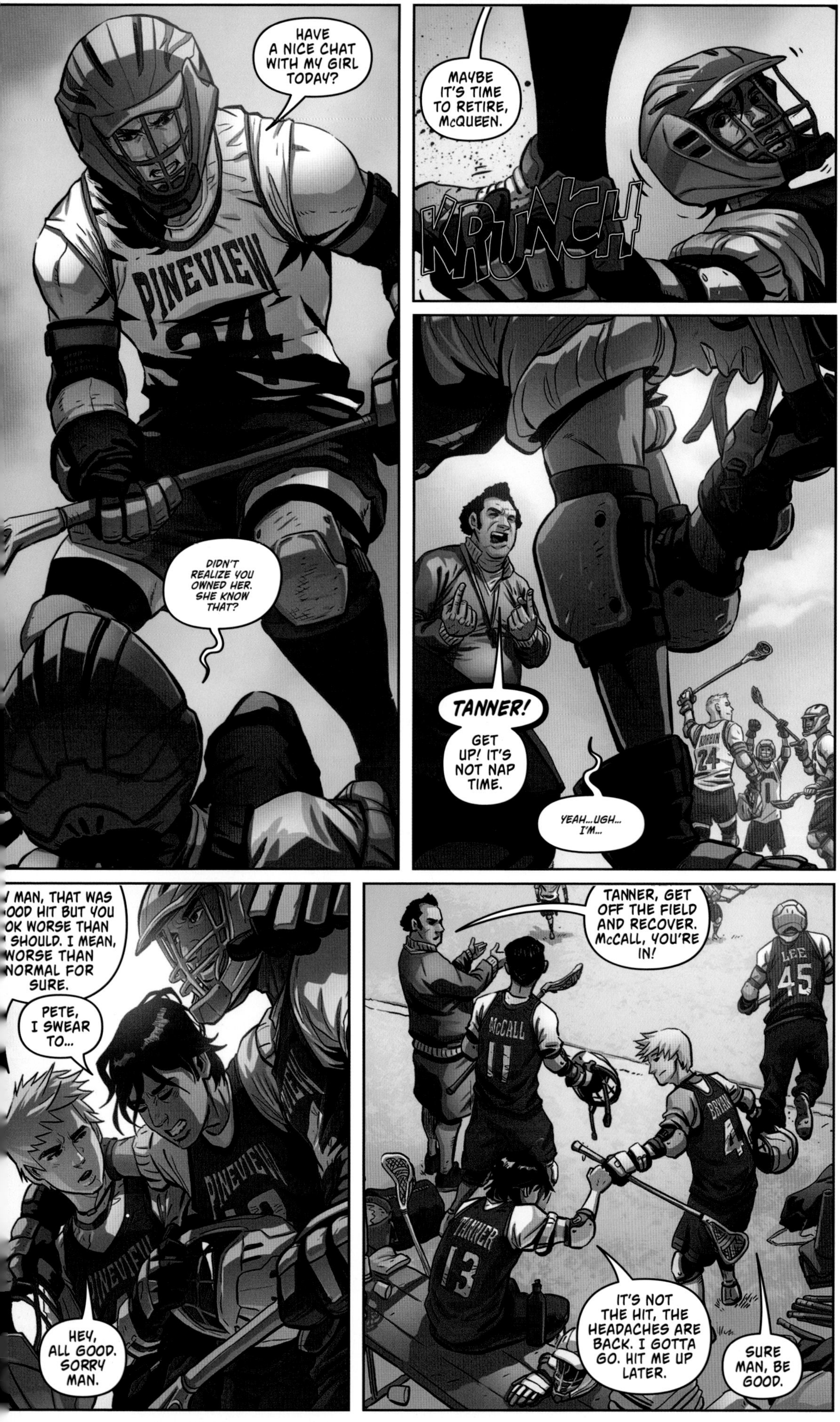
HAVE A NICE CHAT WITH MY GIRL TODAY?
PINEVIEW
DIDN'T REALIZE YOU OWNED HER. SHE KNOW THAT?
MAYBE IT'S TIME TO RETIRE, McQUEEN.
KRUNCH
TANNER!
GET UP! IT'S NOT NAP TIME.
YEAH...UGH... I'M...
MAN, THAT WAS OOD HIT BUT YOU OK WORSE THAN SHOULD. I MEAN, WORSE THAN NORMAL FOR SURE.
PETE, I SWEAR TO...
HEY, ALL GOOD. SORRY MAN.
TANNER, GET OFF THE FIELD AND RECOVER. McCALL, YOU'RE IN!
IT'S NOT THE HIT, THE HEADACHES ARE BACK. I GOTTA GO. HIT ME UP LATER.
SURE MAN, BE GOOD.

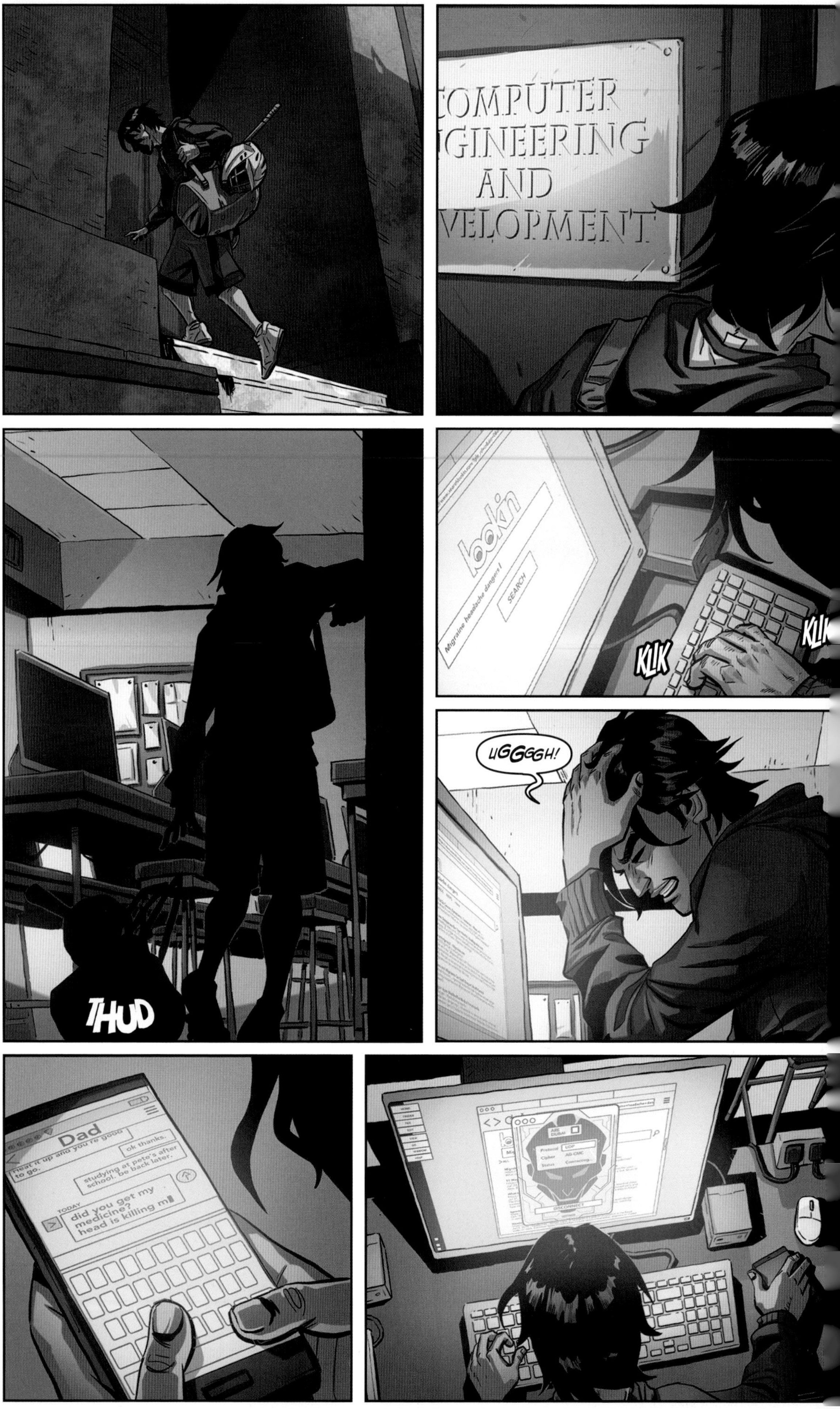
OMPUTER
GINEERING
AND
VELOPMENT
lookn
Migraine headache dangers
SEARCH
KLIK
KLIK
UGGGGH!
THUD
Dad
Heat it up and you're good to go.
ok thanks.
studying at pete's after school. be back later.
TODAY
did you get my medicine? head is killing m
DISCONNECT

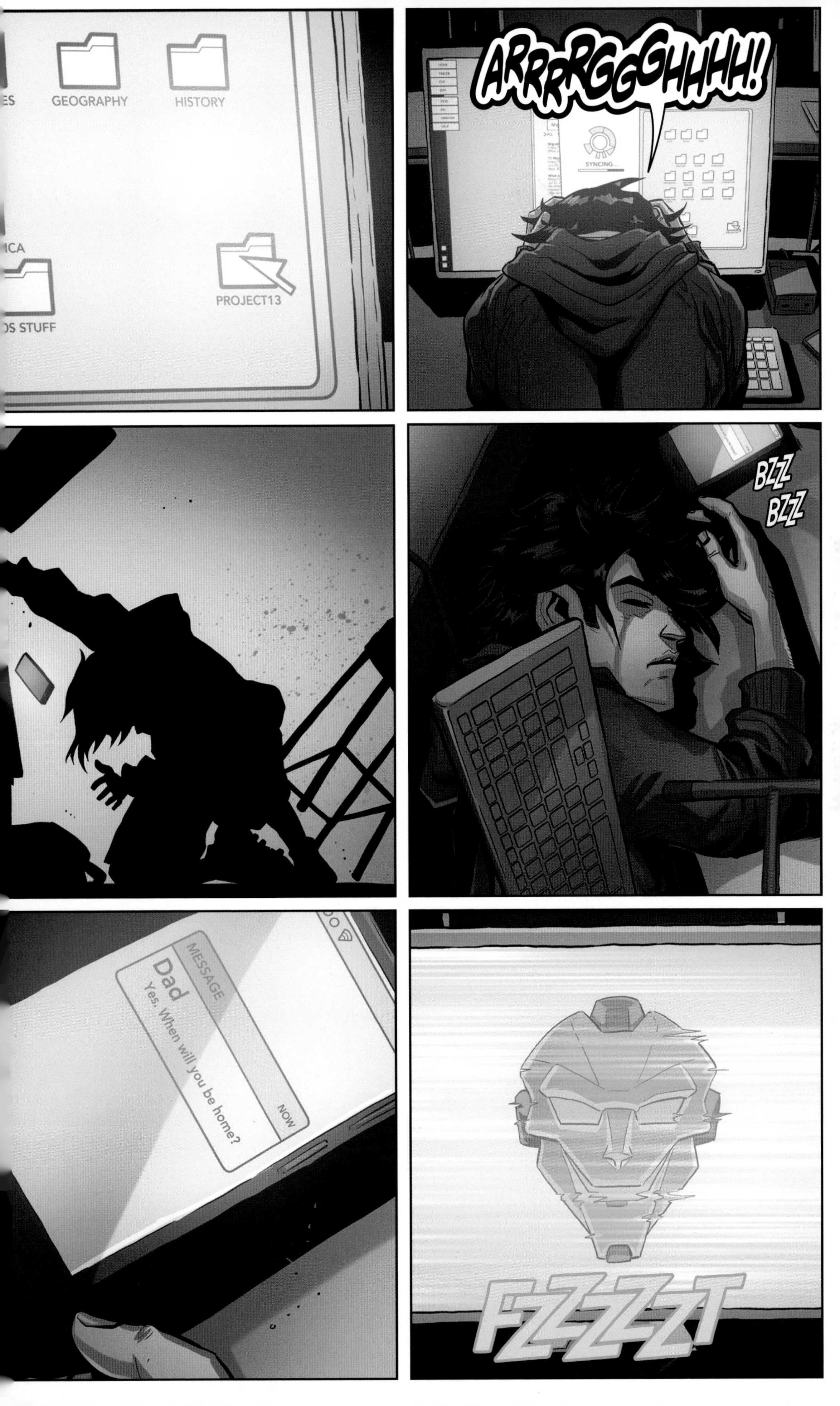
GEOGRAPHY
HISTORY
PROJECT13
ARRRRGGGHHHH!
SYNCING...
BZZZ
BZZZ
MESSAGE
NOW
Dad
Yes. When will you be home?
FZZZZT

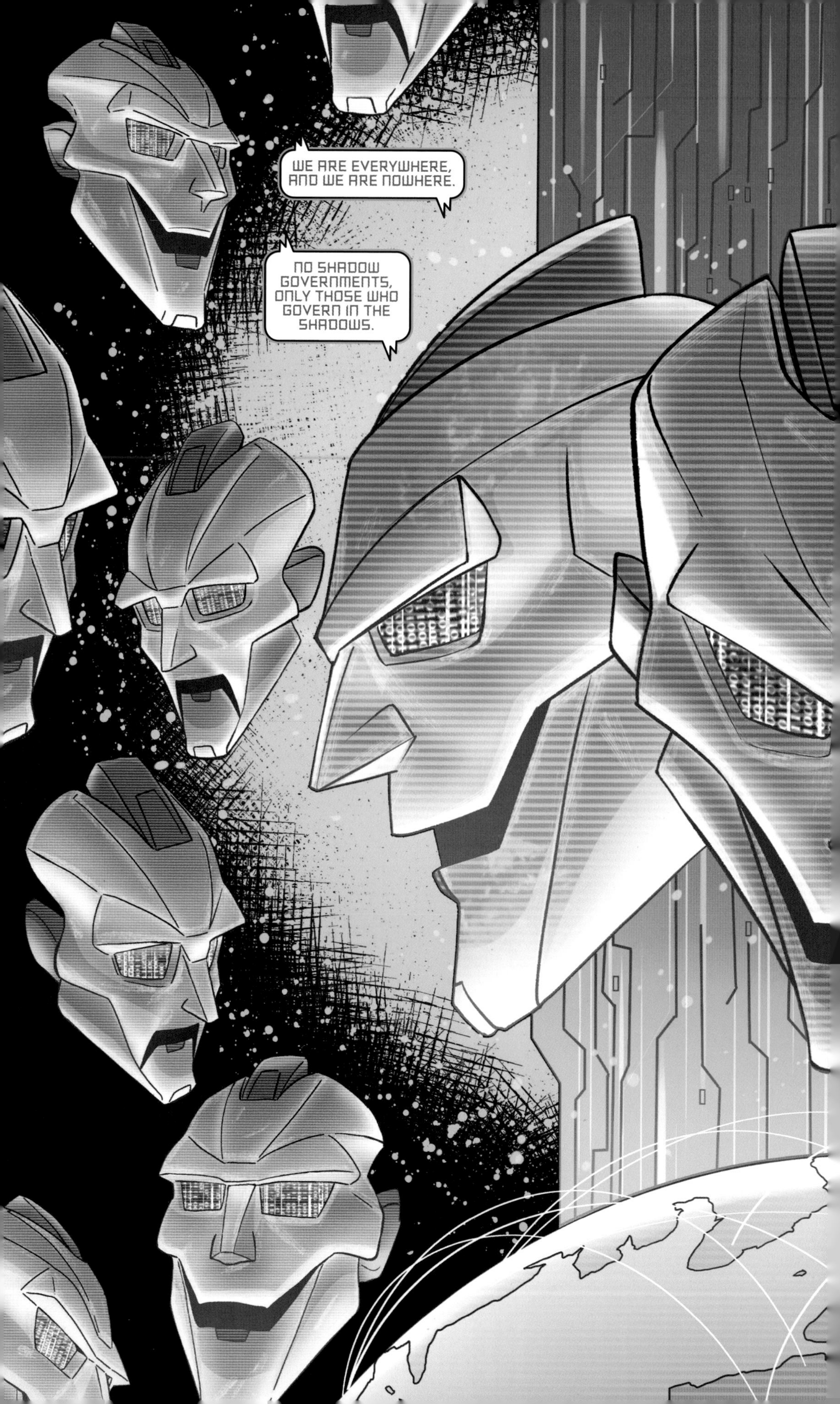
WE ARE EVERYWHERE, AND WE ARE NOWHERE.
NO SHADOW GOVERNMENTS, ONLY THOSE WHO GOVERN IN THE SHADOWS.

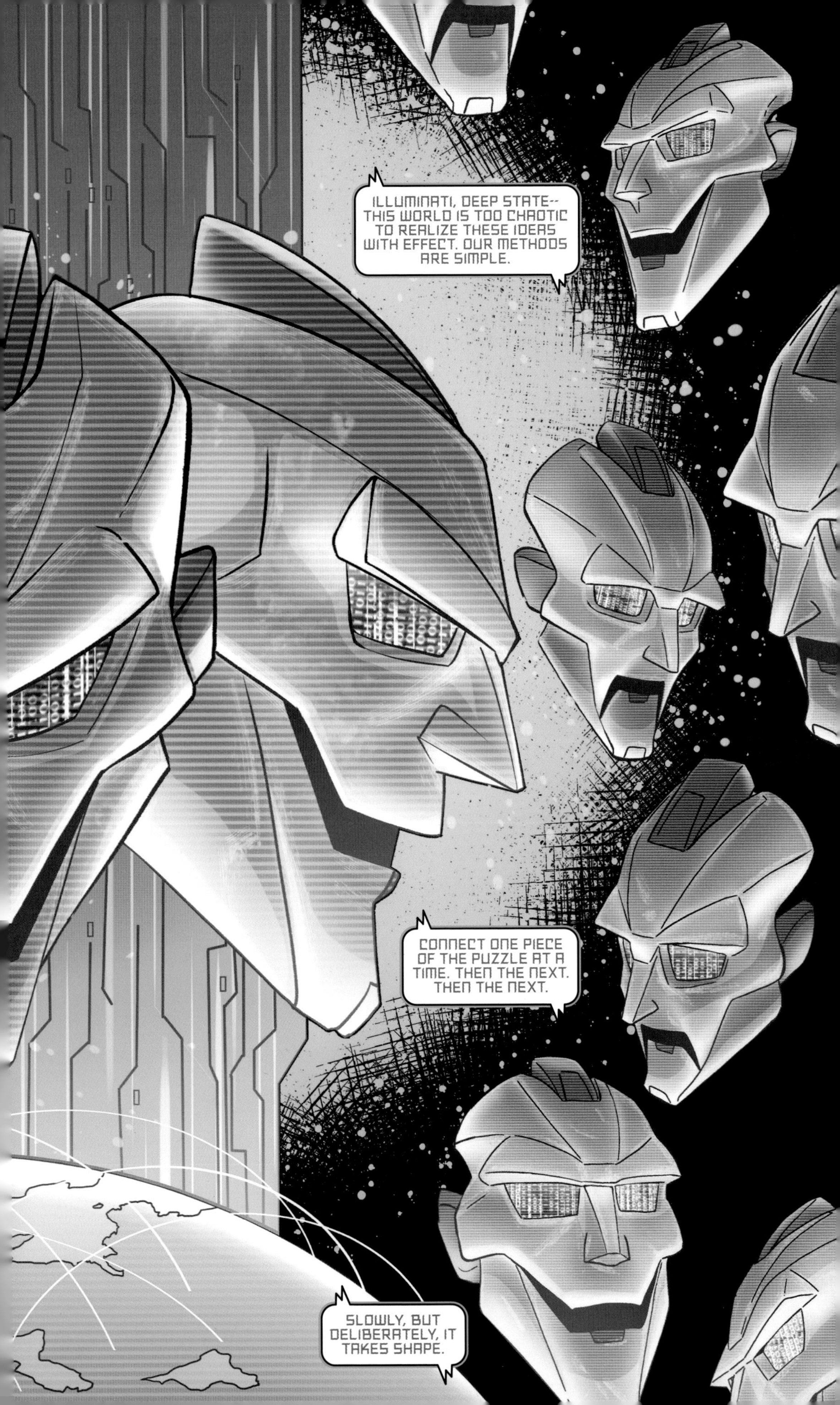
ILLUMINATI, DEEP STATE-- THIS WORLD IS TOO CHAOTIC TO REALIZE THESE IDEAS WITH EFFECT. OUR METHODS ARE SIMPLE.
CONNECT ONE PIECE OF THE PUZZLE AT A TIME. THEN THE NEXT. THEN THE NEXT.
SLOWLY, BUT DELIBERATELY, IT TAKES SHAPE.

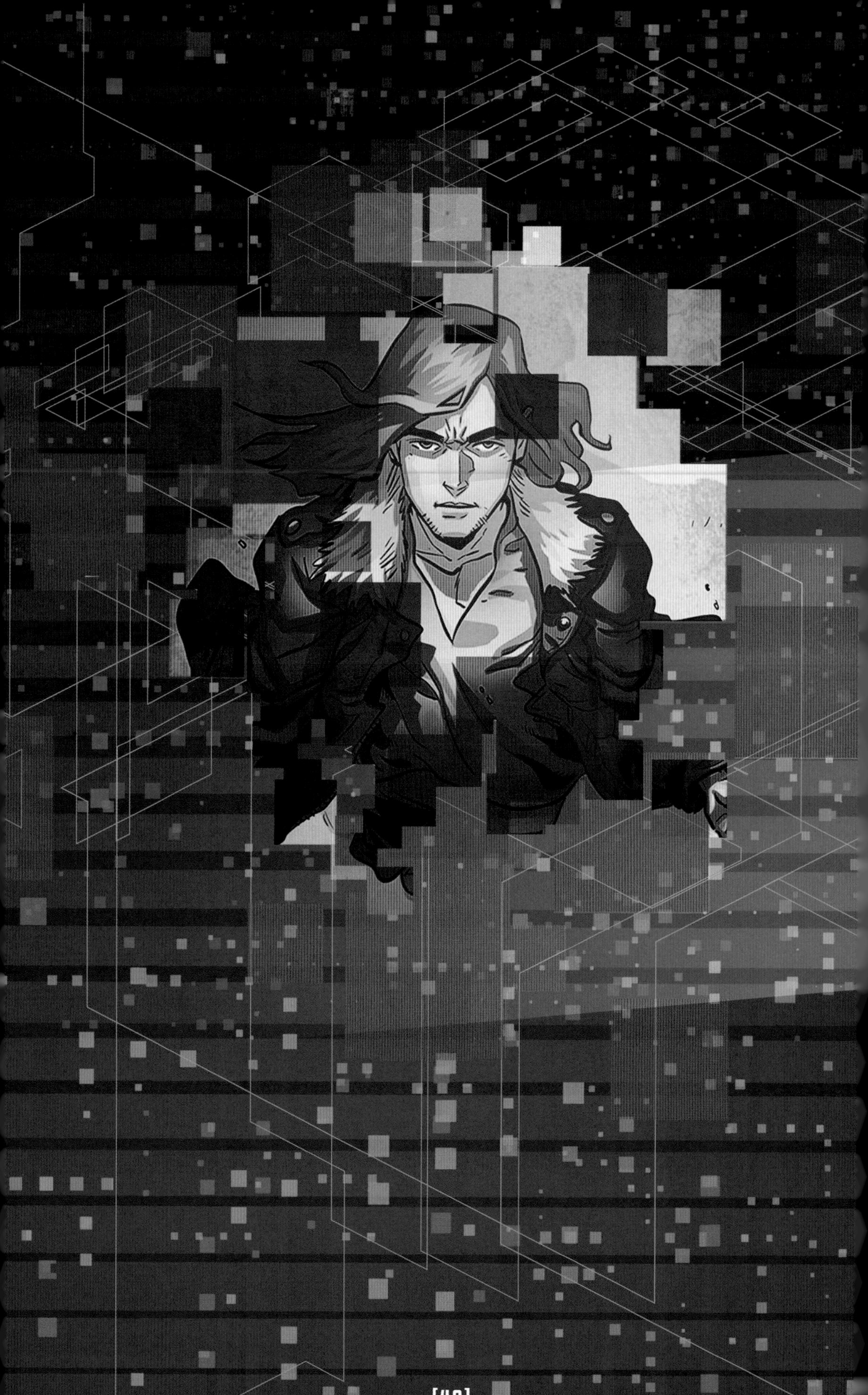

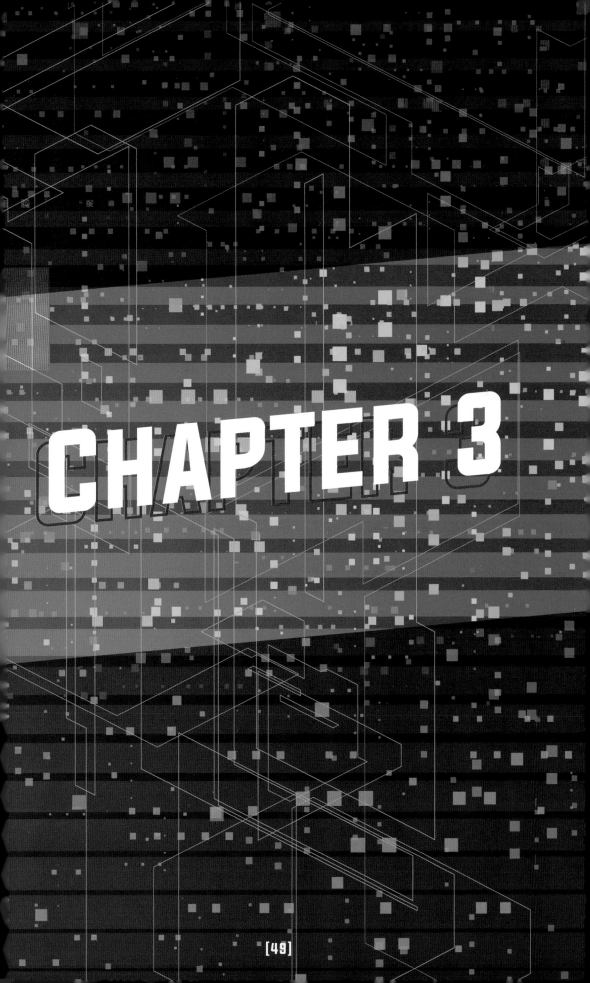

CHAPTER 3

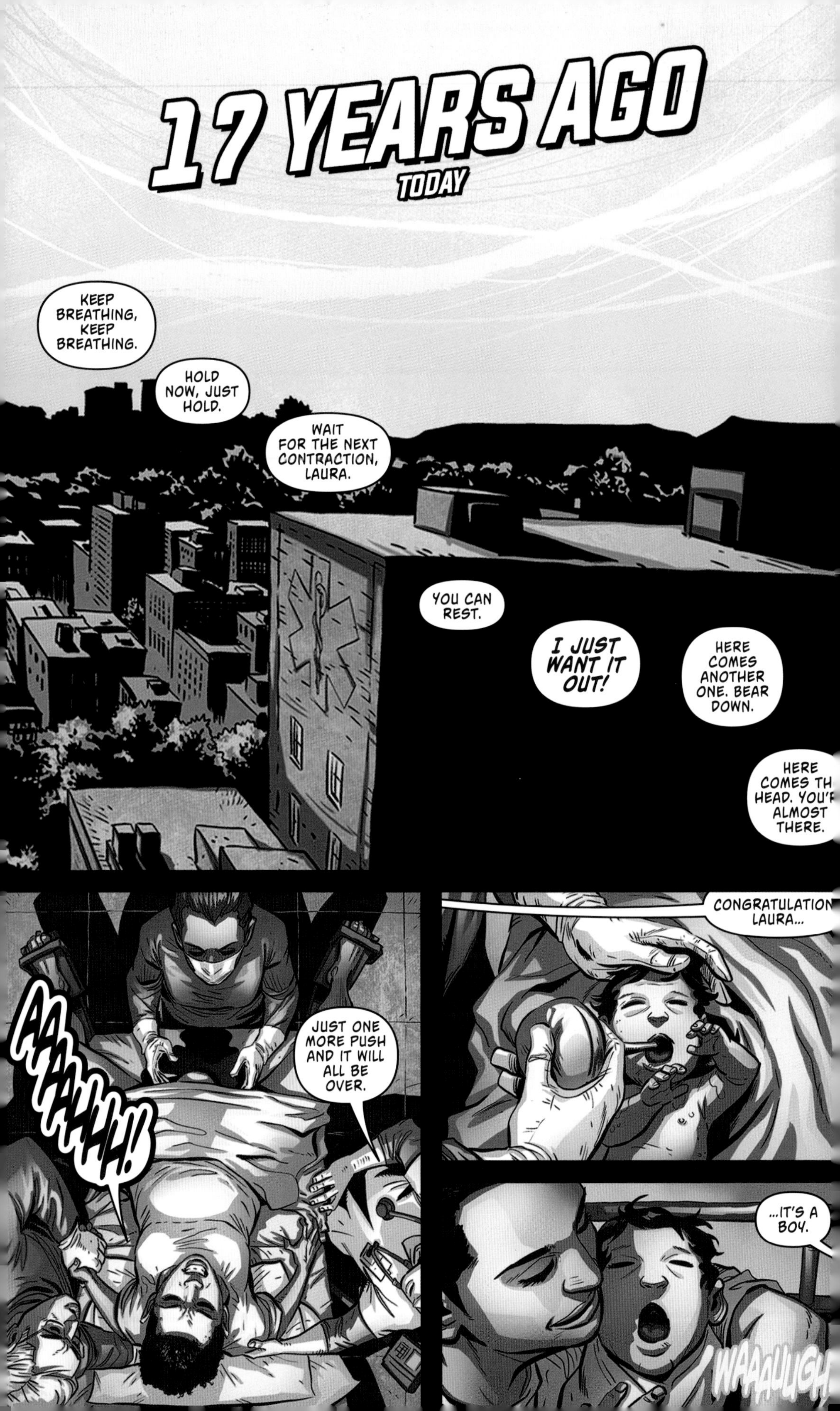

17 YEARS AGO
TODAY
KEEP BREATHING, KEEP BREATHING.
HOLD NOW, JUST HOLD.
WAIT FOR THE NEXT CONTRACTION, LAURA.
YOU CAN REST.
I JUST WANT IT OUT!
HERE COMES ANOTHER ONE. BEAR DOWN.
HERE COMES TH HEAD. YOU'R ALMOST THERE.
AAAAAHHH!
JUST ONE MORE PUSH AND IT WILL ALL BE OVER.
CONGRATULATION LAURA...
...IT'S A BOY.
WAAAUUGH

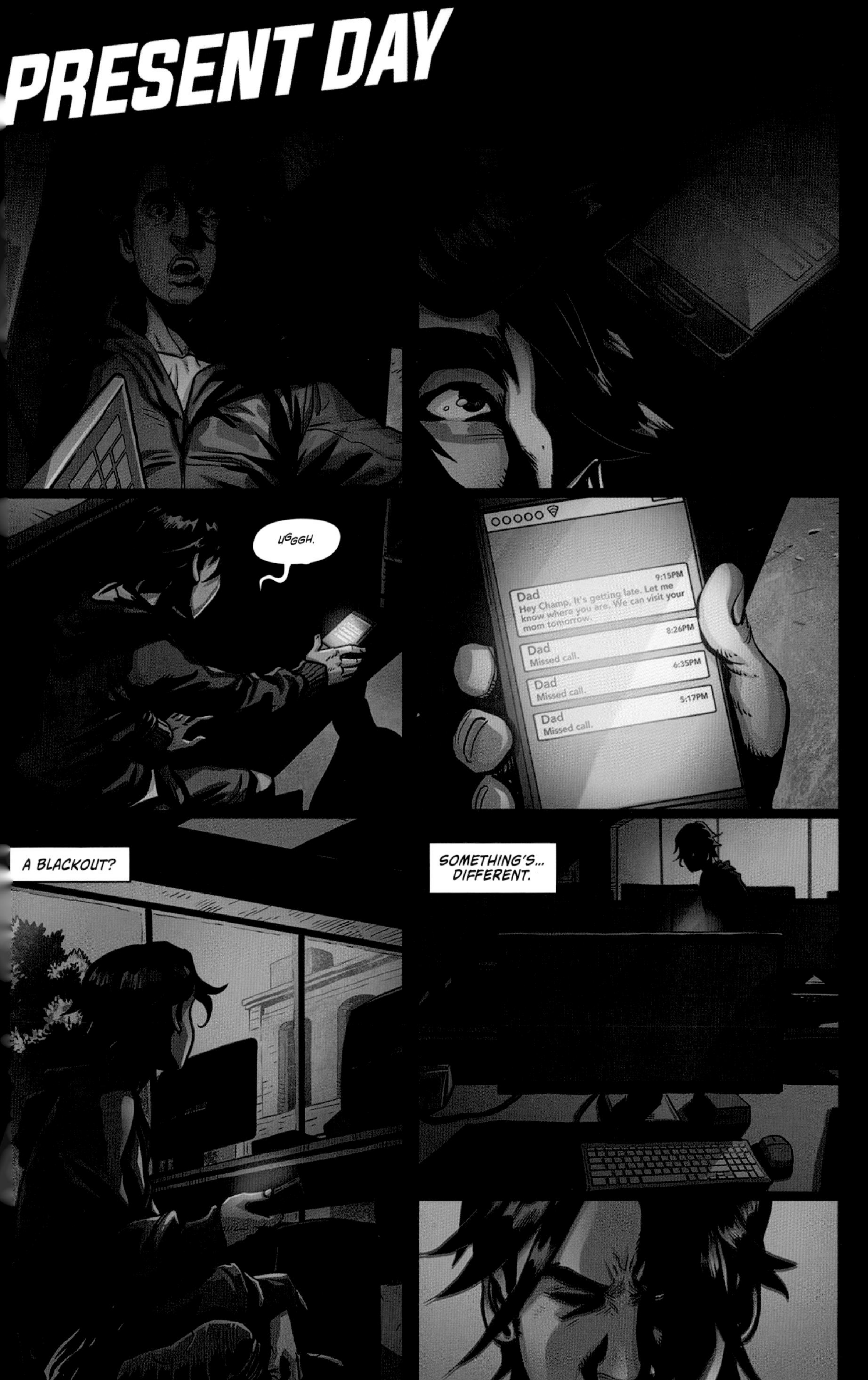
PRESENT DAY
UGGGH.
9:15PM
Dad
Hey Champ, It's getting late. Let me know where you are. We can visit your mom tomorrow.
8:26PM
Dad
Missed call.
6:35PM
Dad
Missed call.
5:17PM
Dad
Missed call.
A BLACKOUT?
SOMETHING'S... DIFFERENT.

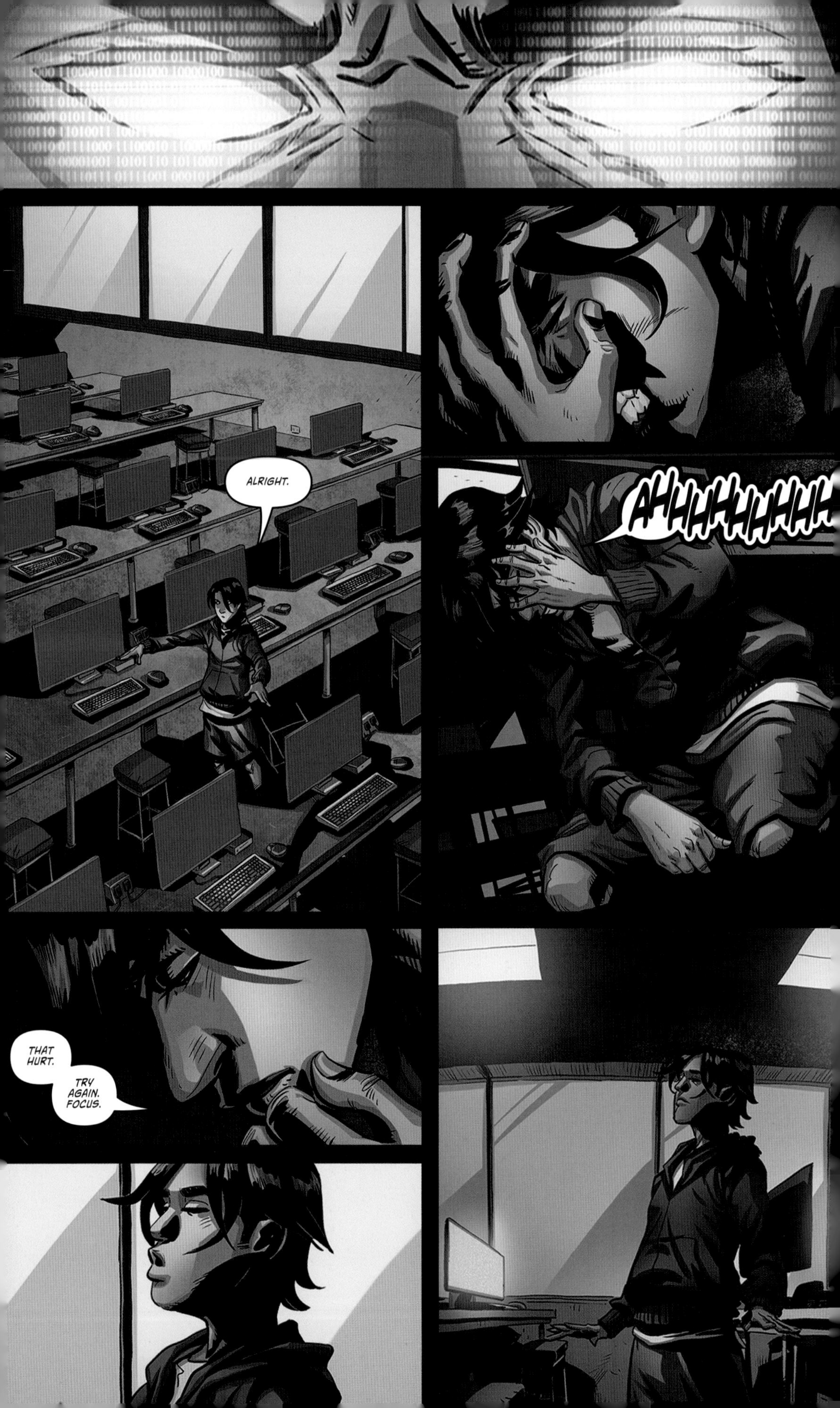
ALRIGHT.
AHHHHHHHHH
THAT HURT.
TRY AGAIN. FOCUS.

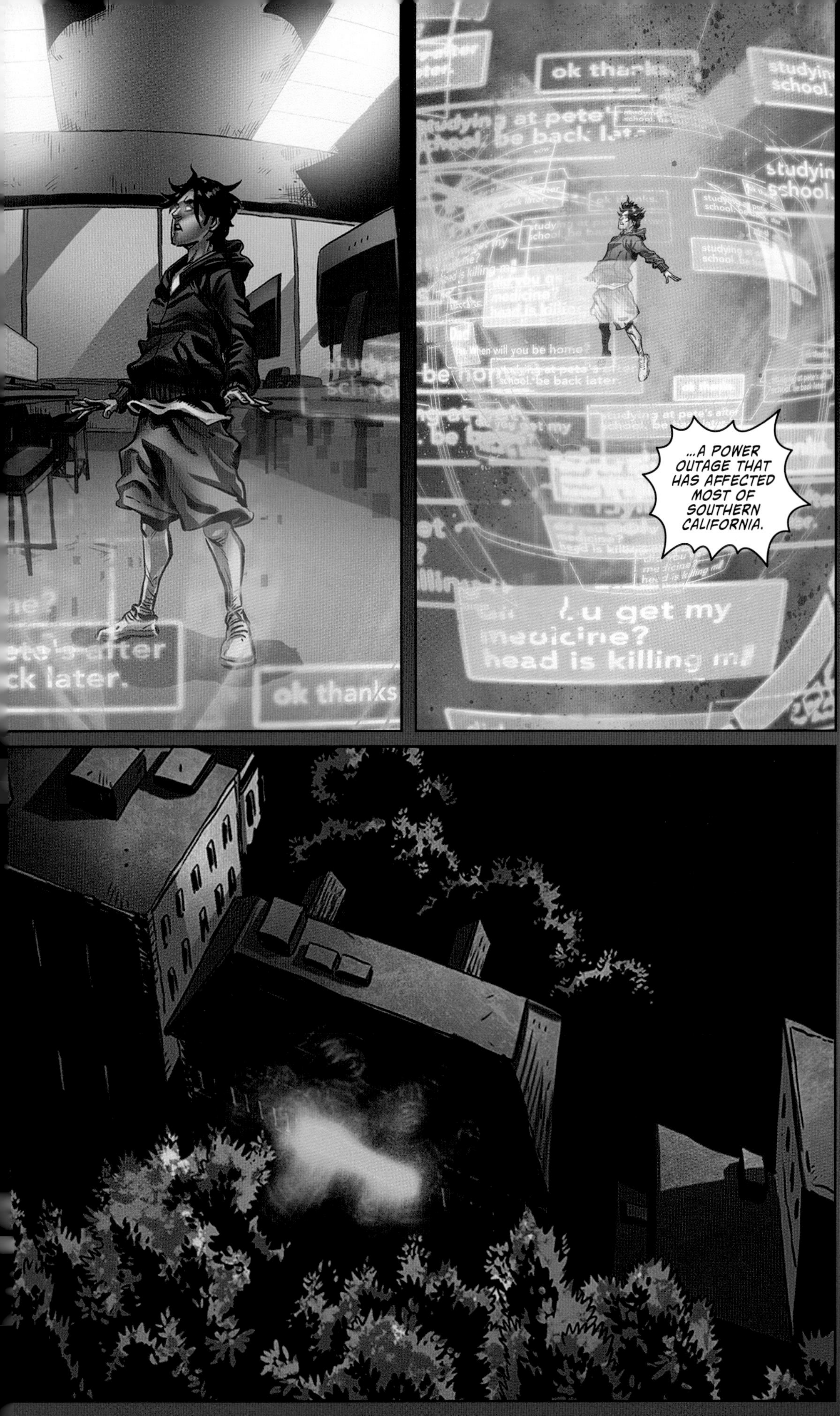
ok thanks.
studying at pete's after school. be back later.
Dad
Yes. When will you be home?
...A POWER OUTAGE THAT HAS AFFECTED MOST OF SOUTHERN CALIFORNIA.

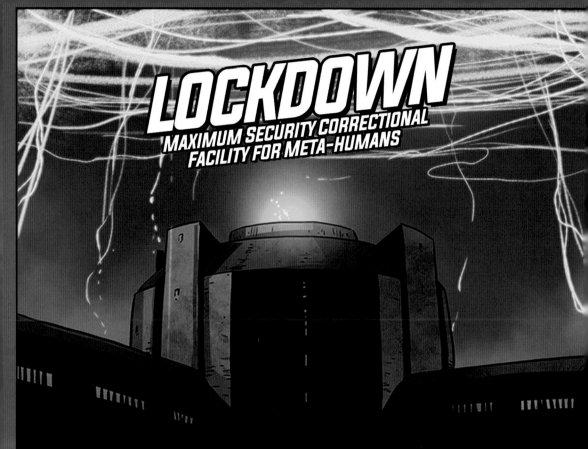

LOCKDOWN
MAXIMUM SECURITY CORRECTIONAL FACILITY FOR META-HUMANS

OK MASTERSON, WE'RE HERE. NOW WHAT?

TRANSIT, MY FRIEND, THE MOST POWERFUL WARRIORS ARE PATIENCE AND TIME.

A MOMENT PLEASE.

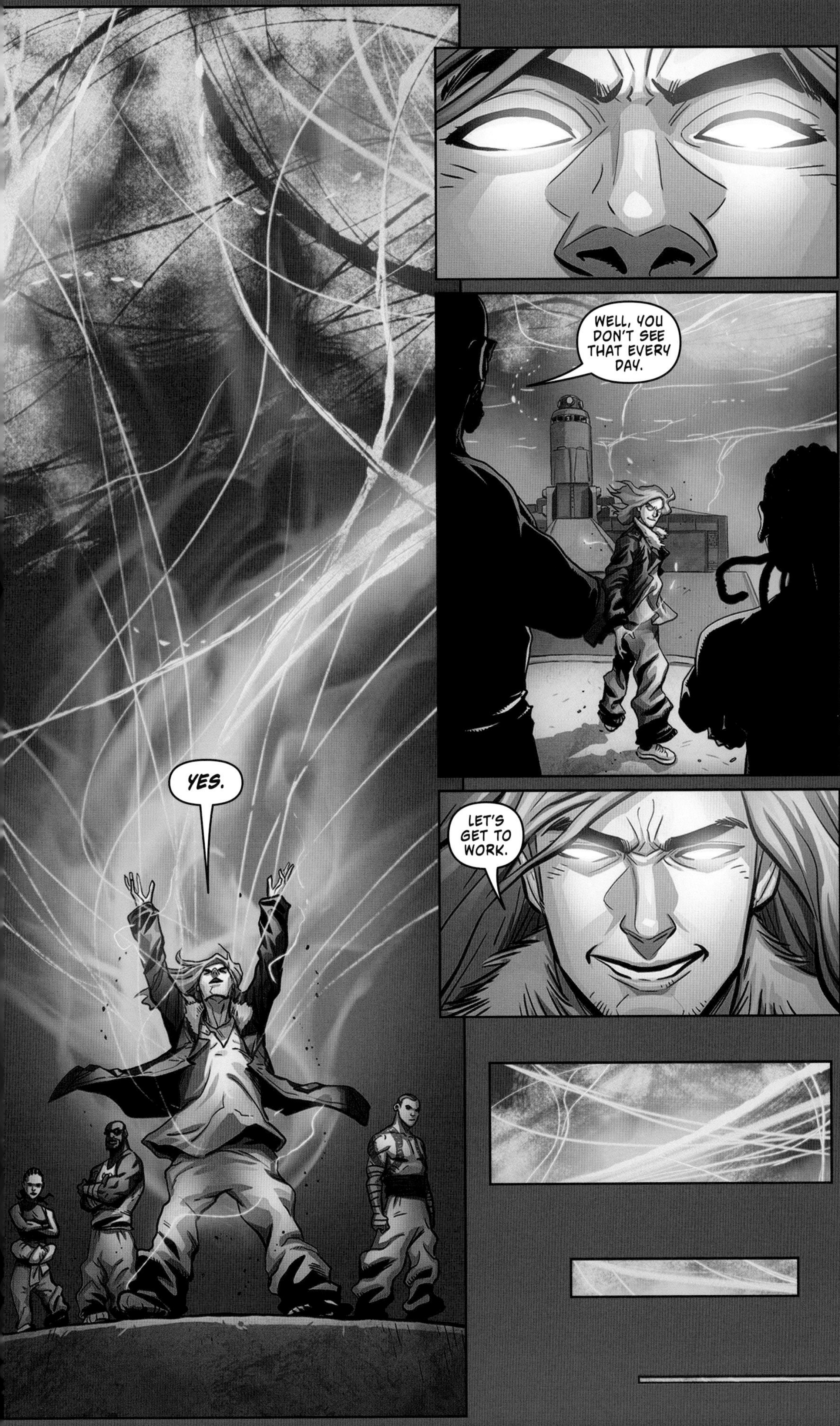
YES.
WELL, YOU DON'T SEE THAT EVERY DAY.
LET'S GET TO WORK.

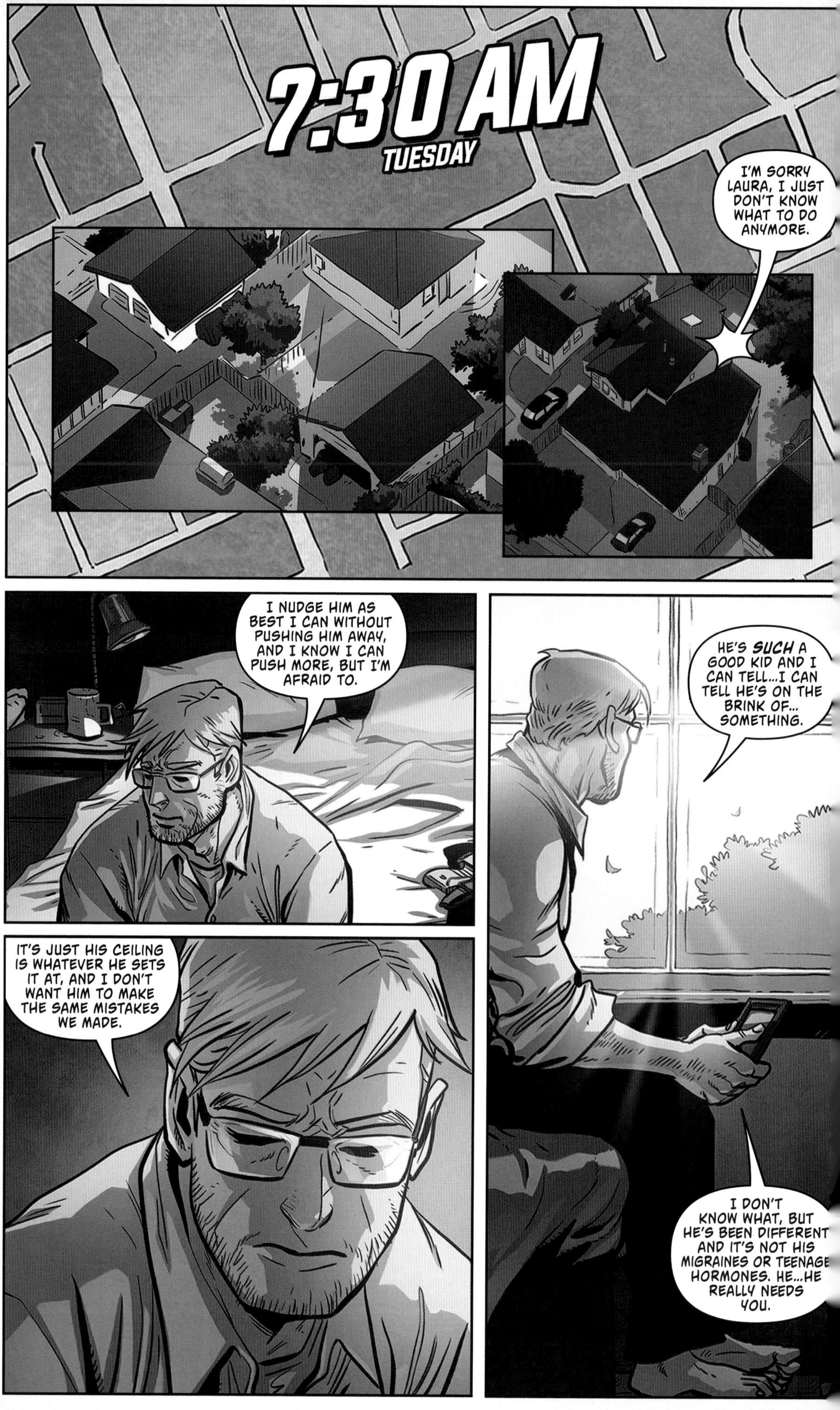
7:30 AM
TUESDAY
I'M SORRY LAURA, I JUST DON'T KNOW WHAT TO DO ANYMORE.
I NUDGE HIM AS BEST I CAN WITHOUT PUSHING HIM AWAY, AND I KNOW I CAN PUSH MORE, BUT I'M AFRAID TO.
IT'S JUST HIS CEILING IS WHATEVER HE SETS IT AT, AND I DON'T WANT HIM TO MAKE THE SAME MISTAKES WE MADE.
HE'S SUCH A GOOD KID AND I CAN TELL...I CAN TELL HE'S ON THE BRINK OF... SOMETHING.
I DON'T KNOW WHAT, BUT HE'S BEEN DIFFERENT AND IT'S NOT HIS MIGRAINES OR TEENAGE HORMONES. HE...HE REALLY NEEDS YOU.

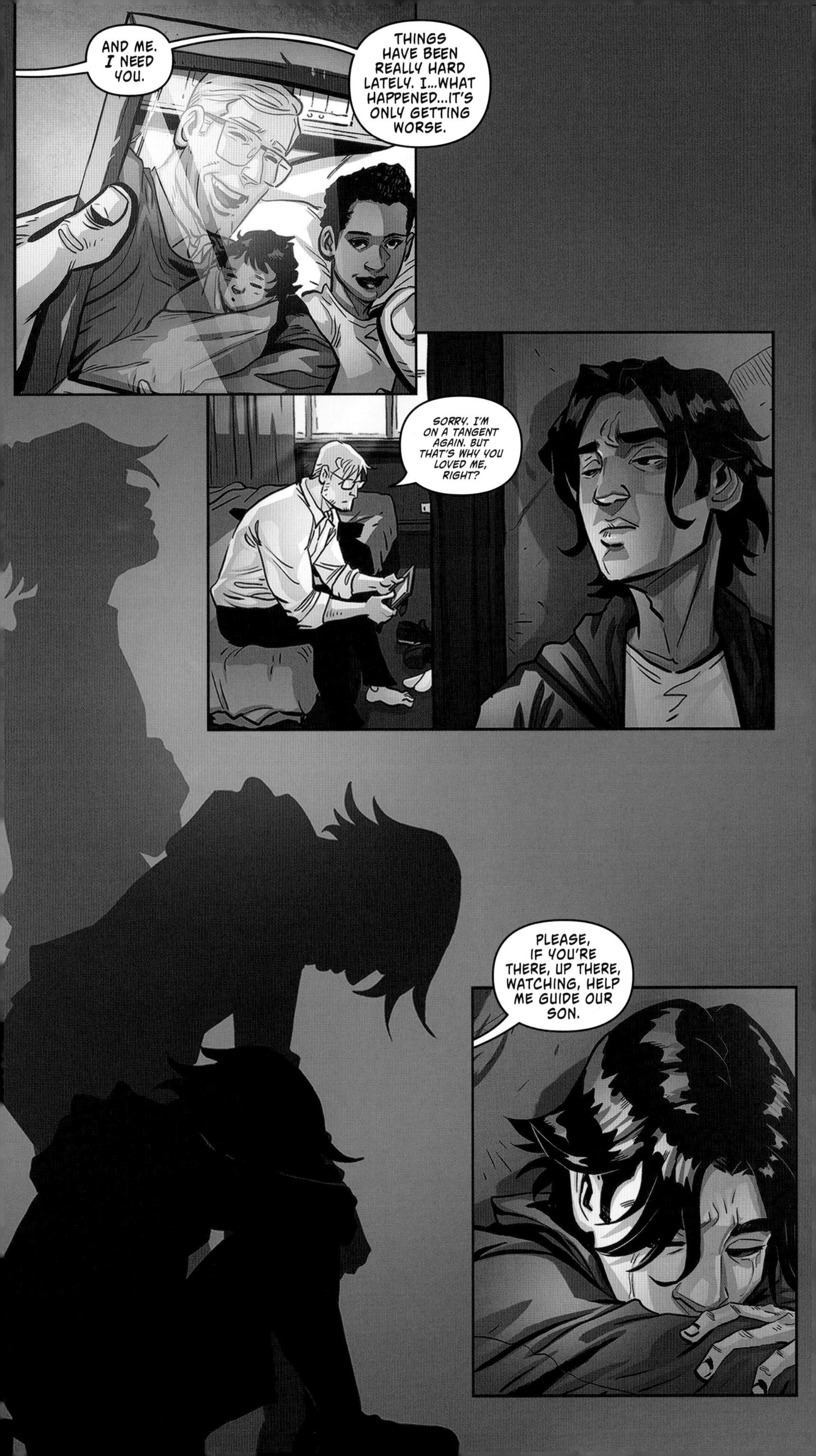

AND ME. I NEED YOU.
THINGS HAVE BEEN REALLY HARD LATELY. I...WHAT HAPPENED...IT'S ONLY GETTING WORSE.
SORRY. I'M ON A TANGENT AGAIN. BUT THAT'S WHY YOU LOVED ME, RIGHT?
PLEASE, IF YOU'RE THERE, UP THERE, WATCHING, HELP ME GUIDE OUR SON.

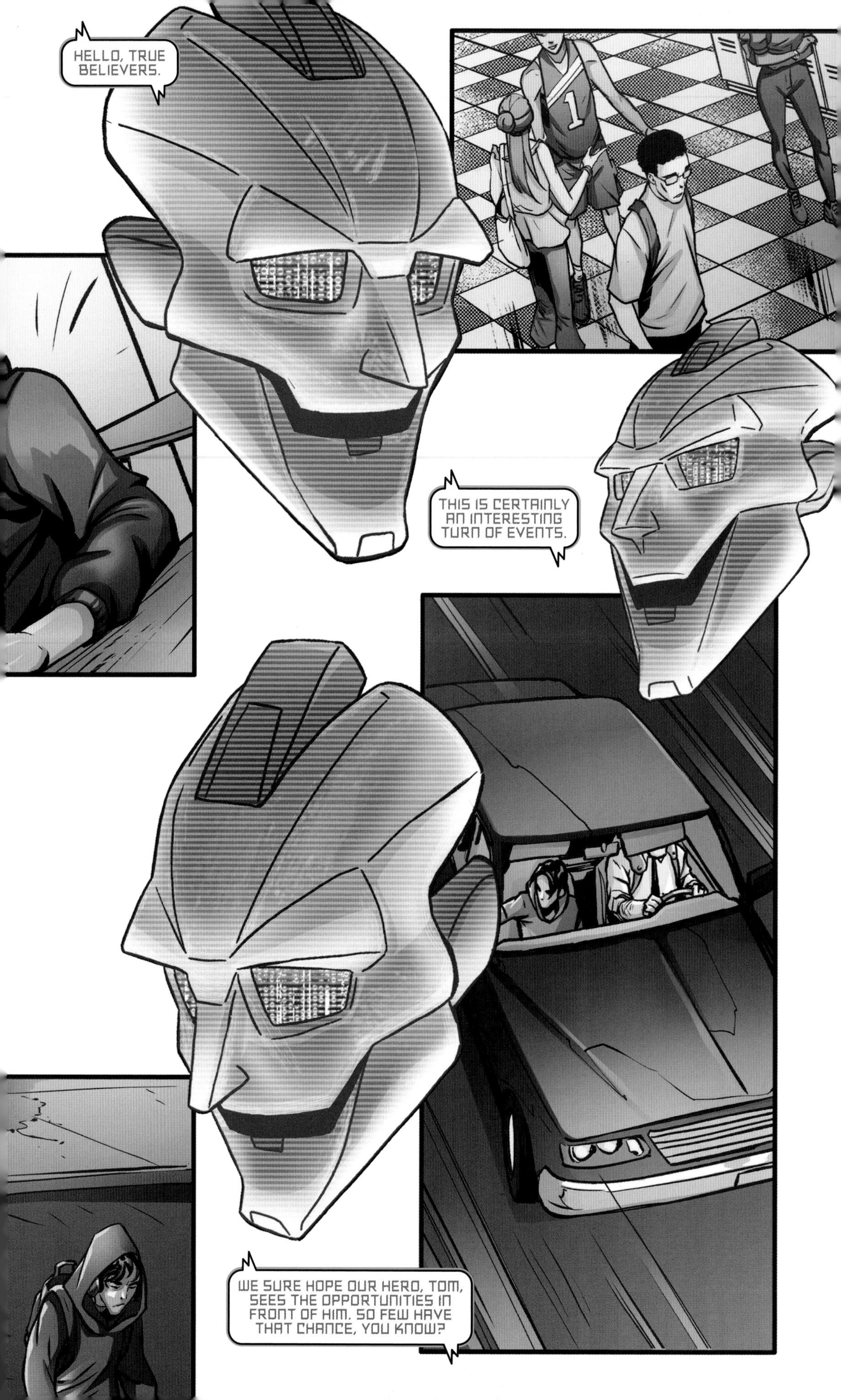
HELLO, TRUE BELIEVERS.
THIS IS CERTAINLY AN INTERESTING TURN OF EVENTS.
WE SURE HOPE OUR HERO, TOM, SEES THE OPPORTUNITIES IN FRONT OF HIM. SO FEW HAVE THAT CHANCE, YOU KNOW?

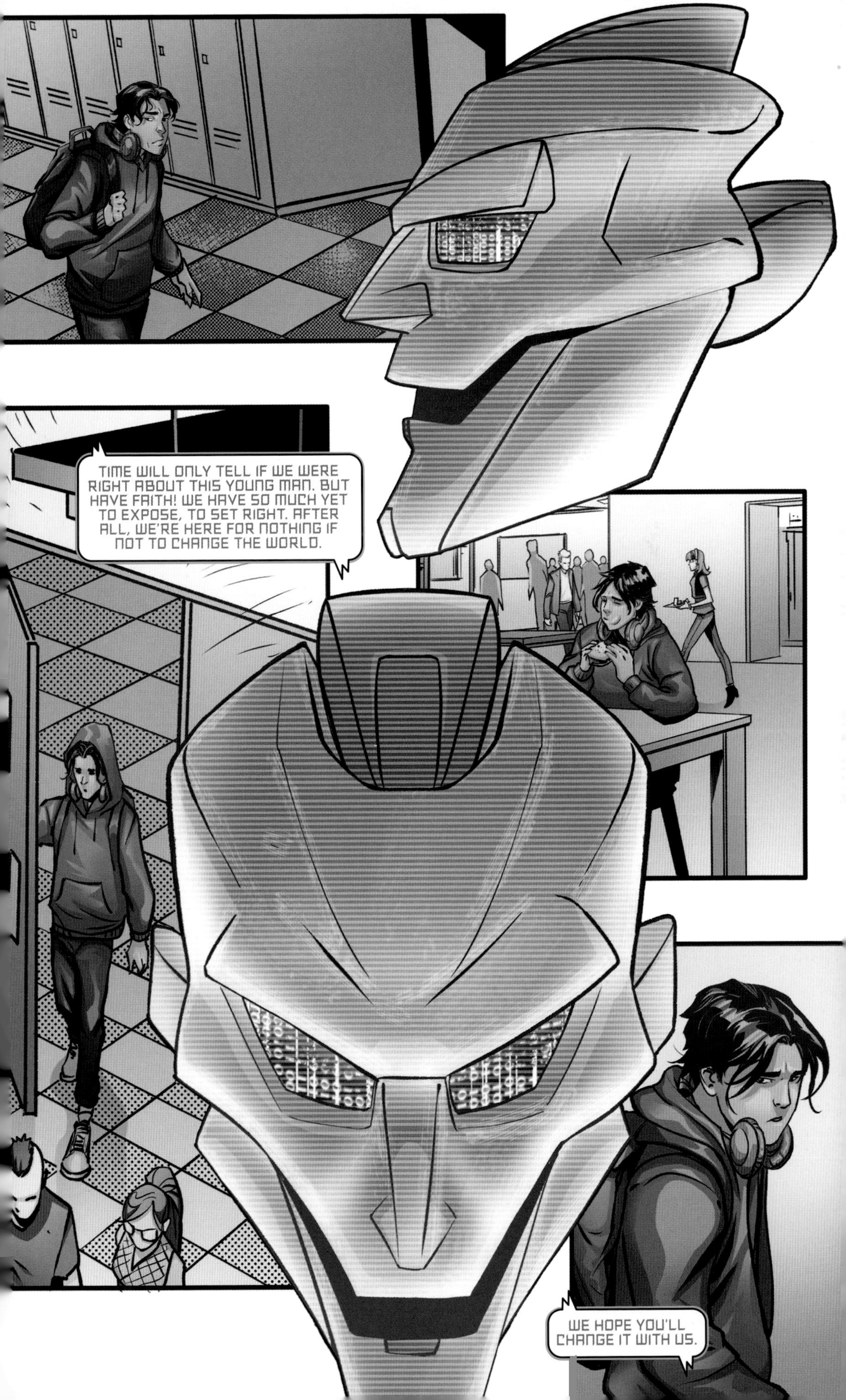
TIME WILL ONLY TELL IF WE WERE RIGHT ABOUT THIS YOUNG MAN. BUT HAVE FAITH! WE HAVE SO MUCH YET TO EXPOSE, TO SET RIGHT. AFTER ALL, WE'RE HERE FOR NOTHING IF NOT TO CHANGE THE WORLD.
WE HOPE YOU'LL CHANGE IT WITH US.

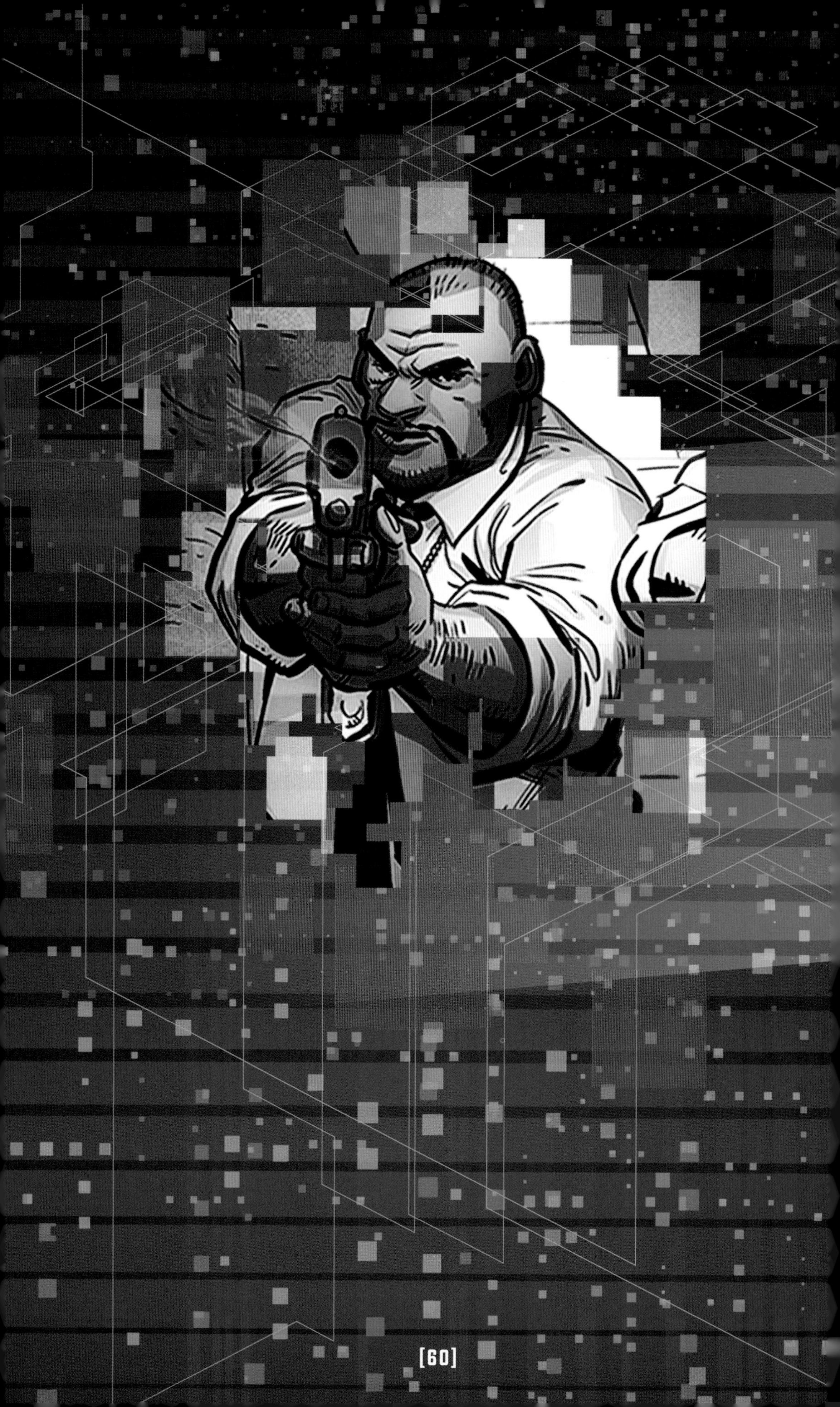

CHAPTER 4

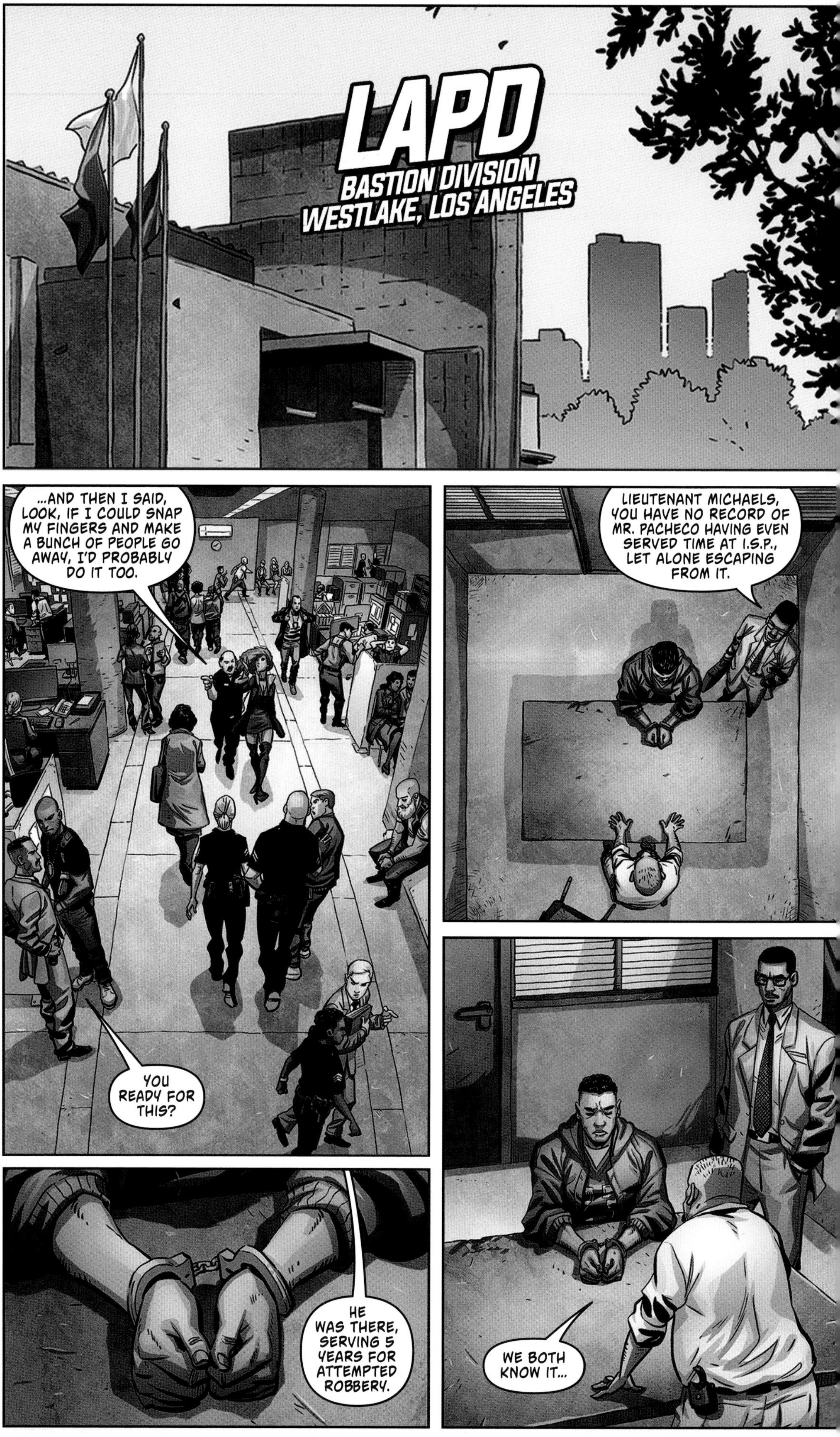
LAPD
BASTION DIVISION
WESTLAKE, LOS ANGELES
...AND THEN I SAID, LOOK, IF I COULD SNAP MY FINGERS AND MAKE A BUNCH OF PEOPLE GO AWAY, I'D PROBABLY DO IT TOO.
YOU READY FOR THIS?
LIEUTENANT MICHAELS, YOU HAVE NO RECORD OF MR. PACHECO HAVING EVEN SERVED TIME AT I.S.P., LET ALONE ESCAPING FROM IT.
HE WAS THERE, SERVING 5 YEARS FOR ATTEMPTED ROBBERY.
WE BOTH KNOW IT...

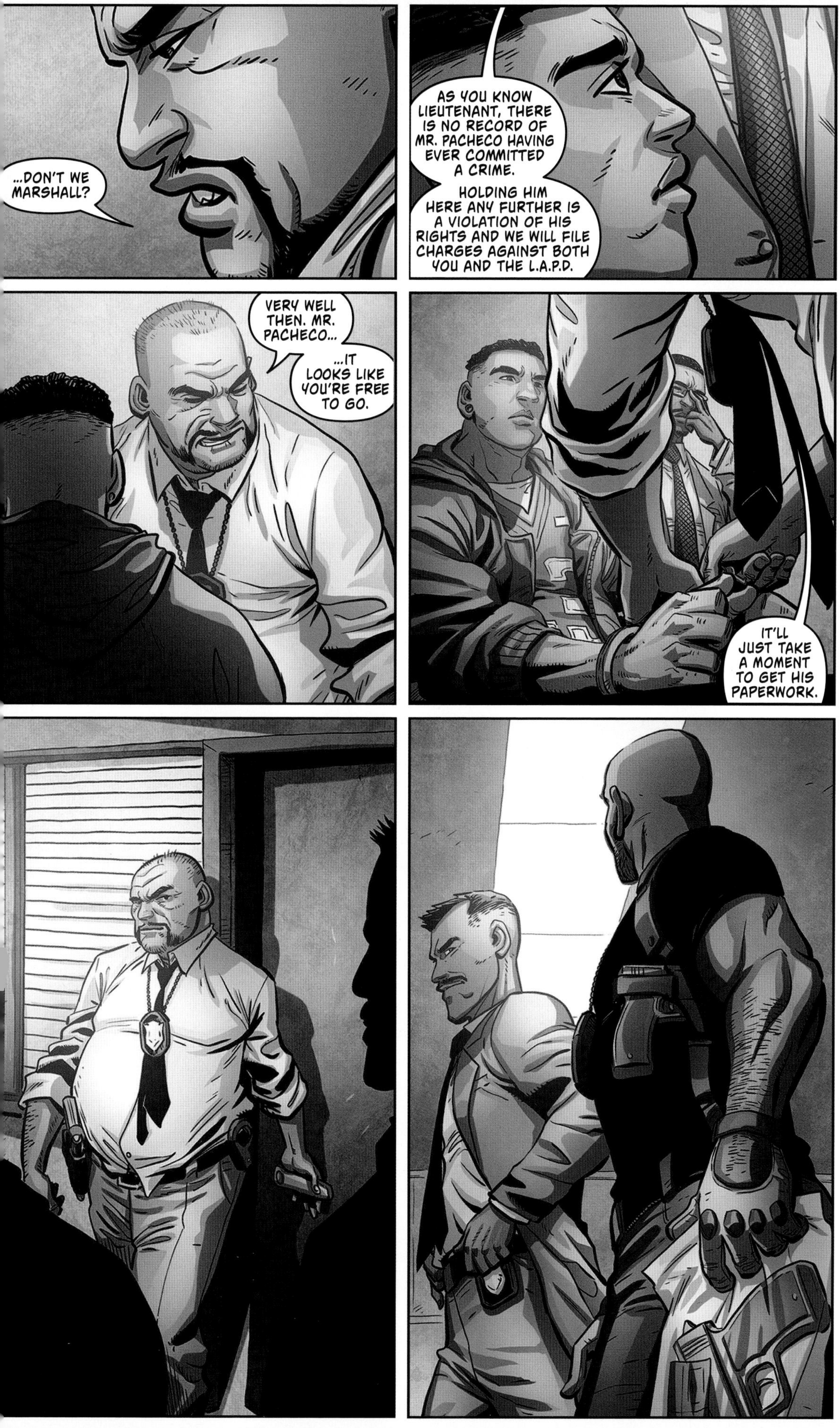

...DON'T WE MARSHALL?
AS YOU KNOW LIEUTENANT, THERE IS NO RECORD OF MR. PACHECO HAVING EVER COMMITTED A CRIME.
HOLDING HIM HERE ANY FURTHER IS A VIOLATION OF HIS RIGHTS AND WE WILL FILE CHARGES AGAINST BOTH YOU AND THE L.A.P.D.
VERY WELL THEN. MR. PACHECO...
...IT LOOKS LIKE YOU'RE FREE TO GO.
IT'LL JUST TAKE A MOMENT TO GET HIS PAPERWORK.

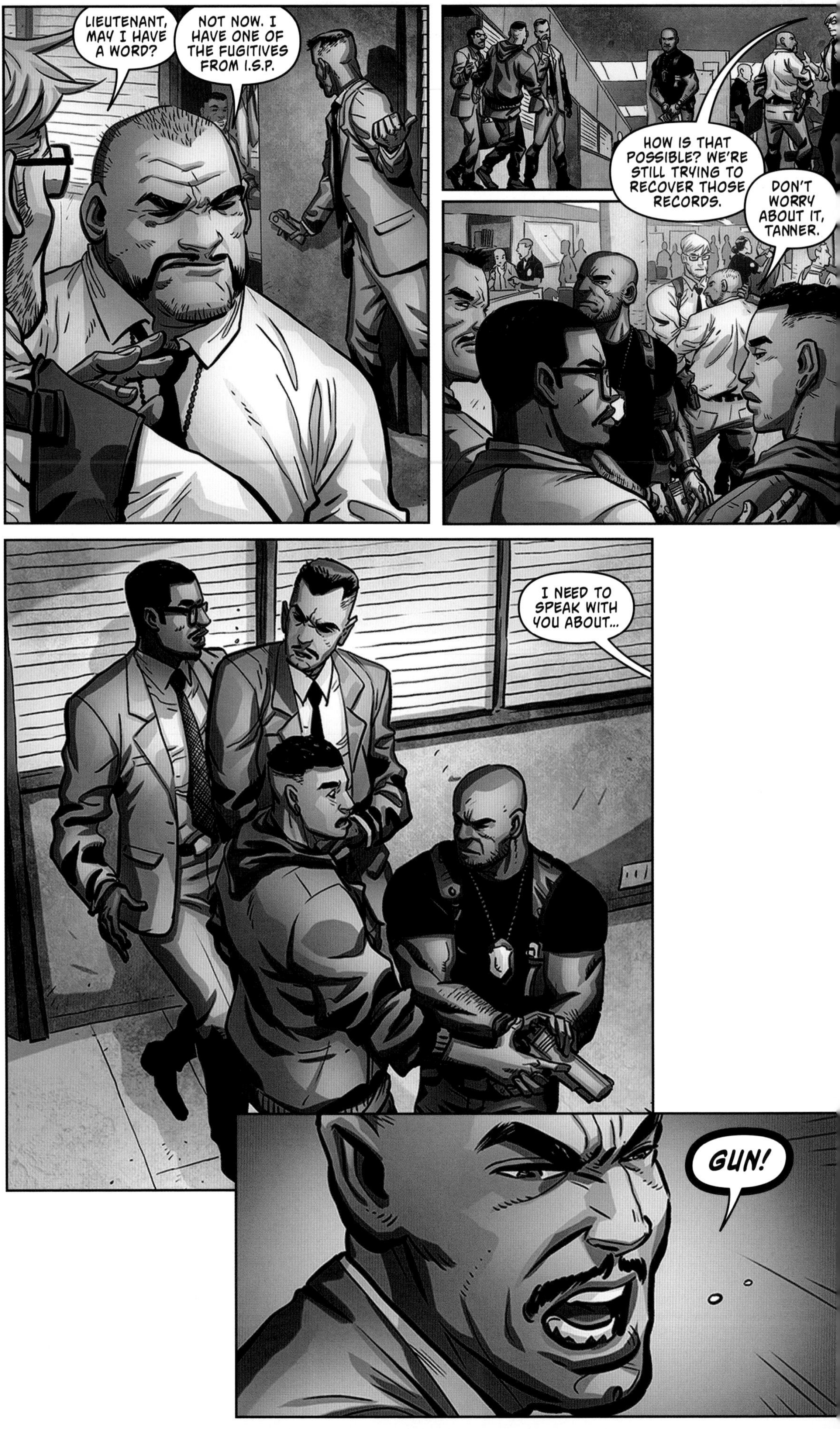
LIEUTENANT, MAY I HAVE A WORD?
NOT NOW. I HAVE ONE OF THE FUGITIVES FROM I.S.P.
HOW IS THAT POSSIBLE? WE'RE STILL TRYING TO RECOVER THOSE RECORDS.
DON'T WORRY ABOUT IT, TANNER.
I NEED TO SPEAK WITH YOU ABOUT...
GUN!

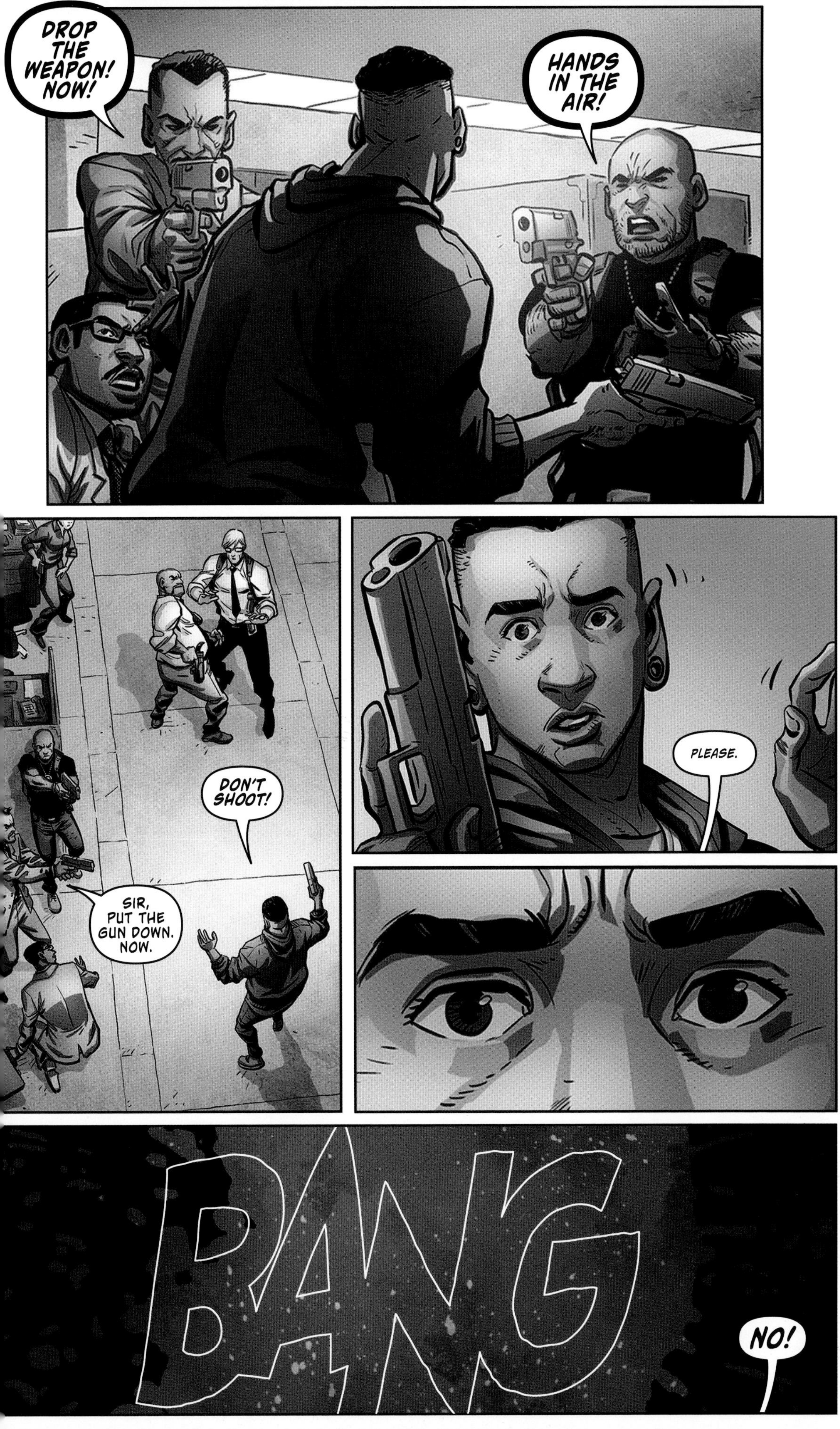
DROP THE WEAPON! NOW!
HANDS IN THE AIR!
DON'T SHOOT!
SIR, PUT THE GUN DOWN. NOW.
PLEASE.
BANG
NO!

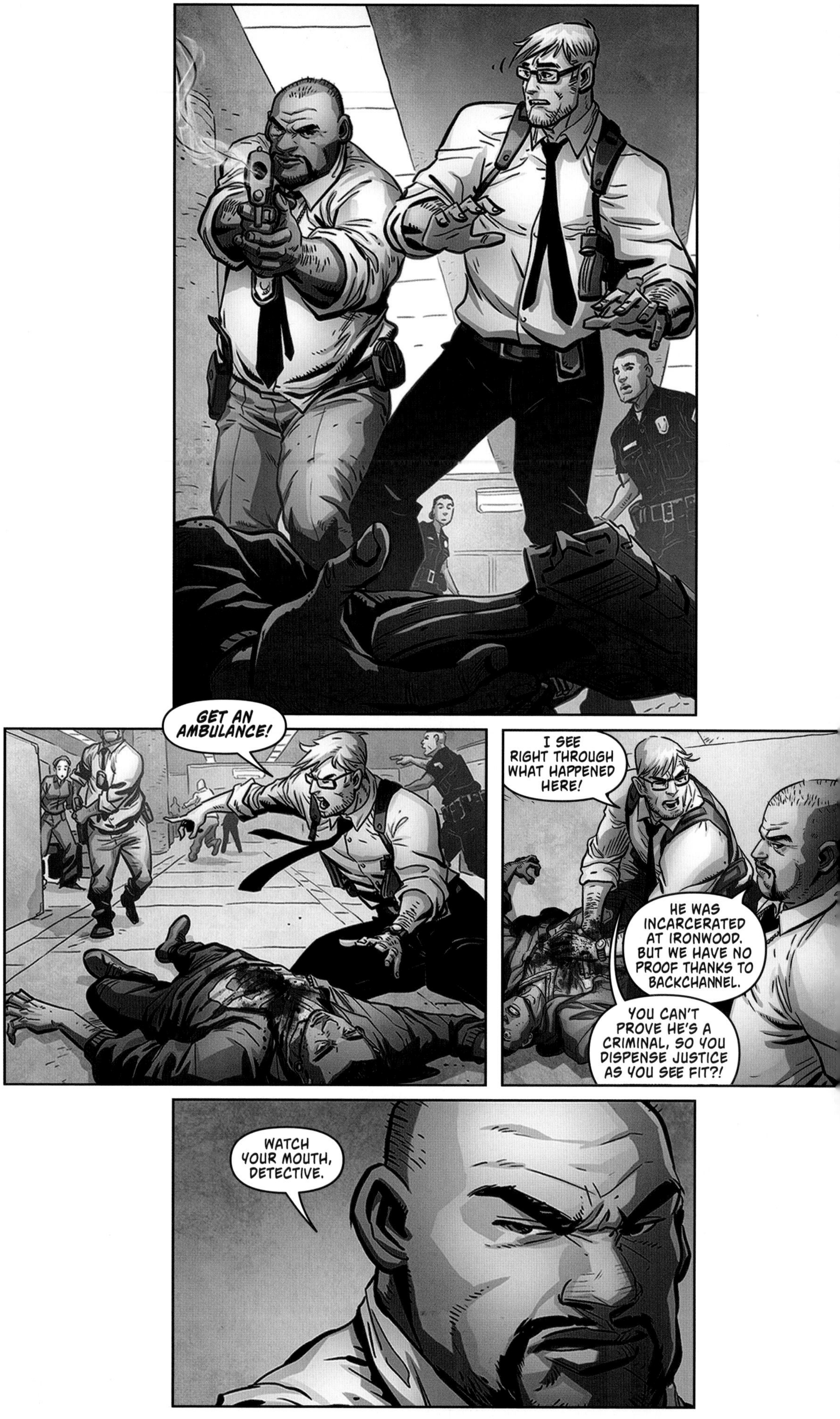
GET AN AMBULANCE!
I SEE RIGHT THROUGH WHAT HAPPENED HERE!
HE WAS INCARCERATED AT IRONWOOD. BUT WE HAVE NO PROOF THANKS TO BACKCHANNEL.
YOU CAN'T PROVE HE'S A CRIMINAL, SO YOU DISPENSE JUSTICE AS YOU SEE FIT?!
WATCH YOUR MOUTH, DETECTIVE.

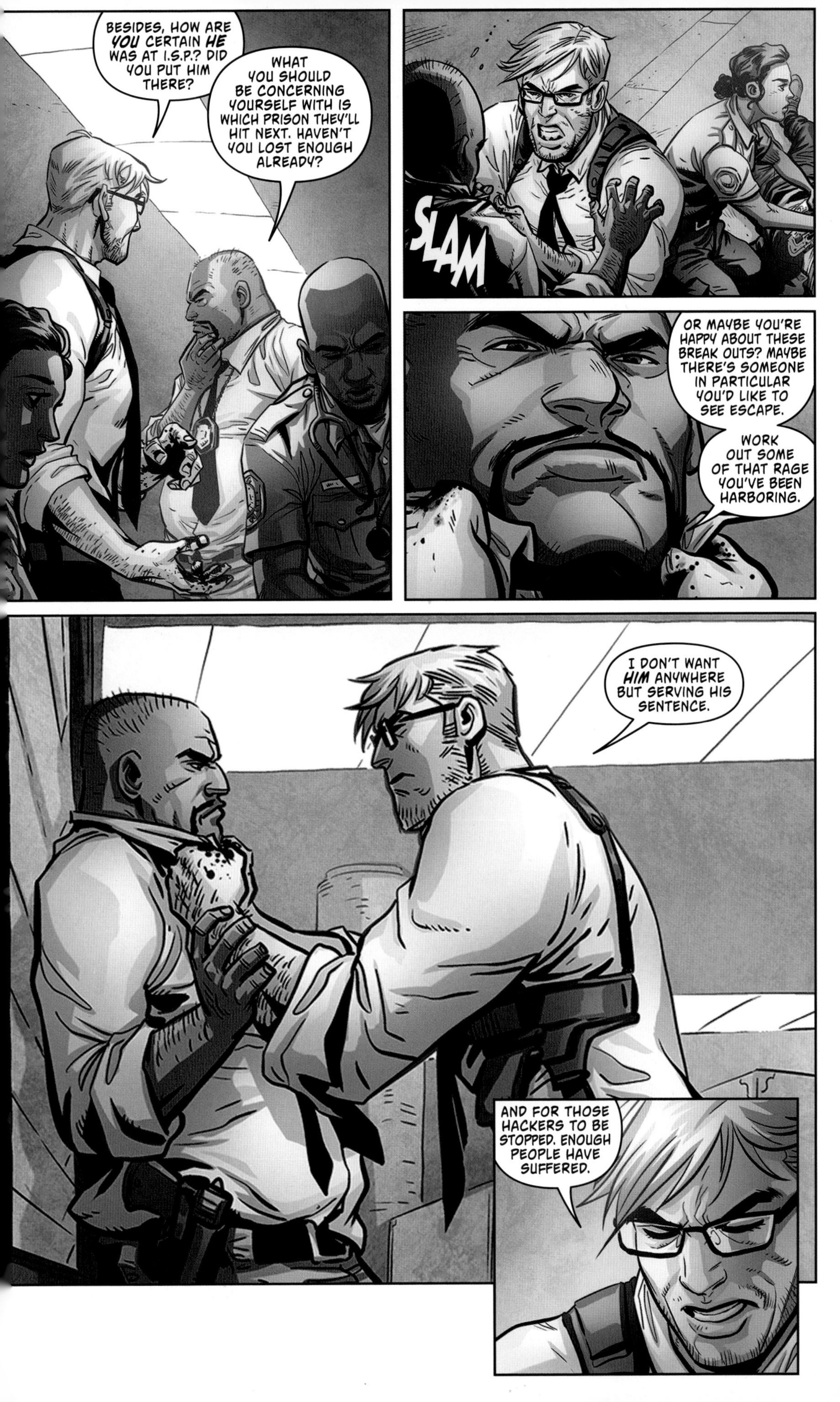
BESIDES, HOW ARE YOU CERTAIN HE WAS AT I.S.P.? DID YOU PUT HIM THERE?
WHAT YOU SHOULD BE CONCERNING YOURSELF WITH IS WHICH PRISON THEY'LL HIT NEXT. HAVEN'T YOU LOST ENOUGH ALREADY?
SLAM
OR MAYBE YOU'RE HAPPY ABOUT THESE BREAK OUTS? MAYBE THERE'S SOMEONE IN PARTICULAR YOU'D LIKE TO SEE ESCAPE.
WORK OUT SOME OF THAT RAGE YOU'VE BEEN HARBORING.
I DON'T WANT HIM ANYWHERE BUT SERVING HIS SENTENCE.
AND FOR THOSE HACKERS TO BE STOPPED. ENOUGH PEOPLE HAVE SUFFERED.

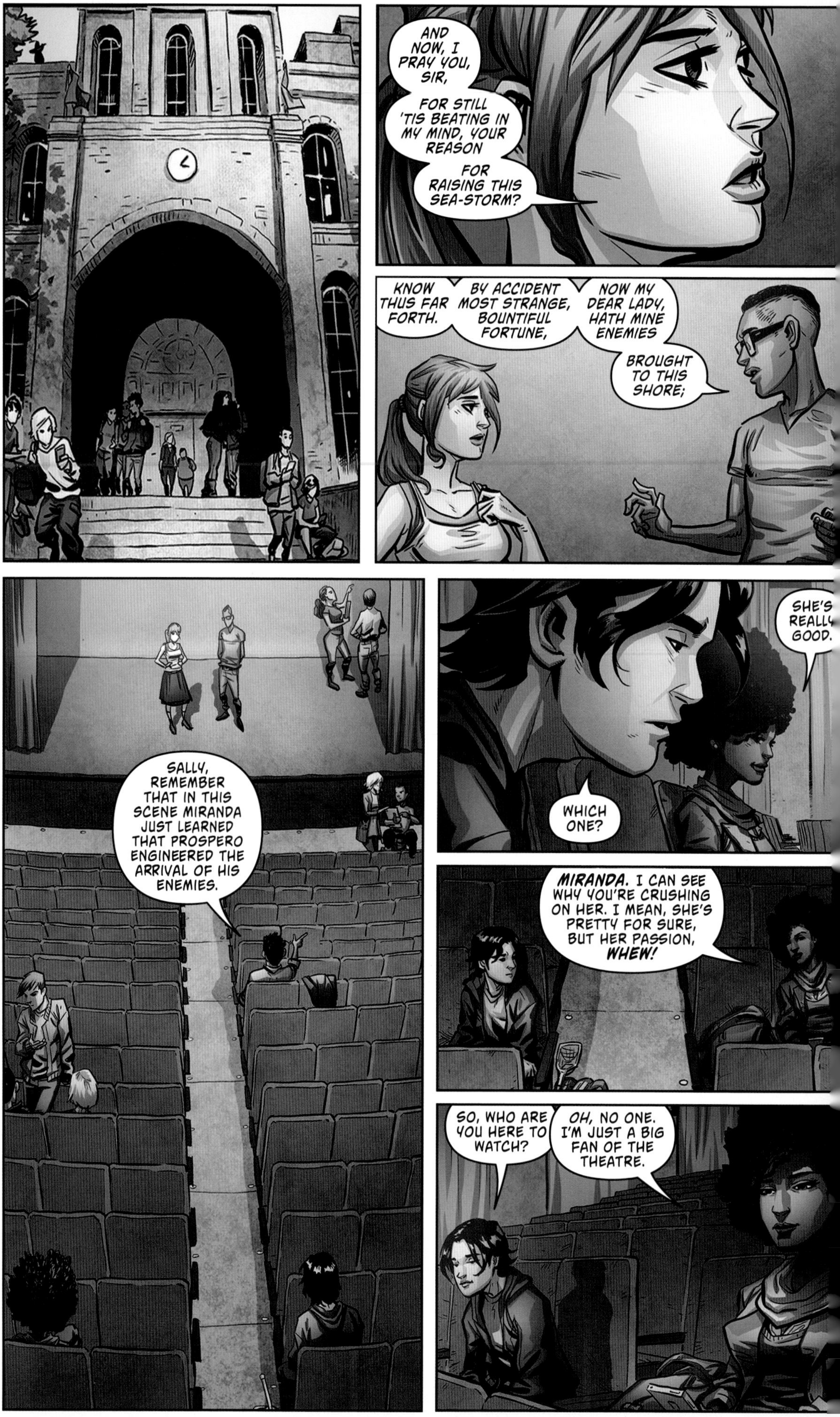
AND NOW, I PRAY YOU, SIR,
FOR STILL 'TIS BEATING IN MY MIND, YOUR REASON
FOR RAISING THIS SEA-STORM?
KNOW THUS FAR FORTH.
BY ACCIDENT MOST STRANGE, BOUNTIFUL FORTUNE,
NOW MY DEAR LADY, HATH MINE ENEMIES
BROUGHT TO THIS SHORE;
SALLY, REMEMBER THAT IN THIS SCENE MIRANDA JUST LEARNED THAT PROSPERO ENGINEERED THE ARRIVAL OF HIS ENEMIES.
SHE'S REALLY GOOD.
WHICH ONE?
MIRANDA. I CAN SEE WHY YOU'RE CRUSHING ON HER. I MEAN, SHE'S PRETTY FOR SURE, BUT HER PASSION, WHEW!
SO, WHO ARE YOU HERE TO WATCH?
OH, NO ONE. I'M JUST A BIG FAN OF THE THEATRE.

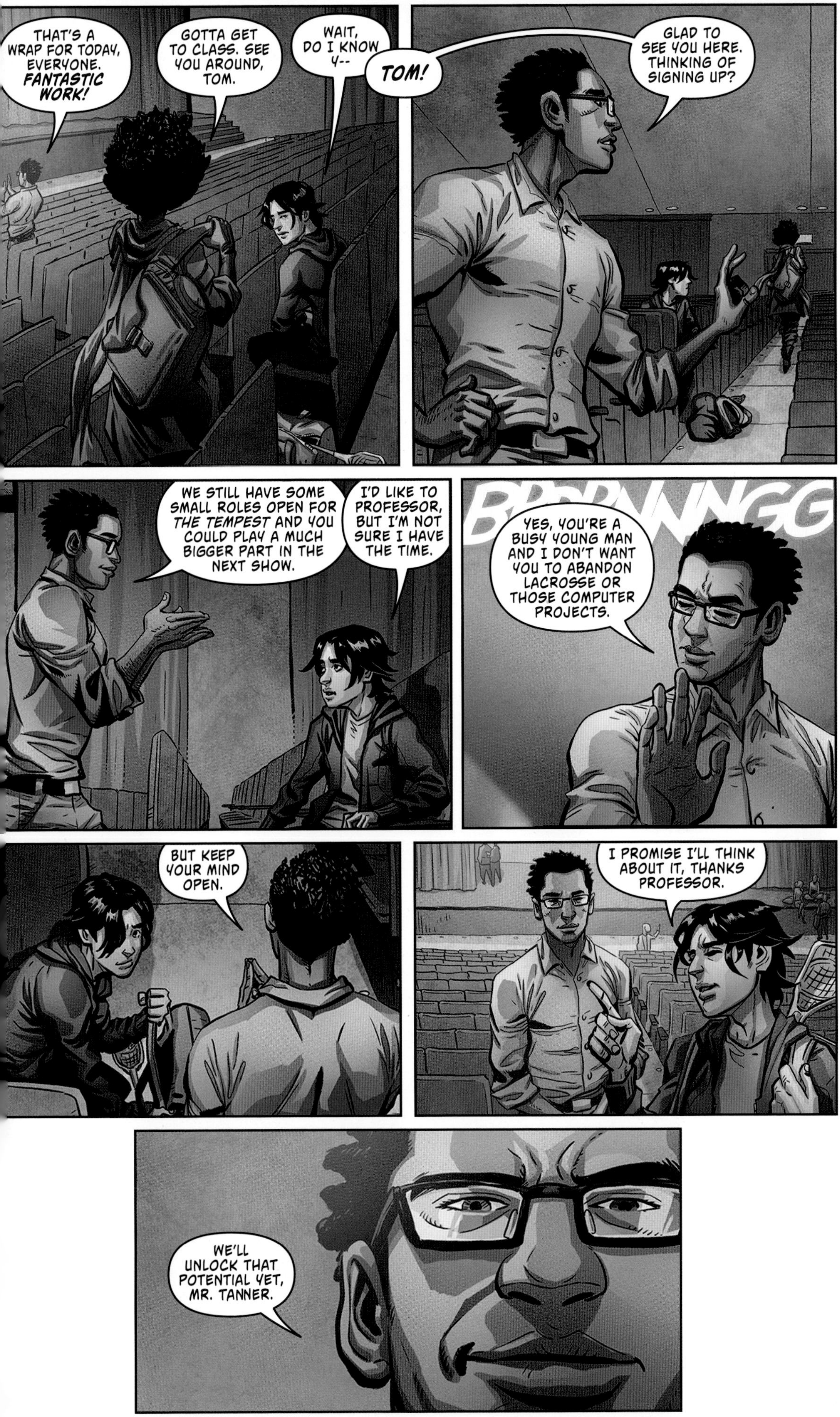

THAT'S A WRAP FOR TODAY, EVERYONE. *FANTASTIC WORK!*
GOTTA GET TO CLASS. SEE YOU AROUND, TOM.
WAIT, DO I KNOW Y--
TOM!
GLAD TO SEE YOU HERE. THINKING OF SIGNING UP?
WE STILL HAVE SOME SMALL ROLES OPEN FOR *THE TEMPEST* AND YOU COULD PLAY A MUCH BIGGER PART IN THE NEXT SHOW.
I'D LIKE TO PROFESSOR, BUT I'M NOT SURE I HAVE THE TIME.
BRRRNNNGG
YES, YOU'RE A BUSY YOUNG MAN AND I DON'T WANT YOU TO ABANDON LACROSSE OR THOSE COMPUTER PROJECTS.
BUT KEEP YOUR MIND OPEN.
I PROMISE I'LL THINK ABOUT IT, THANKS PROFESSOR.
WE'LL UNLOCK THAT POTENTIAL YET, MR. TANNER.

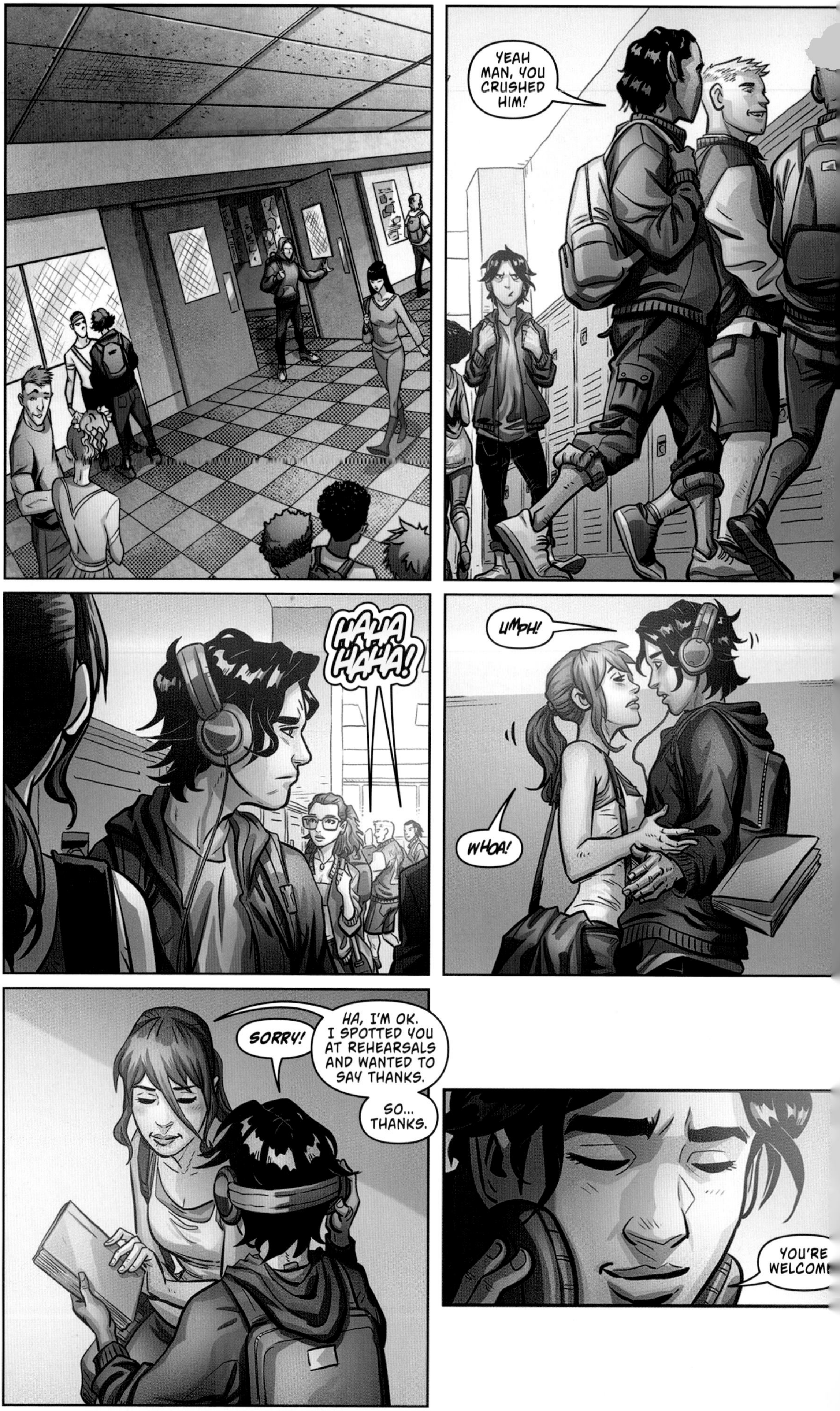
YEAH MAN, YOU CRUSHED HIM!
HAHA HAHA!
UMPH!
WHOA!
SORRY!
HA, I'M OK. I SPOTTED YOU AT REHEARSALS AND WANTED TO SAY THANKS.
SO... THANKS.
YOU'RE WELCOM

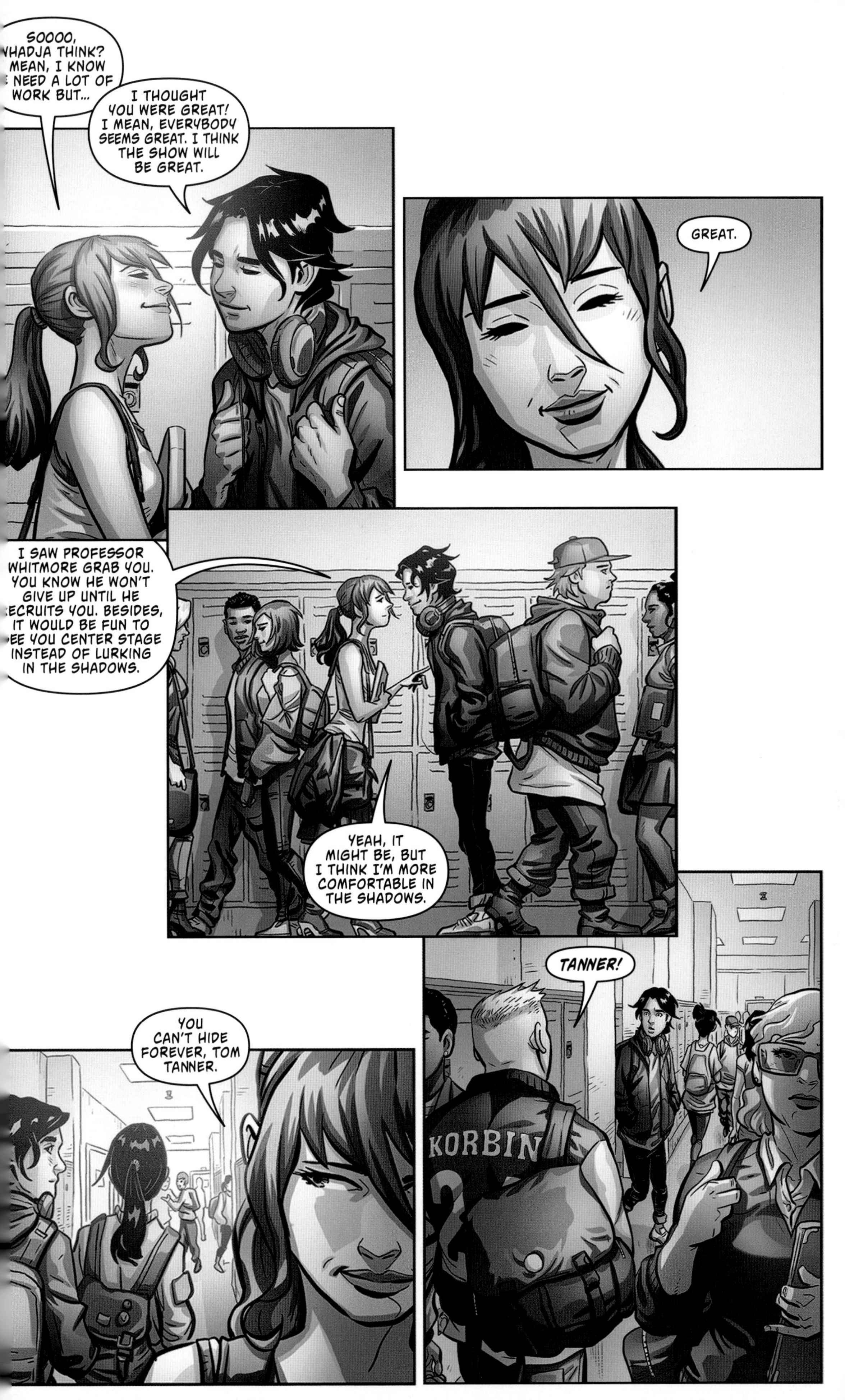
SOOOO, WHADJA THINK? MEAN, I KNOW E NEED A LOT OF WORK BUT...
I THOUGHT YOU WERE GREAT! I MEAN, EVERYBODY SEEMS GREAT. I THINK THE SHOW WILL BE GREAT.
GREAT.
I SAW PROFESSOR WHITMORE GRAB YOU. YOU KNOW HE WON'T GIVE UP UNTIL HE ECRUITS YOU. BESIDES, IT WOULD BE FUN TO EE YOU CENTER STAGE INSTEAD OF LURKING IN THE SHADOWS.
YEAH, IT MIGHT BE, BUT I THINK I'M MORE COMFORTABLE IN THE SHADOWS.
YOU CAN'T HIDE FOREVER, TOM TANNER.
TANNER!
KORBIN

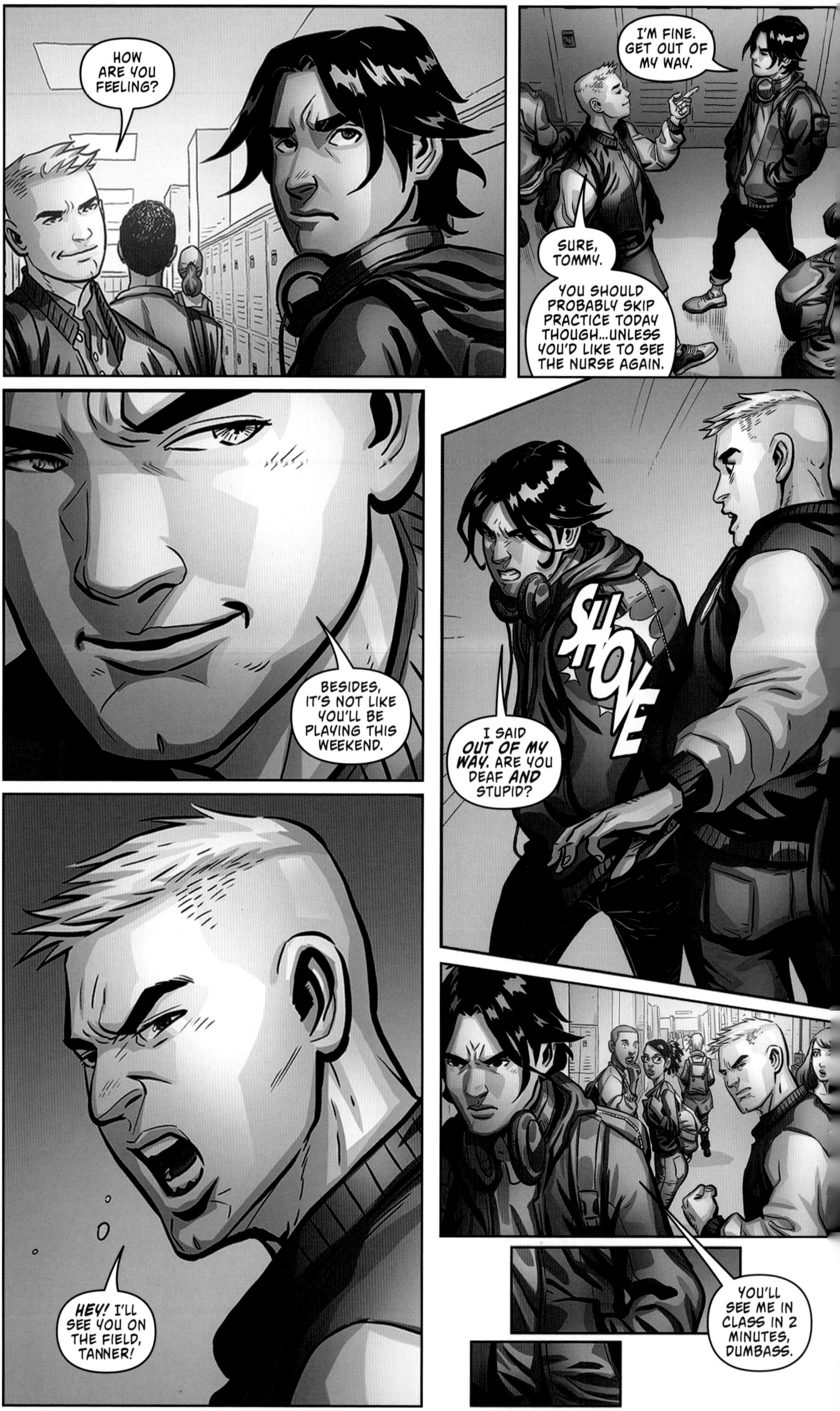

HOW ARE YOU FEELING?
I'M FINE. GET OUT OF MY WAY.
SURE, TOMMY.
YOU SHOULD PROBABLY SKIP PRACTICE TODAY THOUGH...UNLESS YOU'D LIKE TO SEE THE NURSE AGAIN.
BESIDES, IT'S NOT LIKE YOU'LL BE PLAYING THIS WEEKEND.
SHOVE
I SAID *OUT OF MY WAY*. ARE YOU DEAF *AND* STUPID?
HEY! I'LL SEE YOU ON THE FIELD, TANNER!
YOU'LL SEE ME IN CLASS IN 2 MINUTES, DUMBASS.

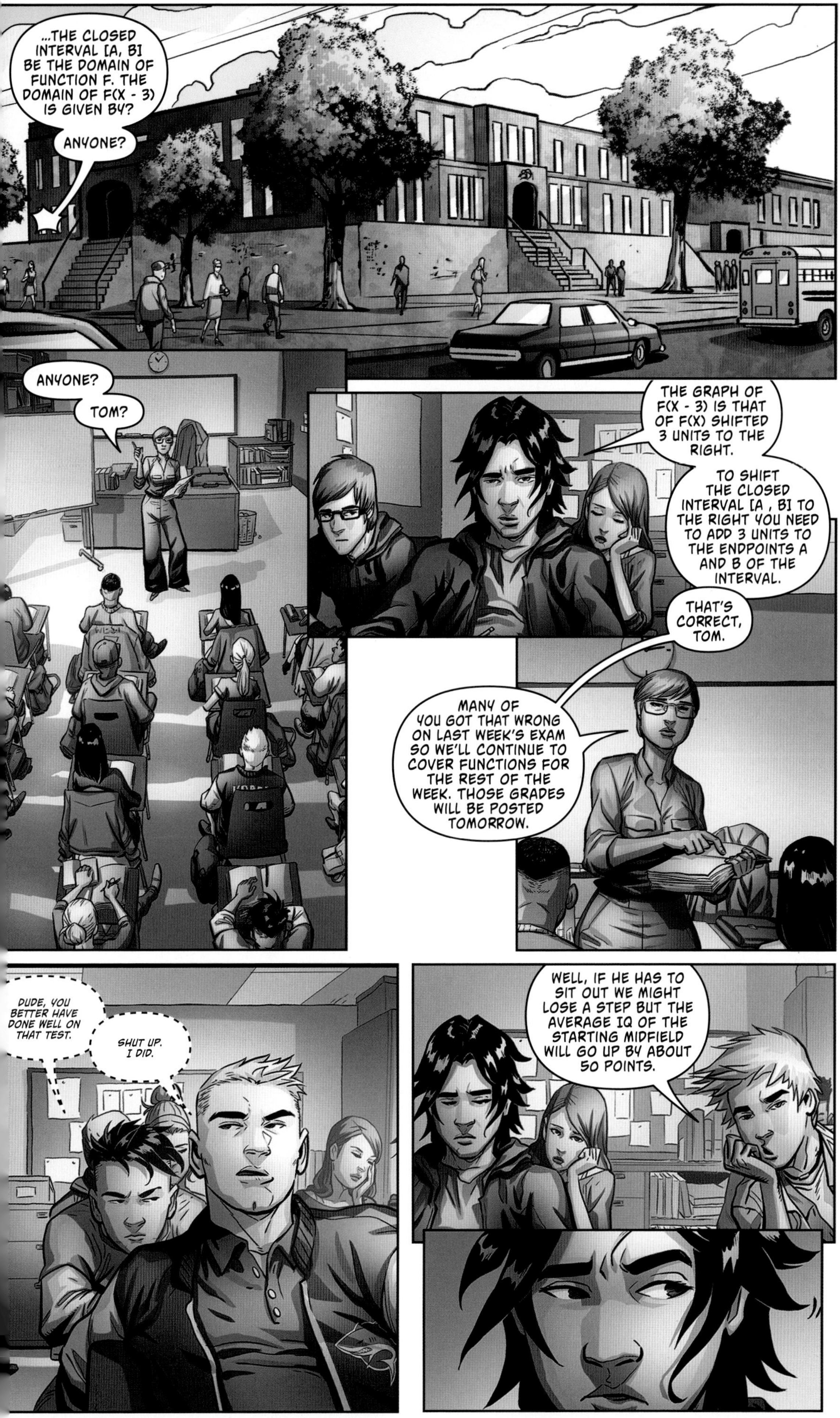

...THE CLOSED INTERVAL [A, B] BE THE DOMAIN OF FUNCTION F. THE DOMAIN OF F(X - 3) IS GIVEN BY?
ANYONE?
ANYONE?
TOM?
THE GRAPH OF F(X - 3) IS THAT OF F(X) SHIFTED 3 UNITS TO THE RIGHT.
TO SHIFT THE CLOSED INTERVAL [A , B] TO THE RIGHT YOU NEED TO ADD 3 UNITS TO THE ENDPOINTS A AND B OF THE INTERVAL.
THAT'S CORRECT, TOM.
MANY OF YOU GOT THAT WRONG ON LAST WEEK'S EXAM SO WE'LL CONTINUE TO COVER FUNCTIONS FOR THE REST OF THE WEEK. THOSE GRADES WILL BE POSTED TOMORROW.
DUDE, YOU BETTER HAVE DONE WELL ON THAT TEST.
SHUT UP. I DID.
WELL, IF HE HAS TO SIT OUT WE MIGHT LOSE A STEP BUT THE AVERAGE IQ OF THE STARTING MIDFIELD WILL GO UP BY ABOUT 50 POINTS.

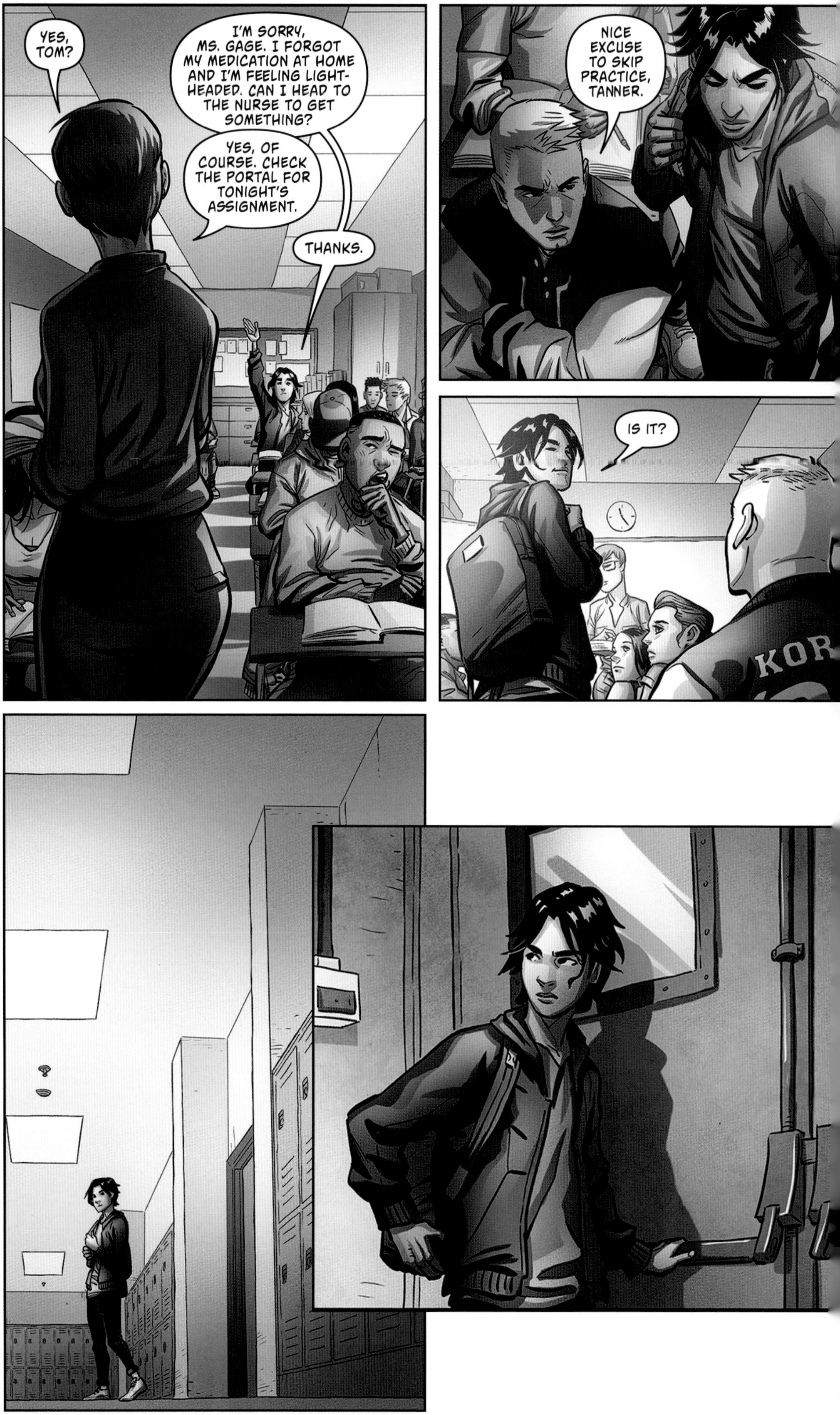
YES, TOM?
I'M SORRY, MS. GAGE. I FORGOT MY MEDICATION AT HOME AND I'M FEELING LIGHT-HEADED. CAN I HEAD TO THE NURSE TO GET SOMETHING?
YES, OF COURSE. CHECK THE PORTAL FOR TONIGHT'S ASSIGNMENT.
THANKS.
NICE EXCUSE TO SKIP PRACTICE, TANNER.
IS IT?

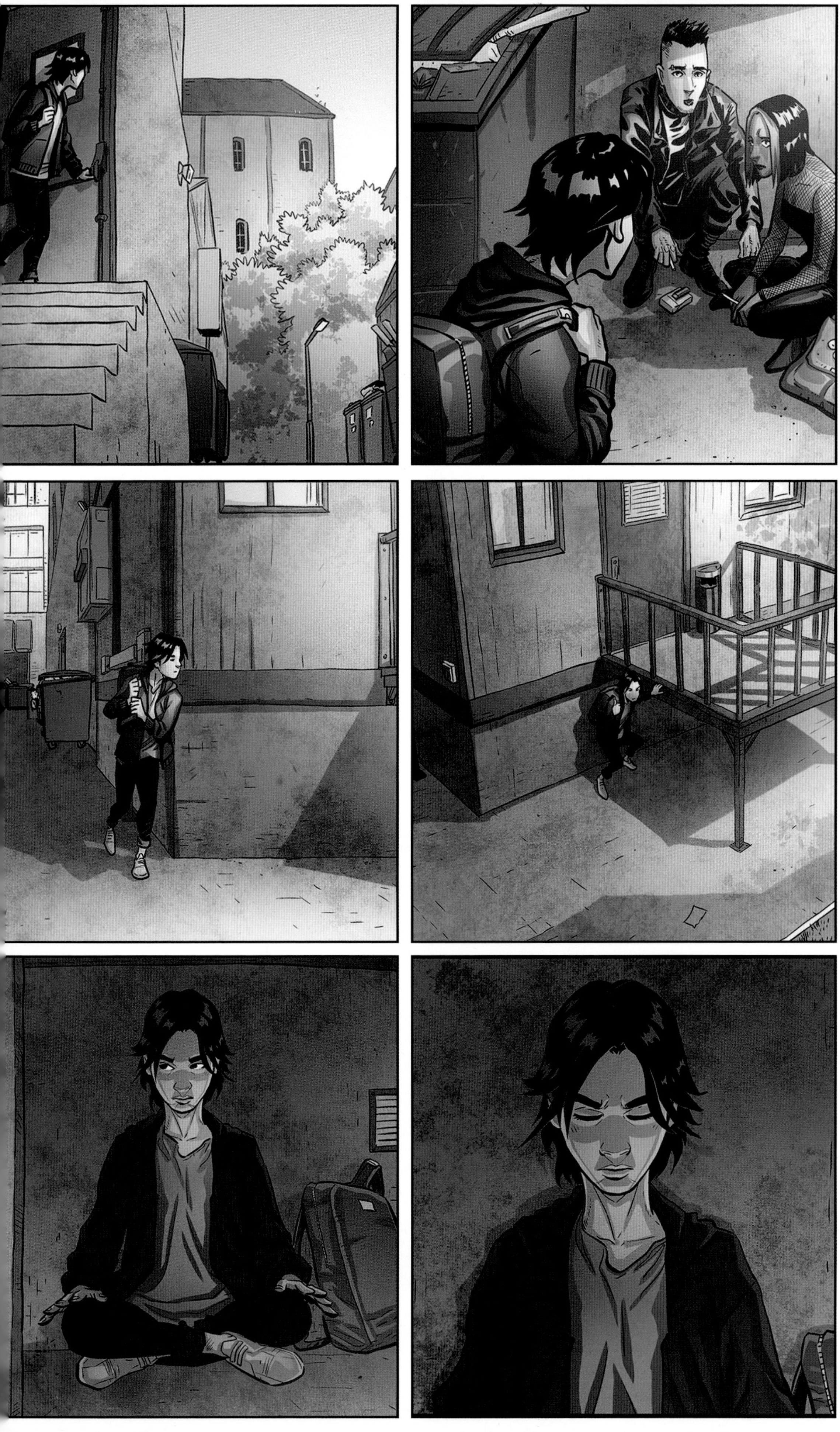

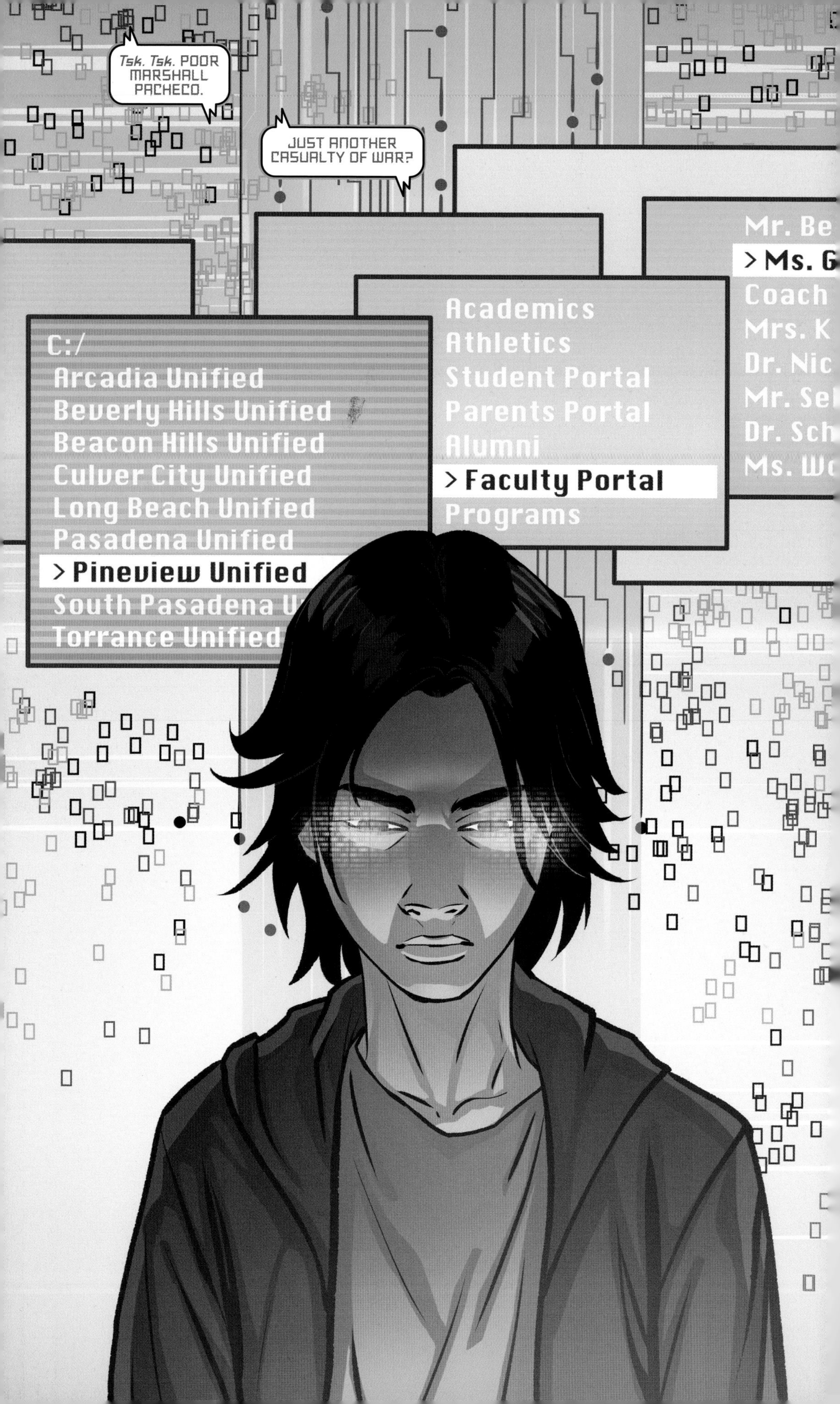
Tsk. Tsk. POOR MARSHALL PACHECO.
JUST ANOTHER CASUALTY OF WAR?
C:/
Arcadia Unified
Beverly Hills Unified
Beacon Hills Unified
Culver City Unified
Long Beach Unified
Pasadena Unified
> Pineview Unified
Torrance Unified
Academics
Athletics
Student Portal
Parents Portal
Alumni
> Faculty Portal
Programs
Coach

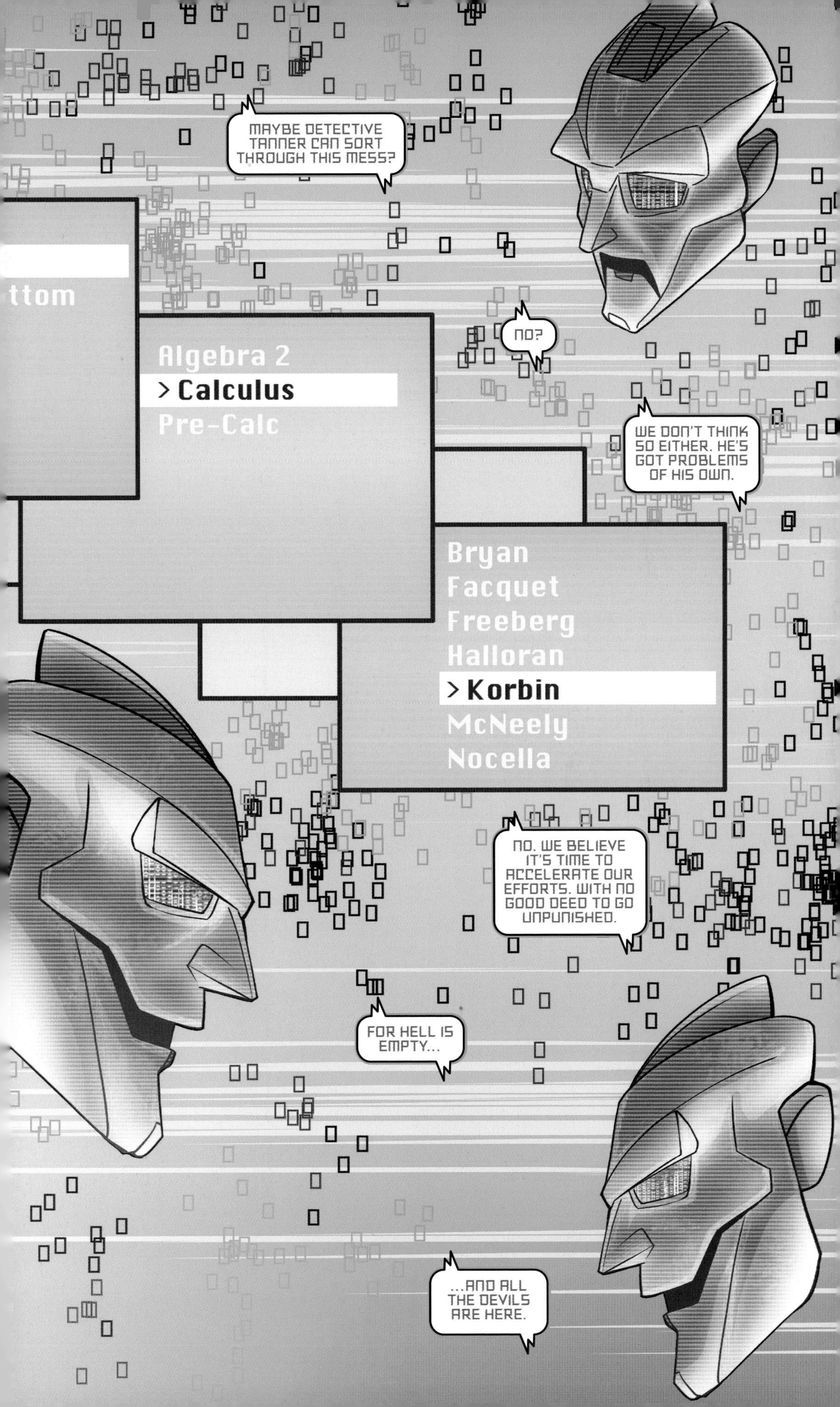
MAYBE DETECTIVE TANNER CAN SORT THROUGH THIS MESS?
ttom
Algebra 2
> Calculus
Pre-Calc
NO?
WE DON'T THINK SO EITHER. HE'S GOT PROBLEMS OF HIS OWN.
Bryan
Facquet
Freeberg
Halloran
> Korbin
McNeely
Nocella
NO. WE BELIEVE IT'S TIME TO ACCELERATE OUR EFFORTS. WITH NO GOOD DEED TO GO UNPUNISHED.
FOR HELL IS EMPTY...
...AND ALL THE DEVILS ARE HERE.

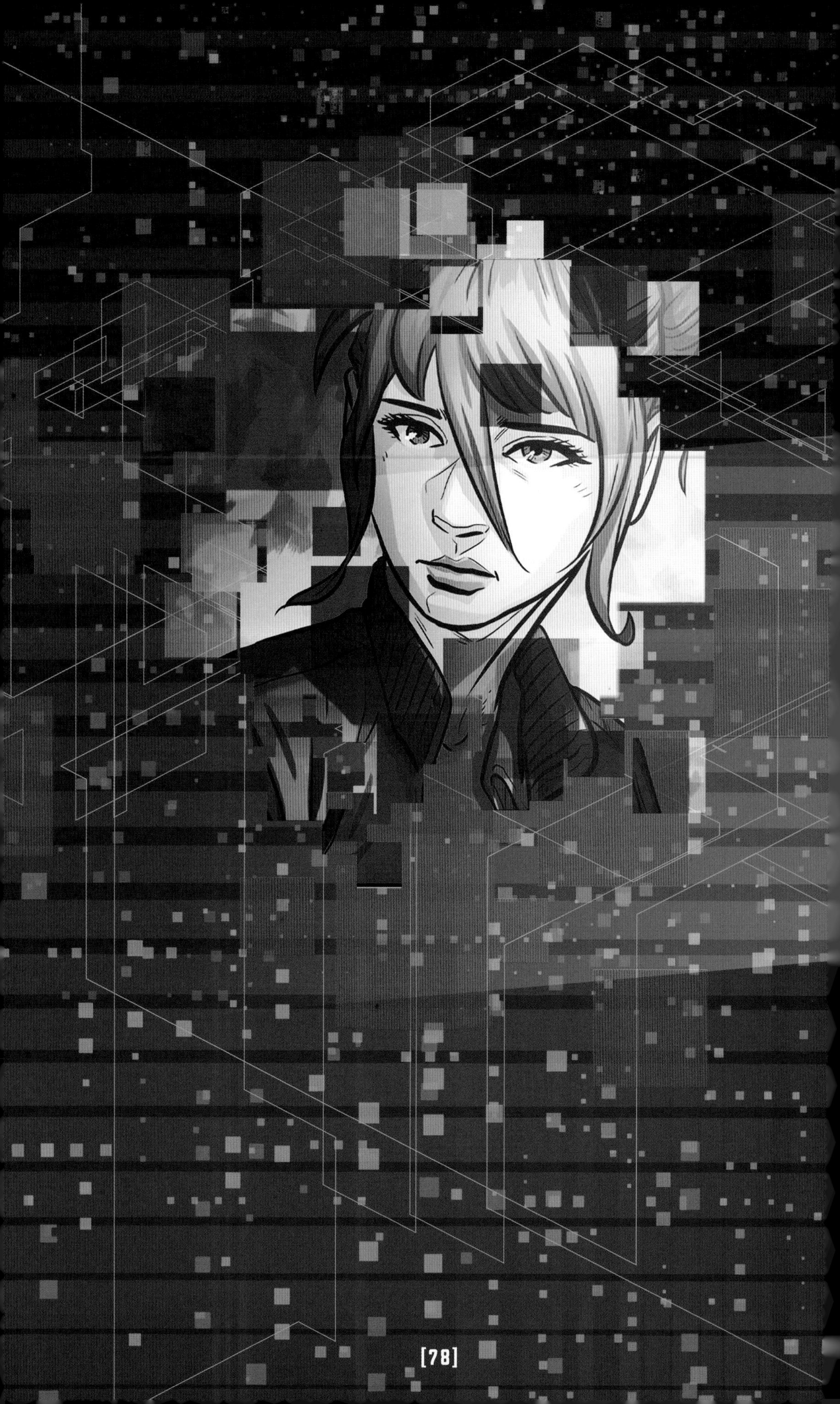

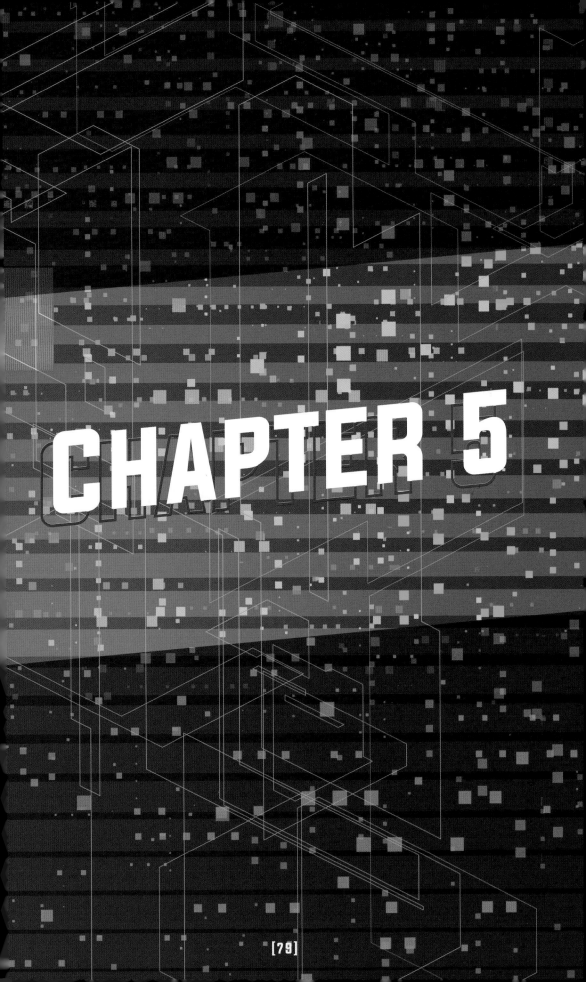

CHAPTER 5

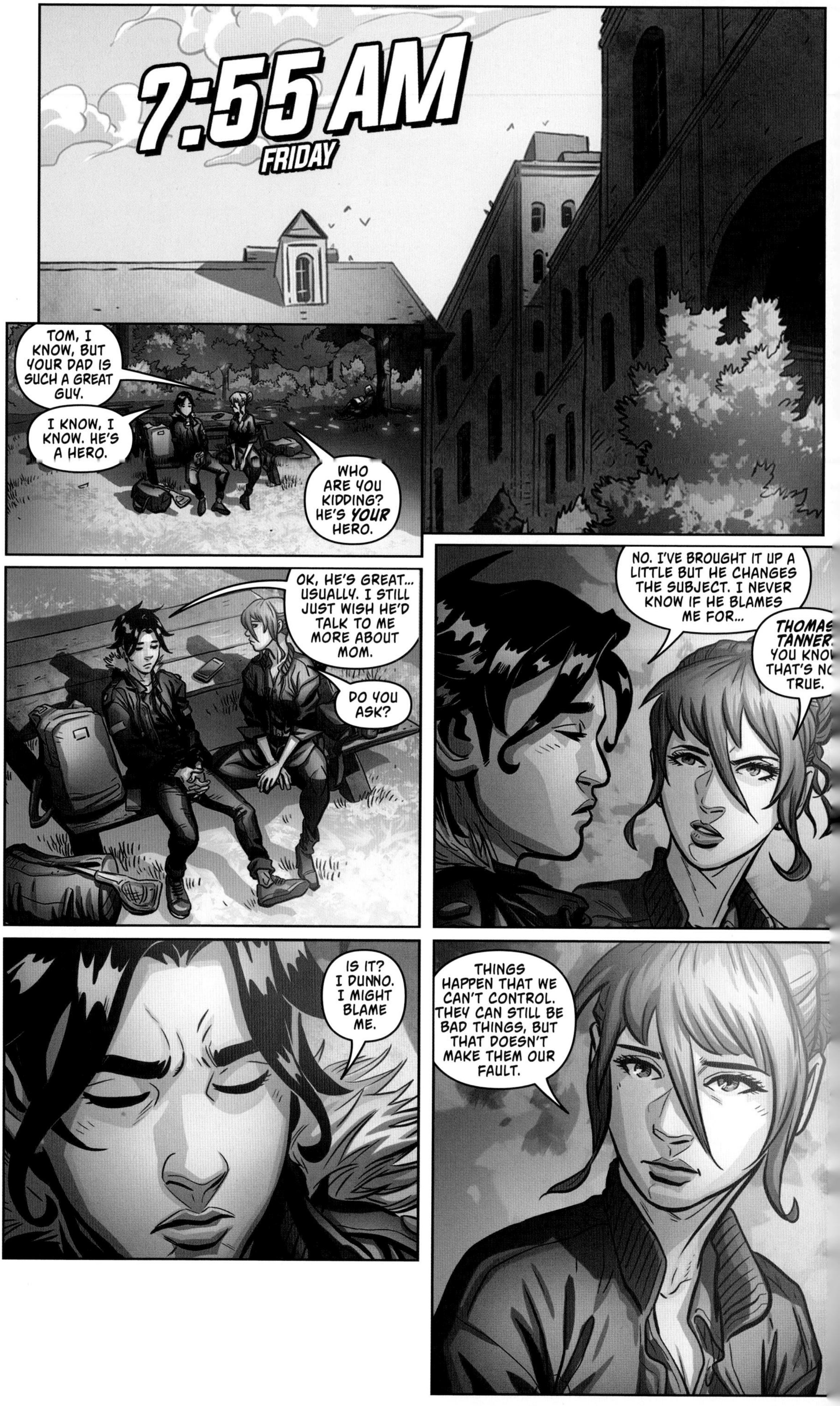
7:55 AM
FRIDAY
TOM, I KNOW, BUT YOUR DAD IS SUCH A GREAT GUY.
I KNOW, I KNOW. HE'S A HERO.
WHO ARE YOU KIDDING? HE'S *YOUR* HERO.
OK, HE'S GREAT... USUALLY. I STILL JUST WISH HE'D TALK TO ME MORE ABOUT MOM.
DO YOU ASK?
NO. I'VE BROUGHT IT UP A LITTLE BUT HE CHANGES THE SUBJECT. I NEVER KNOW IF HE BLAMES ME FOR...
THOMAS TANNER. YOU KNOW THAT'S NOT TRUE.
IS IT? I DUNNO. I MIGHT BLAME ME.
THINGS HAPPEN THAT WE CAN'T CONTROL. THEY CAN STILL BE BAD THINGS, BUT THAT DOESN'T MAKE THEM OUR FAULT.

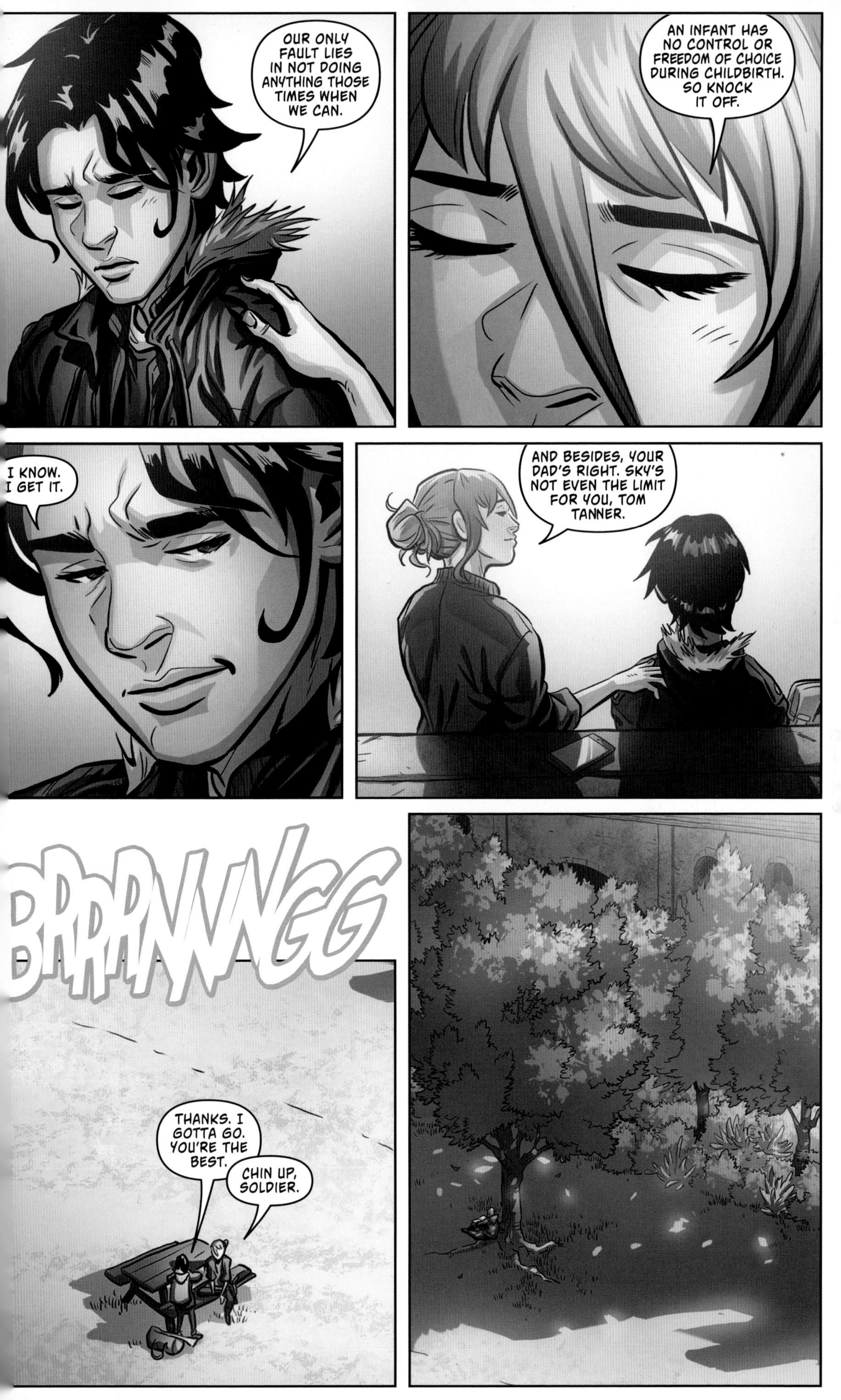
OUR ONLY FAULT LIES IN NOT DOING ANYTHING THOSE TIMES WHEN WE CAN.
AN INFANT HAS NO CONTROL OR FREEDOM OF CHOICE DURING CHILDBIRTH. SO KNOCK IT OFF.
I KNOW. I GET IT.
AND BESIDES, YOUR DAD'S RIGHT. SKY'S NOT EVEN THE LIMIT FOR YOU, TOM TANNER.
BRRRNNGG
THANKS. I GOTTA GO. YOU'RE THE BEST.
CHIN UP, SOLDIER.

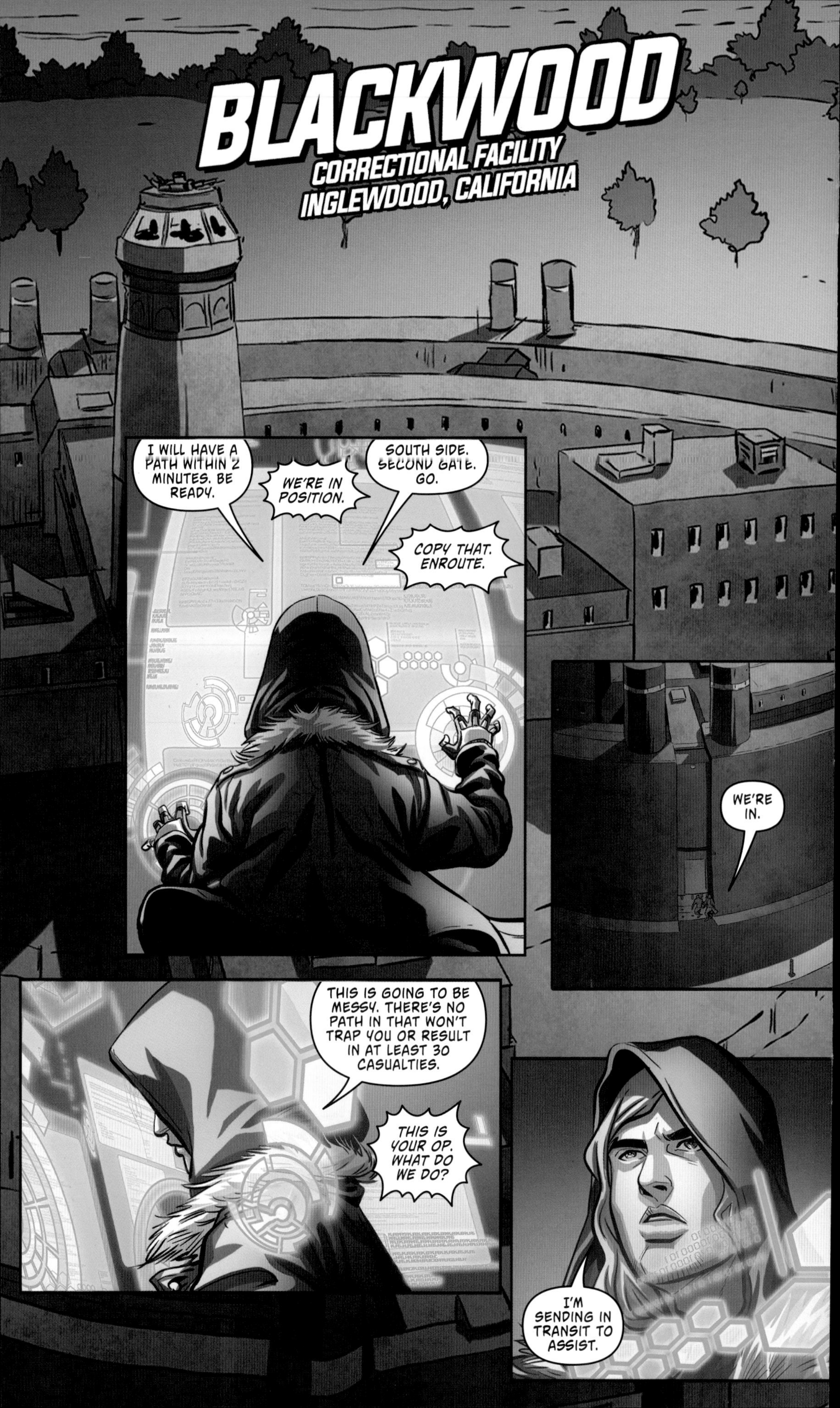
BLACKWOOD
CORRECTIONAL FACILITY
INGLEWOOD, CALIFORNIA
I WILL HAVE A PATH WITHIN 2 MINUTES. BE READY.
WE'RE IN POSITION.
SOUTH SIDE. SECOND GATE. GO.
COPY THAT. ENROUTE.
WE'RE IN.
THIS IS GOING TO BE MESSY. THERE'S NO PATH IN THAT WON'T TRAP YOU OR RESULT IN AT LEAST 30 CASUALTIES.
THIS IS YOUR OP. WHAT DO WE DO?
I'M SENDING IN TRANSIT TO ASSIST.

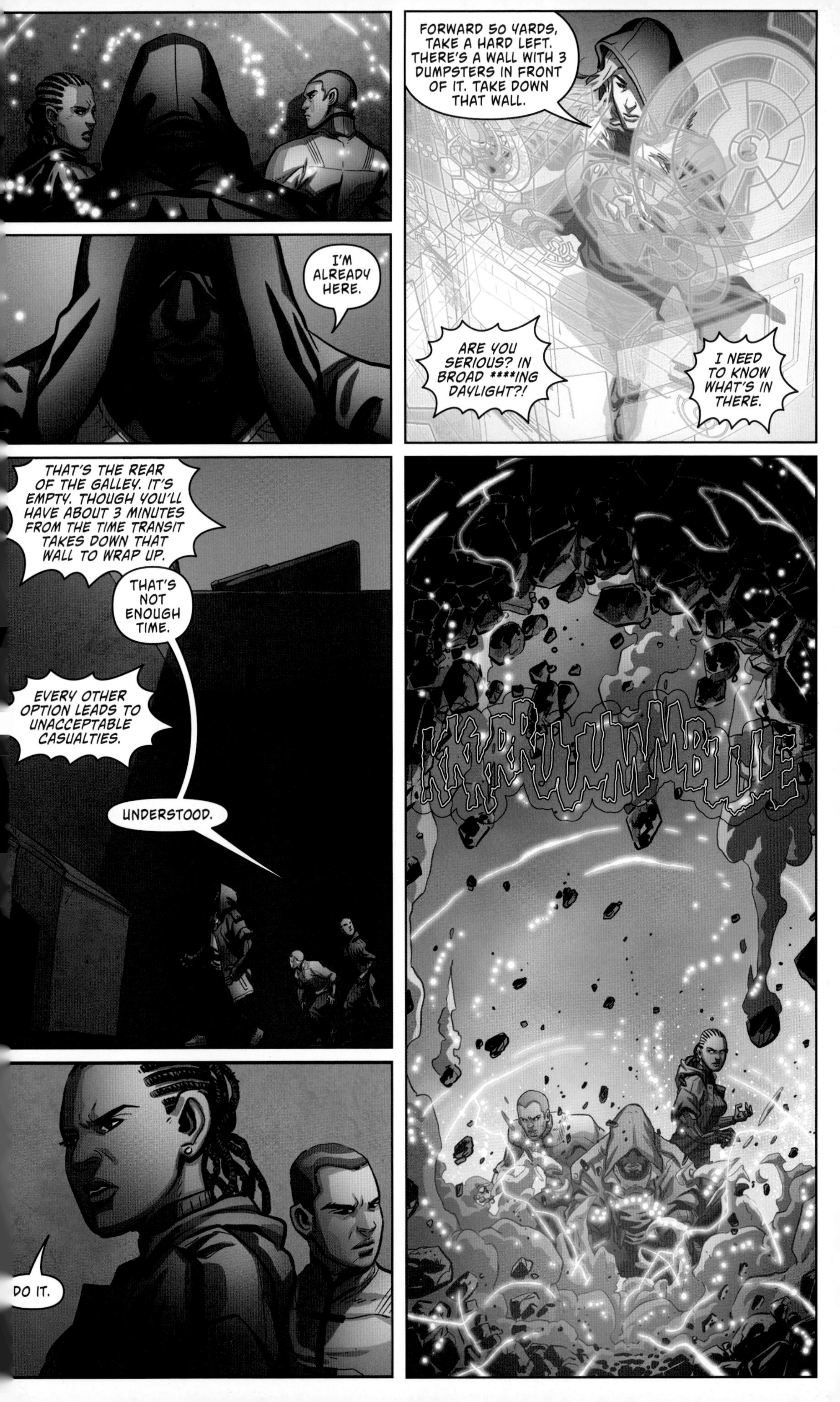
FORWARD 50 YARDS, TAKE A HARD LEFT. THERE'S A WALL WITH 3 DUMPSTERS IN FRONT OF IT. TAKE DOWN THAT WALL.
I'M ALREADY HERE.
ARE YOU SERIOUS? IN BROAD ****ING DAYLIGHT?!
I NEED TO KNOW WHAT'S IN THERE.
THAT'S THE REAR OF THE GALLEY. IT'S EMPTY. THOUGH YOU'LL HAVE ABOUT 3 MINUTES FROM THE TIME TRANSIT TAKES DOWN THAT WALL TO WRAP UP.
THAT'S NOT ENOUGH TIME.
EVERY OTHER OPTION LEADS TO UNACCEPTABLE CASUALTIES.
UNDERSTOOD.
DO IT.
KKRRUUUMMBLLE

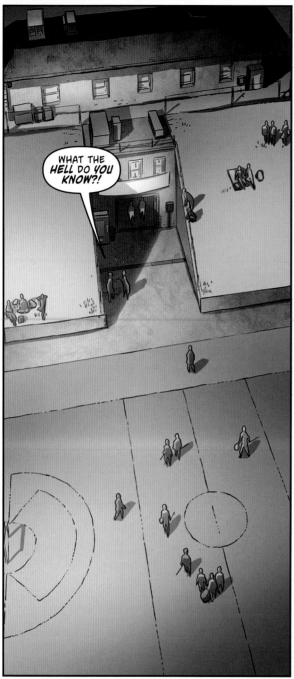

WHAT THE *HELL* DO *YOU* KNOW?!

I KNOW THAT YOU *SHOULDN'T* HAVE SCREWED AROUND IN YOUR CLASSES--

--AND YOU *COULD* HAVE AVOIDED THIS.

RIGHT. BECAUSE I *HAVE* TIME FOR THAT.

WHAT? DO YOU THINK YOU'RE *SPECIAL* BECAUSE YOU START ON THE LACROSSE TEAM? YOU DON'T HAVE TO DO THE WORK THE REST OF US DO?

I HAVE THEATRE *FIVE* DAYS A WEEK. IT DOESN'T EXCUSE ME FROM *STUDYING.*

WASTING YOUR TIME ON THAT GARBAGE IS *NOT* THE SAME AS THE RESPONSIBILITY I HAVE TO THE TEAM.

EXCUSE ME?

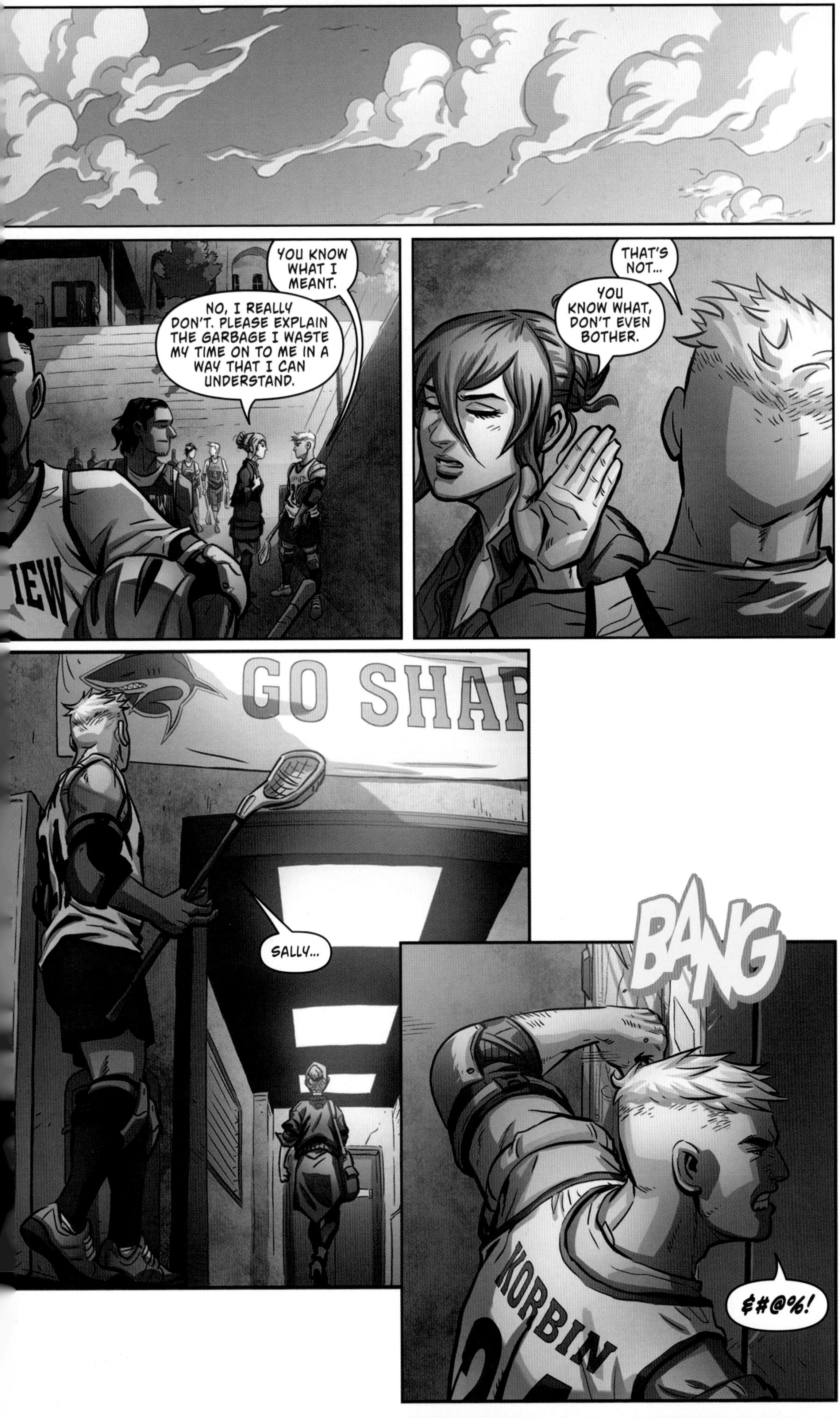
YOU KNOW WHAT I MEANT.
NO, I REALLY DON'T. PLEASE EXPLAIN THE GARBAGE I WASTE MY TIME ON TO ME IN A WAY THAT I CAN UNDERSTAND.
THAT'S NOT...
YOU KNOW WHAT, DON'T EVEN BOTHER.
GO SHAR
SALLY...
BANG
KORBIN
$#@%!

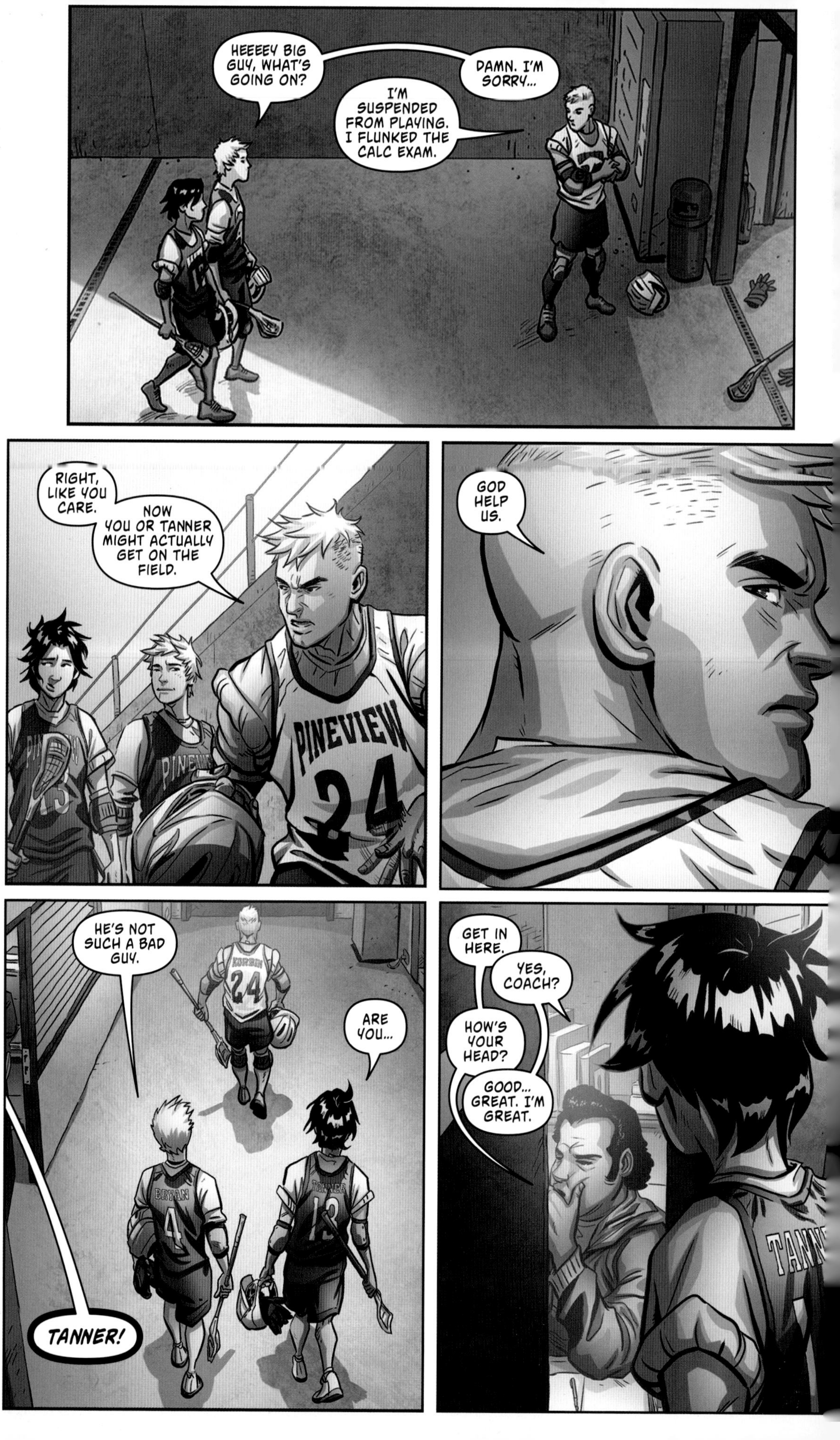
HEEEEY BIG GUY, WHAT'S GOING ON?
DAMN. I'M SORRY...
I'M SUSPENDED FROM PLAYING. I FLUNKED THE CALC EXAM.
RIGHT, LIKE YOU CARE.
NOW YOU OR TANNER MIGHT ACTUALLY GET ON THE FIELD.
PINEVIEW
24
GOD HELP US.
HE'S NOT SUCH A BAD GUY.
KORBIN
24
ARE YOU...
BRYAN
4
TANNER
13
TANNER!
GET IN HERE.
YES, COACH?
HOW'S YOUR HEAD?
GOOD... GREAT. I'M GREAT.

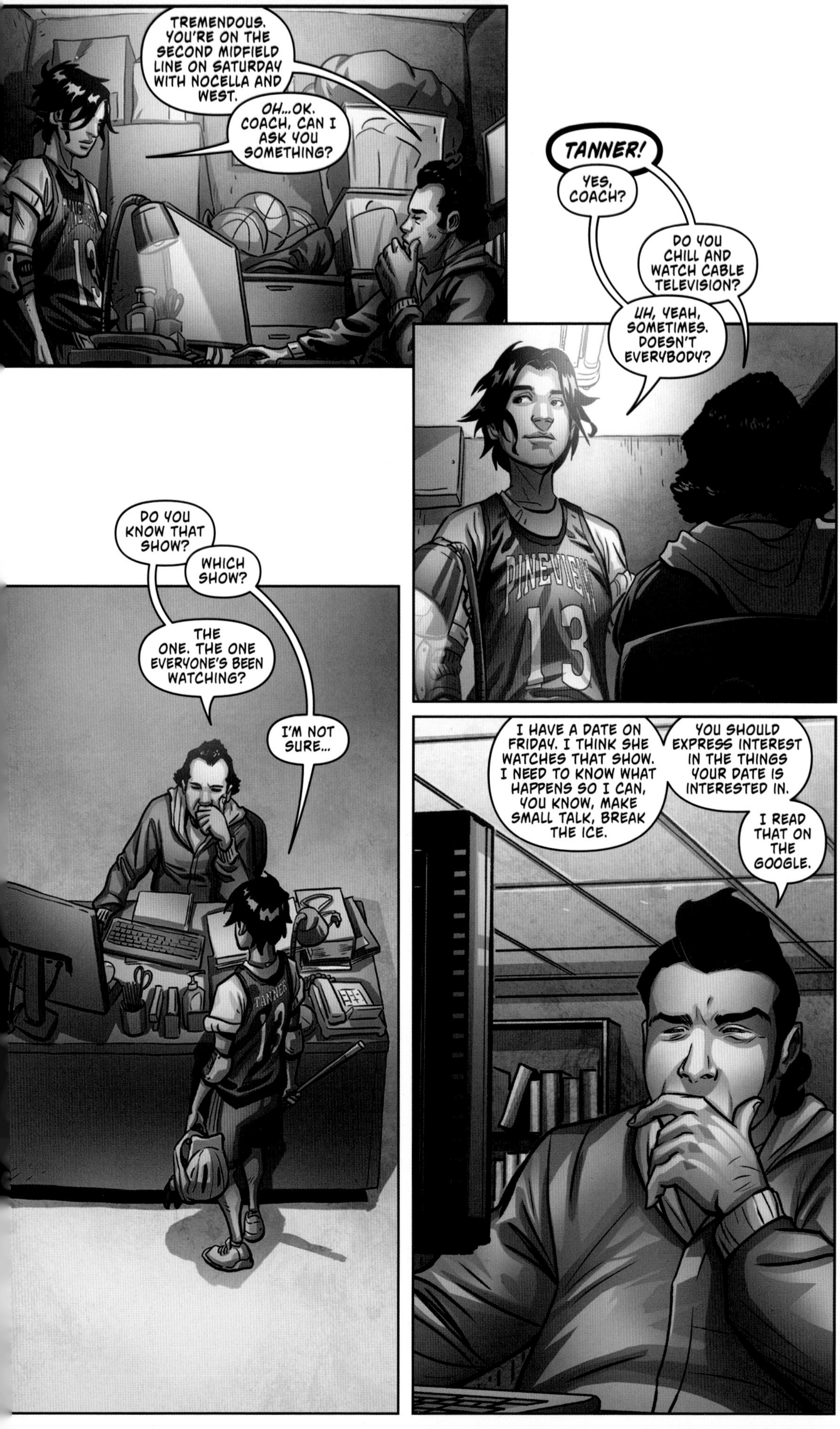
TREMENDOUS. YOU'RE ON THE SECOND MIDFIELD LINE ON SATURDAY WITH NOCELLA AND WEST.
OH...OK. COACH, CAN I ASK YOU SOMETHING?
TANNER!
YES, COACH?
DO YOU CHILL AND WATCH CABLE TELEVISION?
UH, YEAH, SOMETIMES. DOESN'T EVERYBODY?
PINEVIEW 13
DO YOU KNOW THAT SHOW?
WHICH SHOW?
THE ONE. THE ONE EVERYONE'S BEEN WATCHING?
I'M NOT SURE...
TANNER 13
I HAVE A DATE ON FRIDAY. I THINK SHE WATCHES THAT SHOW. I NEED TO KNOW WHAT HAPPENS SO I CAN, YOU KNOW, MAKE SMALL TALK, BREAK THE ICE.
YOU SHOULD EXPRESS INTEREST IN THE THINGS YOUR DATE IS INTERESTED IN.
I READ THAT ON THE GOOGLE.

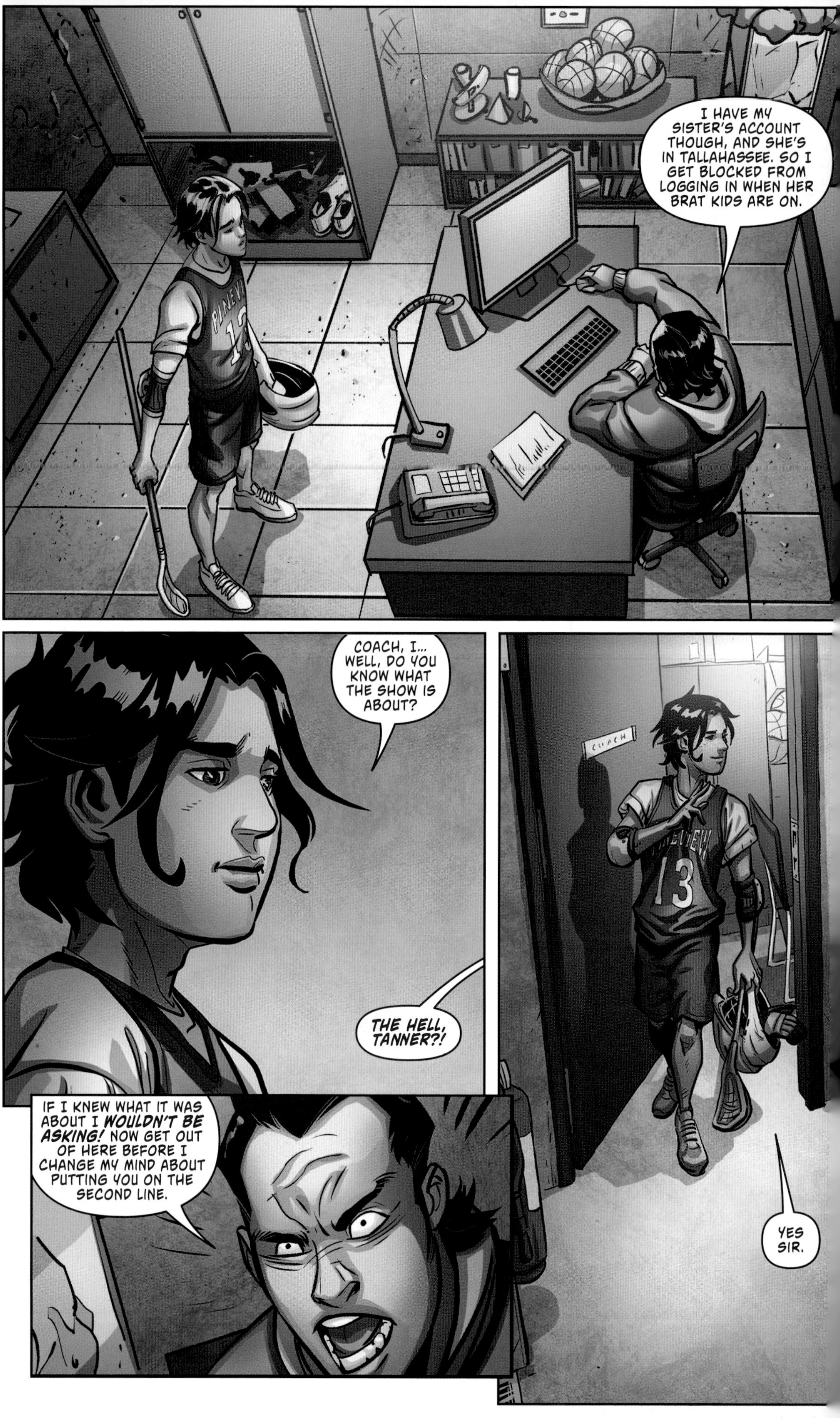

I HAVE MY SISTER'S ACCOUNT THOUGH, AND SHE'S IN TALLAHASSEE. SO I GET BLOCKED FROM LOGGING IN WHEN HER BRAT KIDS ARE ON.
COACH, I... WELL, DO YOU KNOW WHAT THE SHOW IS ABOUT?
THE HELL, TANNER?!
IF I KNEW WHAT IT WAS ABOUT I WOULDN'T BE ASKING! NOW GET OUT OF HERE BEFORE I CHANGE MY MIND ABOUT PUTTING YOU ON THE SECOND LINE.
YES SIR.

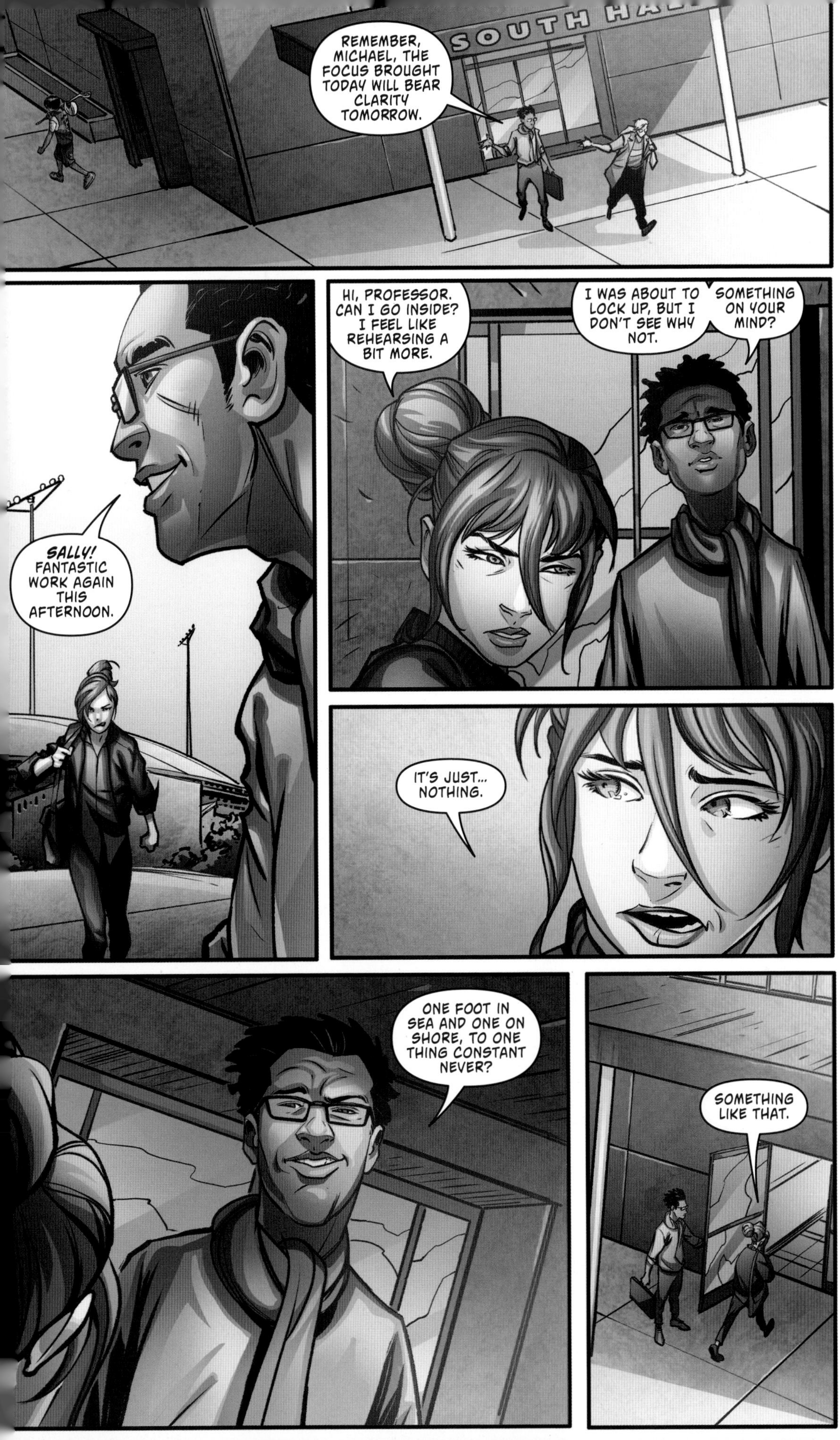
SOUTH HA
REMEMBER, MICHAEL, THE FOCUS BROUGHT TODAY WILL BEAR CLARITY TOMORROW.
SALLY! FANTASTIC WORK AGAIN THIS AFTERNOON.
HI, PROFESSOR. CAN I GO INSIDE? I FEEL LIKE REHEARSING A BIT MORE.
I WAS ABOUT TO LOCK UP, BUT I DON'T SEE WHY NOT.
SOMETHING ON YOUR MIND?
IT'S JUST... NOTHING.
ONE FOOT IN SEA AND ONE ON SHORE, TO ONE THING CONSTANT NEVER?
SOMETHING LIKE THAT.

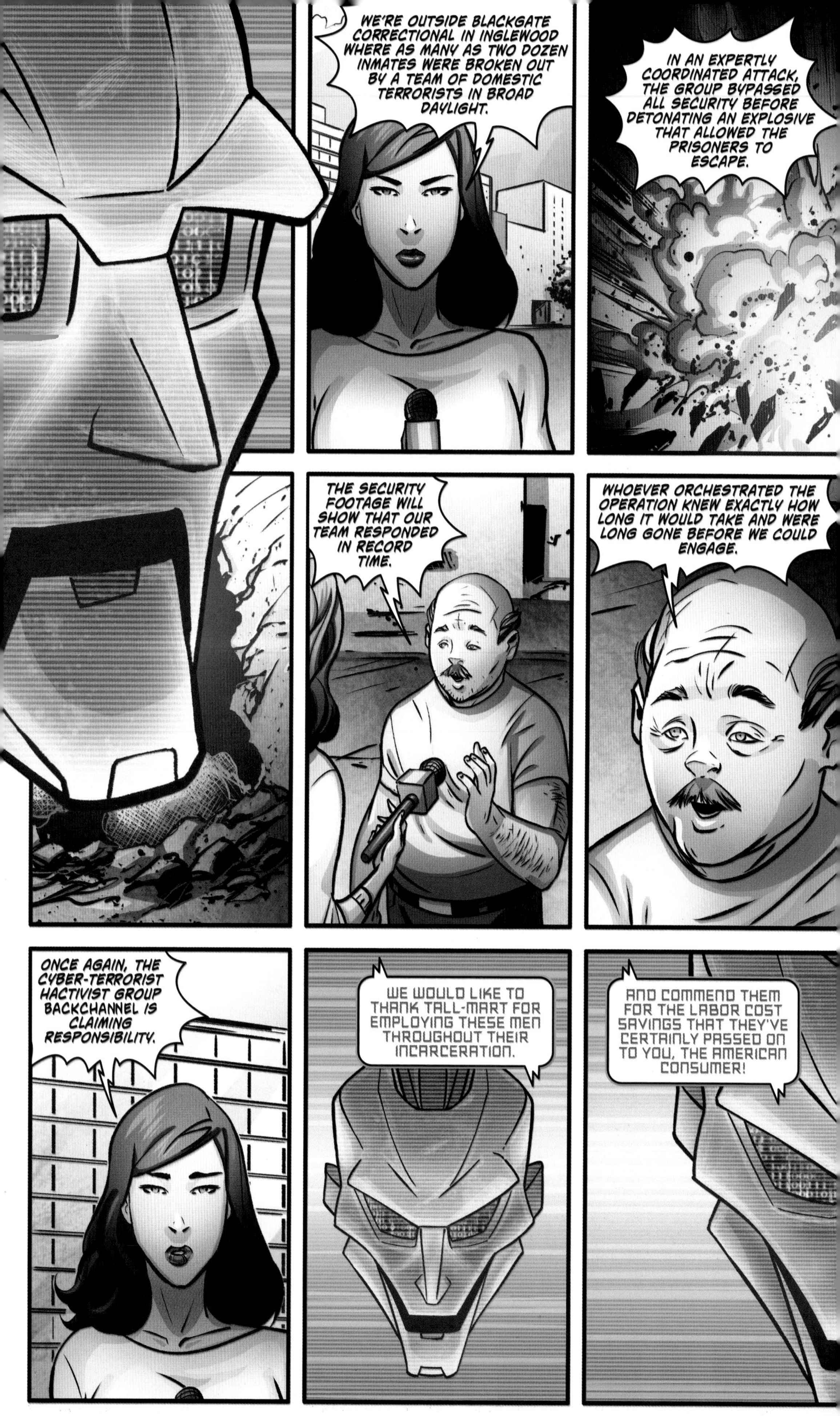
WE'RE OUTSIDE BLACKGATE CORRECTIONAL IN INGLEWOOD WHERE AS MANY AS TWO DOZEN INMATES WERE BROKEN OUT BY A TEAM OF DOMESTIC TERRORISTS IN BROAD DAYLIGHT.
IN AN EXPERTLY COORDINATED ATTACK, THE GROUP BYPASSED ALL SECURITY BEFORE DETONATING AN EXPLOSIVE THAT ALLOWED THE PRISONERS TO ESCAPE.
THE SECURITY FOOTAGE WILL SHOW THAT OUR TEAM RESPONDED IN RECORD TIME.
WHOEVER ORCHESTRATED THE OPERATION KNEW EXACTLY HOW LONG IT WOULD TAKE AND WERE LONG GONE BEFORE WE COULD ENGAGE.
ONCE AGAIN, THE CYBER-TERRORIST HACTIVIST GROUP BACKCHANNEL IS CLAIMING RESPONSIBILITY.
WE WOULD LIKE TO THANK TALL-MART FOR EMPLOYING THESE MEN THROUGHOUT THEIR INCARCERATION.
AND COMMEND THEM FOR THE LABOR COST SAVINGS THAT THEY'VE CERTAINLY PASSED ON TO YOU, THE AMERICAN CONSUMER!

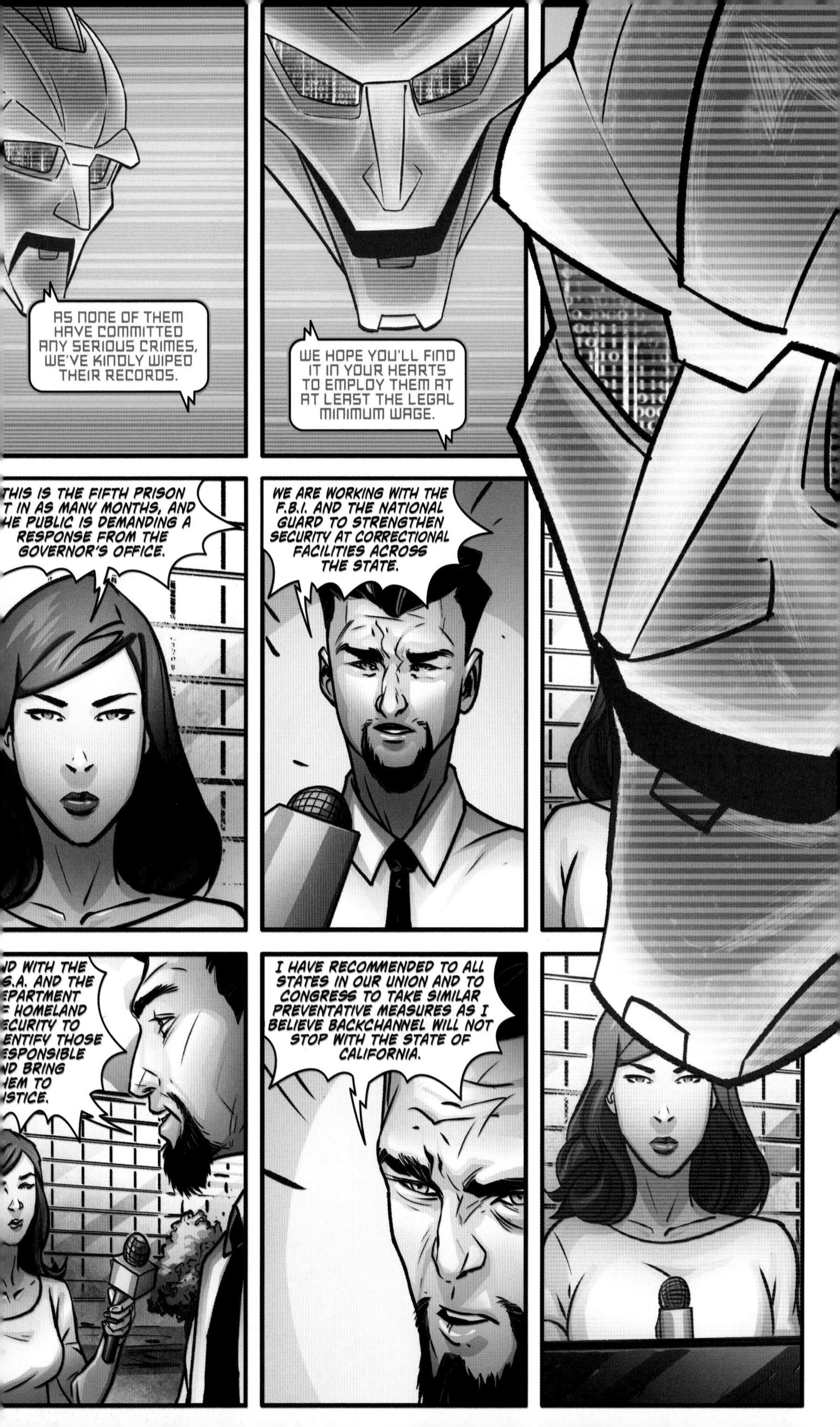
AS NONE OF THEM HAVE COMMITTED ANY SERIOUS CRIMES, WE'VE KINDLY WIPED THEIR RECORDS.
WE HOPE YOU'LL FIND IT IN YOUR HEARTS TO EMPLOY THEM AT AT LEAST THE LEGAL MINIMUM WAGE.
THIS IS THE FIFTH PRISON T IN AS MANY MONTHS, AND HE PUBLIC IS DEMANDING A RESPONSE FROM THE GOVERNOR'S OFFICE.
WE ARE WORKING WITH THE F.B.I. AND THE NATIONAL GUARD TO STRENGTHEN SECURITY AT CORRECTIONAL FACILITIES ACROSS THE STATE.
ND WITH THE S.A. AND THE EPARTMENT HOMELAND ECURITY TO ENTIFY THOSE ESPONSIBLE ND BRING HEM TO STICE.
I HAVE RECOMMENDED TO ALL STATES IN OUR UNION AND TO CONGRESS TO TAKE SIMILAR PREVENTATIVE MEASURES AS I BELIEVE BACKCHANNEL WILL NOT STOP WITH THE STATE OF CALIFORNIA.

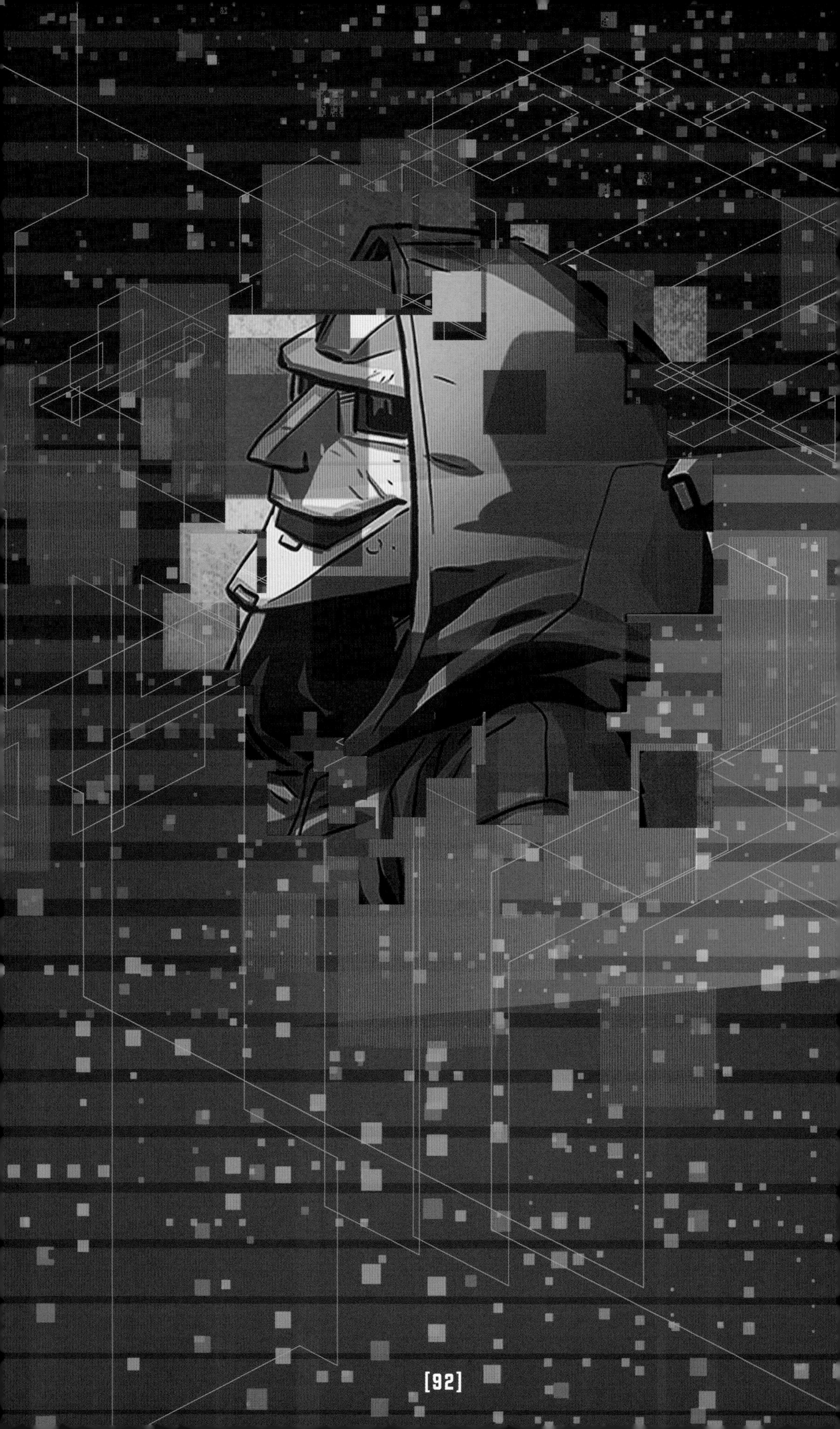

CHAPTER 6

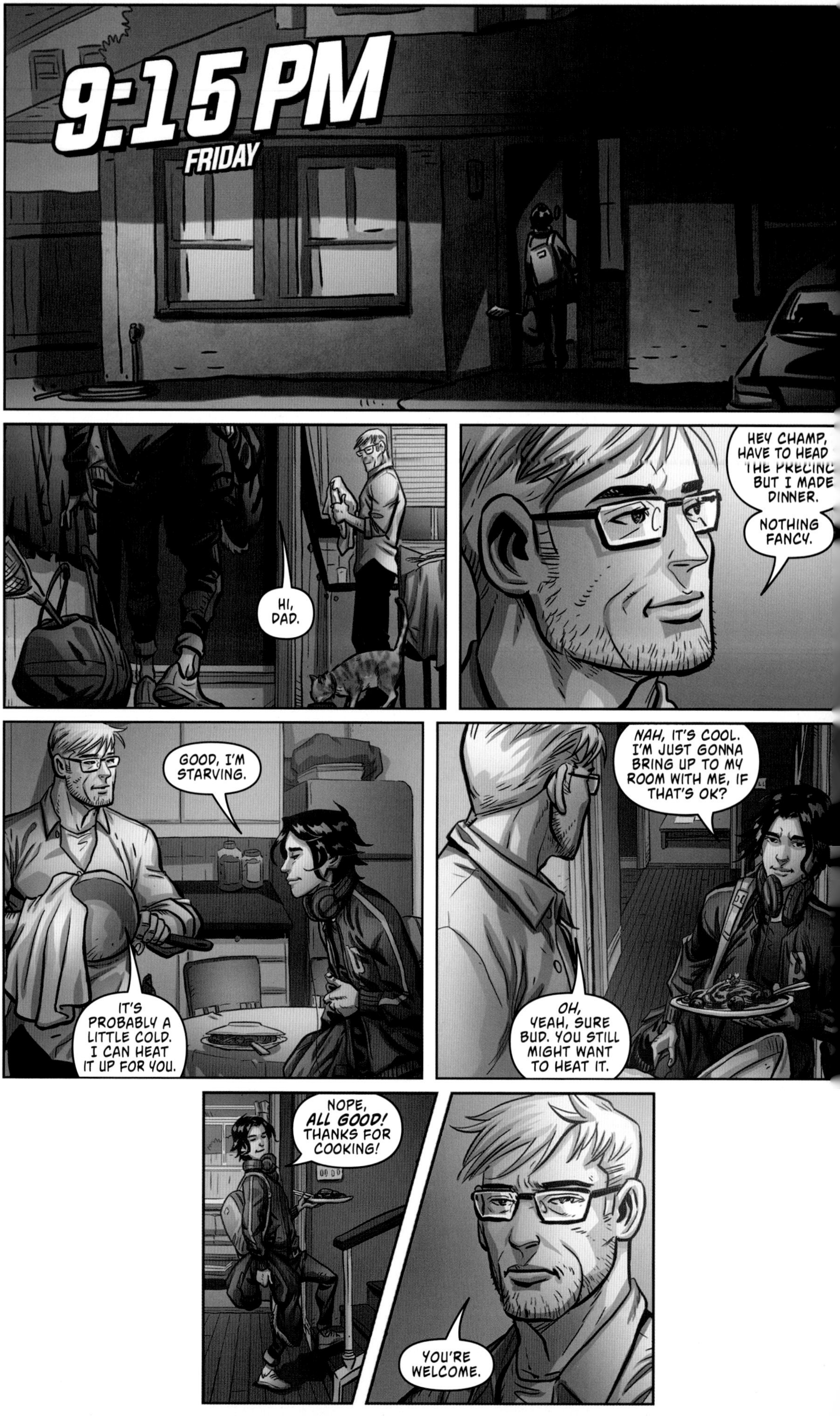
9:15 PM
FRIDAY
HI, DAD.
HEY CHAMP, HAVE TO HEAD TO THE PRECINCT BUT I MADE DINNER.
NOTHING FANCY.
GOOD, I'M STARVING.
IT'S PROBABLY A LITTLE COLD. I CAN HEAT IT UP FOR YOU.
NAH, IT'S COOL. I'M JUST GONNA BRING UP TO MY ROOM WITH ME, IF THAT'S OK?
OH, YEAH, SURE BUD. YOU STILL MIGHT WANT TO HEAT IT.
NOPE, ALL GOOD! THANKS FOR COOKING!
YOU'RE WELCOME.

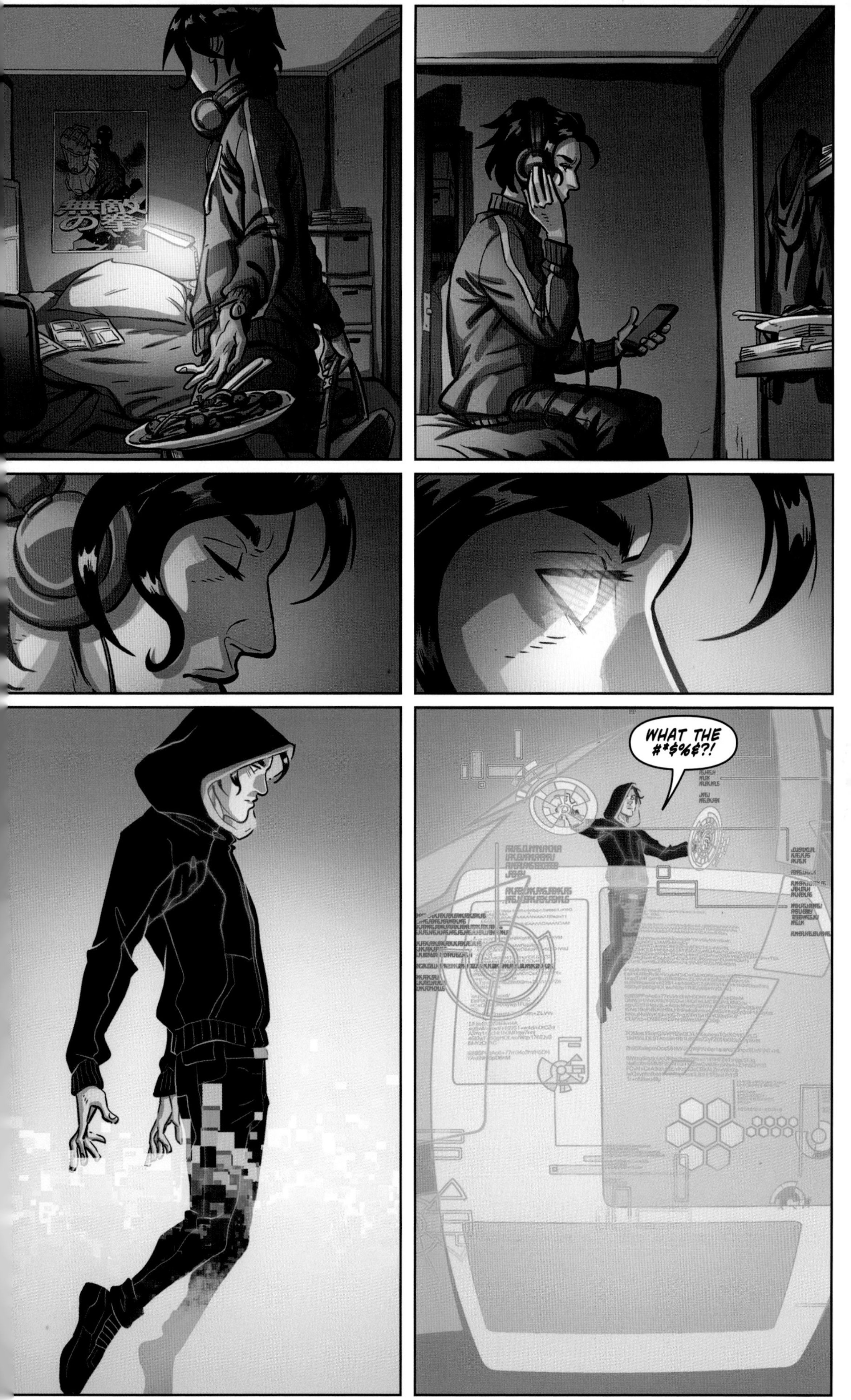

無敵の拳
WHAT THE #*$%¢?!

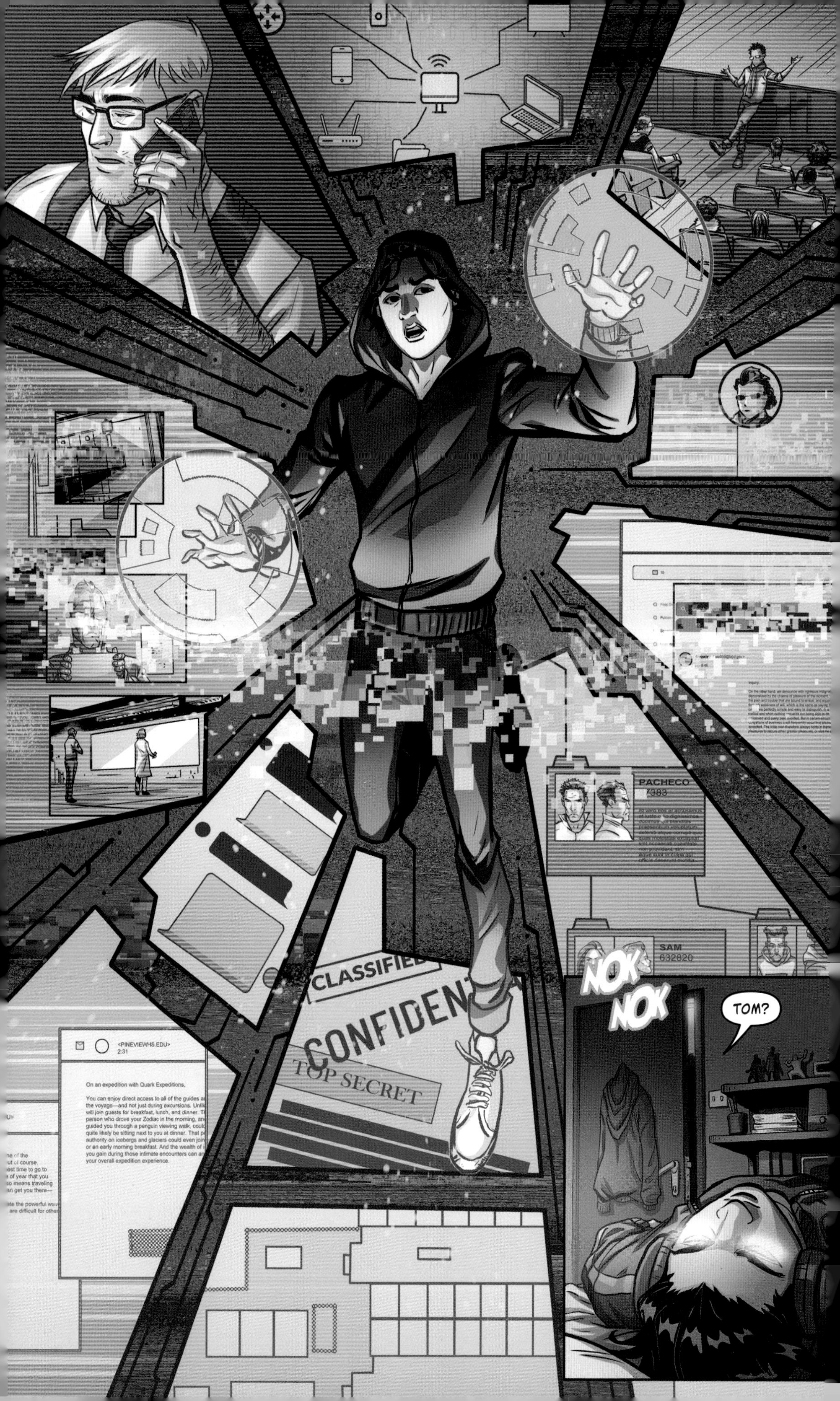

PACHECO
SAM
632820
CLASSIFIED
CONFIDENT
TOP SECRET
<PINEVIEWHS.EDU>
2:31
On an expedition with Quark Expeditions,
NOK NOK
TOM?

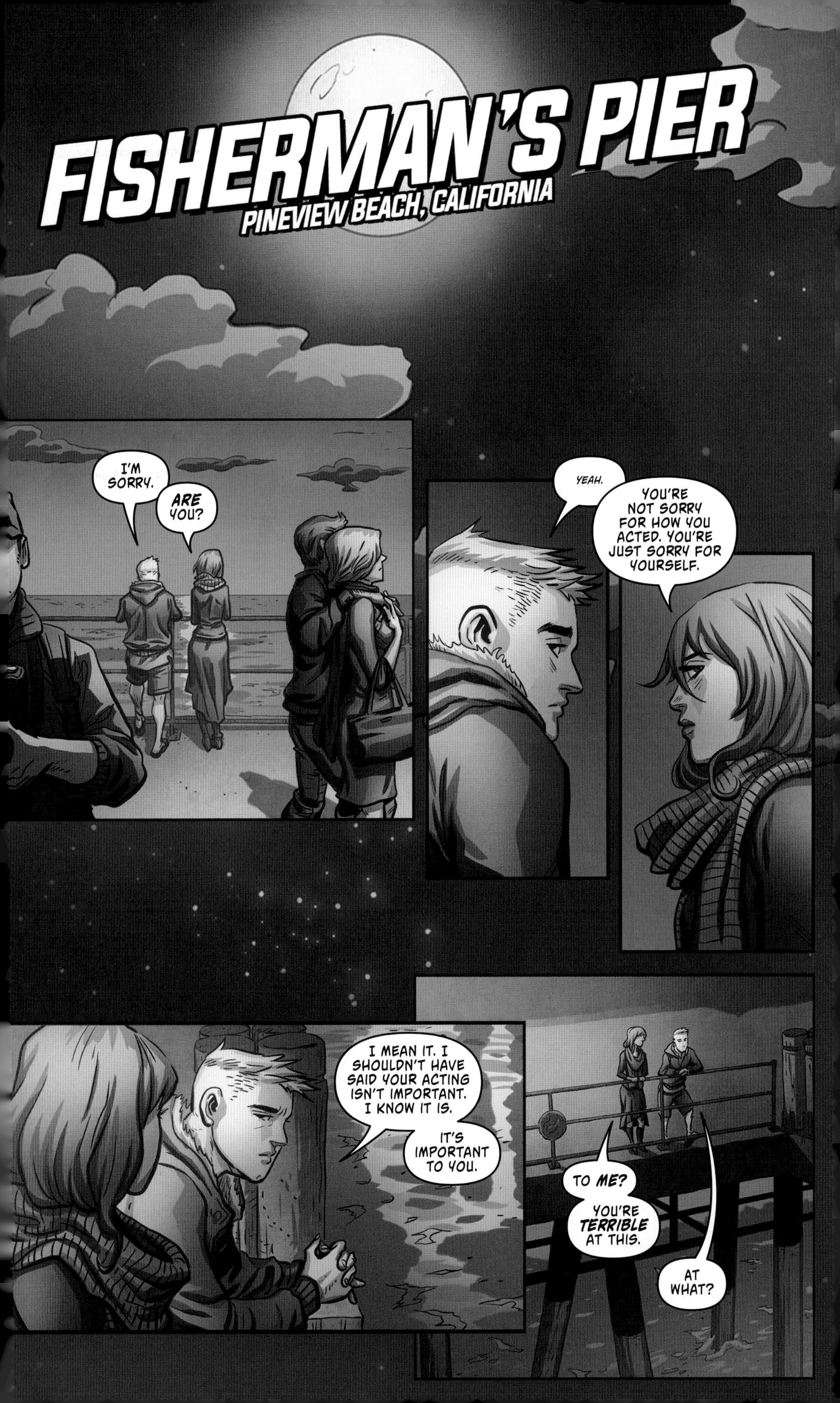
FISHERMAN'S PIER
PINEVIEW BEACH, CALIFORNIA
I'M SORRY.
ARE YOU?
YEAH.
YOU'RE NOT SORRY FOR HOW YOU ACTED. YOU'RE JUST SORRY FOR YOURSELF.
I MEAN IT. I SHOULDN'T HAVE SAID YOUR ACTING ISN'T IMPORTANT. I KNOW IT IS.
IT'S IMPORTANT TO YOU.
TO ME?
YOU'RE TERRIBLE AT THIS.
AT WHAT?

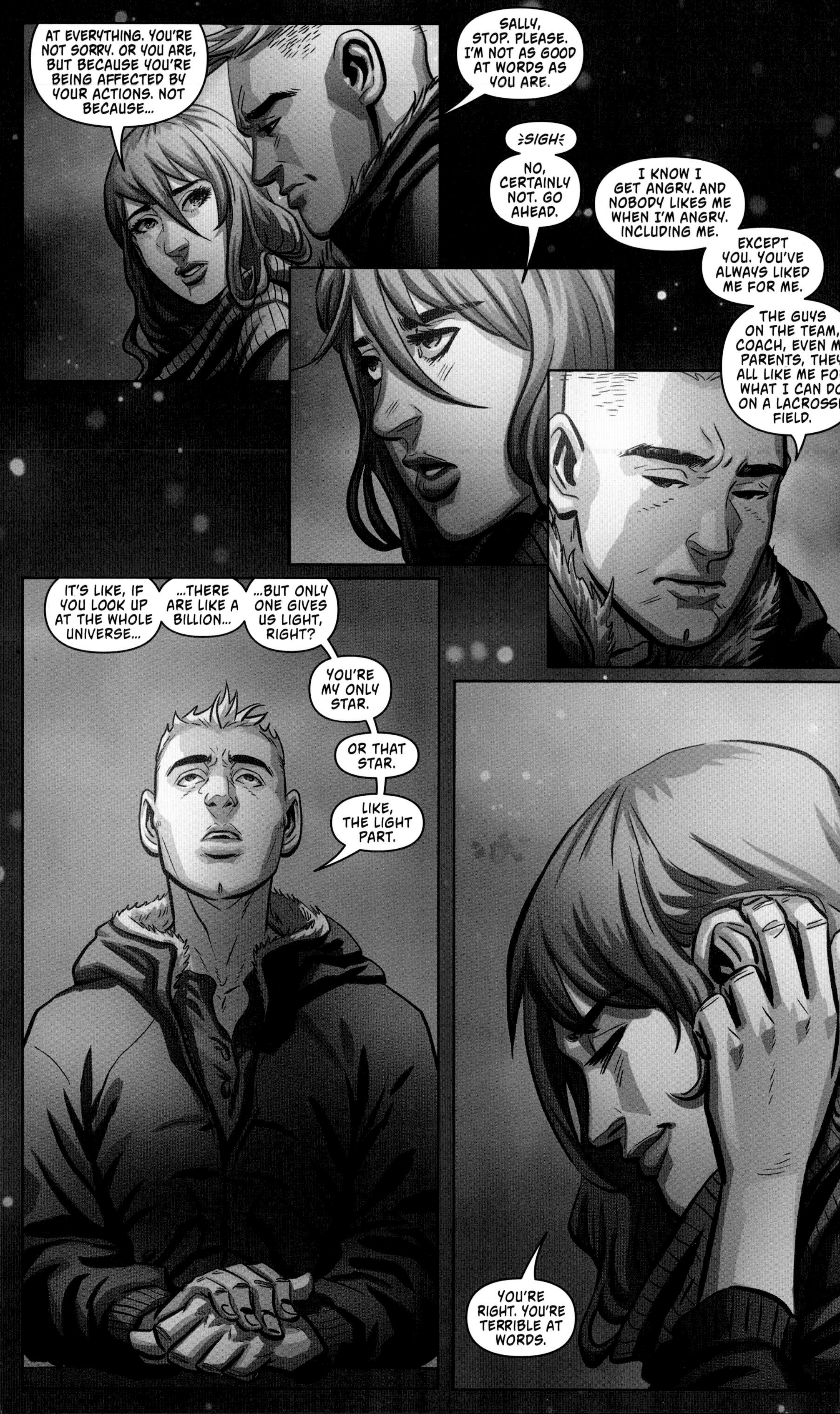
AT EVERYTHING. YOU'RE NOT SORRY. OR YOU ARE, BUT BECAUSE YOU'RE BEING AFFECTED BY YOUR ACTIONS. NOT BECAUSE...
SALLY, STOP. PLEASE. I'M NOT AS GOOD AT WORDS AS YOU ARE.
SIGH
NO, CERTAINLY NOT. GO AHEAD.
I KNOW I GET ANGRY. AND NOBODY LIKES ME WHEN I'M ANGRY. INCLUDING ME.
EXCEPT YOU. YOU'VE ALWAYS LIKED ME FOR ME.
THE GUYS ON THE TEAM, COACH, EVEN M PARENTS, THE ALL LIKE ME FO WHAT I CAN DO ON A LACROSS FIELD.
IT'S LIKE, IF YOU LOOK UP AT THE WHOLE UNIVERSE...
...THERE ARE LIKE A BILLION...
...BUT ONLY ONE GIVES US LIGHT, RIGHT?
YOU'RE MY ONLY STAR.
OR THAT STAR.
LIKE, THE LIGHT PART.
YOU'RE RIGHT. YOU'RE TERRIBLE AT WORDS.

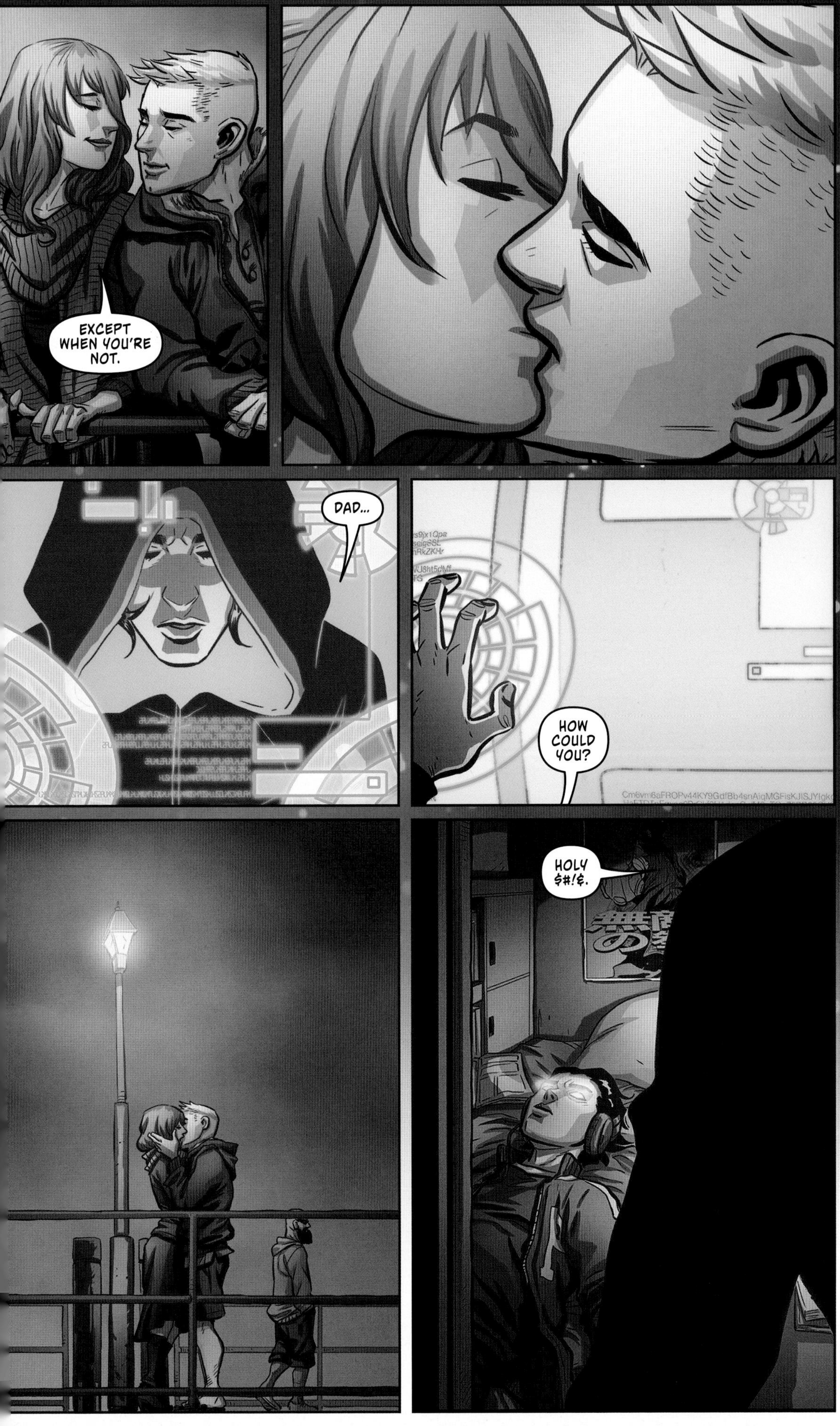
EXCEPT WHEN YOU'RE NOT.
DAD...
HOW COULD YOU?
HOLY $#!&.

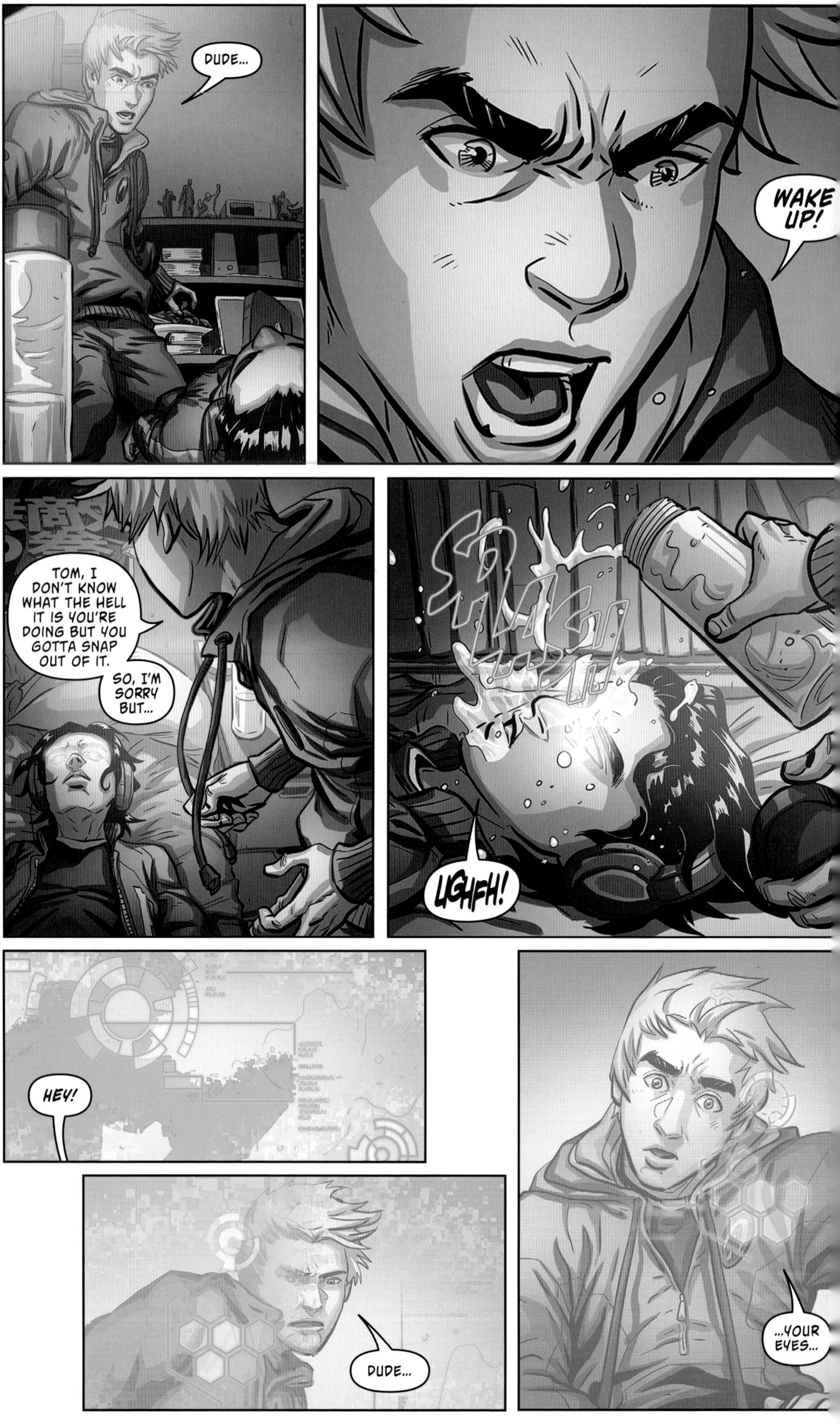
DUDE...
WAKE UP!
TOM, I DON'T KNOW WHAT THE HELL IT IS YOU'RE DOING BUT YOU GOTTA SNAP OUT OF IT.
SO, I'M SORRY BUT...
UGHFH!
HEY!
DUDE...
...YOUR EYES...

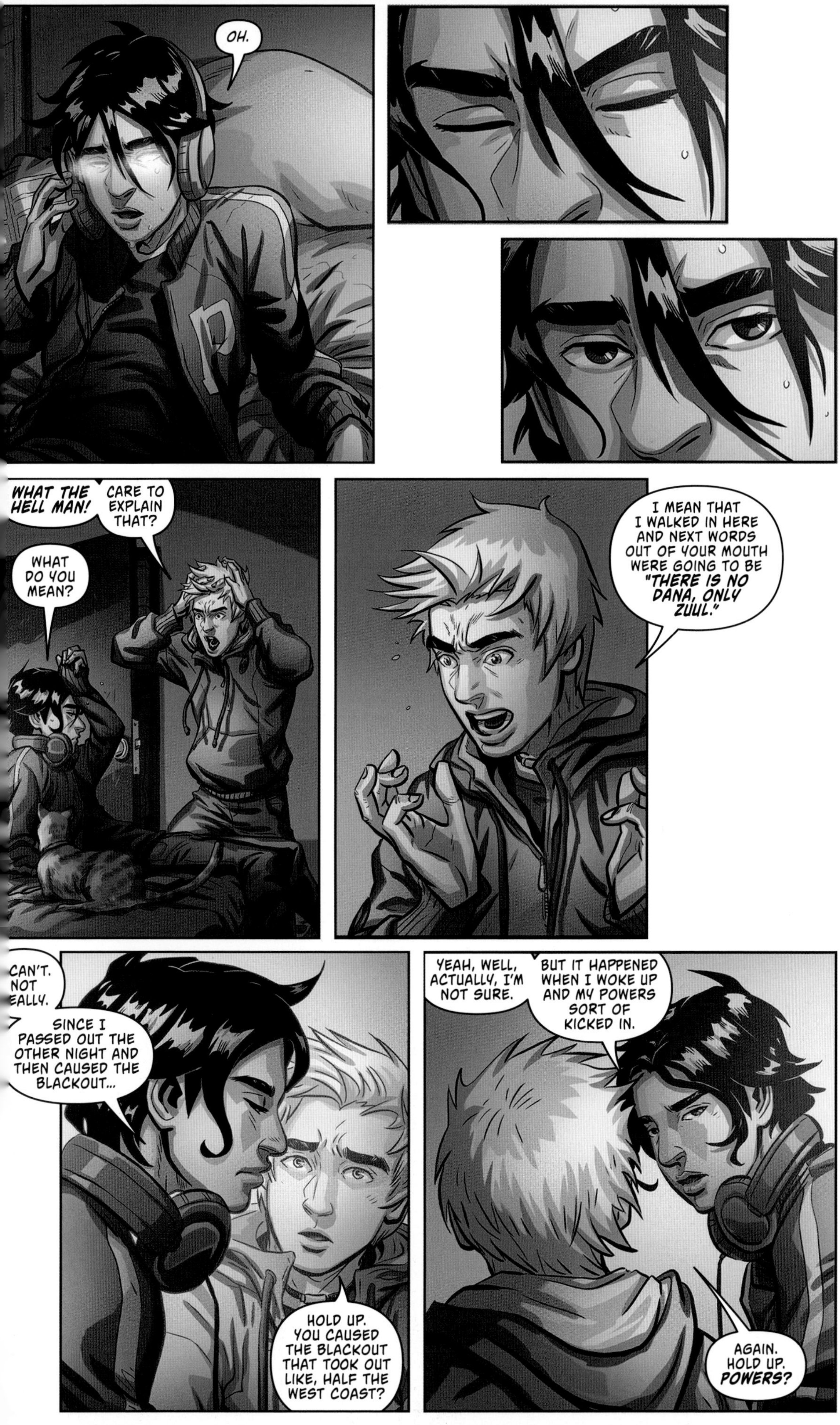
OH.
WHAT THE HELL MAN!
CARE TO EXPLAIN THAT?
WHAT DO YOU MEAN?
I MEAN THAT I WALKED IN HERE AND NEXT WORDS OUT OF YOUR MOUTH WERE GOING TO BE "THERE IS NO DANA, ONLY ZUUL."
CAN'T. NOT EALLY.
SINCE I PASSED OUT THE OTHER NIGHT AND THEN CAUSED THE BLACKOUT...
HOLD UP. YOU CAUSED THE BLACKOUT THAT TOOK OUT LIKE, HALF THE WEST COAST?
YEAH, WELL, ACTUALLY, I'M NOT SURE.
BUT IT HAPPENED WHEN I WOKE UP AND MY POWERS SORT OF KICKED IN.
AGAIN. HOLD UP. POWERS?

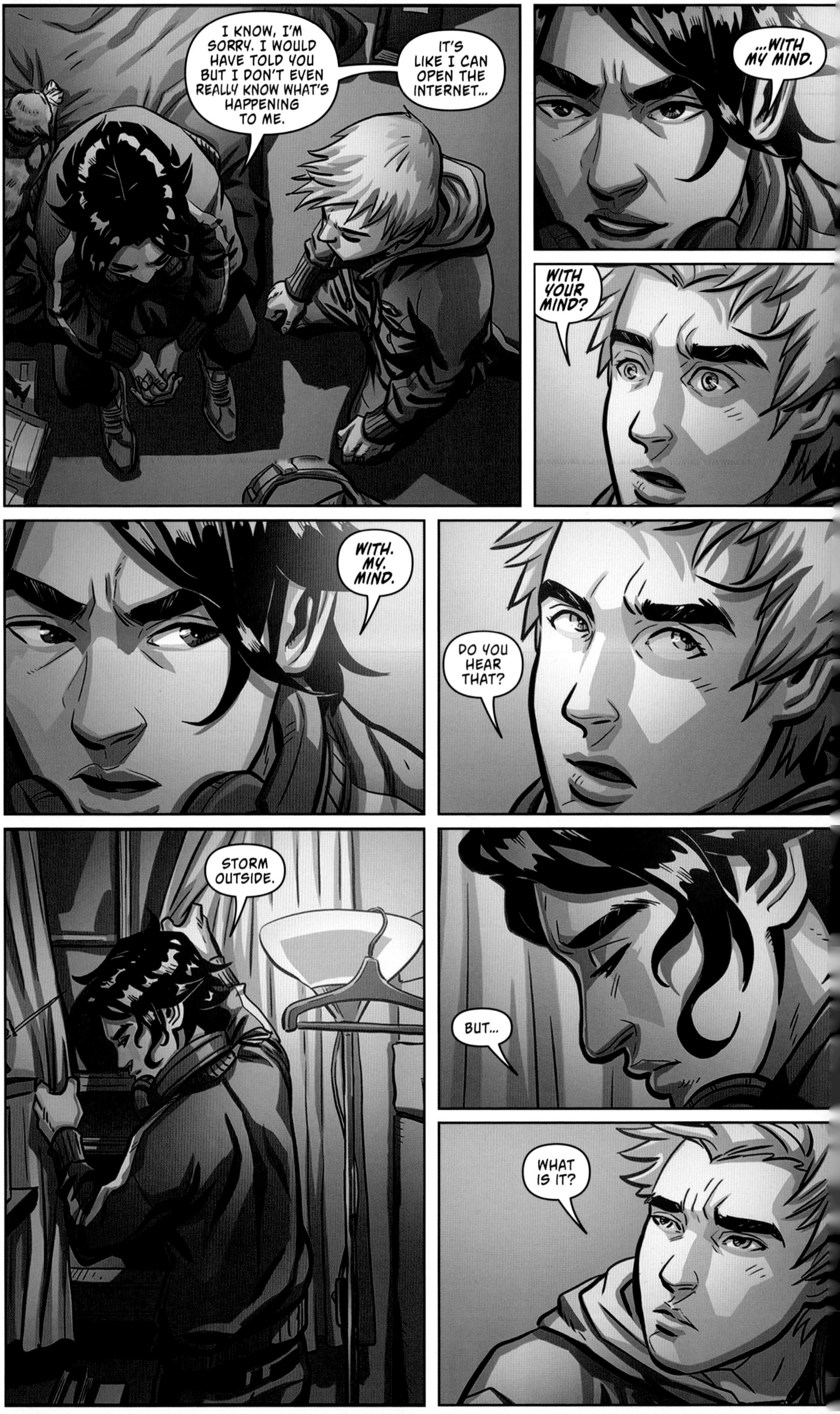
I KNOW, I'M SORRY. I WOULD HAVE TOLD YOU BUT I DON'T EVEN REALLY KNOW WHAT'S HAPPENING TO ME.
IT'S LIKE I CAN OPEN THE INTERNET...
...WITH MY MIND.
WITH YOUR MIND?
WITH. MY. MIND.
DO YOU HEAR THAT?
STORM OUTSIDE.
BUT...
WHAT IS IT?

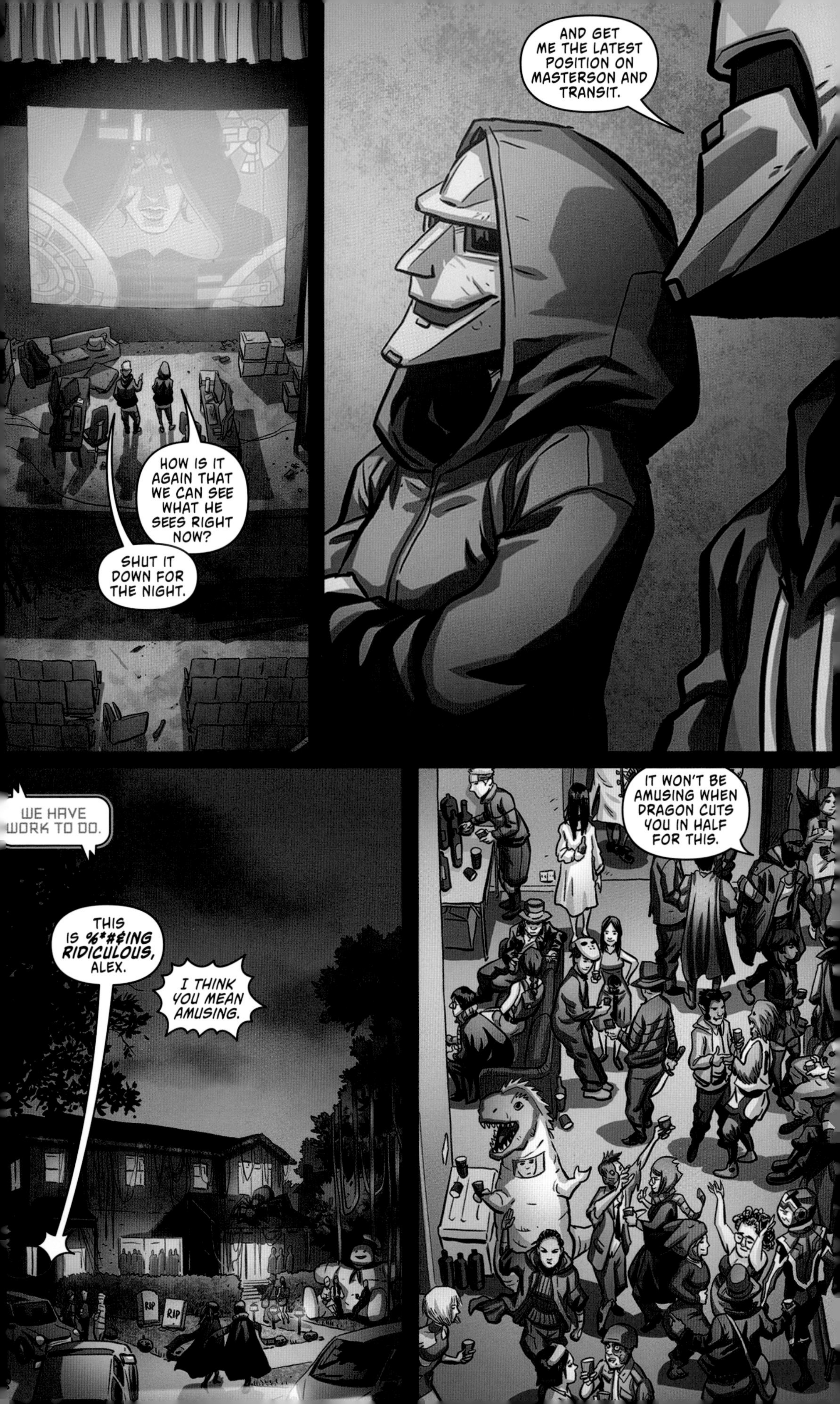
HOW IS IT AGAIN THAT WE CAN SEE WHAT HE SEES RIGHT NOW?
SHUT IT DOWN FOR THE NIGHT.
AND GET ME THE LATEST POSITION ON MASTERSON AND TRANSIT.
WE HAVE WORK TO DO.
THIS IS %*#$ING RIDICULOUS, ALEX.
I THINK YOU MEAN AMUSING.
IT WON'T BE AMUSING WHEN DRAGON CUTS YOU IN HALF FOR THIS.
RIP
RIP

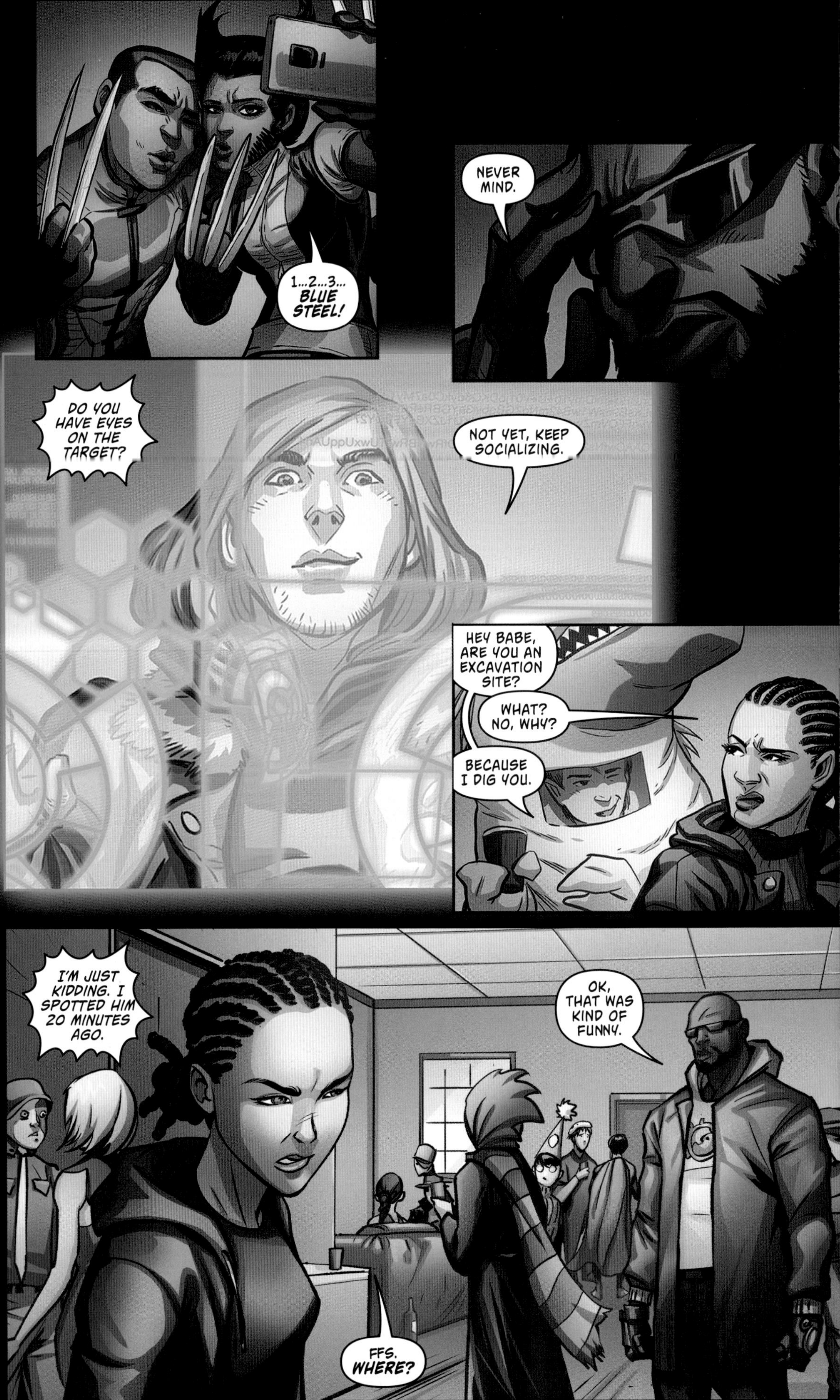
1...2...3... BLUE STEEL!
NEVER MIND.
DO YOU HAVE EYES ON THE TARGET?
NOT YET, KEEP SOCIALIZING.
HEY BABE, ARE YOU AN EXCAVATION SITE?
WHAT? NO, WHY?
BECAUSE I DIG YOU.
I'M JUST KIDDING. I SPOTTED HIM 20 MINUTES AGO.
OK, THAT WAS KIND OF FUNNY.
FFS. WHERE?

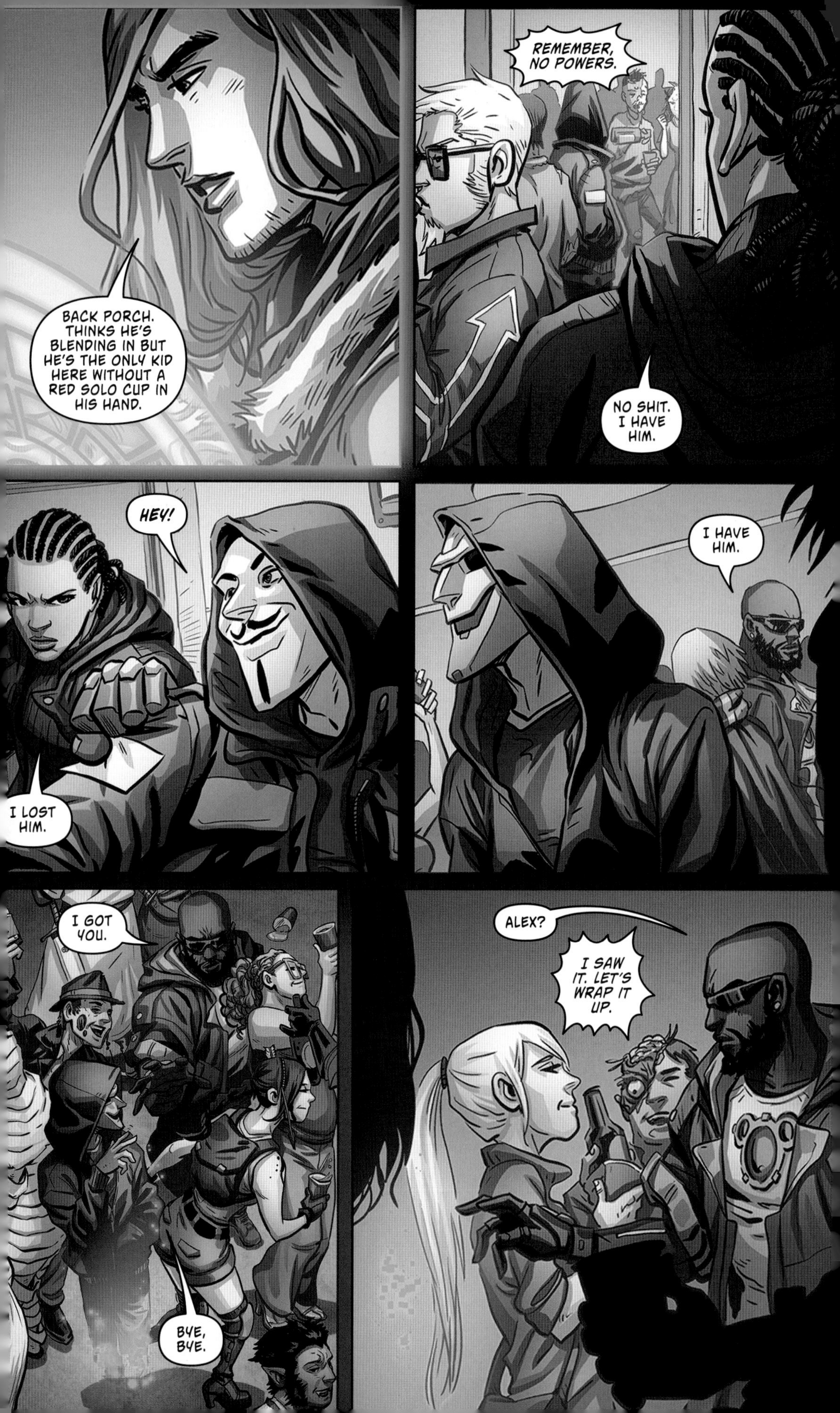
BACK PORCH. THINKS HE'S BLENDING IN BUT HE'S THE ONLY KID HERE WITHOUT A RED SOLO CUP IN HIS HAND.
REMEMBER, NO POWERS.
NO SHIT. I HAVE HIM.
HEY!
I LOST HIM.
I HAVE HIM.
I GOT YOU.
BYE, BYE.
ALEX?
I SAW IT. LET'S WRAP IT UP.

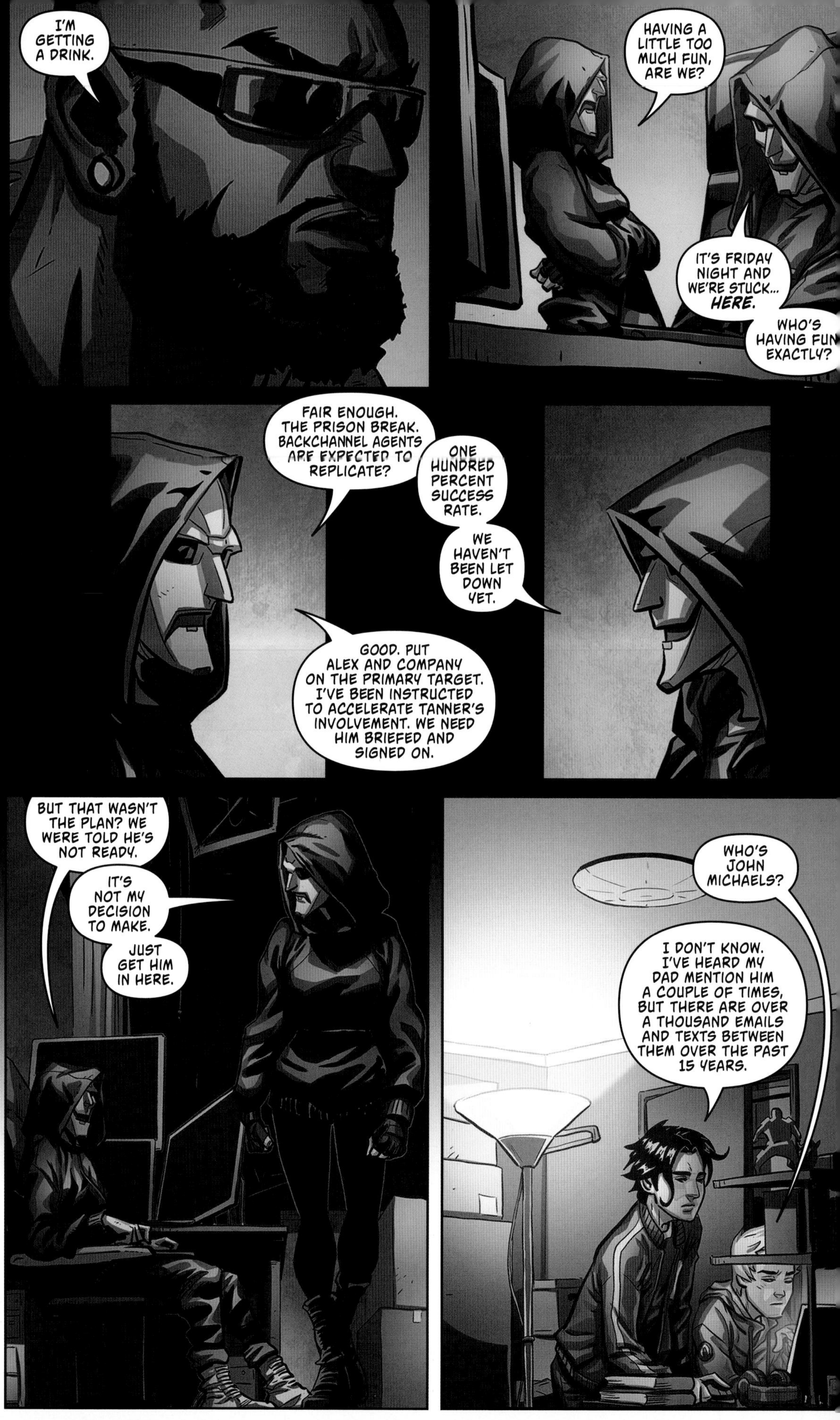

I'M GETTING A DRINK.
HAVING A LITTLE TOO MUCH FUN, ARE WE?
IT'S FRIDAY NIGHT AND WE'RE STUCK... **HERE.**
WHO'S HAVING FUN EXACTLY?
FAIR ENOUGH. THE PRISON BREAK. BACKCHANNEL AGENTS ARE EXPECTED TO REPLICATE?
ONE HUNDRED PERCENT SUCCESS RATE.
WE HAVEN'T BEEN LET DOWN YET.
GOOD. PUT ALEX AND COMPANY ON THE PRIMARY TARGET. I'VE BEEN INSTRUCTED TO ACCELERATE TANNER'S INVOLVEMENT. WE NEED HIM BRIEFED AND SIGNED ON.
BUT THAT WASN'T THE PLAN? WE WERE TOLD HE'S NOT READY.
IT'S NOT MY DECISION TO MAKE.
JUST GET HIM IN HERE.
WHO'S JOHN MICHAELS?
I DON'T KNOW. I'VE HEARD MY DAD MENTION HIM A COUPLE OF TIMES, BUT THERE ARE OVER A THOUSAND EMAILS AND TEXTS BETWEEN THEM OVER THE PAST 15 YEARS.

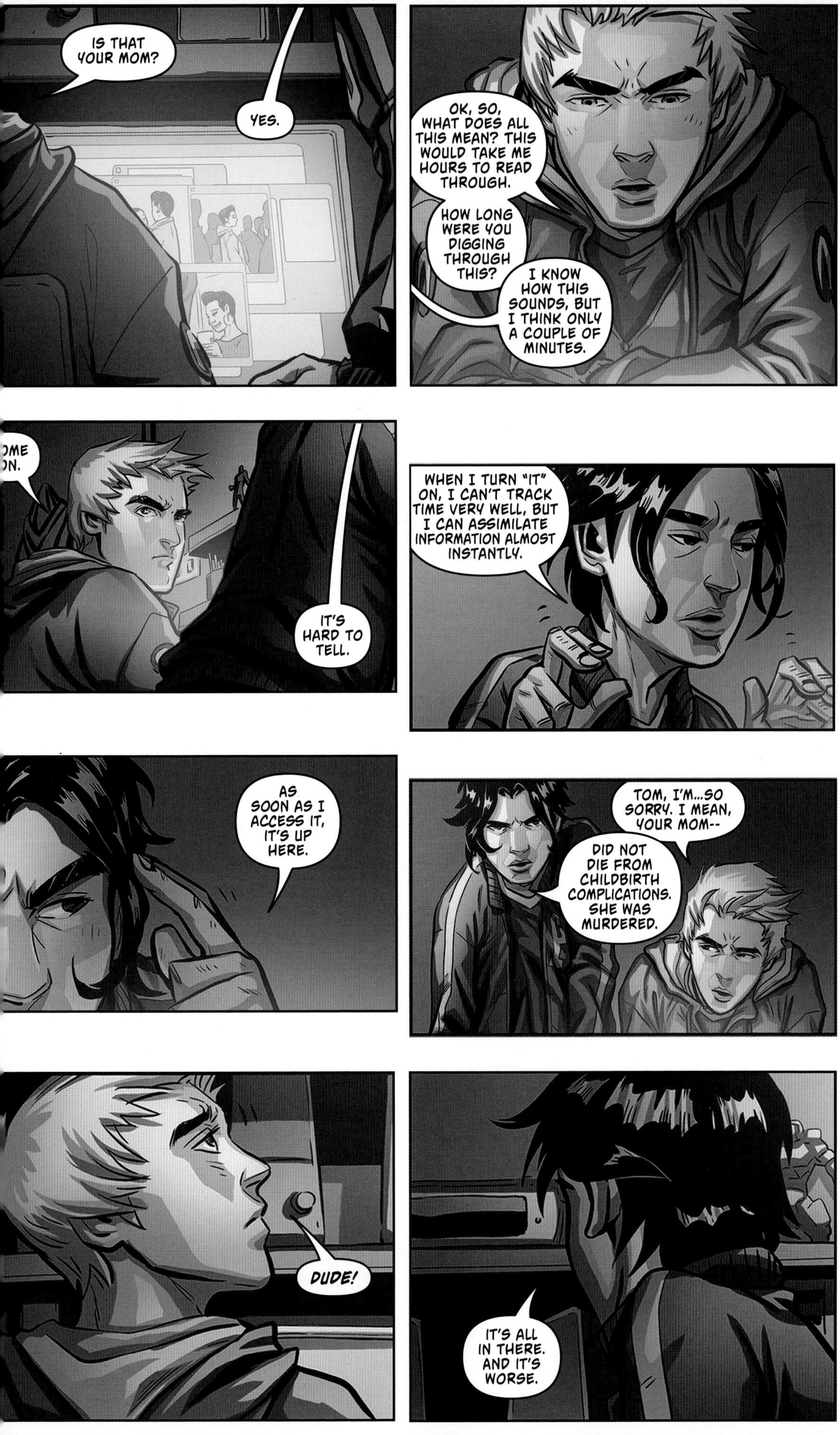
IS THAT YOUR MOM?
YES.
OK, SO, WHAT DOES ALL THIS MEAN? THIS WOULD TAKE ME HOURS TO READ THROUGH.
HOW LONG WERE YOU DIGGING THROUGH THIS?
I KNOW HOW THIS SOUNDS, BUT I THINK ONLY A COUPLE OF MINUTES.
IT'S HARD TO TELL.
WHEN I TURN "IT" ON, I CAN'T TRACK TIME VERY WELL, BUT I CAN ASSIMILATE INFORMATION ALMOST INSTANTLY.
AS SOON AS I ACCESS IT, IT'S UP HERE.
TOM, I'M...SO SORRY. I MEAN, YOUR MOM--
DID NOT DIE FROM CHILDBIRTH COMPLICATIONS. SHE WAS MURDERED.
DUDE!
IT'S ALL IN THERE. AND IT'S WORSE.

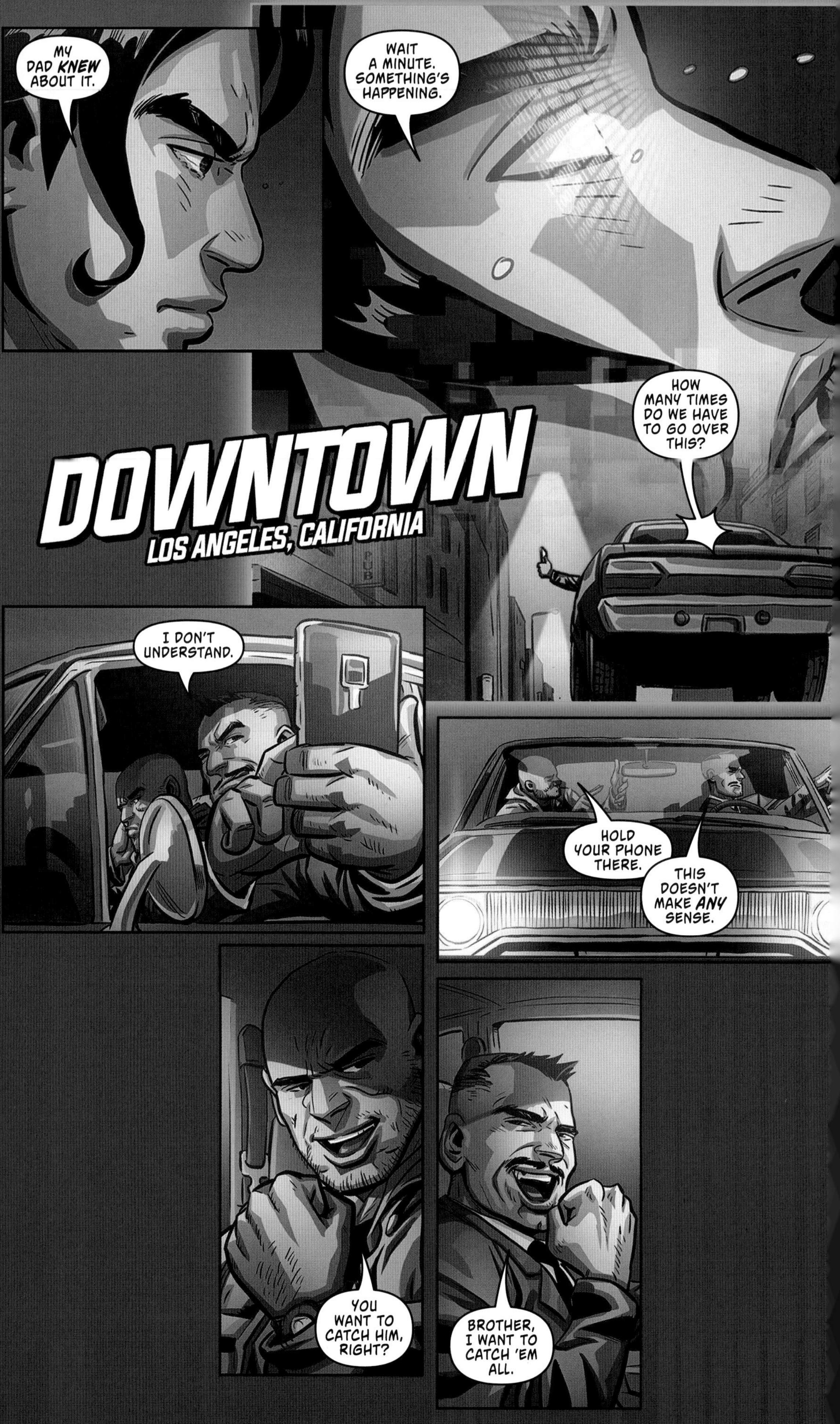
MY DAD KNEW ABOUT IT.
WAIT A MINUTE. SOMETHING'S HAPPENING.
DOWNTOWN
LOS ANGELES, CALIFORNIA
HOW MANY TIMES DO WE HAVE TO GO OVER THIS?
PUB
I DON'T UNDERSTAND.
HOLD YOUR PHONE THERE.
THIS DOESN'T MAKE ANY SENSE.
YOU WANT TO CATCH HIM, RIGHT?
BROTHER, I WANT TO CATCH 'EM ALL.

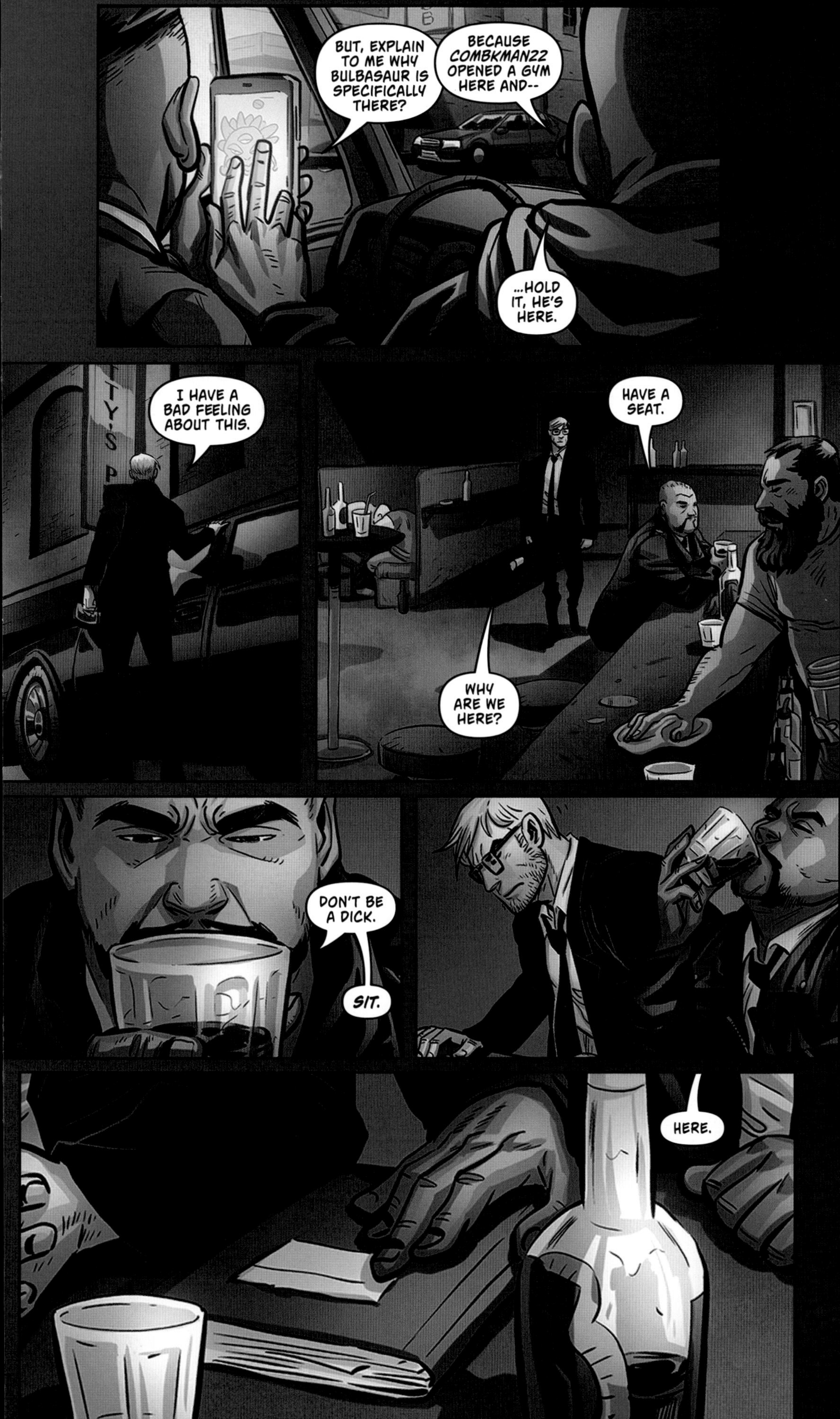
BUT, EXPLAIN TO ME WHY BULBASAUR IS SPECIFICALLY THERE?
BECAUSE COMBKMAN22 OPENED A GYM HERE AND--
...HOLD IT, HE'S HERE.
I HAVE A BAD FEELING ABOUT THIS.
HAVE A SEAT.
WHY ARE WE HERE?
DON'T BE A DICK.
SIT.
HERE.

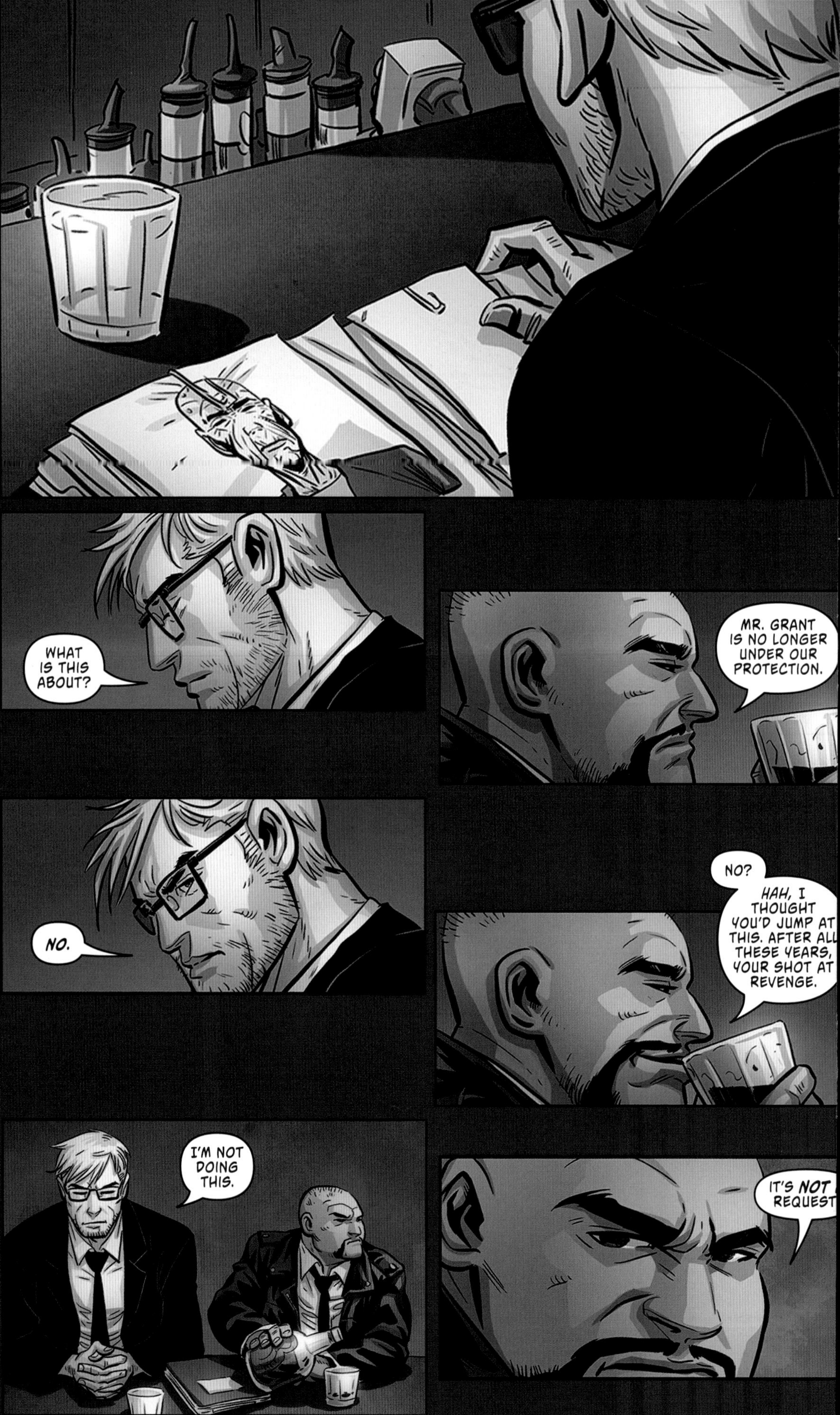
WHAT IS THIS ABOUT?
MR. GRANT IS NO LONGER UNDER OUR PROTECTION.
NO.
NO?
HAH, I THOUGHT YOU'D JUMP AT THIS. AFTER ALL THESE YEARS, YOUR SHOT AT REVENGE.
I'M NOT DOING THIS.

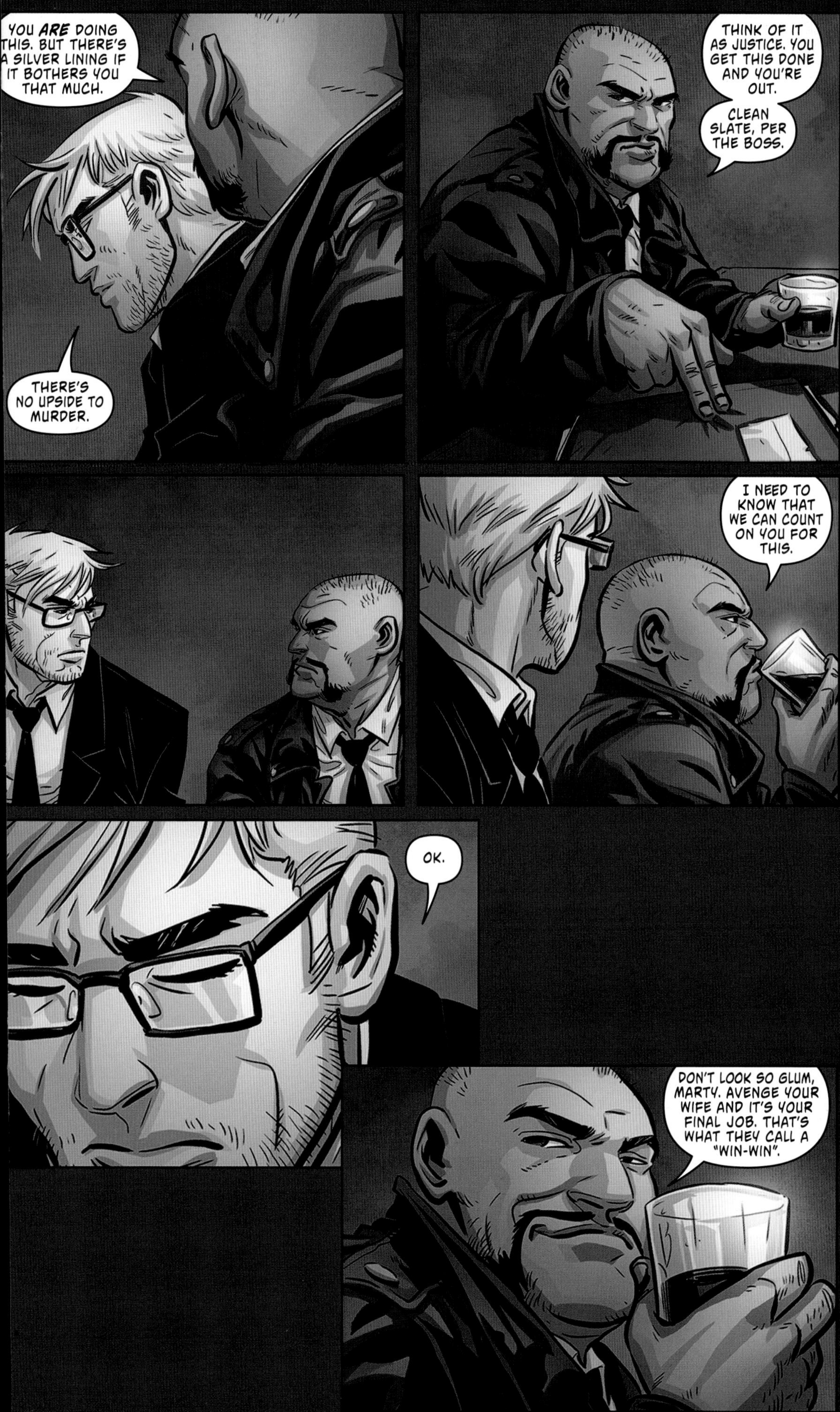
YOU *ARE* DOING THIS. BUT THERE'S A SILVER LINING IF IT BOTHERS YOU THAT MUCH.
THERE'S NO UPSIDE TO MURDER.
THINK OF IT AS JUSTICE. YOU GET THIS DONE AND YOU'RE OUT.
CLEAN SLATE, PER THE BOSS.
I NEED TO KNOW THAT WE CAN COUNT ON YOU FOR THIS.
OK.
DON'T LOOK SO GLUM, MARTY. AVENGE YOUR WIFE AND IT'S YOUR FINAL JOB. THAT'S WHAT THEY CALL A "WIN-WIN".

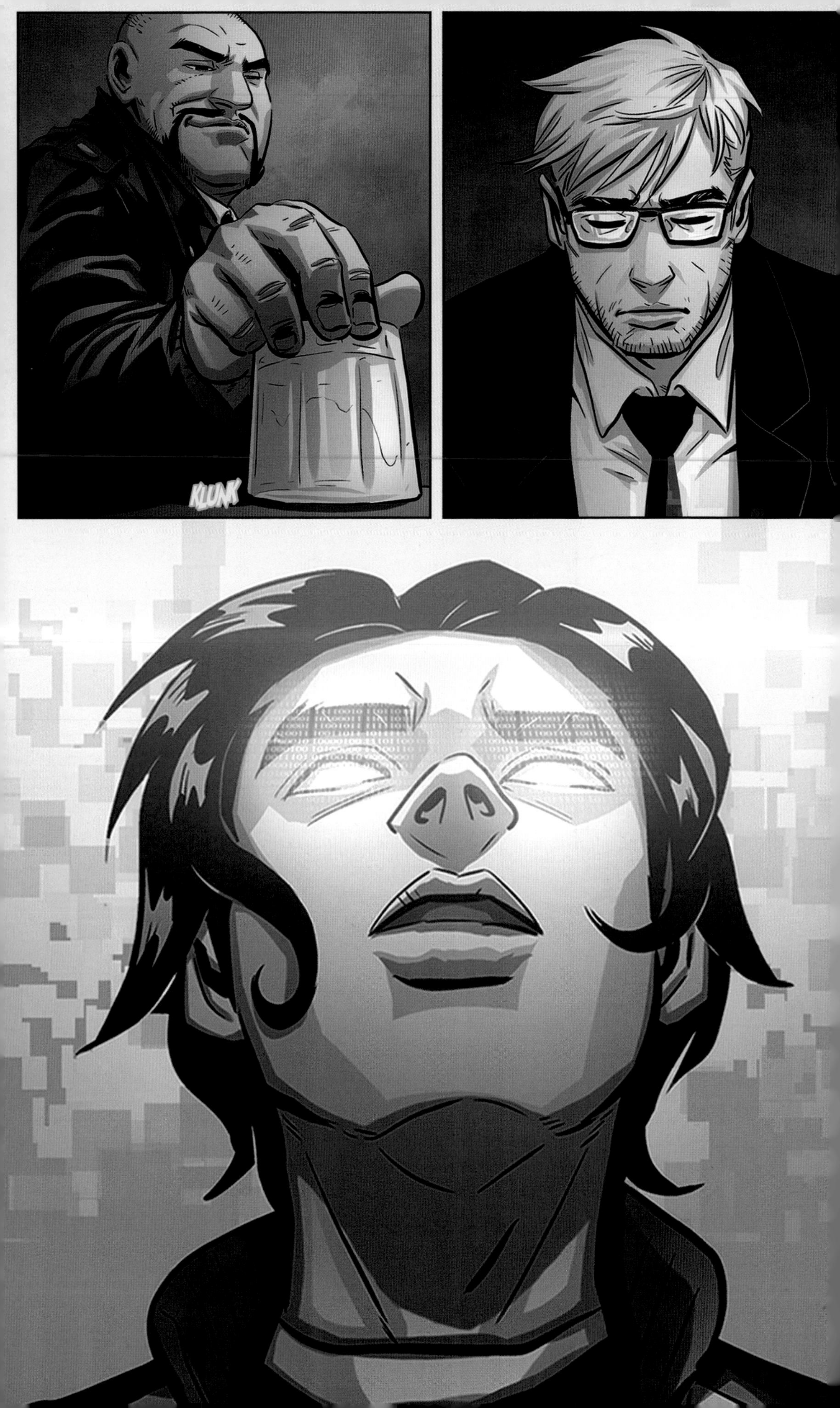
KLUNK

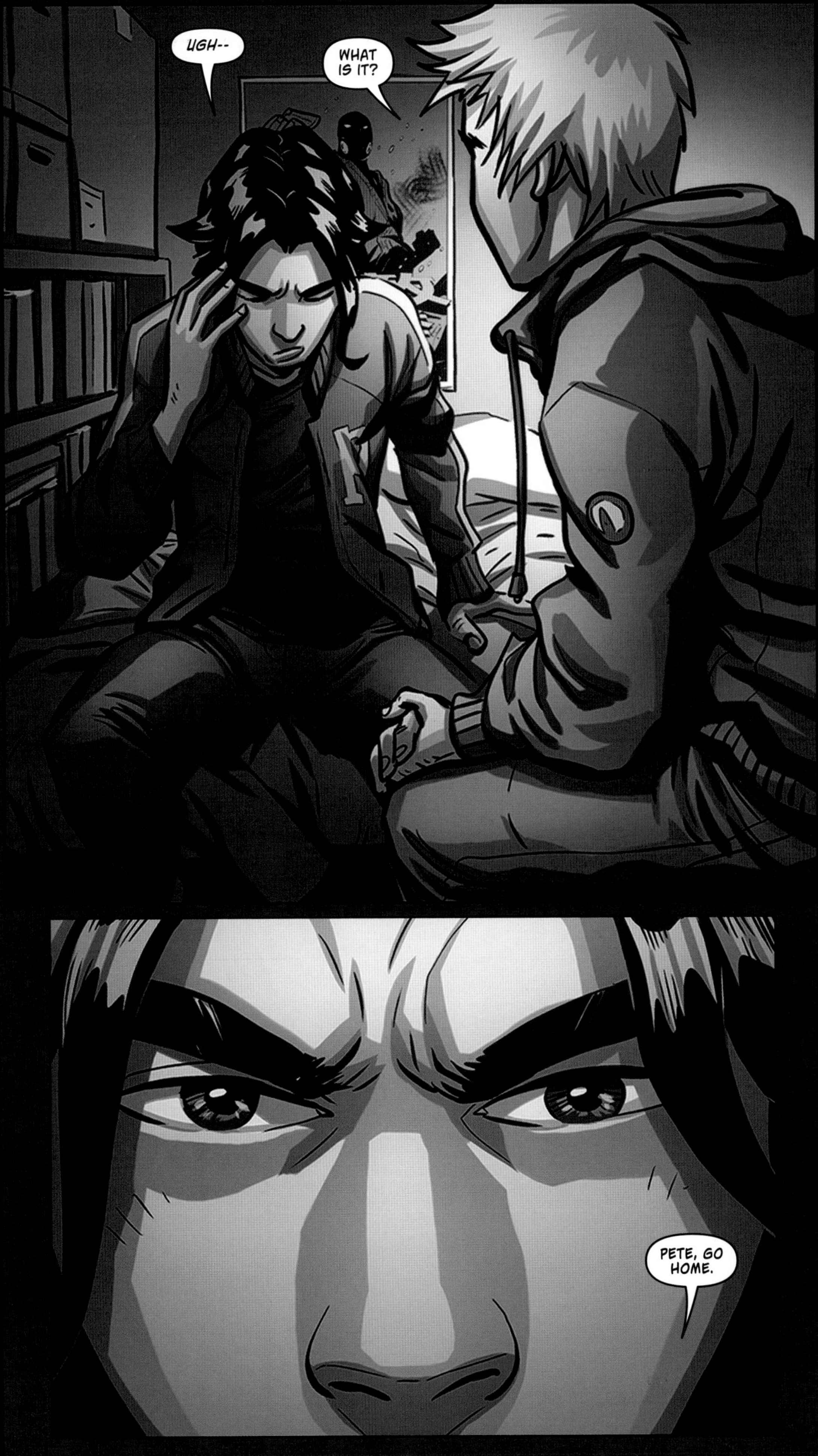
UGH--
WHAT IS IT?
PETE, GO HOME.

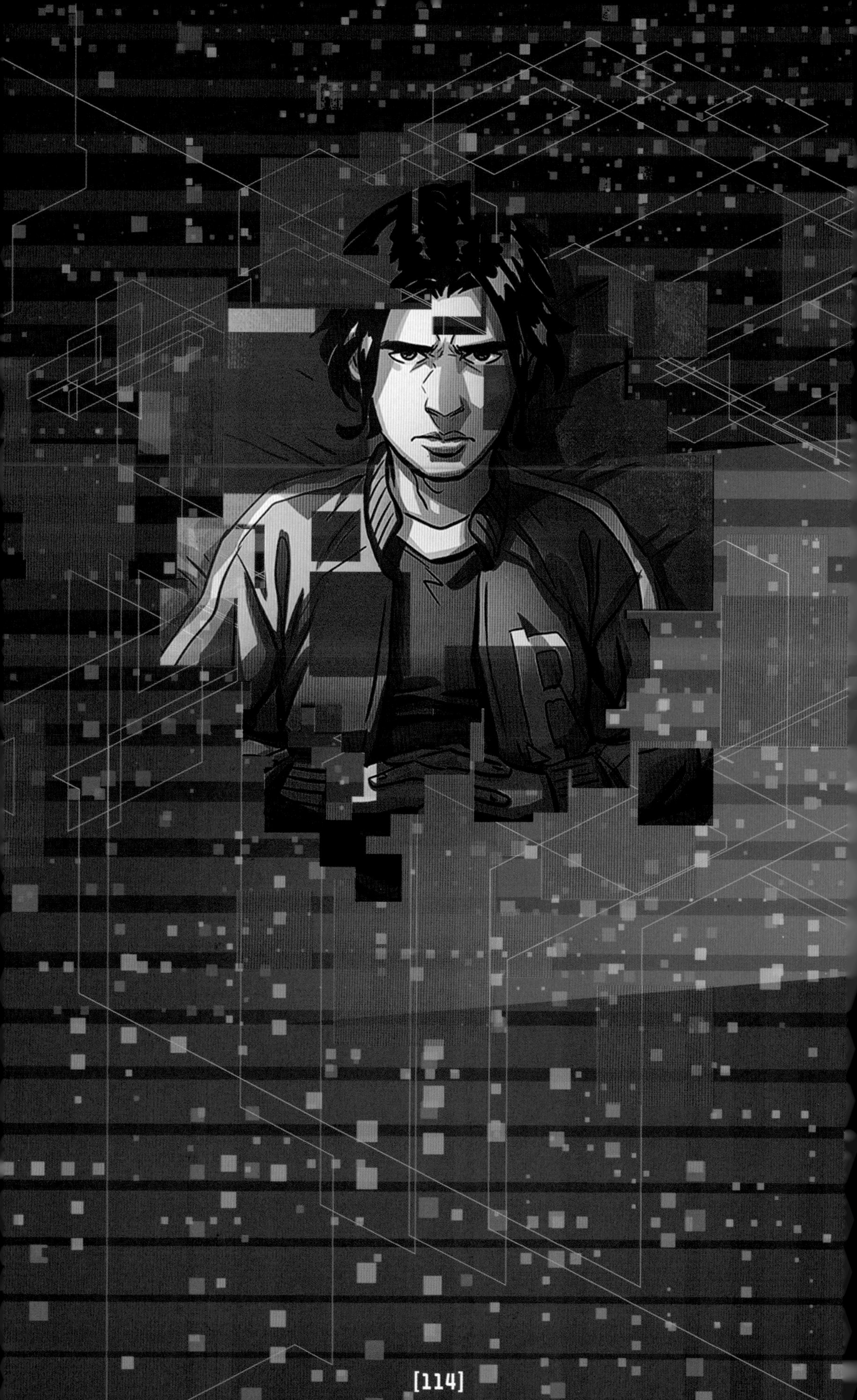

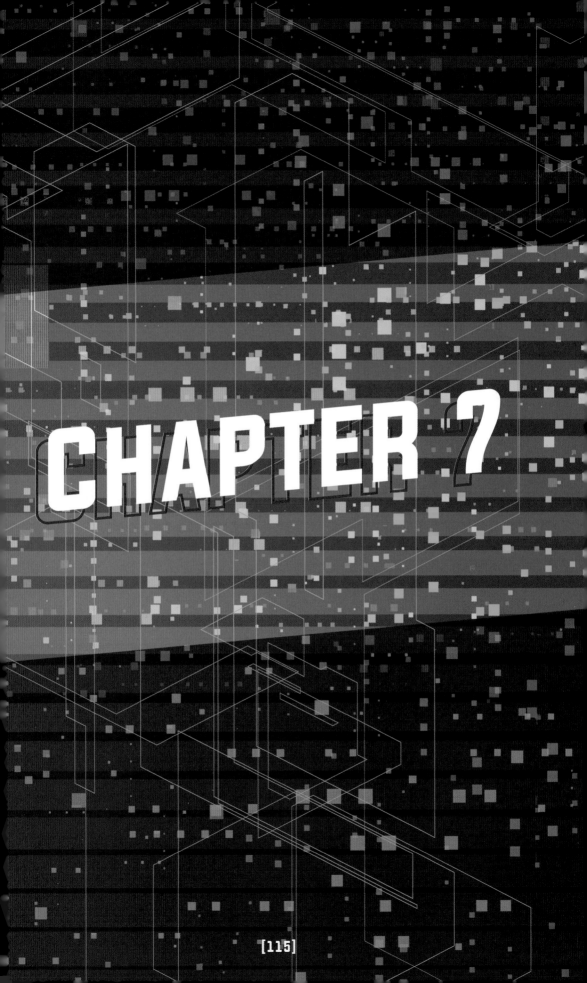

CHAPTER 7

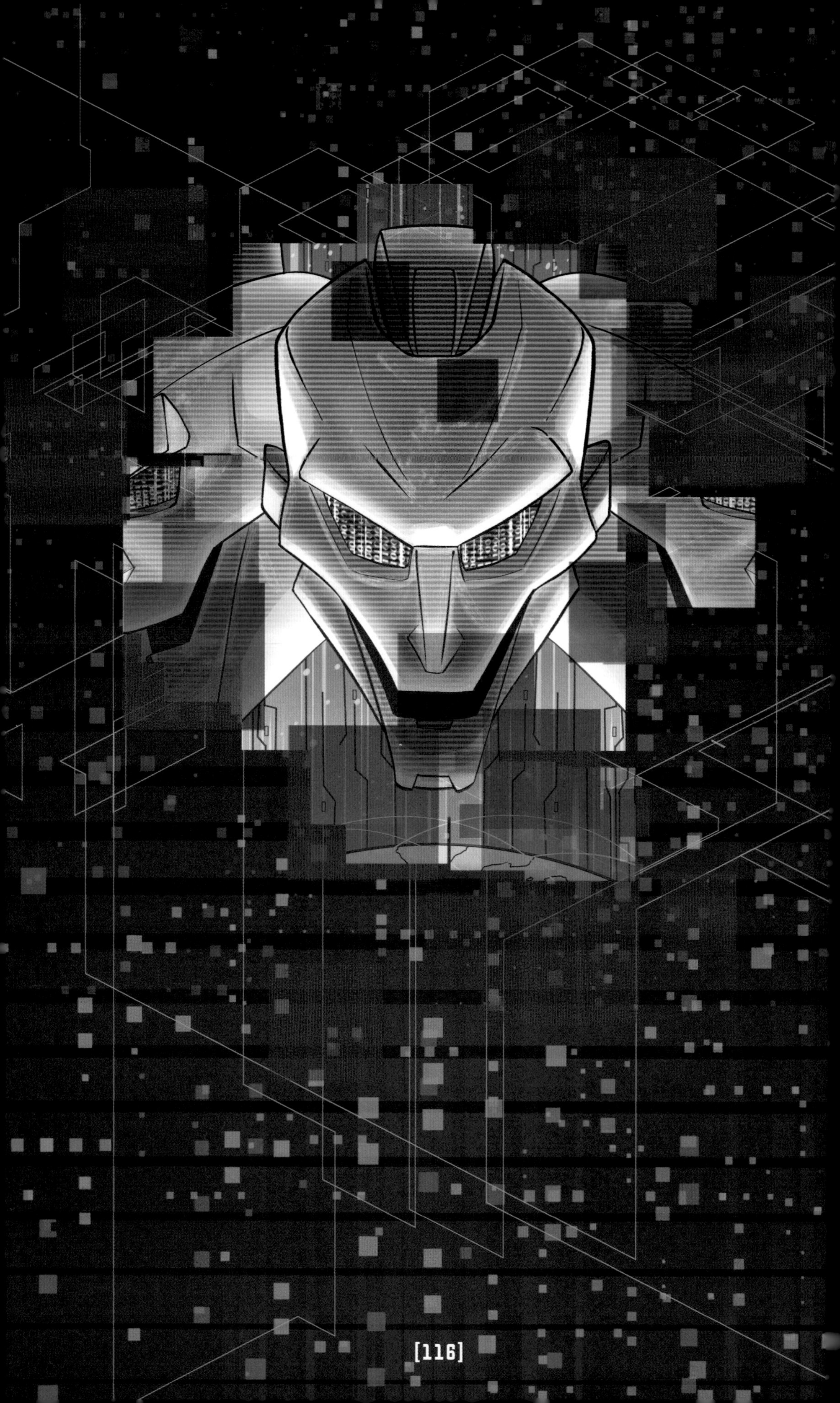

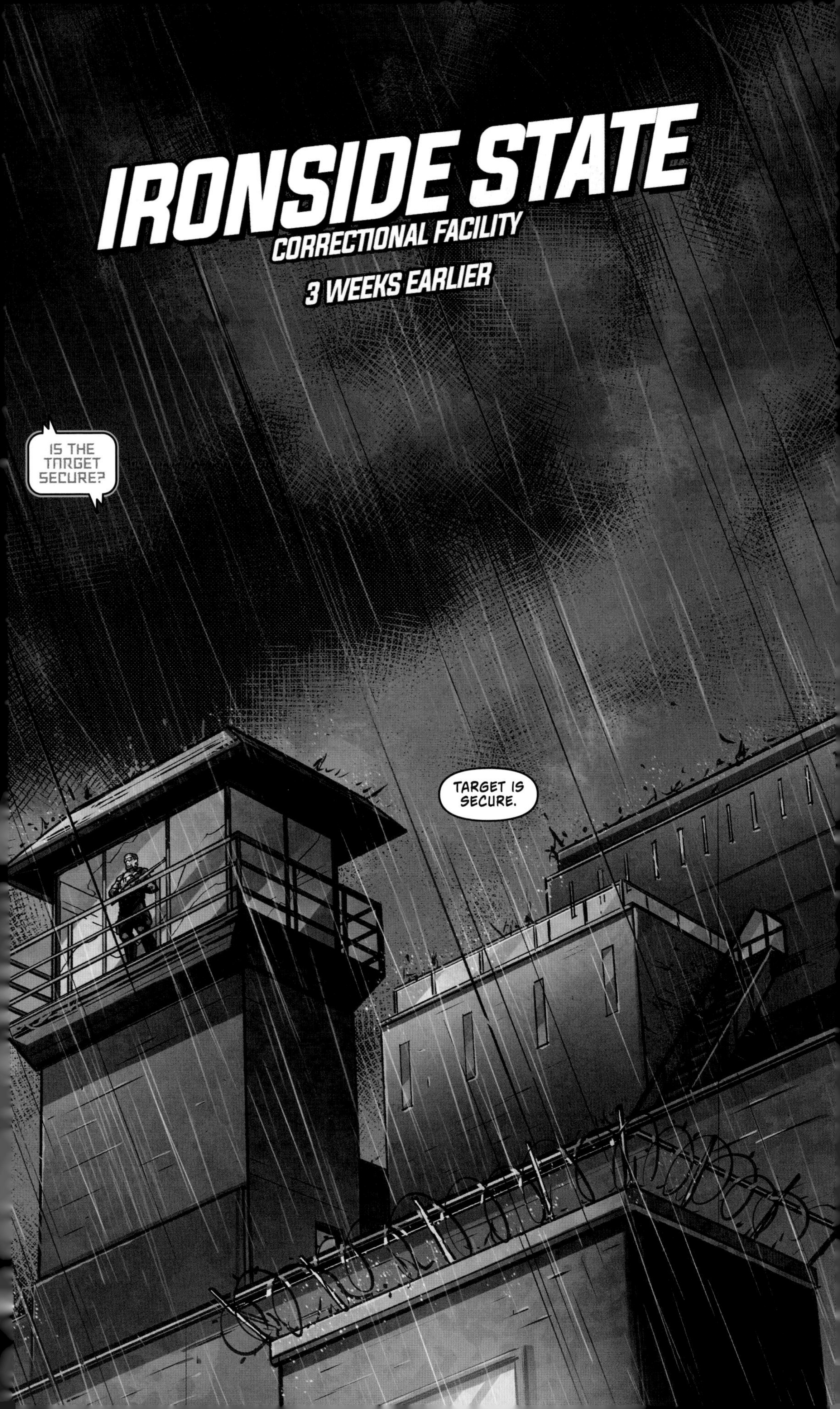
IRONSIDE STATE
CORRECTIONAL FACILITY
3 WEEKS EARLIER
IS THE TARGET SECURE?
TARGET IS SECURE.

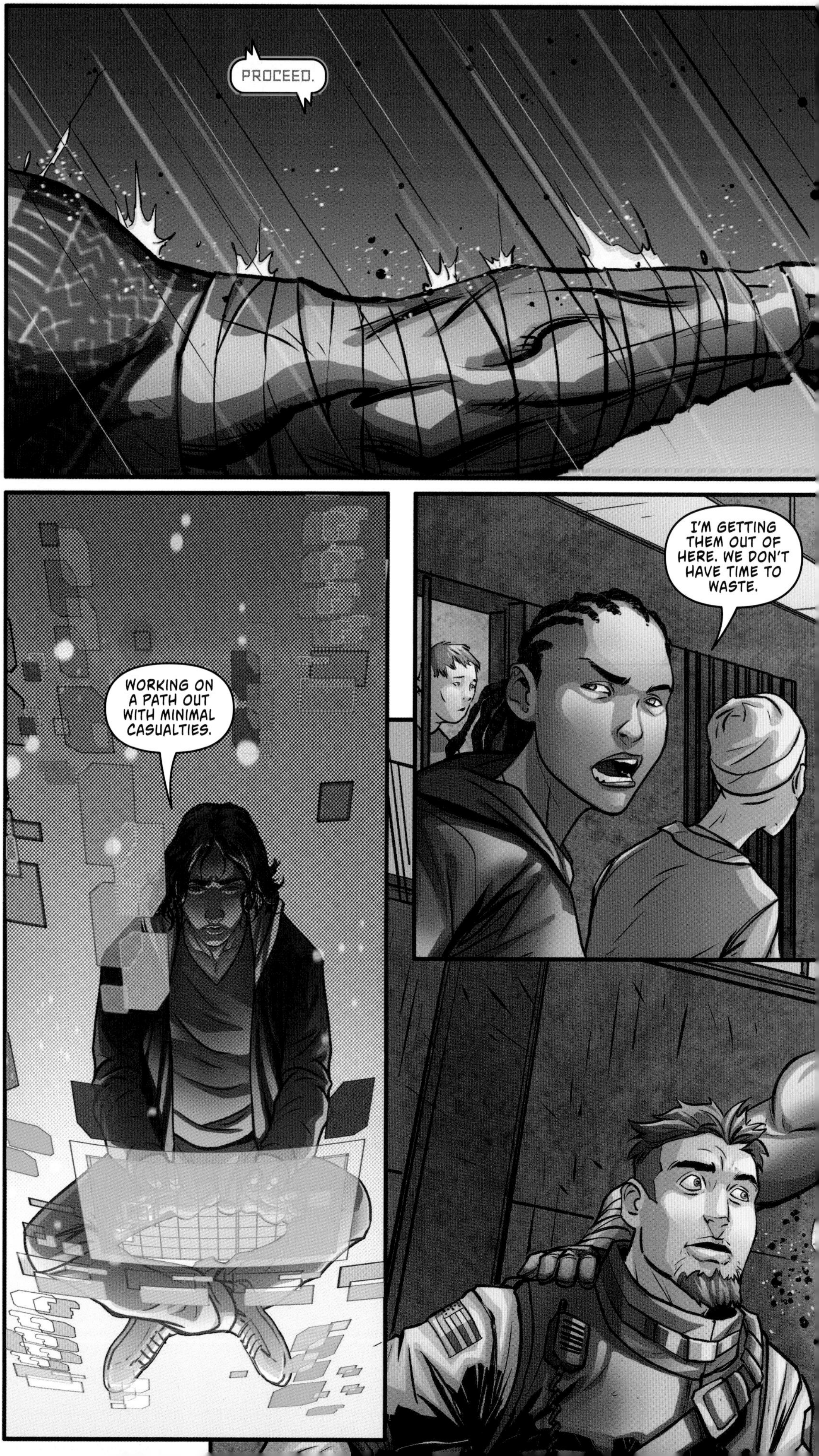
PROCEED.
WORKING ON A PATH OUT WITH MINIMAL CASUALTIES.
I'M GETTING THEM OUT OF HERE. WE DON'T HAVE TIME TO WASTE.

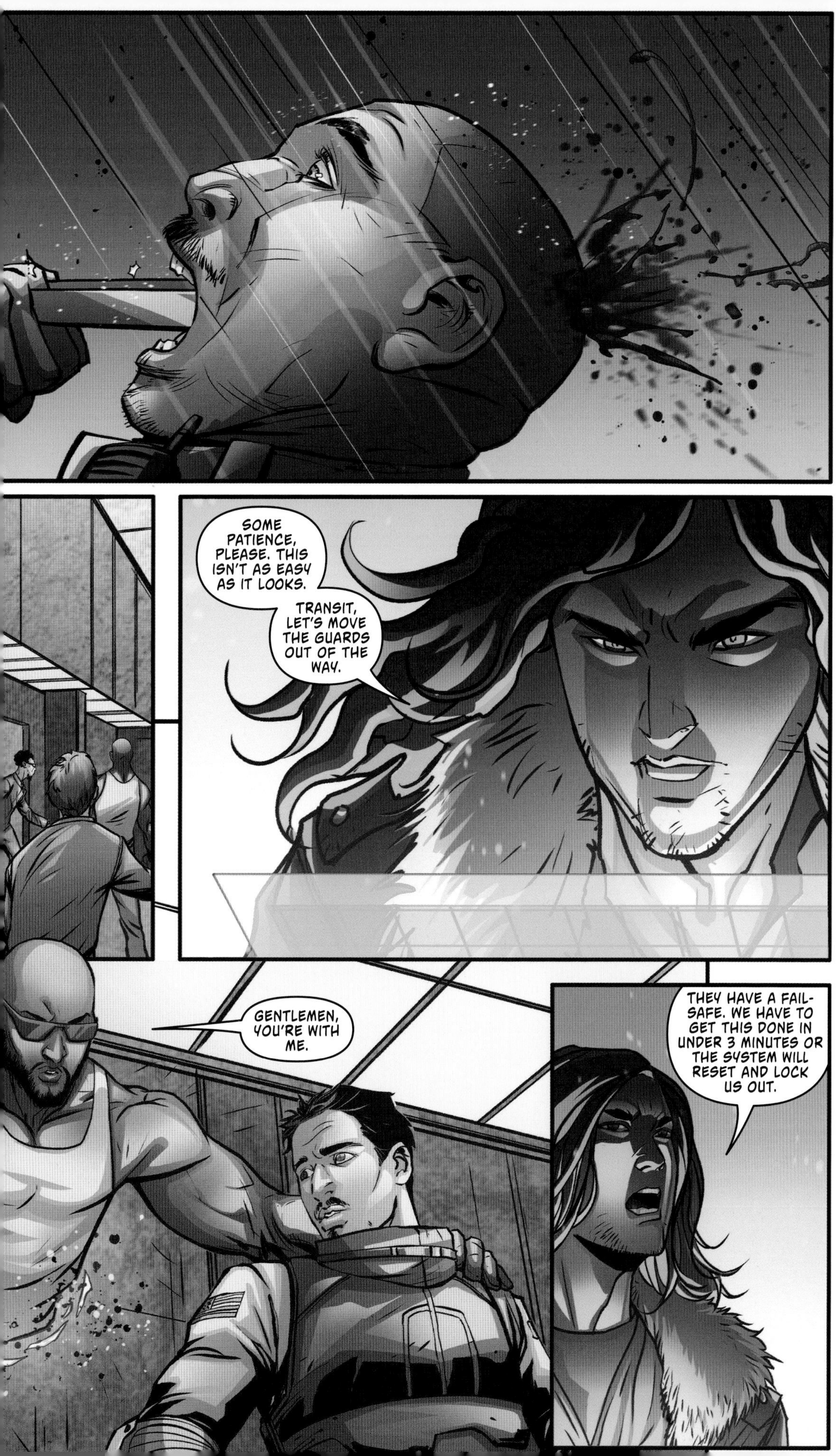
SOME PATIENCE, PLEASE. THIS ISN'T AS EASY AS IT LOOKS.
TRANSIT, LET'S MOVE THE GUARDS OUT OF THE WAY.
GENTLEMEN, YOU'RE WITH ME.
THEY HAVE A FAIL-SAFE. WE HAVE TO GET THIS DONE IN UNDER 3 MINUTES OR THE SYSTEM WILL RESET AND LOCK US OUT.

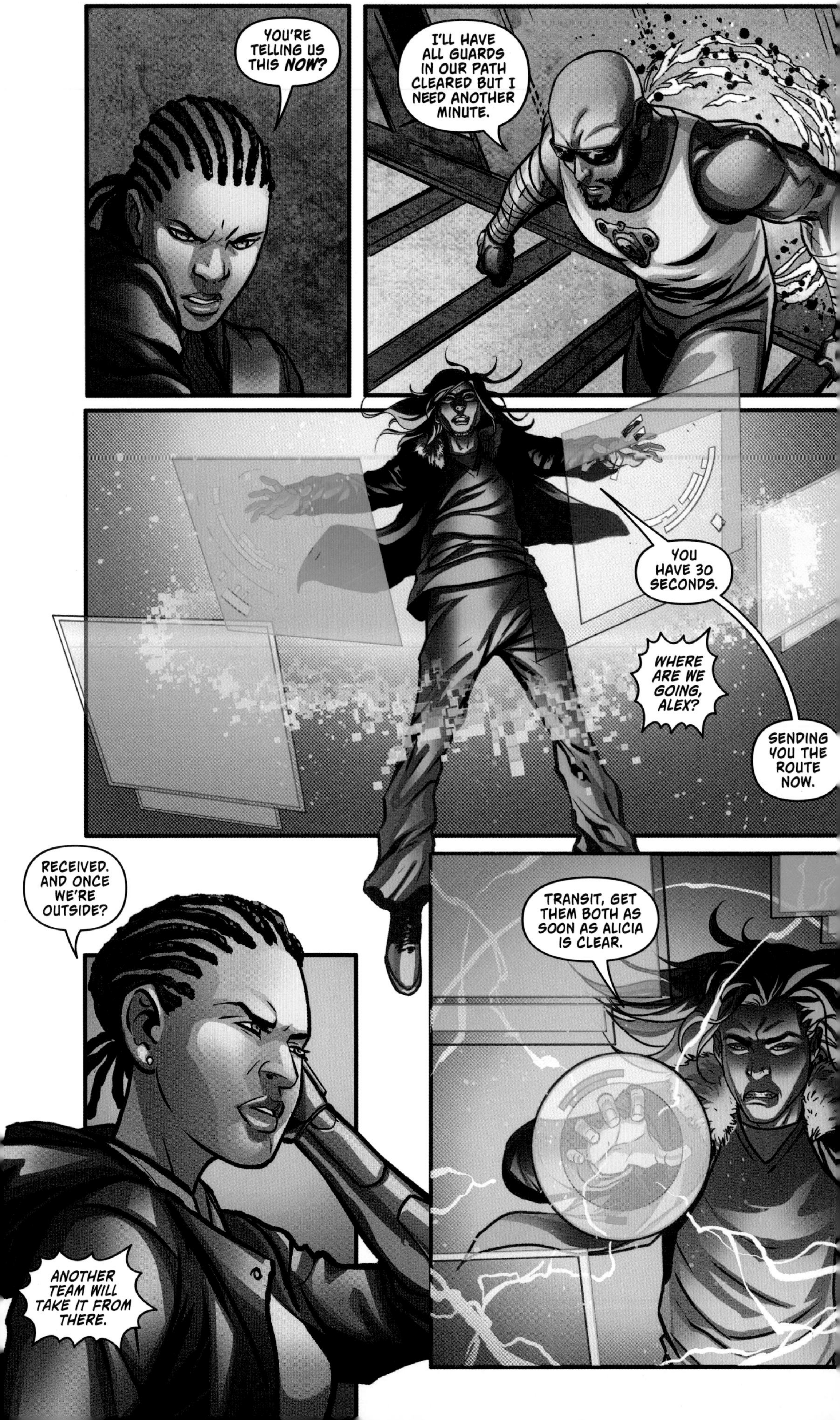
YOU'RE TELLING US THIS NOW?
I'LL HAVE ALL GUARDS IN OUR PATH CLEARED BUT I NEED ANOTHER MINUTE.
YOU HAVE 30 SECONDS.
WHERE ARE WE GOING, ALEX?
SENDING YOU THE ROUTE NOW.
RECEIVED. AND ONCE WE'RE OUTSIDE?
ANOTHER TEAM WILL TAKE IT FROM THERE.
TRANSIT, GET THEM BOTH AS SOON AS ALICIA IS CLEAR.

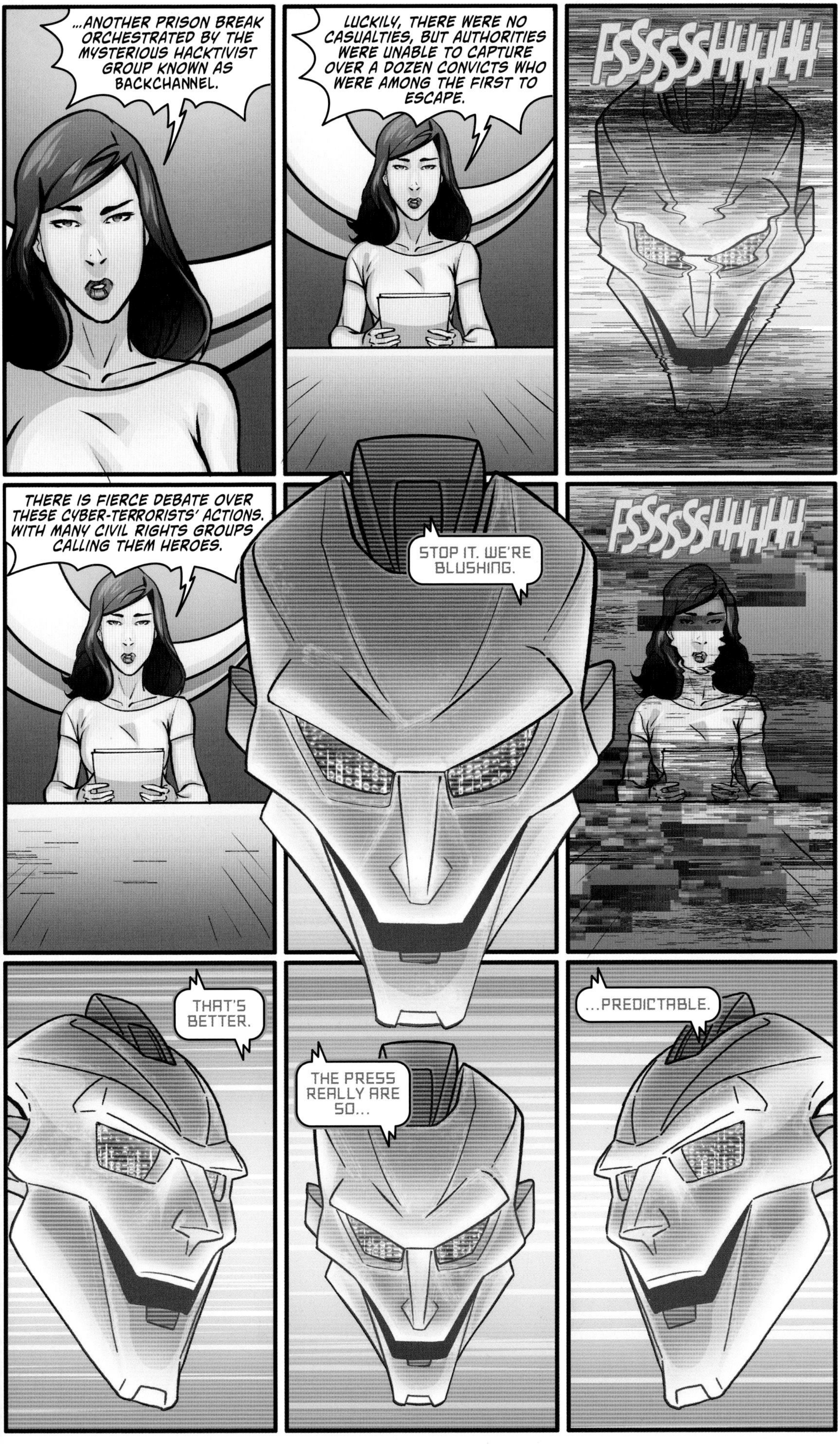
...ANOTHER PRISON BREAK ORCHESTRATED BY THE MYSTERIOUS HACKTIVIST GROUP KNOWN AS BACKCHANNEL.
LUCKILY, THERE WERE NO CASUALTIES, BUT AUTHORITIES WERE UNABLE TO CAPTURE OVER A DOZEN CONVICTS WHO WERE AMONG THE FIRST TO ESCAPE.
FSSSSSHHHHH
THERE IS FIERCE DEBATE OVER THESE CYBER-TERRORISTS' ACTIONS. WITH MANY CIVIL RIGHTS GROUPS CALLING THEM HEROES.
STOP IT. WE'RE BLUSHING.
FSSSSSHHHHH
THAT'S BETTER.
THE PRESS REALLY ARE SO...
...PREDICTABLE.

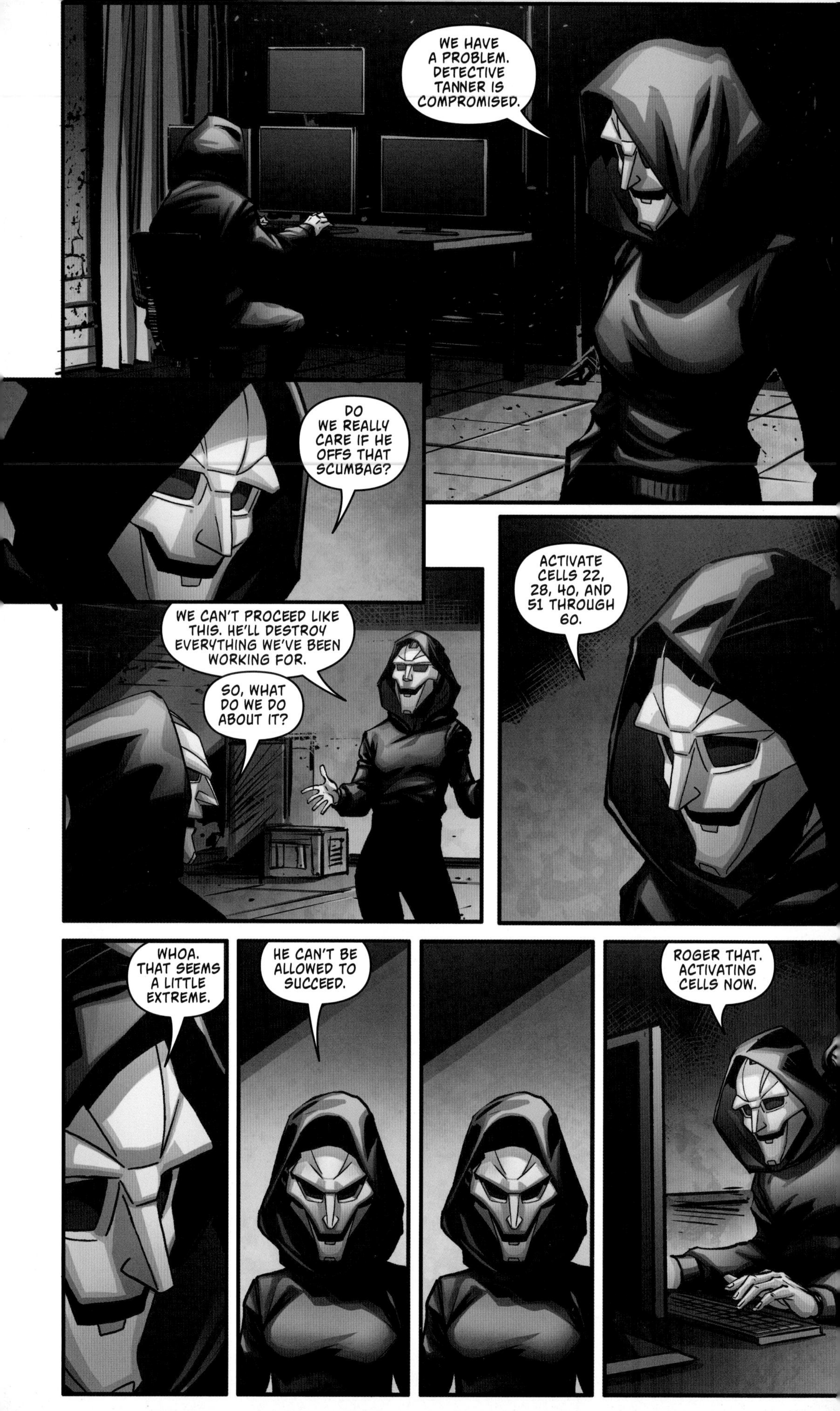
WE HAVE A PROBLEM. DETECTIVE TANNER IS COMPROMISED.
DO WE REALLY CARE IF HE OFFS THAT SCUMBAG?
WE CAN'T PROCEED LIKE THIS. HE'LL DESTROY EVERYTHING WE'VE BEEN WORKING FOR.
SO, WHAT DO WE DO ABOUT IT?
ACTIVATE CELLS 22, 28, 40, AND 51 THROUGH 60.
WHOA. THAT SEEMS A LITTLE EXTREME.
HE CAN'T BE ALLOWED TO SUCCEED.
ROGER THAT. ACTIVATING CELLS NOW.

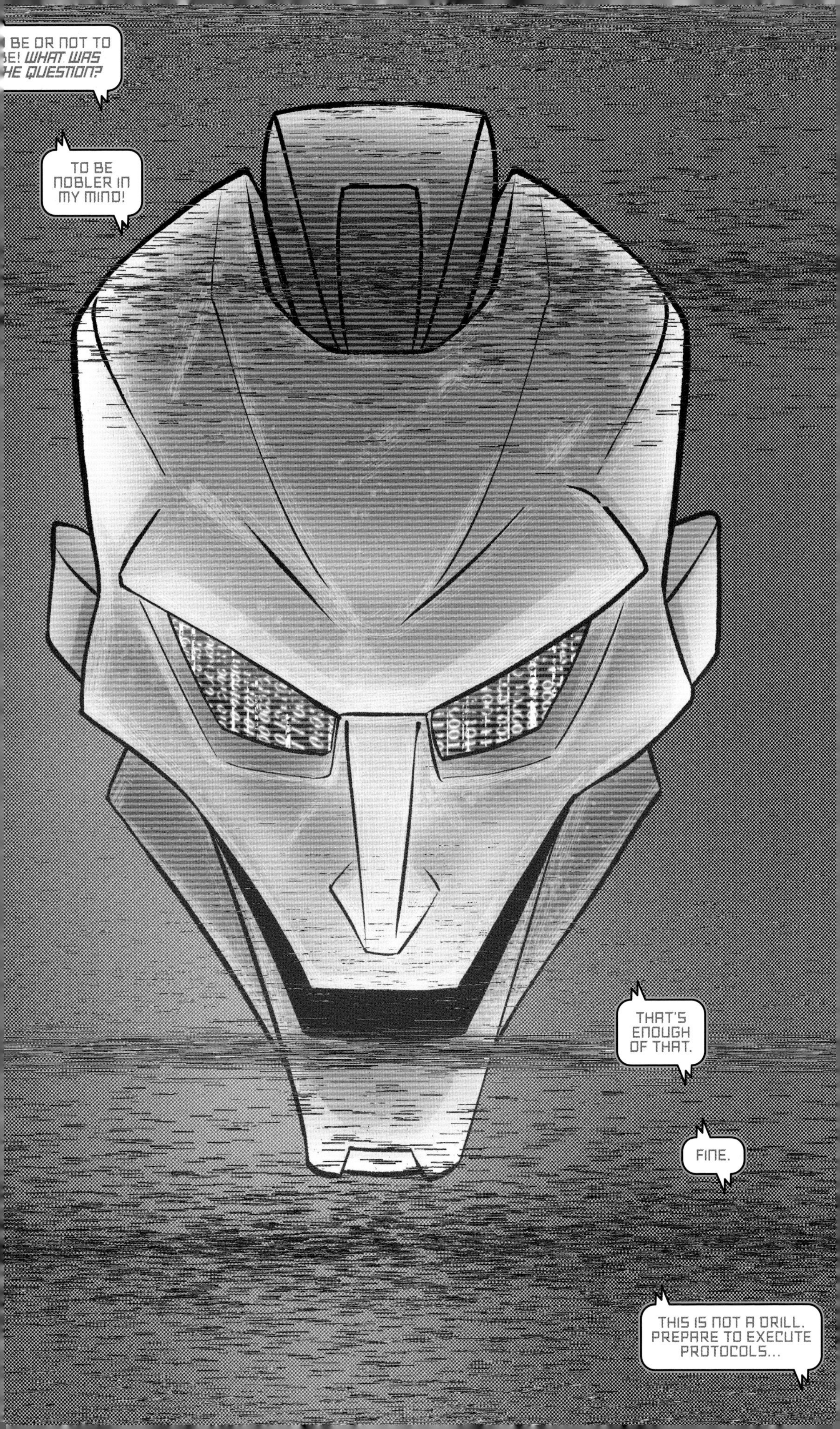

BE OR NOT TO
BE! *WHAT WAS*
HE QUESTION?
TO BE NOBLER IN MY MIND!
THAT'S ENOUGH OF THAT.
FINE.
THIS IS NOT A DRILL. PREPARE TO EXECUTE PROTOCOLS...

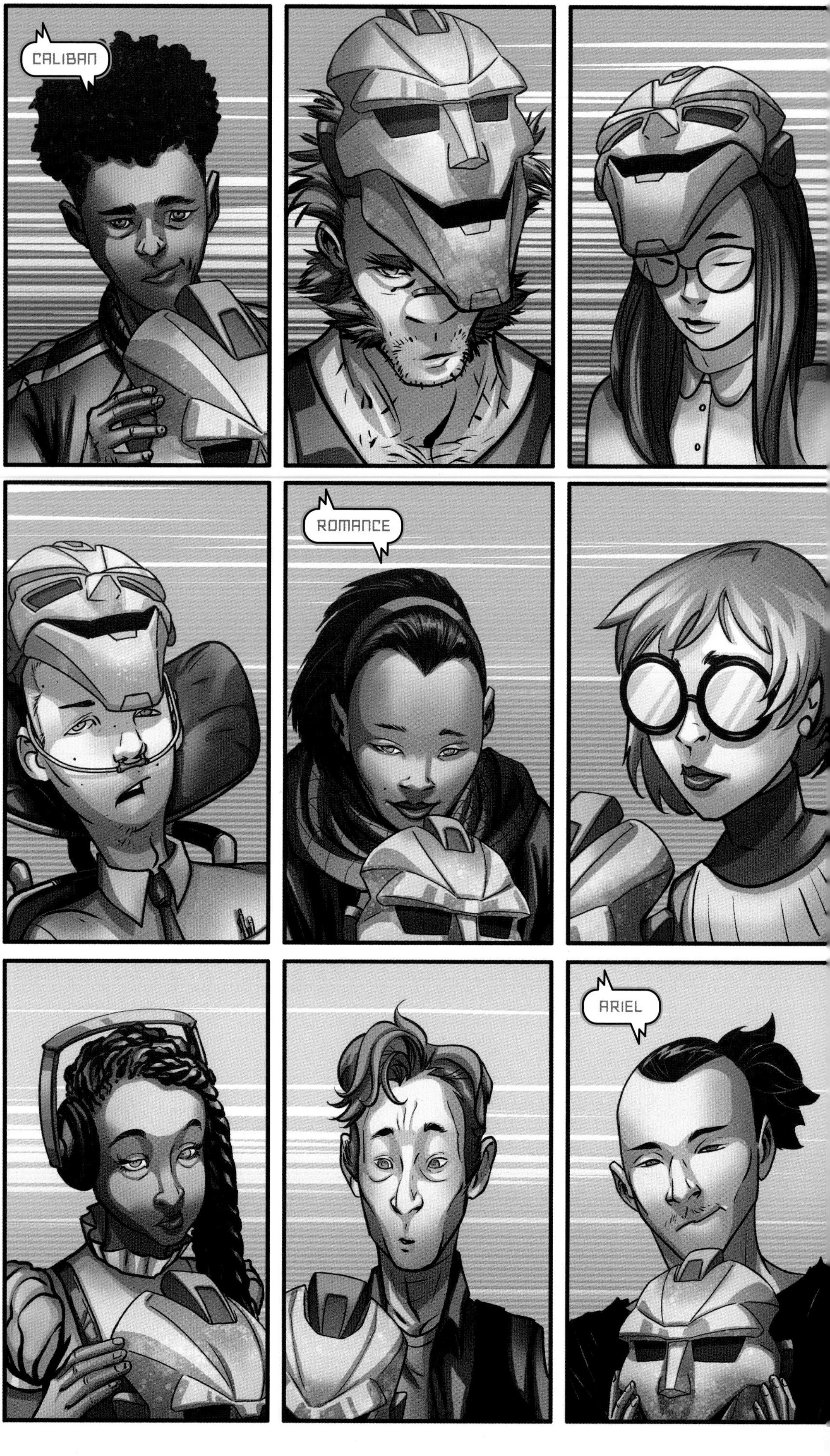
CALIBAN
ROMANCE
ARIEL

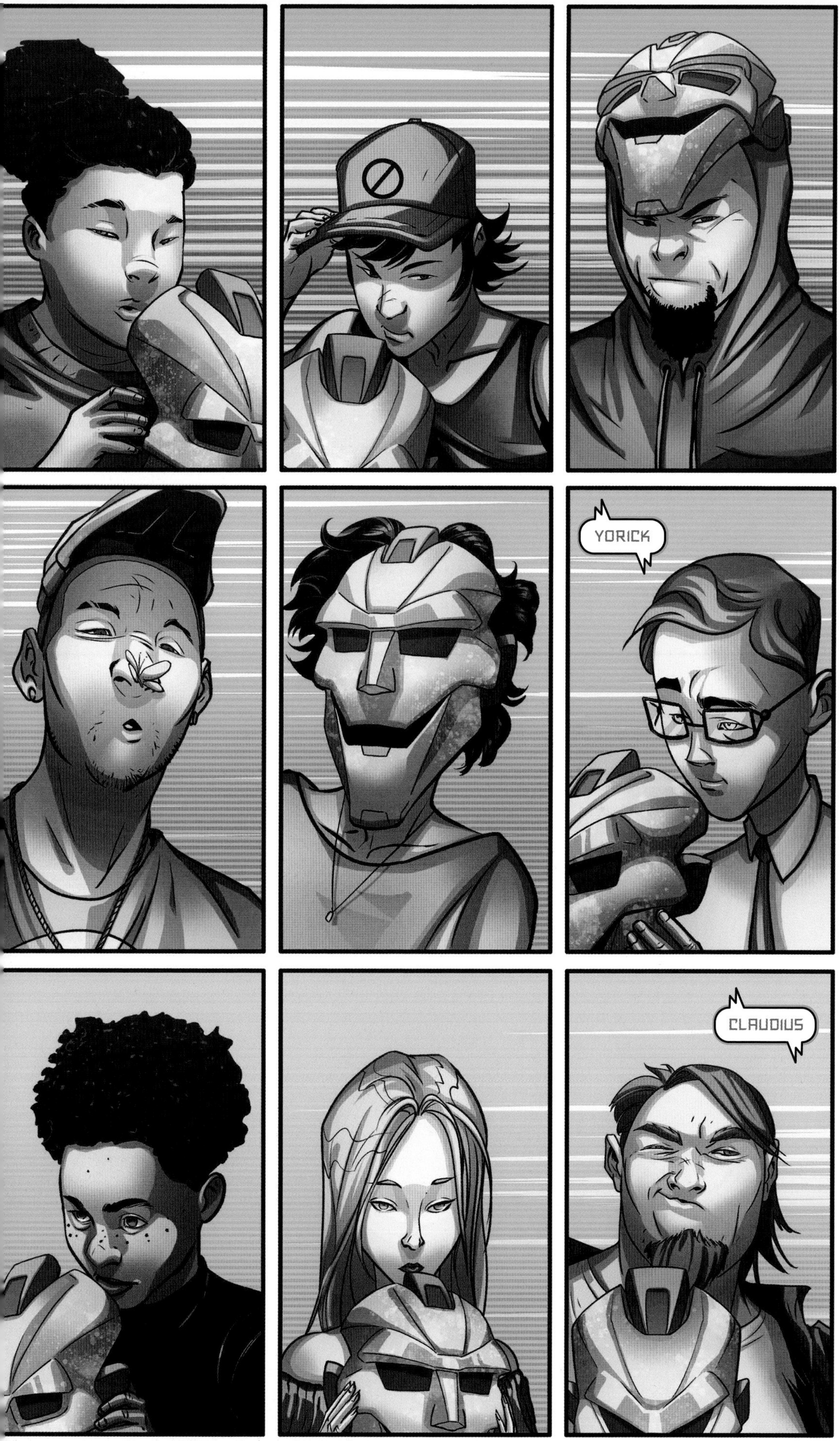
YORICK
CLAUDIUS

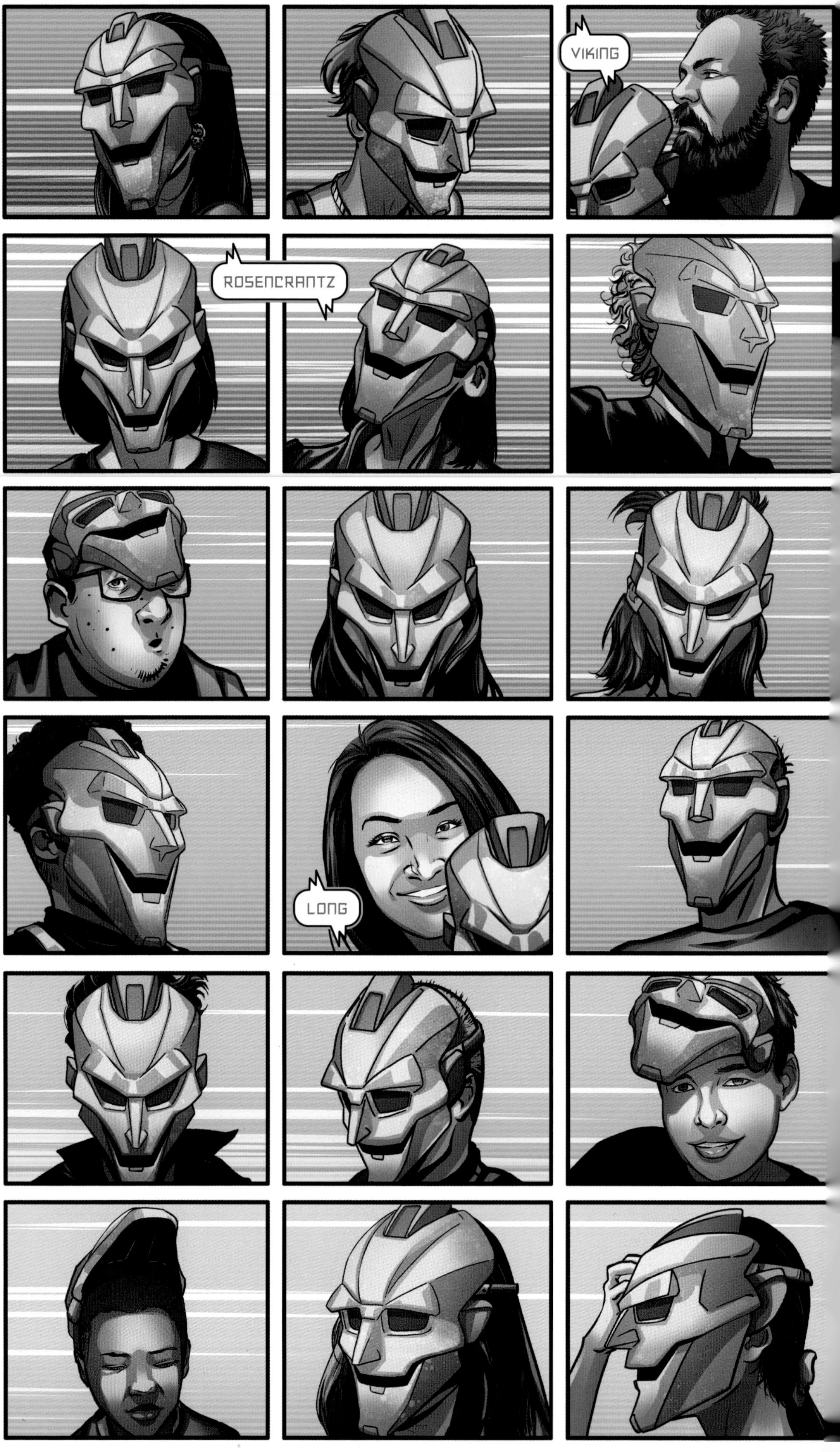
VIKING
ROSENCRANTZ
LONG

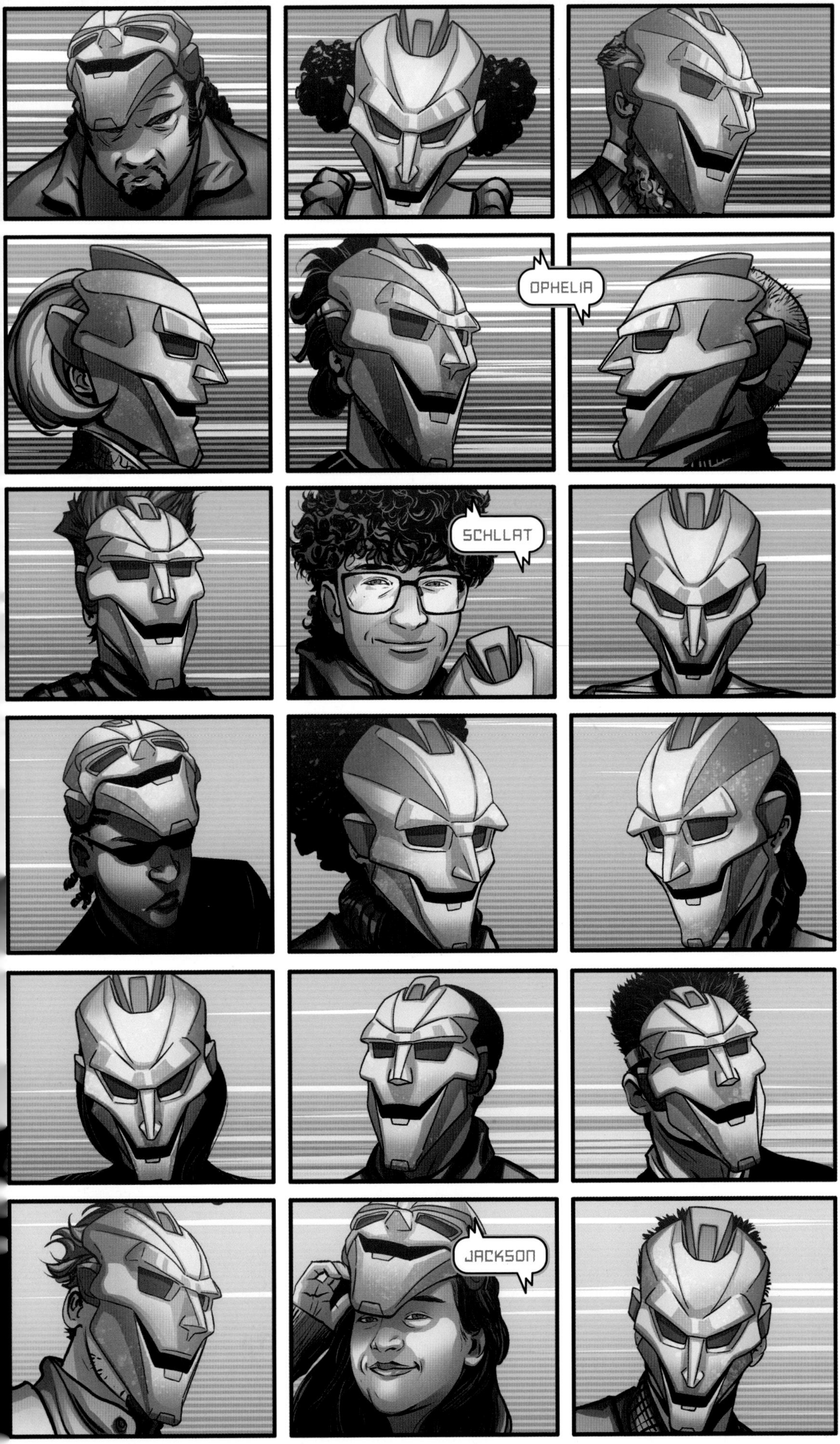
OPHELIA
SCHLLAT
JACKSON

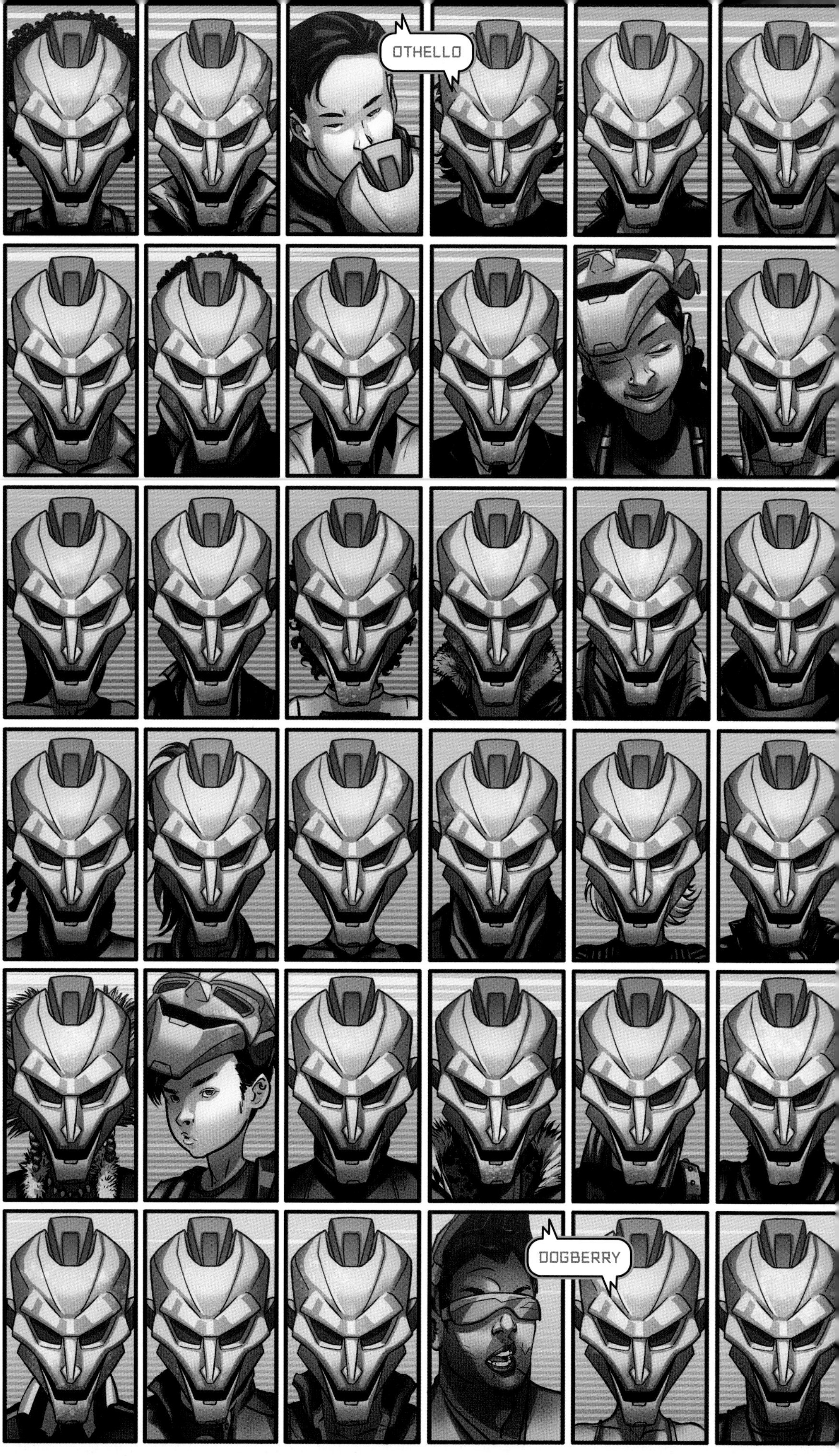
OTHELLO
DOGBERRY

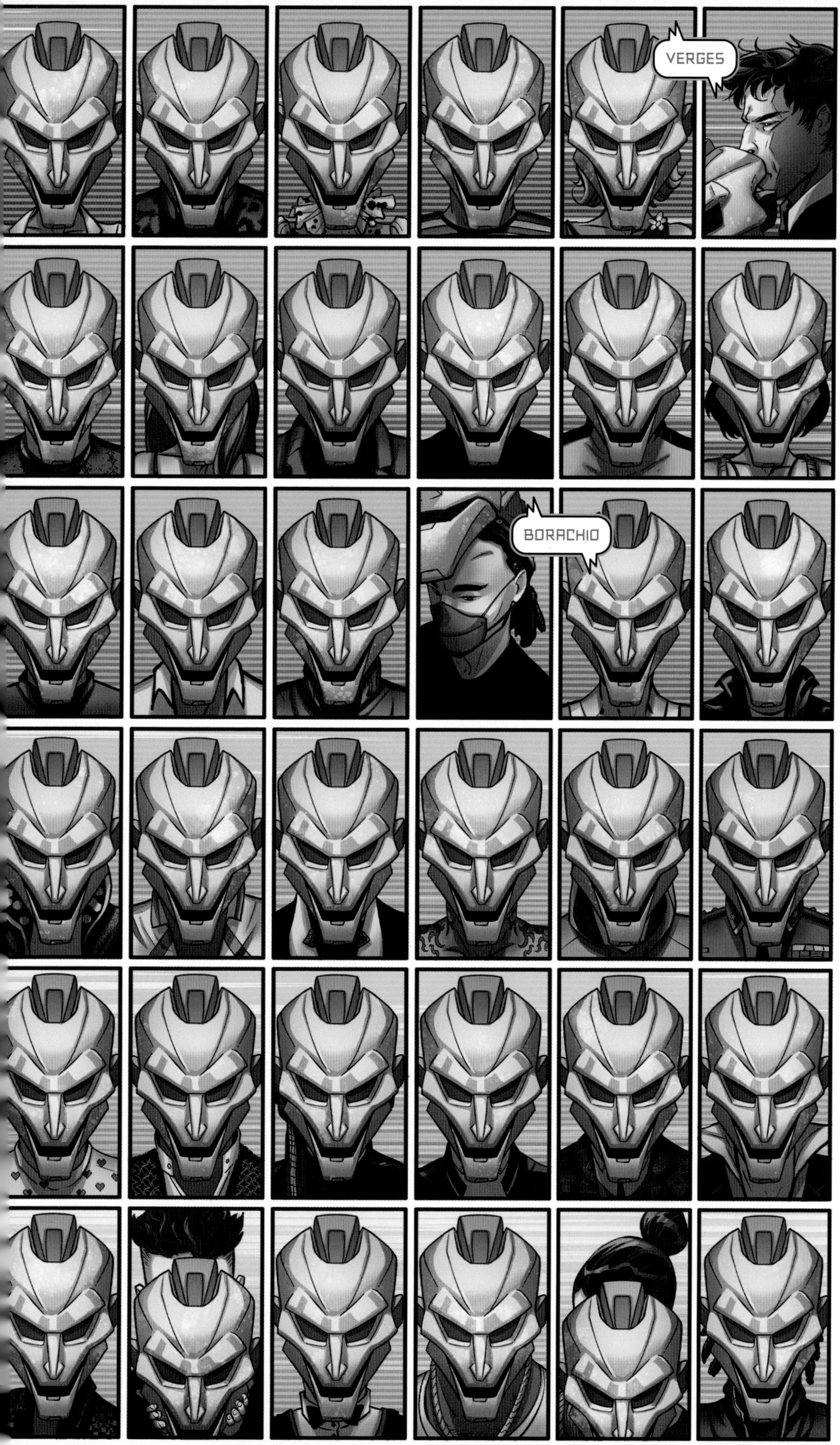
VERGES
BORACHIO

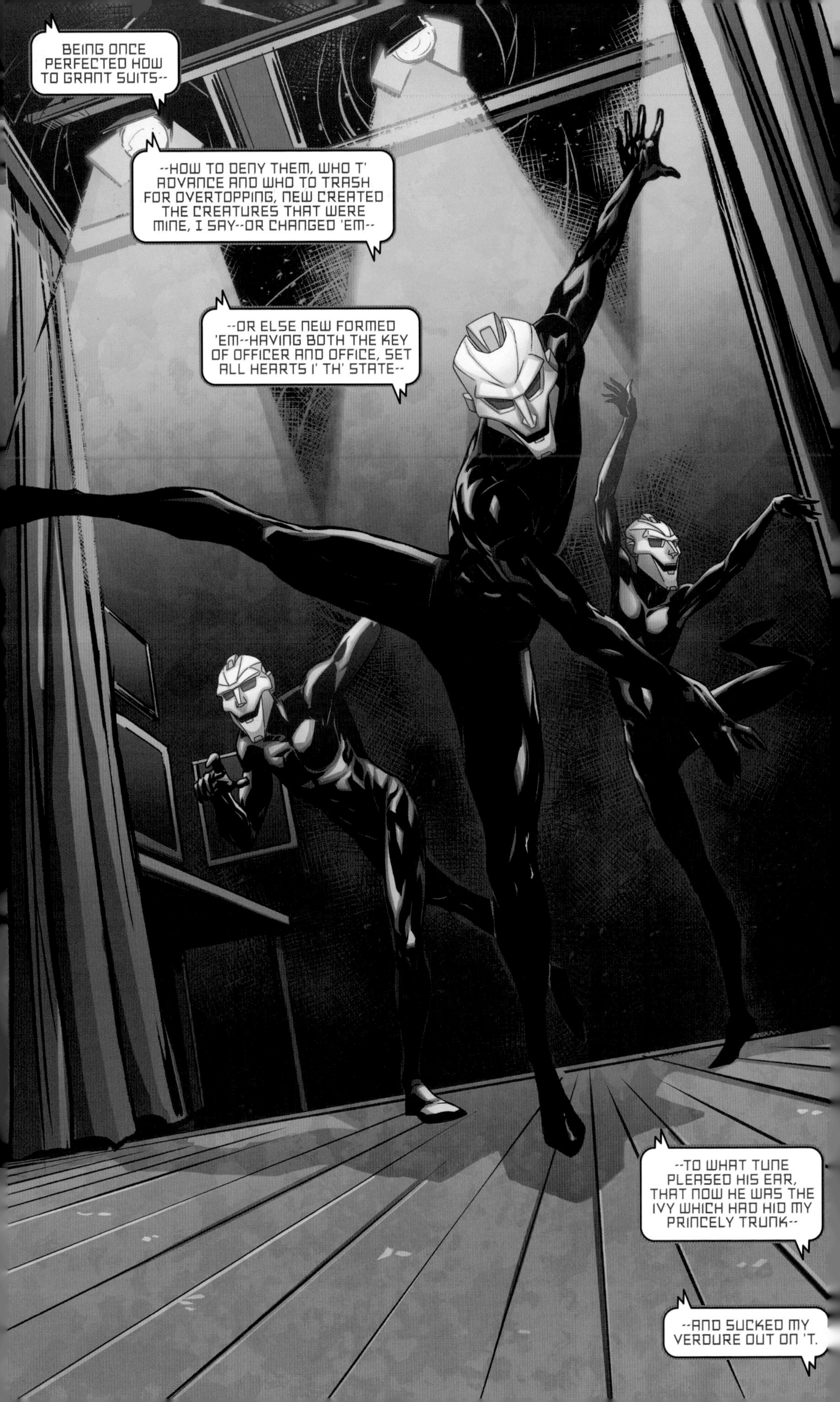
BEING ONCE PERFECTED HOW TO GRANT SUITS--
--HOW TO DENY THEM, WHO T' ADVANCE AND WHO TO TRASH FOR OVERTOPPING, NEW CREATED THE CREATURES THAT WERE MINE, I SAY--OR CHANGED 'EM--
--OR ELSE NEW FORMED 'EM--HAVING BOTH THE KEY OF OFFICER AND OFFICE, SET ALL HEARTS I' TH' STATE--
--TO WHAT TUNE PLEASED HIS EAR, THAT NOW HE WAS THE IVY WHICH HAD HID MY PRINCELY TRUNK--
--AND SUCKED MY VERDURE OUT ON 'T.

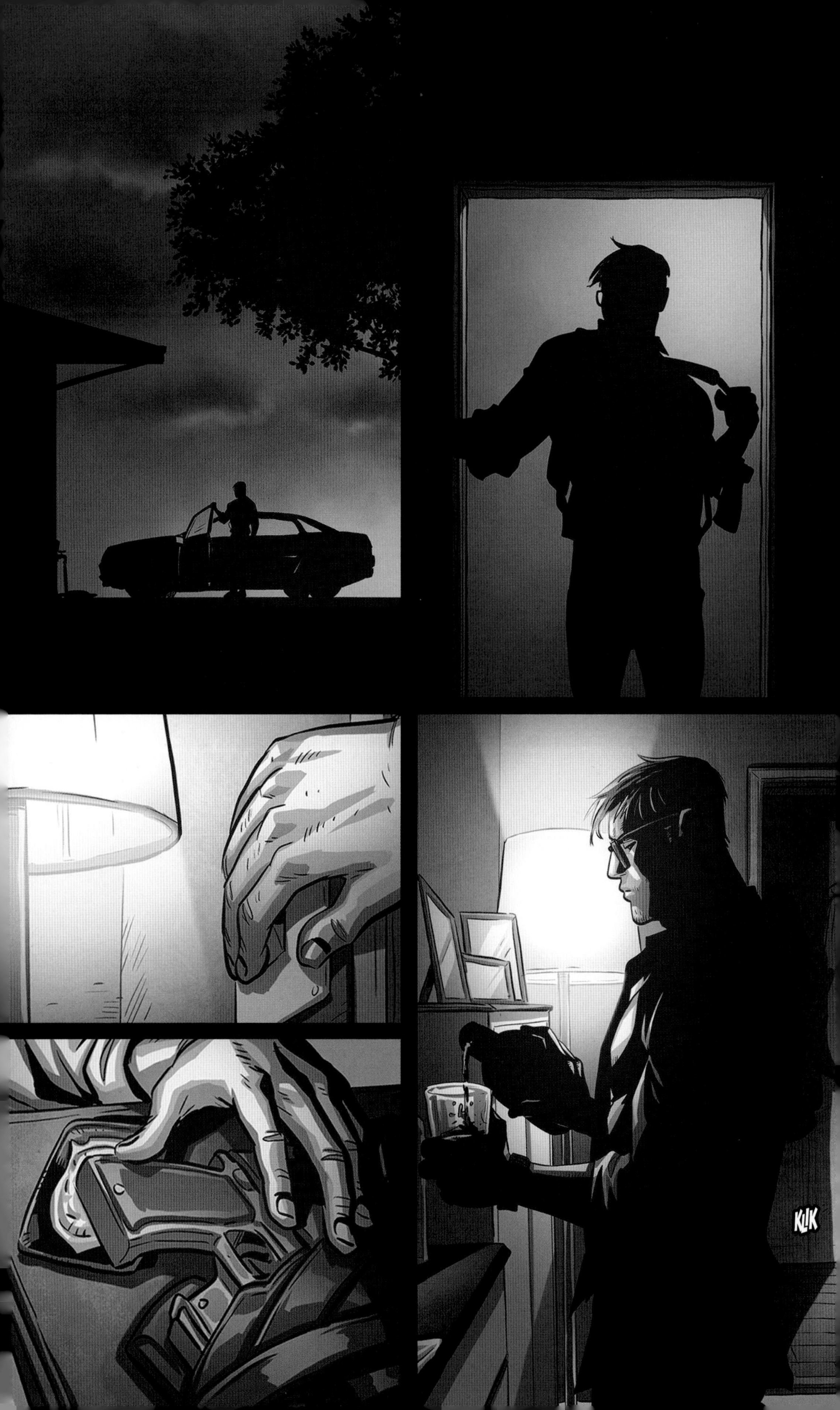
KLIK

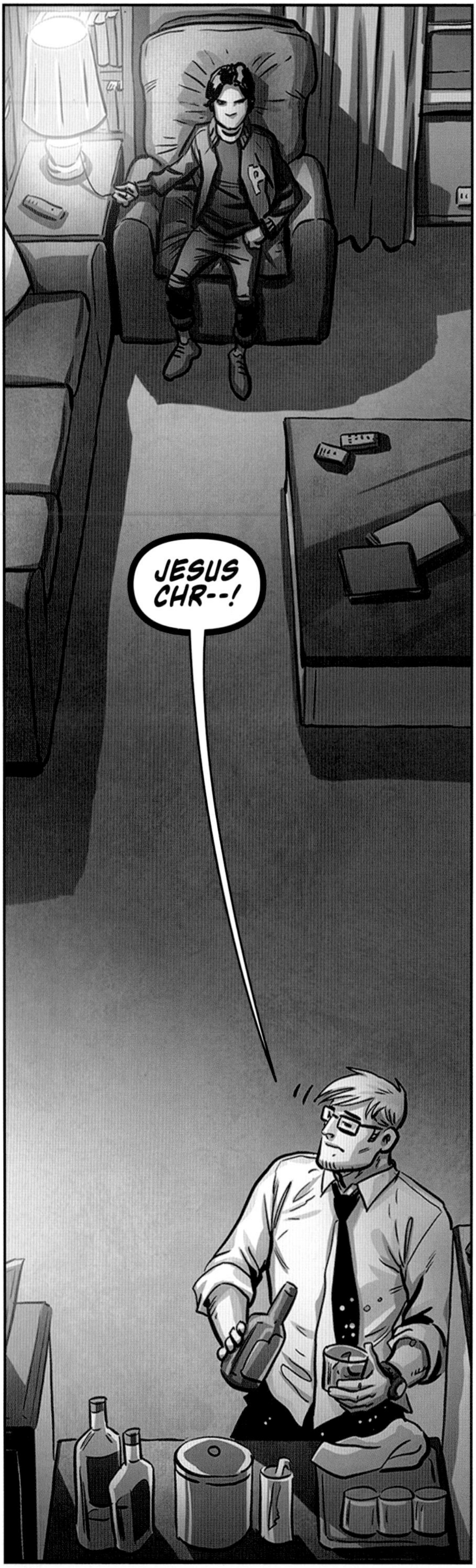
JESUS CHR--!

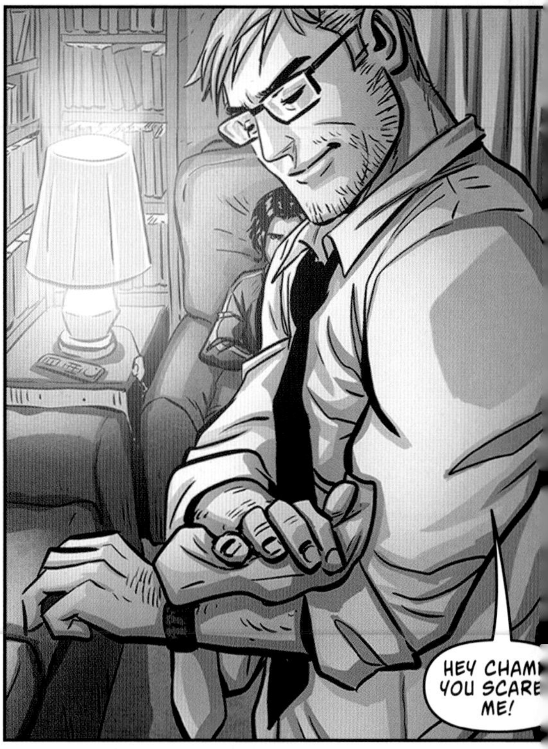
HEY CHAM
YOU SCARE
ME!

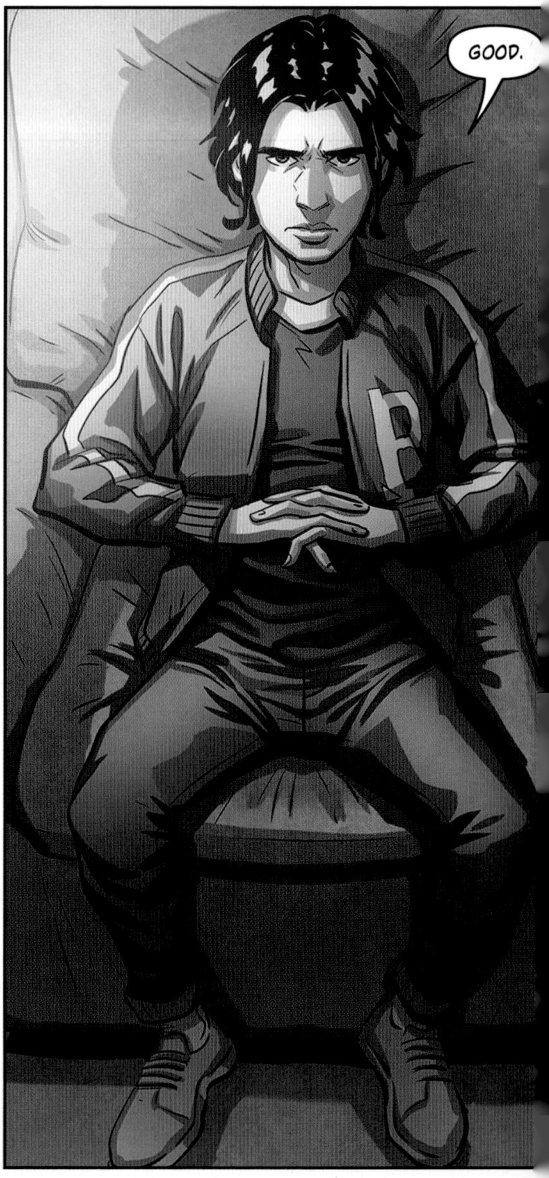
GOOD.

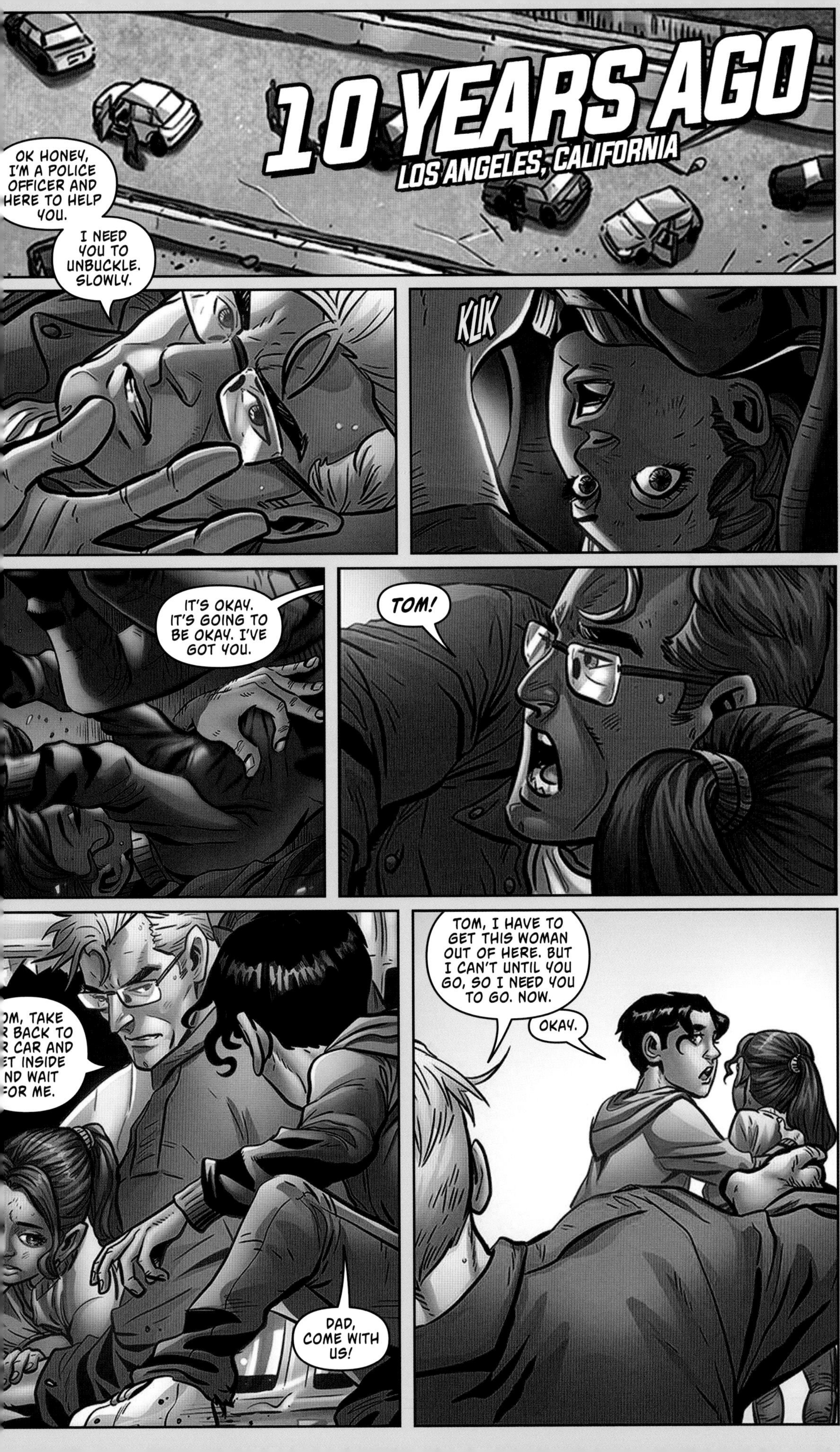
10 YEARS AGO
LOS ANGELES, CALIFORNIA
OK HONEY, I'M A POLICE OFFICER AND HERE TO HELP YOU.
I NEED YOU TO UNBUCKLE. SLOWLY.
KLIK
IT'S OKAY. IT'S GOING TO BE OKAY. I'VE GOT YOU.
TOM!
OM, TAKE R BACK TO R CAR AND ET INSIDE ND WAIT FOR ME.
DAD, COME WITH US!
TOM, I HAVE TO GET THIS WOMAN OUT OF HERE. BUT I CAN'T UNTIL YOU GO, SO I NEED YOU TO GO. NOW.
OKAY.

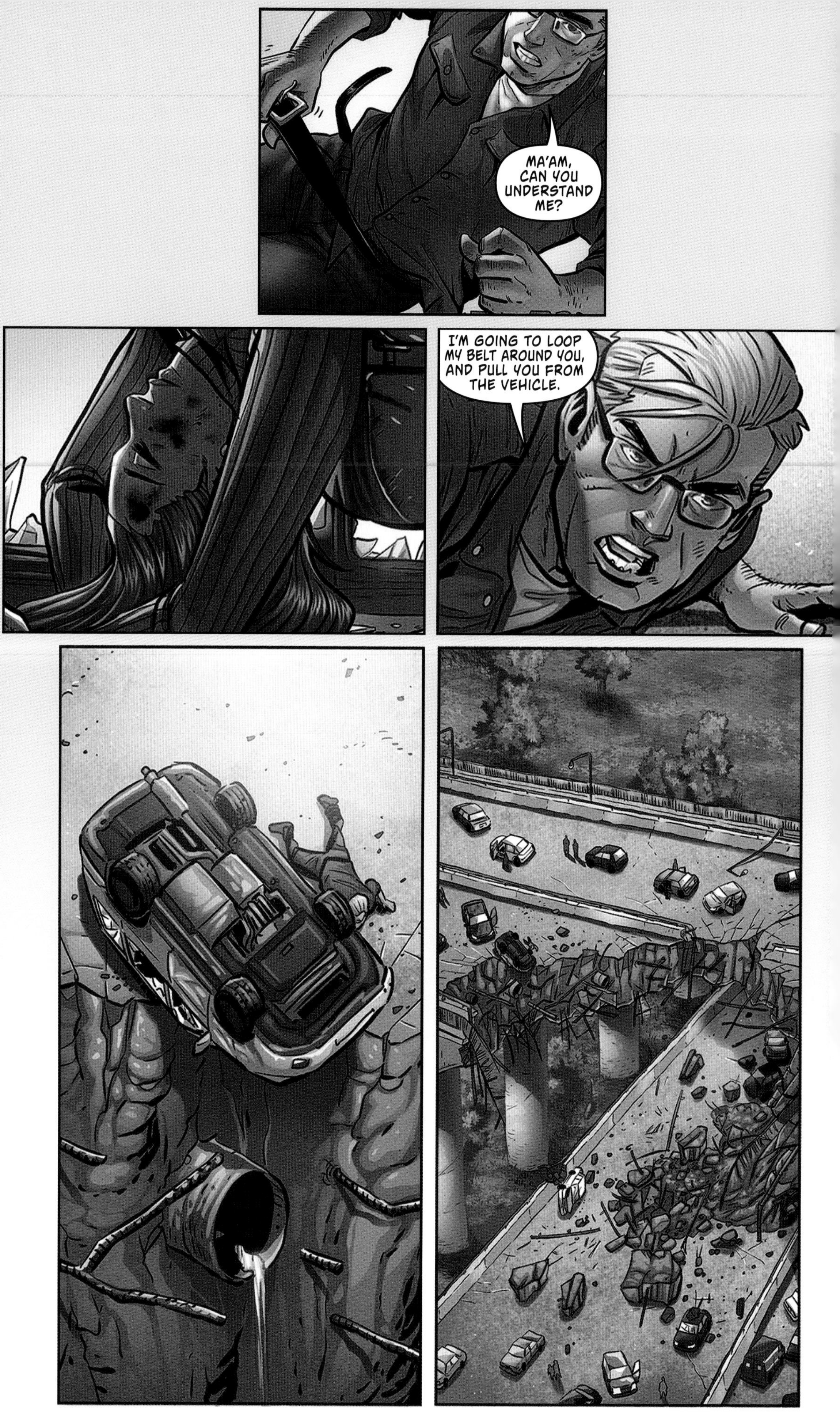
MA'AM, CAN YOU UNDERSTAND ME?
I'M GOING TO LOOP MY BELT AROUND YOU, AND PULL YOU FROM THE VEHICLE.

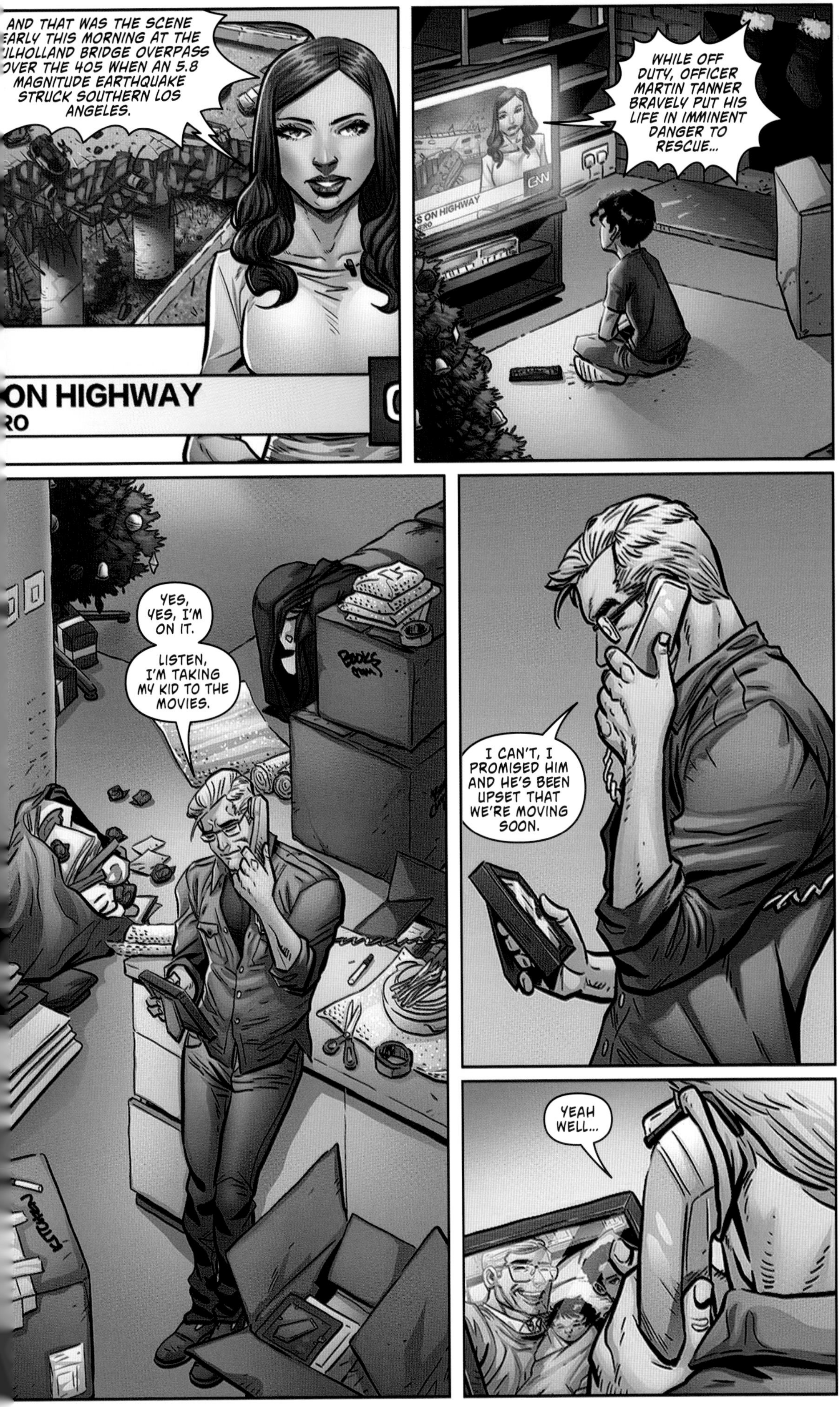
AND THAT WAS THE SCENE EARLY THIS MORNING AT THE MULHOLLAND BRIDGE OVERPASS OVER THE 405 WHEN AN 5.8 MAGNITUDE EARTHQUAKE STRUCK SOUTHERN LOS ANGELES.
ON HIGHWAY
RO
WHILE OFF DUTY, OFFICER MARTIN TANNER BRAVELY PUT HIS LIFE IN IMMINENT DANGER TO RESCUE...
YES, YES, I'M ON IT.
LISTEN, I'M TAKING MY KID TO THE MOVIES.
I CAN'T, I PROMISED HIM AND HE'S BEEN UPSET THAT WE'RE MOVING SOON.
YEAH WELL...

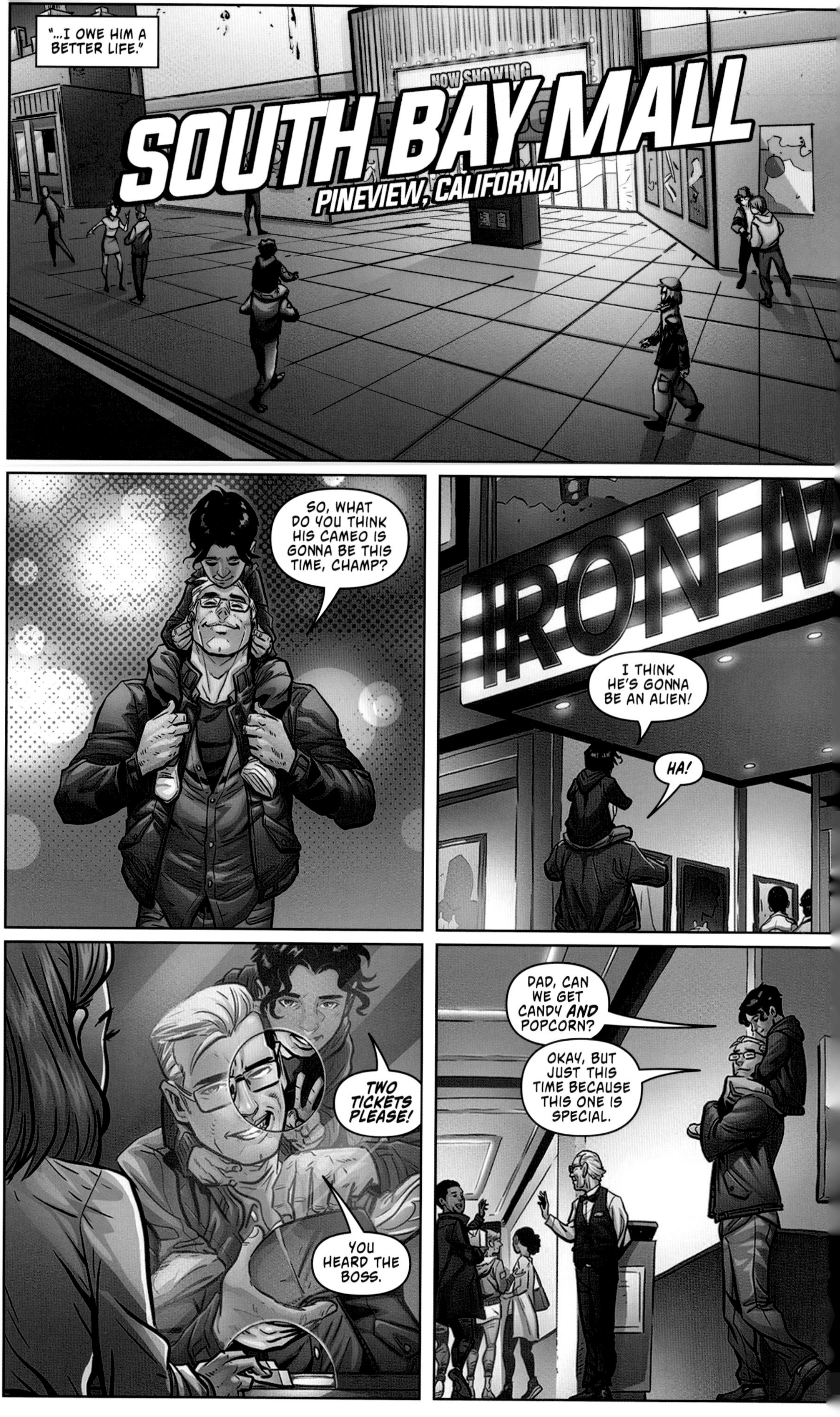

"...I OWE HIM A BETTER LIFE."
NOW SHOWING
SOUTH BAY MALL
PINEVIEW, CALIFORNIA
SO, WHAT DO YOU THINK HIS CAMEO IS GONNA BE THIS TIME, CHAMP?
IRON M
I THINK HE'S GONNA BE AN ALIEN!
HA!
TWO TICKETS PLEASE!
YOU HEARD THE BOSS.
DAD, CAN WE GET CANDY AND POPCORN?
OKAY, BUT JUST THIS TIME BECAUSE THIS ONE IS SPECIAL.

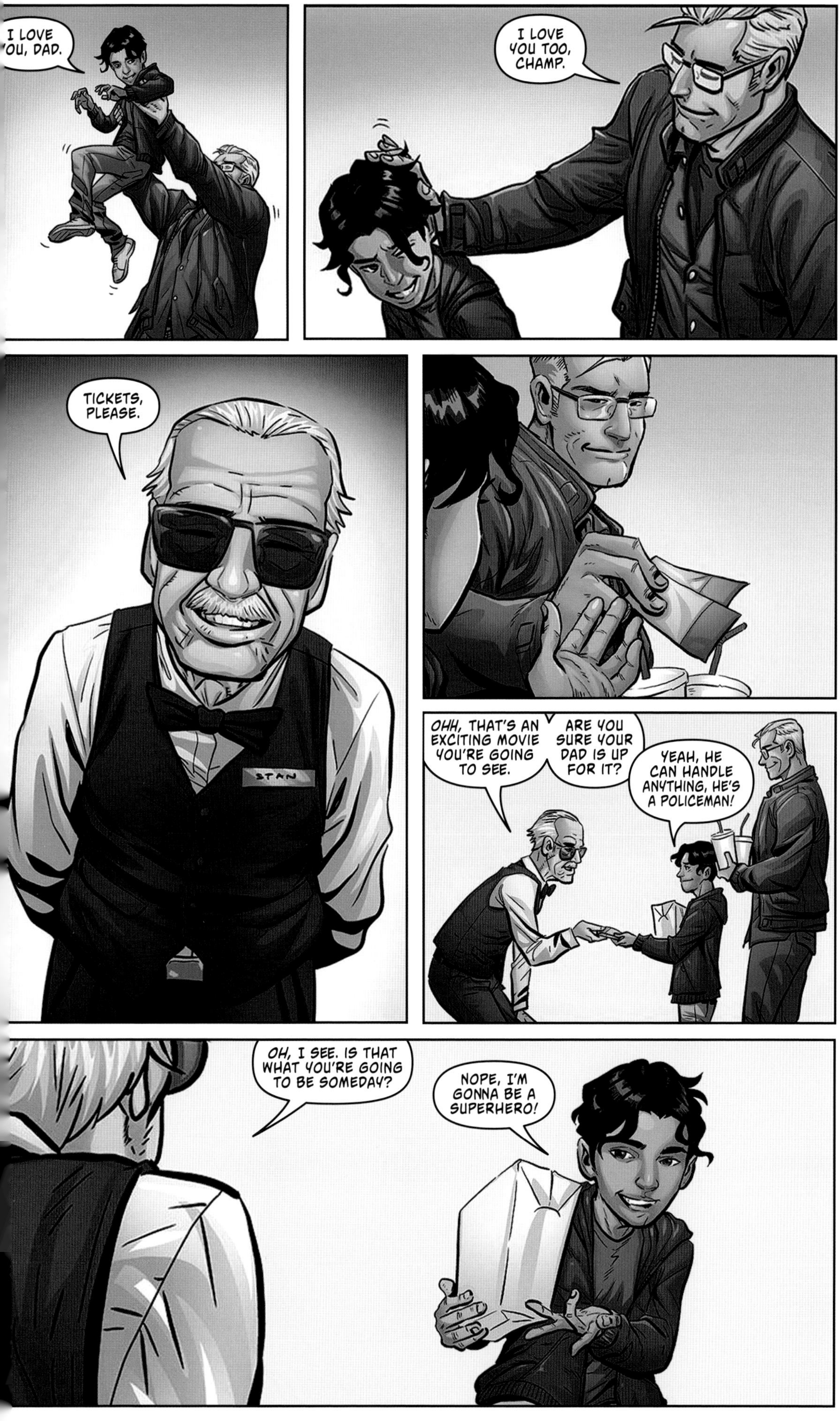
I LOVE
YOU, DAD.
I LOVE YOU TOO, CHAMP.
TICKETS, PLEASE.
STAN
OHH, THAT'S AN EXCITING MOVIE YOU'RE GOING TO SEE.
ARE YOU SURE YOUR DAD IS UP FOR IT?
YEAH, HE CAN HANDLE ANYTHING, HE'S A POLICEMAN!
OH, I SEE. IS THAT WHAT YOU'RE GOING TO BE SOMEDAY?
NOPE, I'M GONNA BE A SUPERHERO!

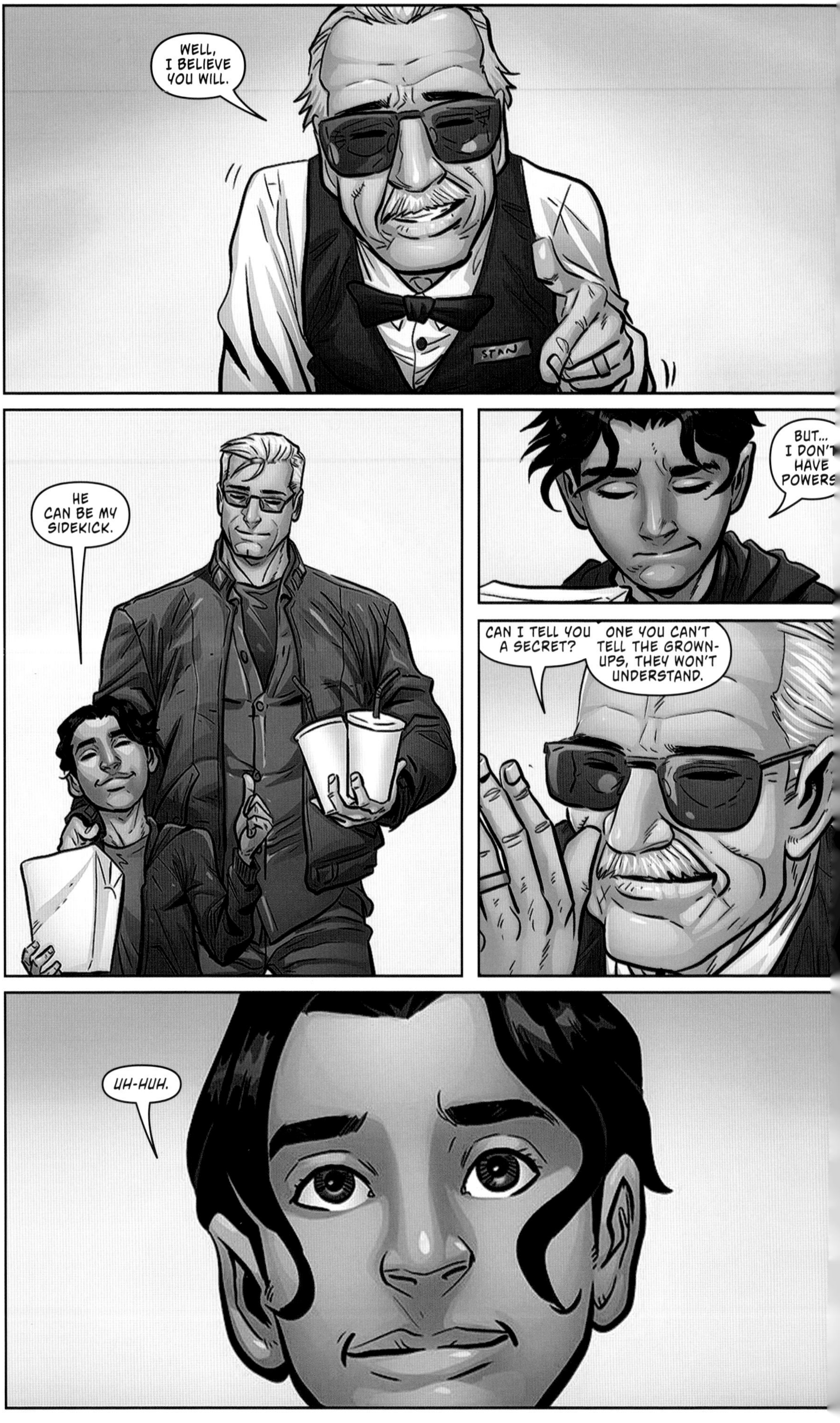
WELL, I BELIEVE YOU WILL.
HE CAN BE MY SIDEKICK.
BUT... I DON'T HAVE POWERS
CAN I TELL YOU A SECRET?
ONE YOU CAN'T TELL THE GROWN-UPS, THEY WON'T UNDERSTAND.
UH-HUH.

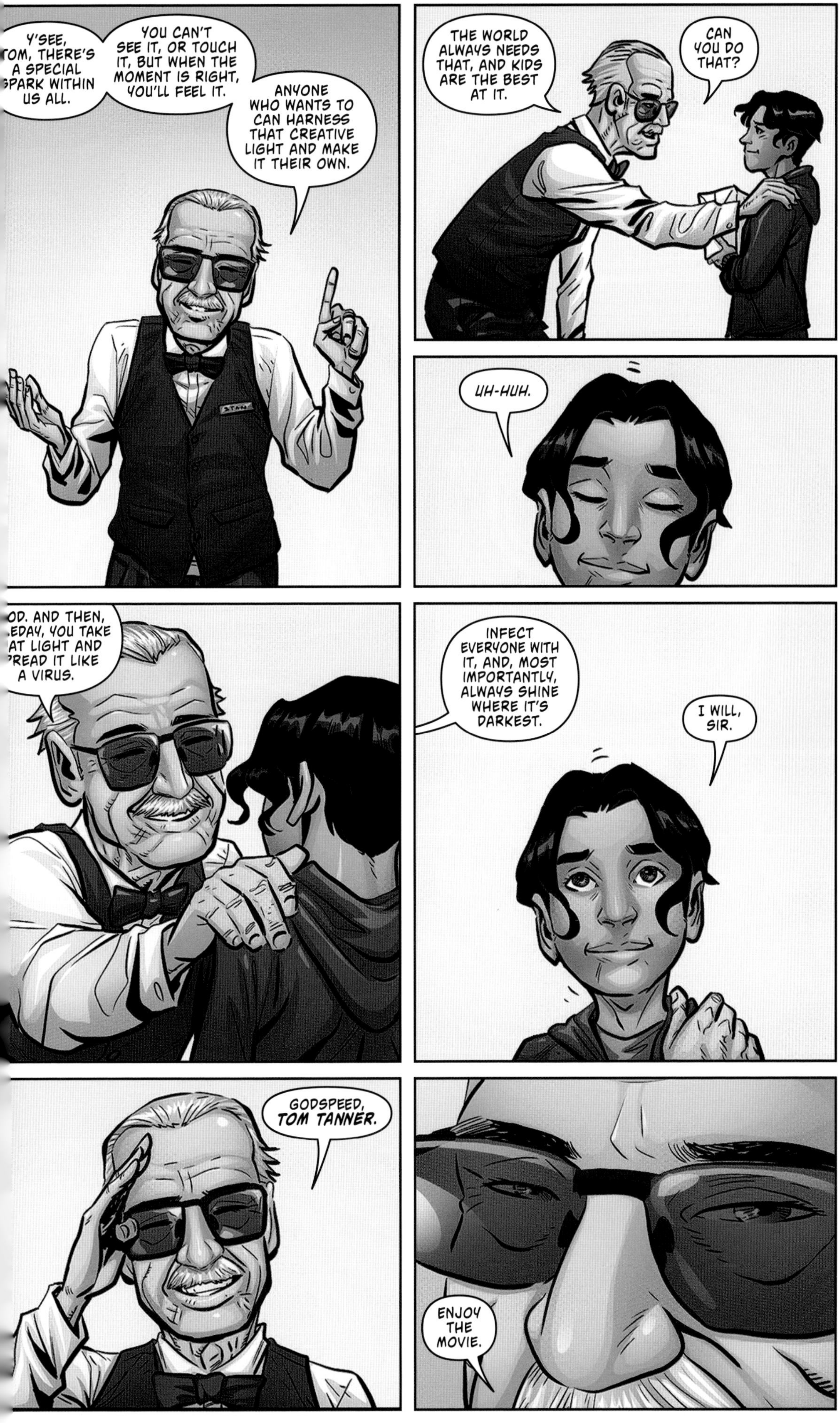

Y'SEE, TOM, THERE'S A SPECIAL SPARK WITHIN US ALL.
YOU CAN'T SEE IT, OR TOUCH IT, BUT WHEN THE MOMENT IS RIGHT, YOU'LL FEEL IT.
ANYONE WHO WANTS TO CAN HARNESS THAT CREATIVE LIGHT AND MAKE IT THEIR OWN.
THE WORLD ALWAYS NEEDS THAT, AND KIDS ARE THE BEST AT IT.
CAN YOU DO THAT?
UH-HUH.
OD. AND THEN, EDAY, YOU TAKE AT LIGHT AND READ IT LIKE A VIRUS.
INFECT EVERYONE WITH IT, AND, MOST IMPORTANTLY, ALWAYS SHINE WHERE IT'S DARKEST.
I WILL, SIR.
GODSPEED, TOM TANNER.
ENJOY THE MOVIE.

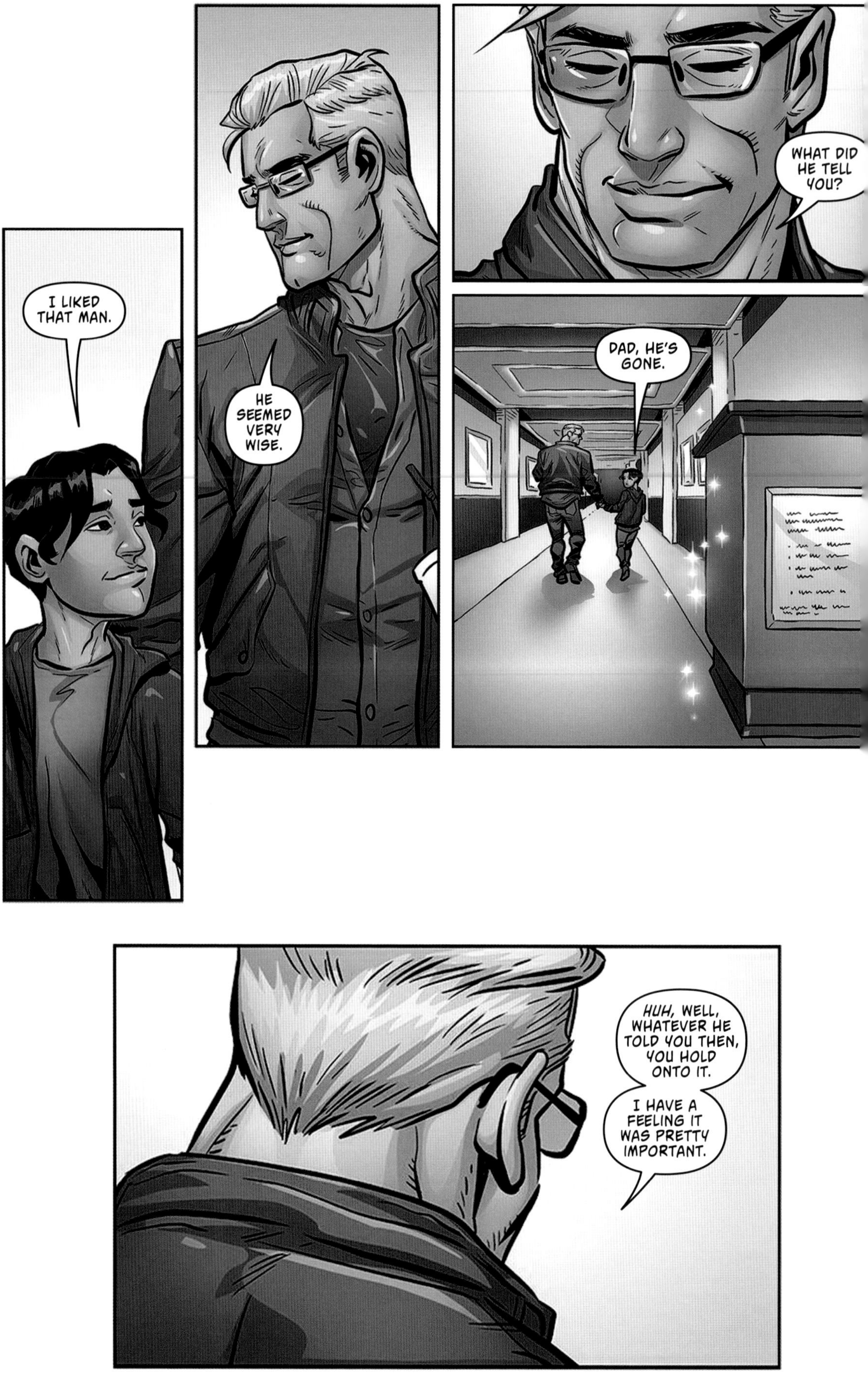
I LIKED THAT MAN.
HE SEEMED VERY WISE.
WHAT DID HE TELL YOU?
DAD, HE'S GONE.
HUH, WELL, WHATEVER HE TOLD YOU THEN, YOU HOLD ONTO IT.
I HAVE A FEELING IT WAS PRETTY IMPORTANT.

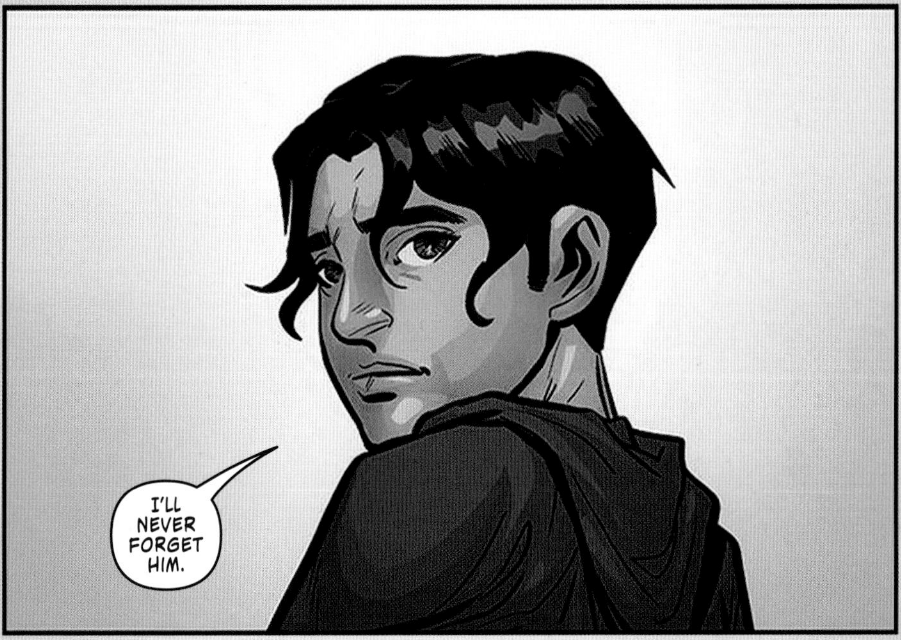
I'LL NEVER FORGET HIM.

TO BE CONTINUED IN STAN LEE'S
BACKCHANNEL VOLUME 2

BACKMATTER

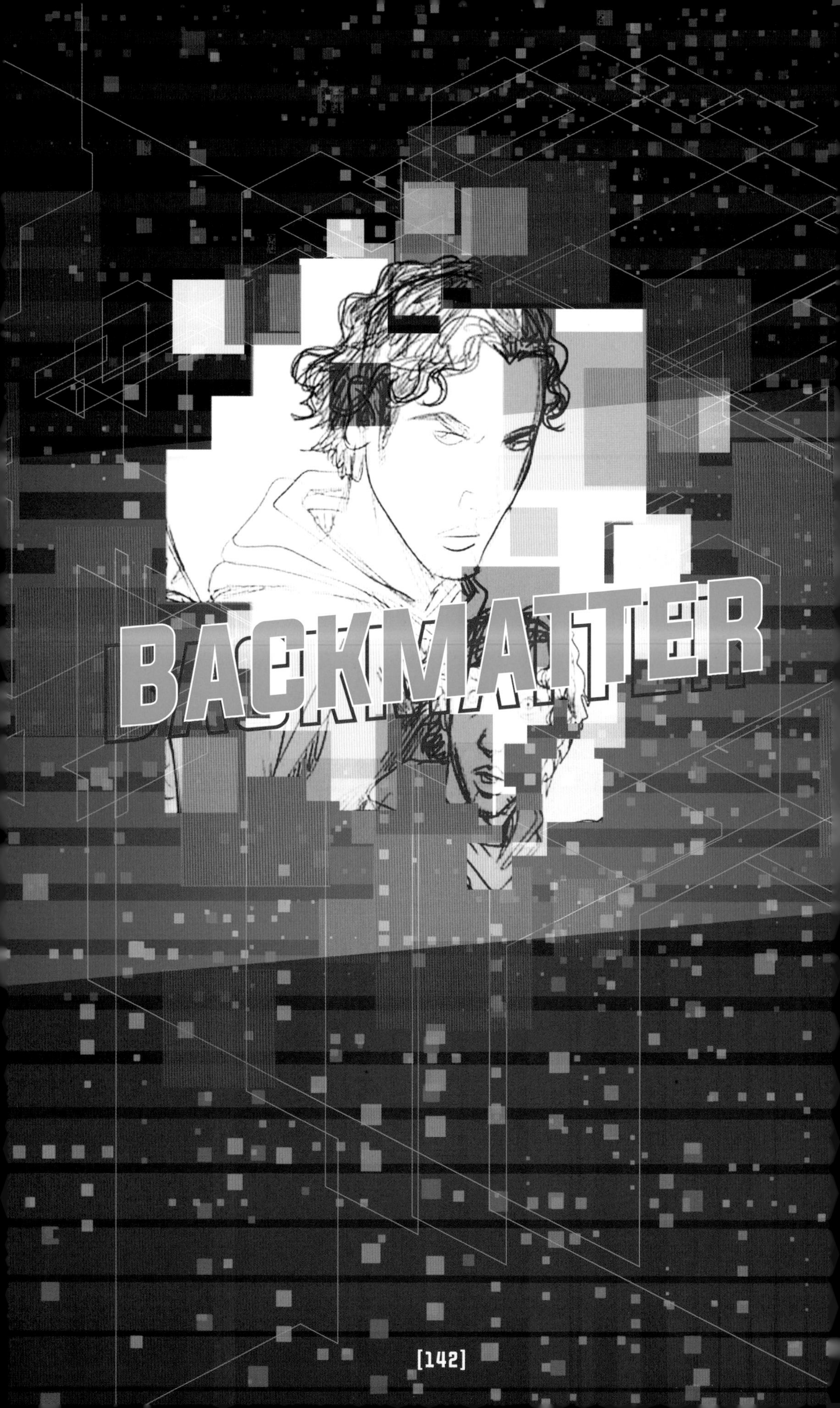

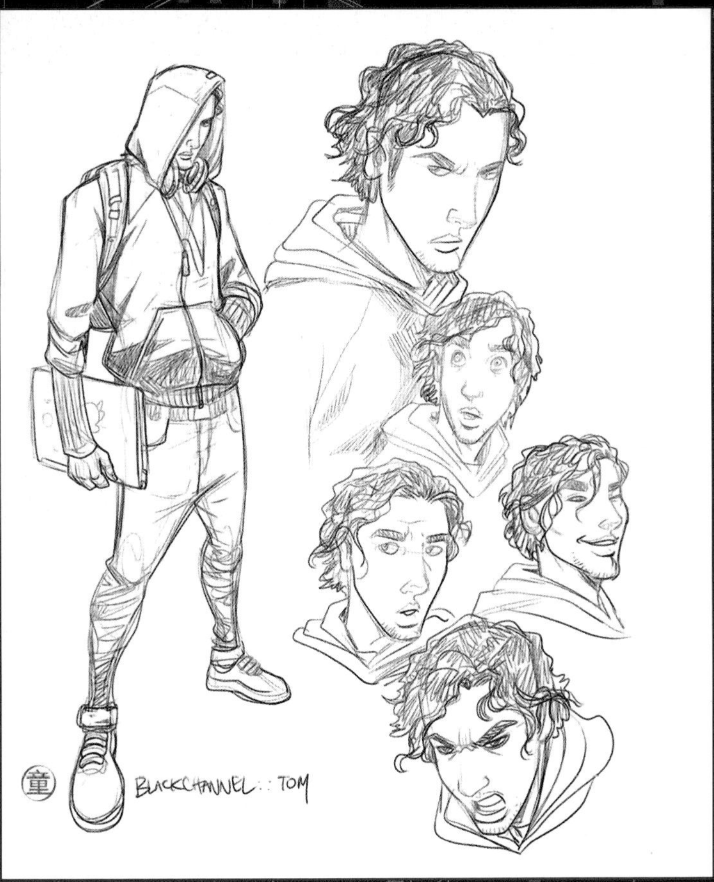
BLACKCHANNEL :: TOM

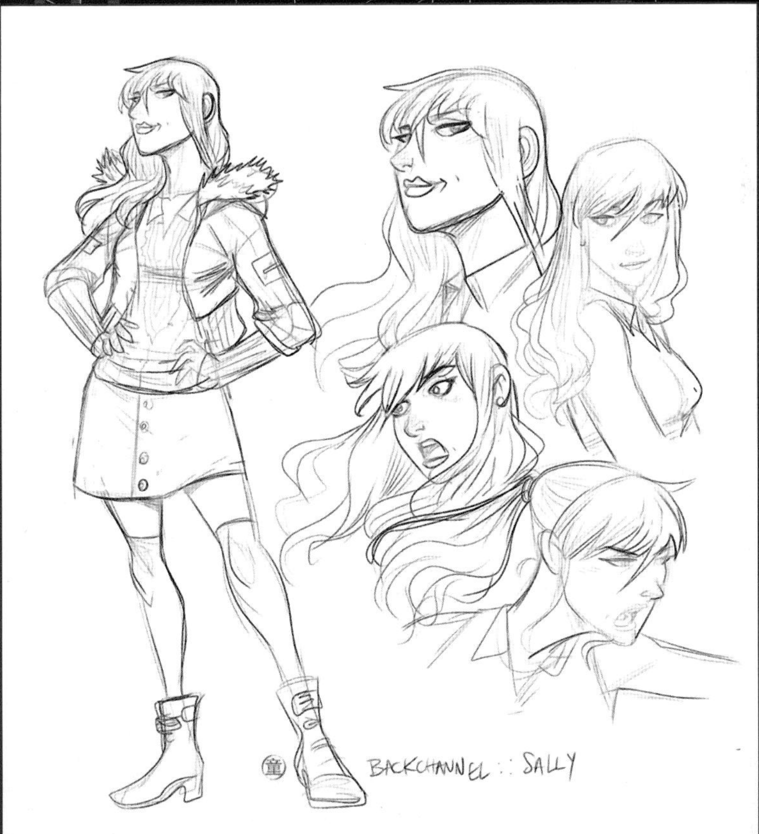
BACKCHANNEL :: SALLY

CHARACTER SKETCHES BY **ANDIE TONG**

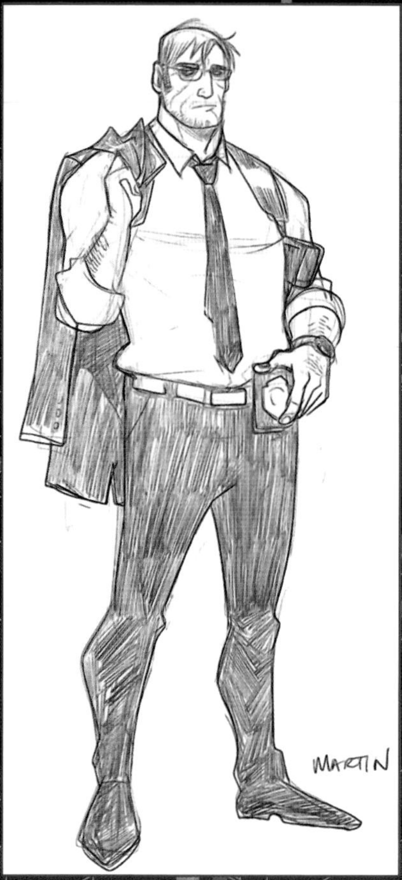
MARTIN

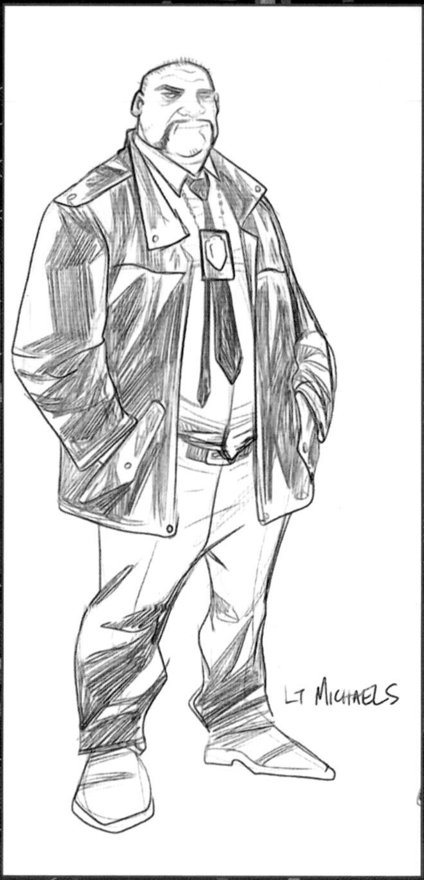
LT MICHAELS

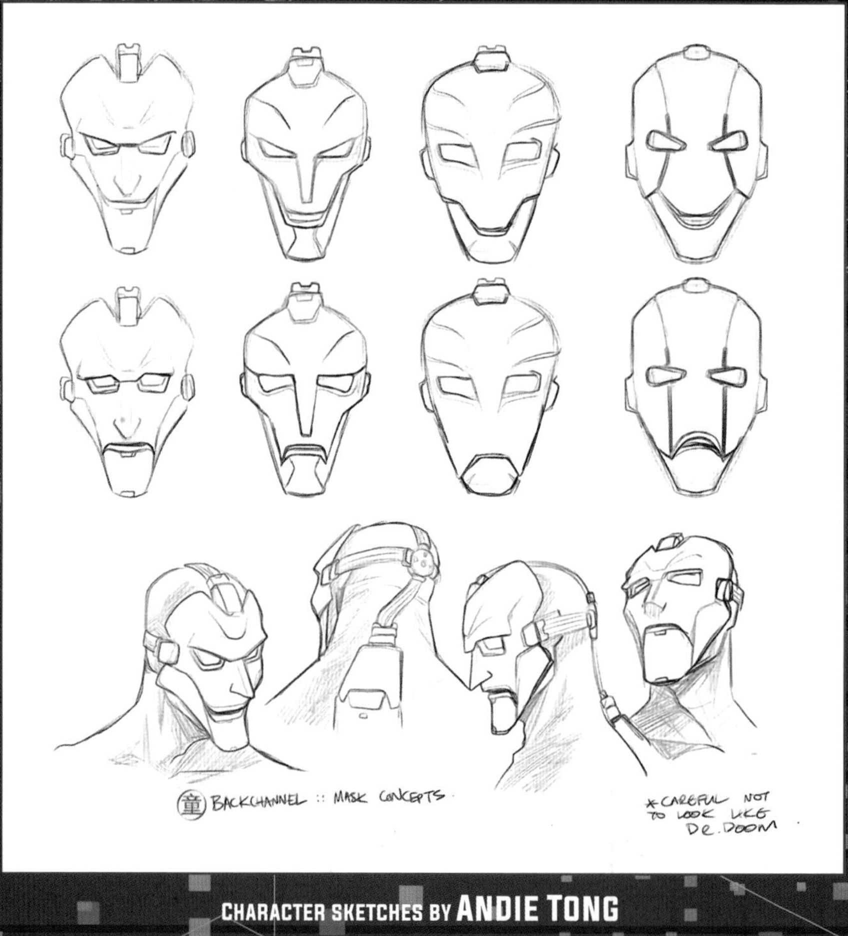
BACKCHANNEL :: MASK CONCEPTS
*CAREFUL NOT TO LOOK LIKE DR. DOOM

CHARACTER SKETCHES BY ANDIE TONG

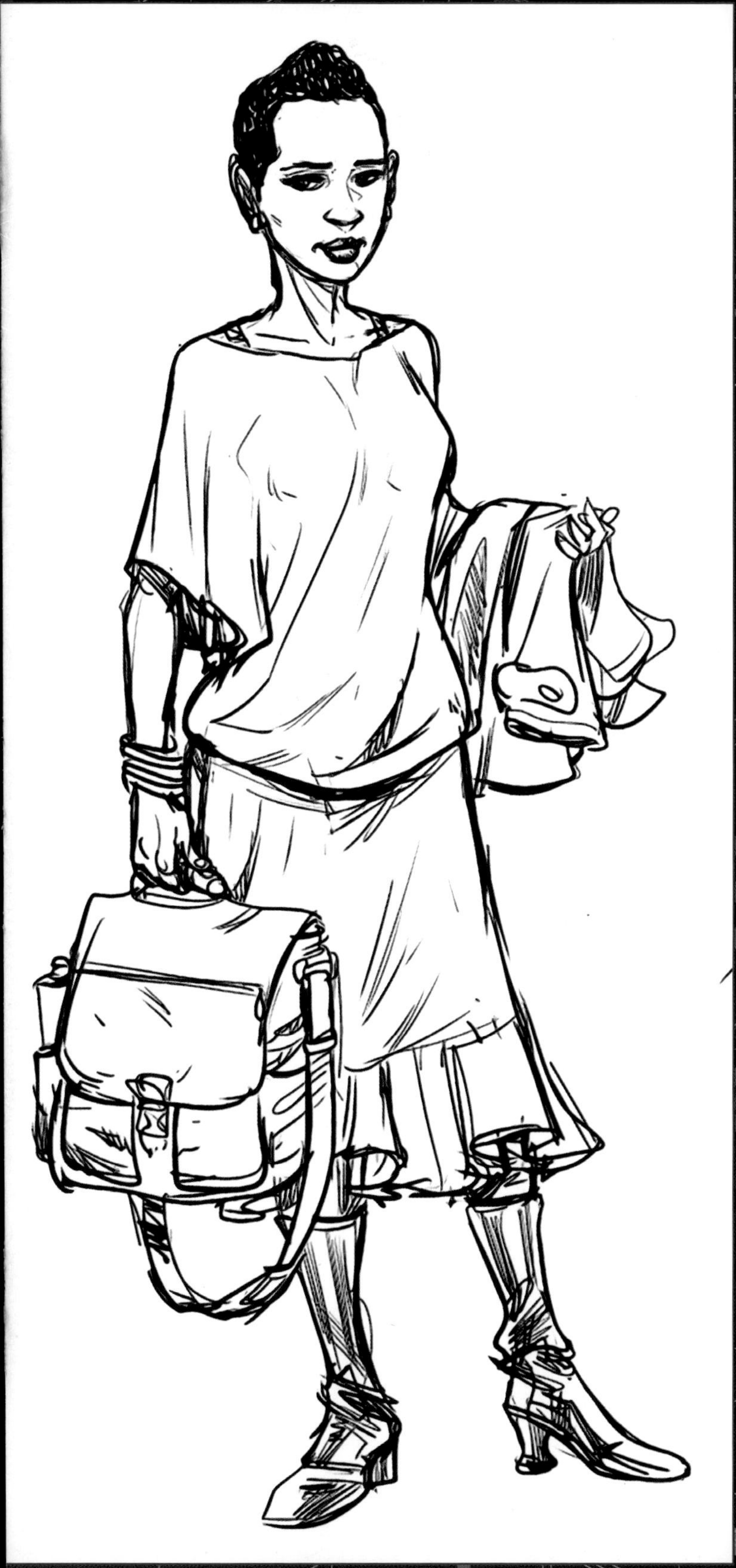

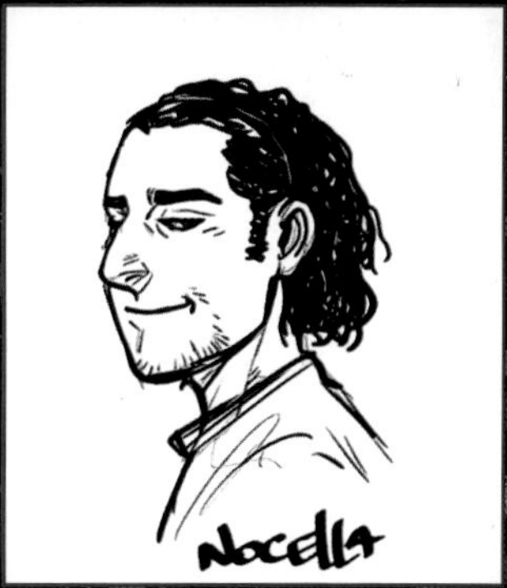
NOCELLA

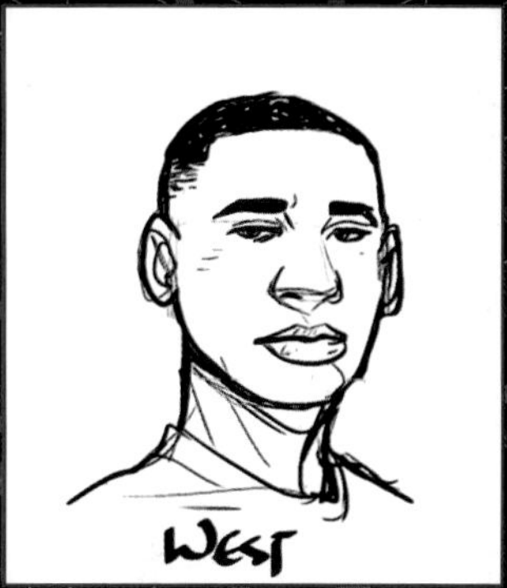
WEST

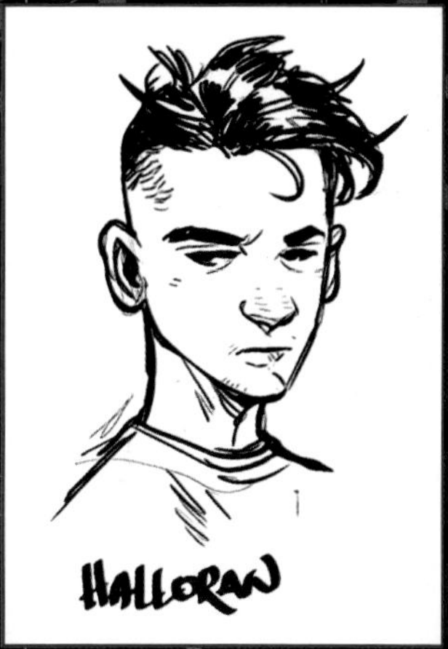
HALLORAN

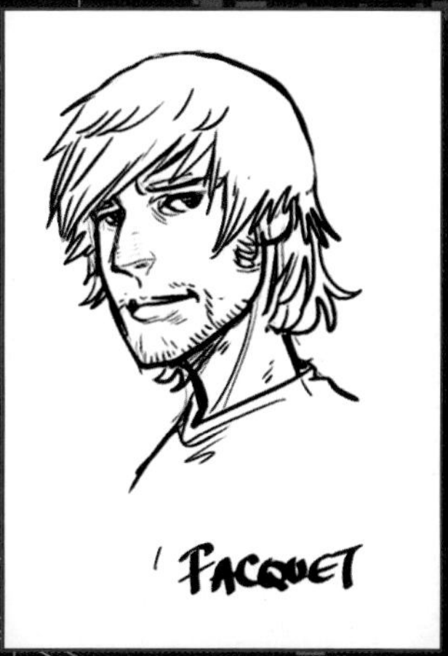
FACQUET

CHARACTER AND CONCEPT ART BY **ANDIE TONG**

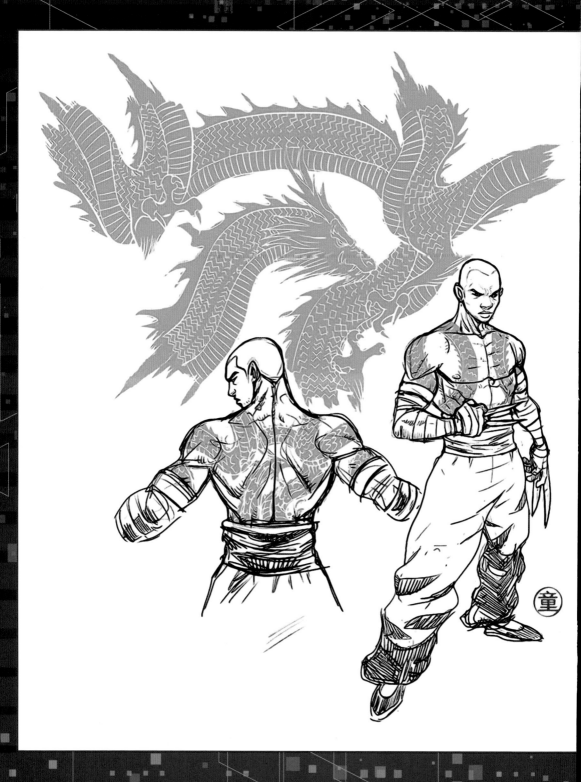

CHARACTER AND CONCEPT ART BY **ANDIE TONG**

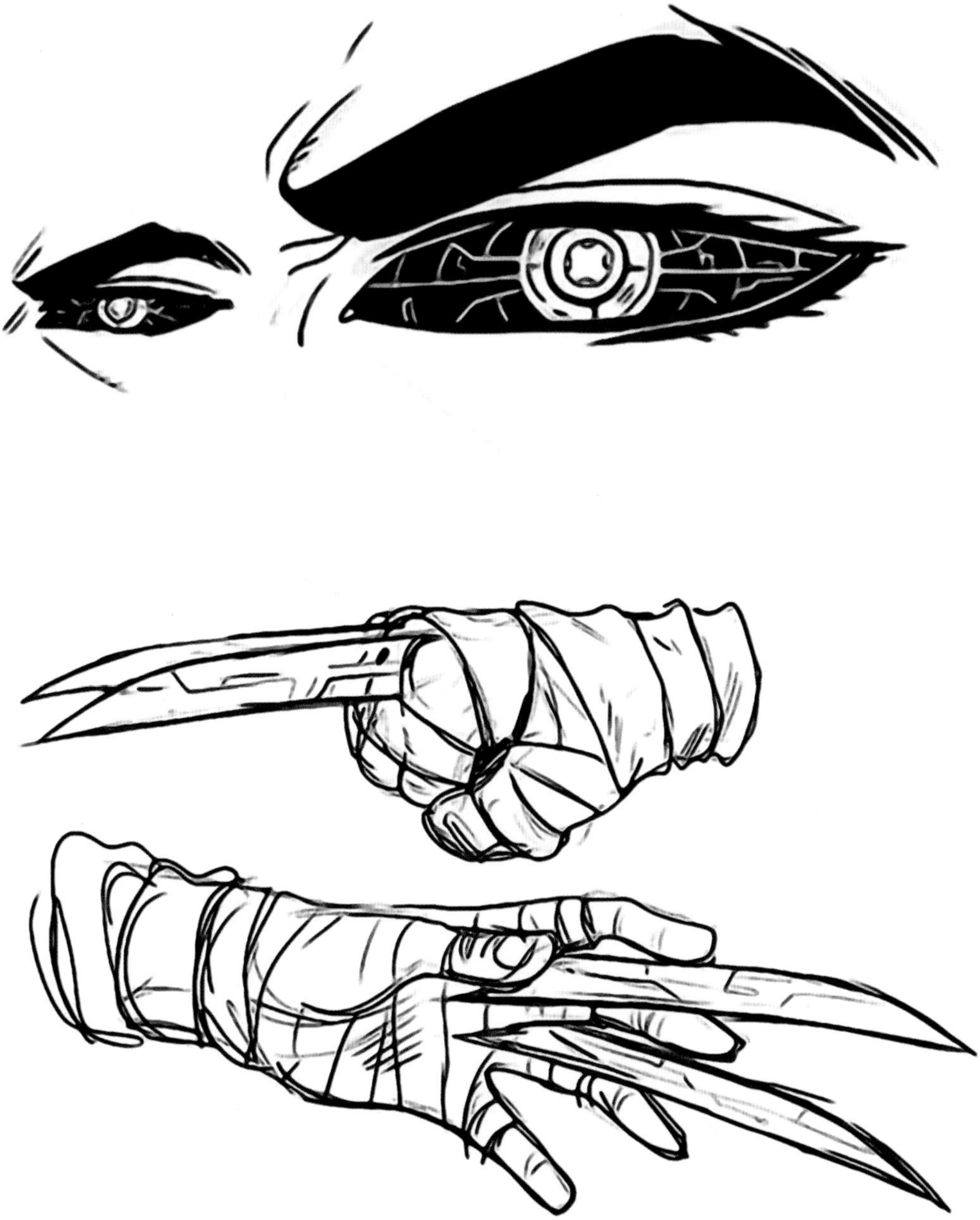

CHARACTER AND CONCEPT ART BY **ANDIE TONG**

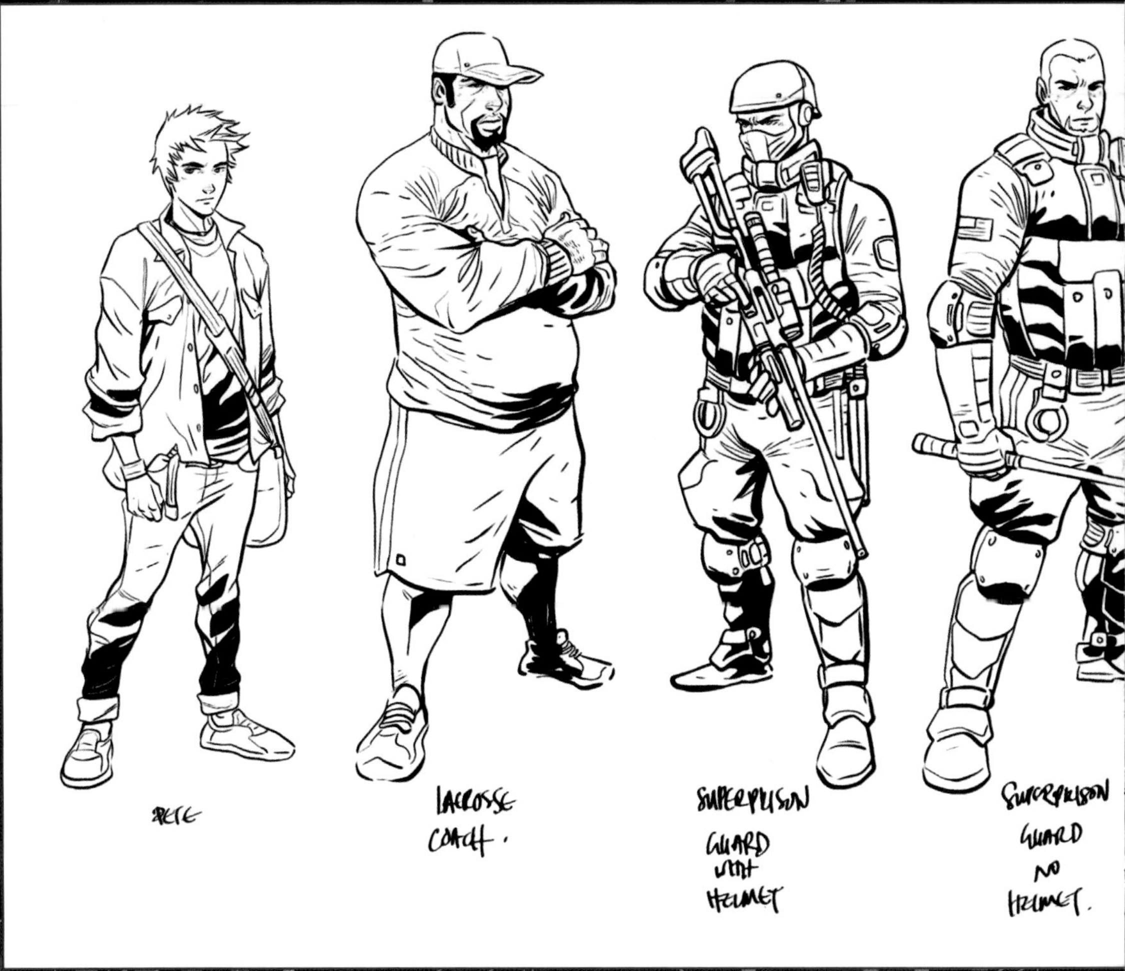
PETE
LACROSSE COACH.
SUPERPRISON GUARD WITH HELMET
SUPERPRISON GUARD NO HELMET.

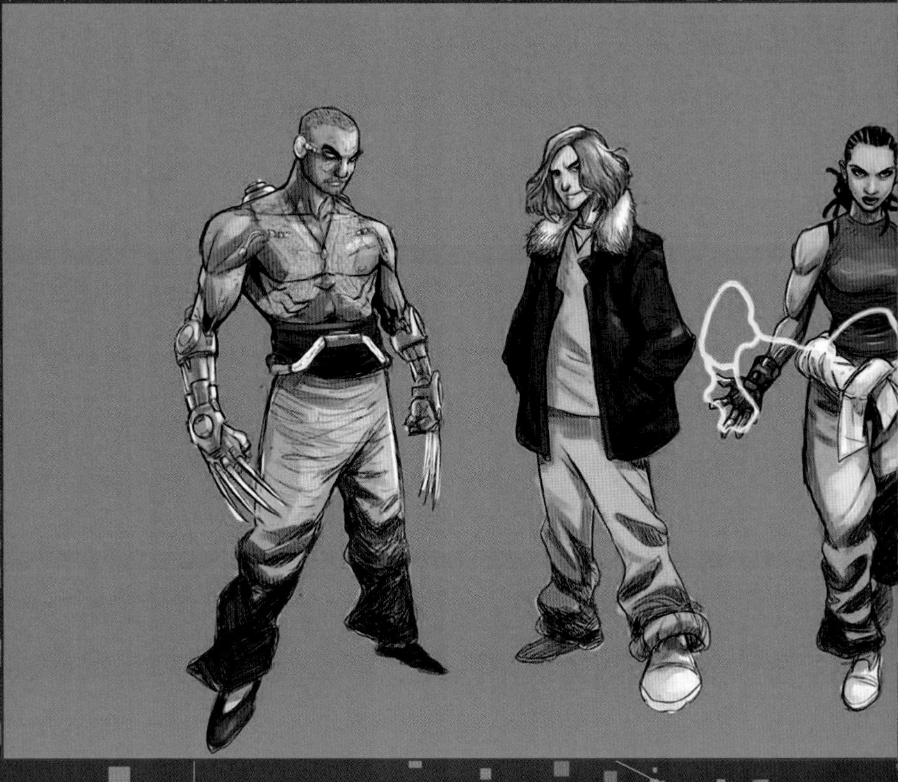

CHARACTER AND CONCEPT ART BY **ANDIE TONG**

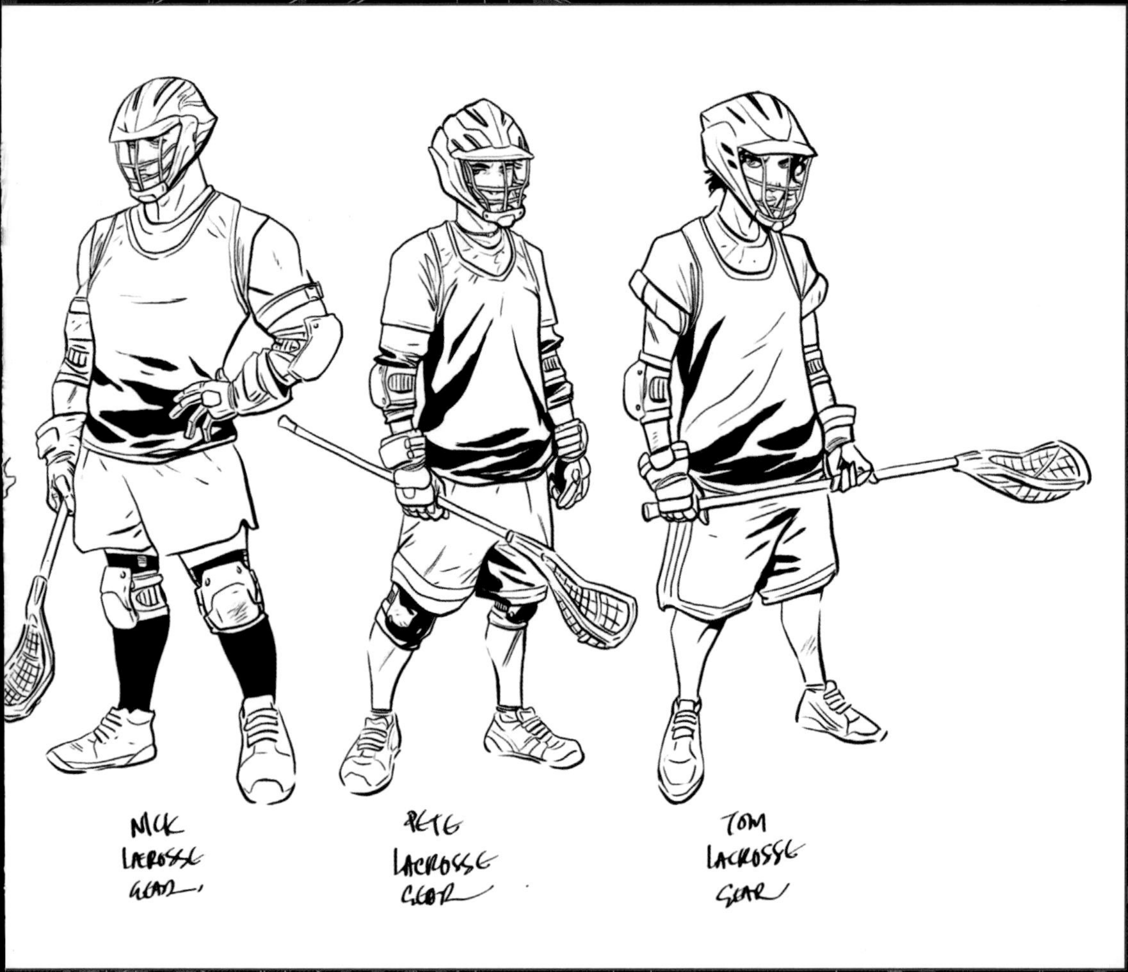
NICK
LACROSSE
GEAR
PETE
LACROSSE
GEAR
TOM
LACROSSE
GEAR

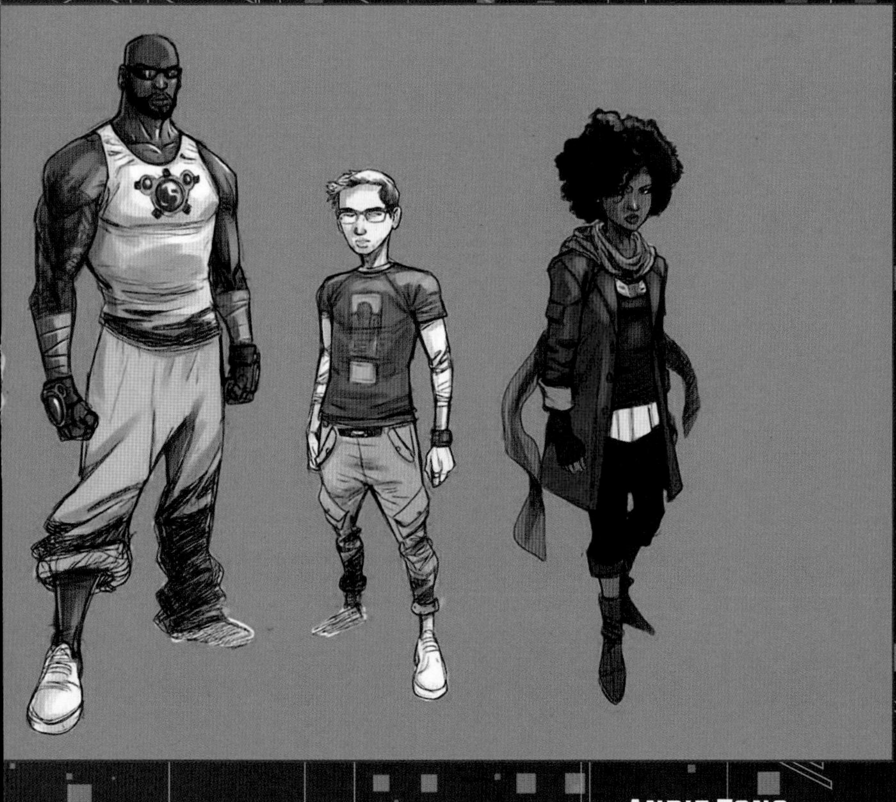

CHARACTER AND CONCEPT ART BY **ANDIE TONG**

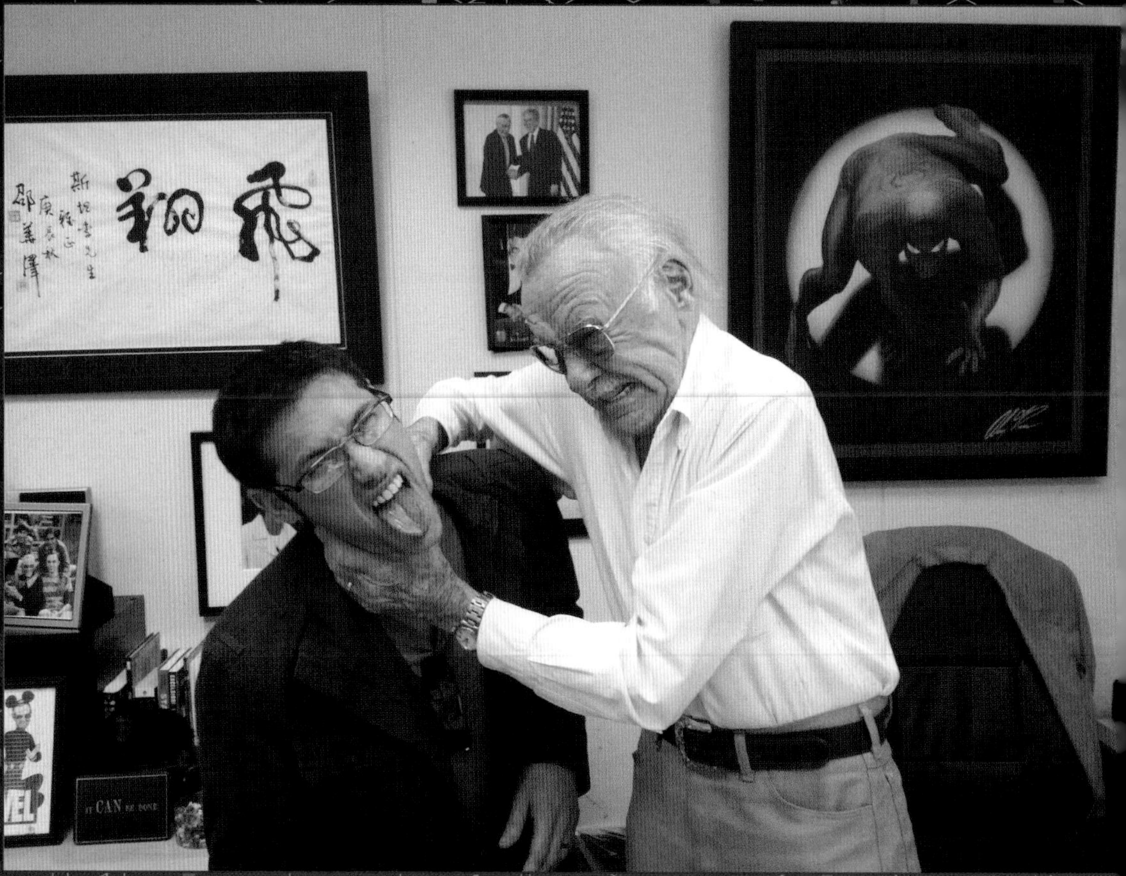
CAN

TOM AKEL AND STAN LEE WORK OUT A DISAGREEMENT ON THE SCRIPT.

Stan Lee's back channel

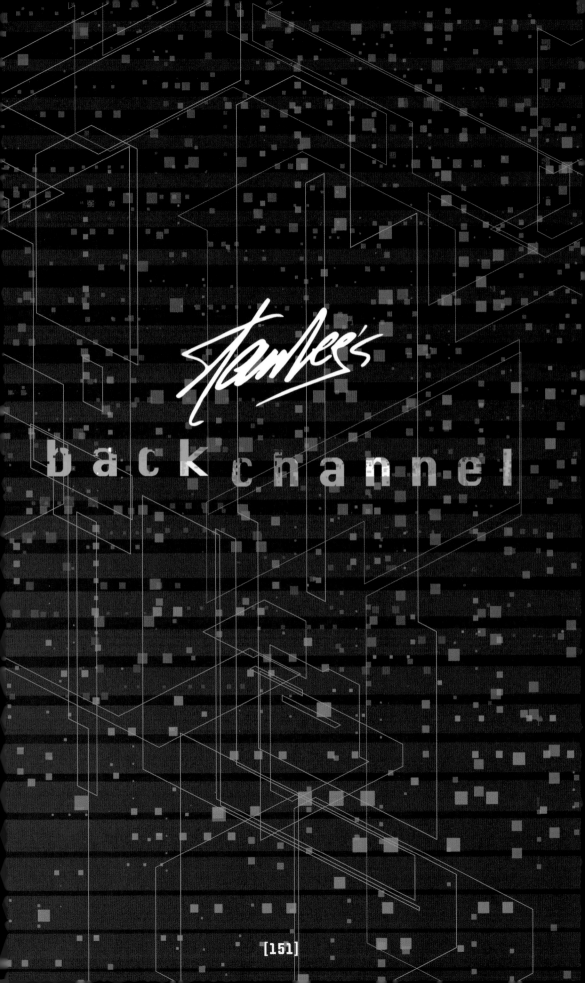

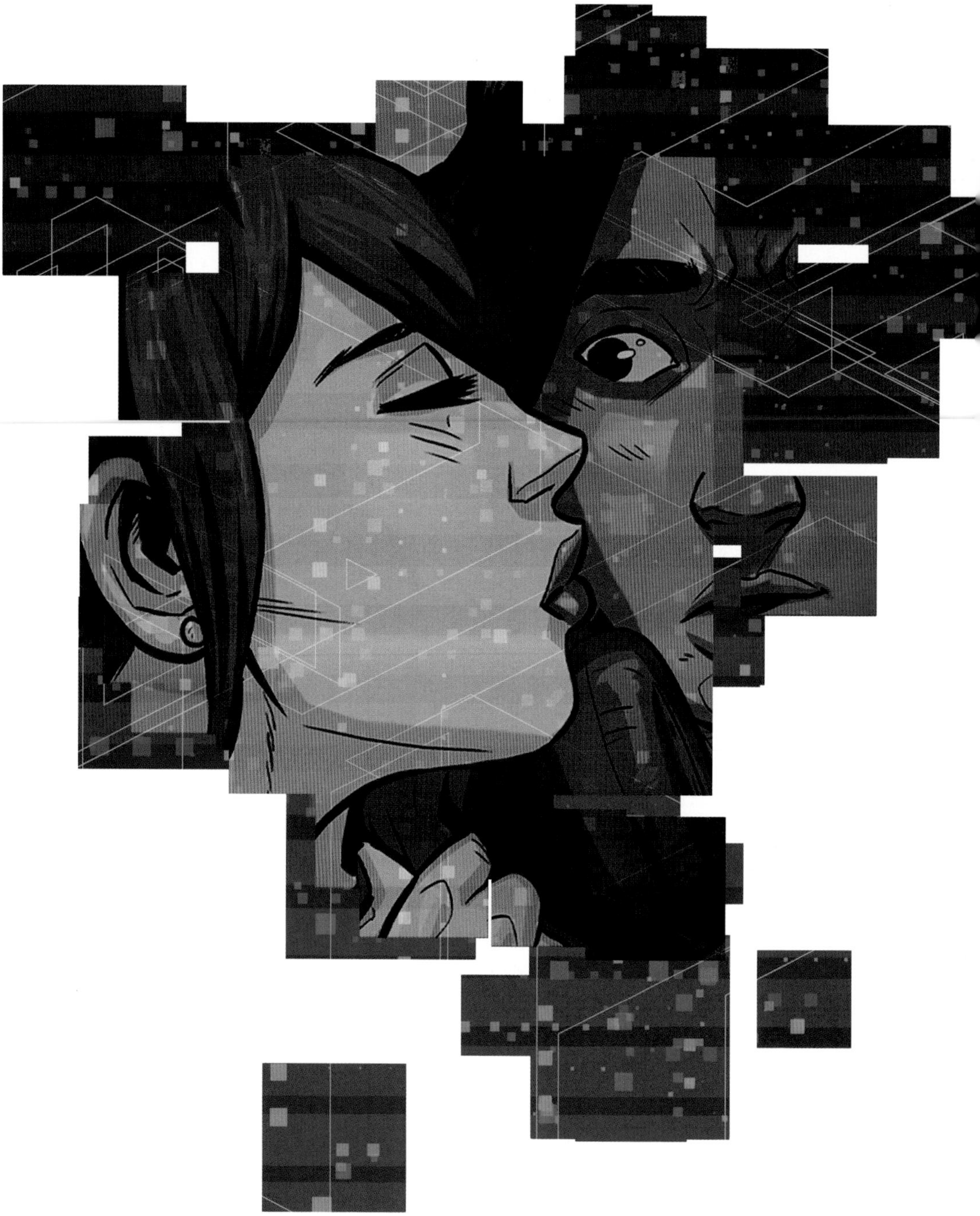

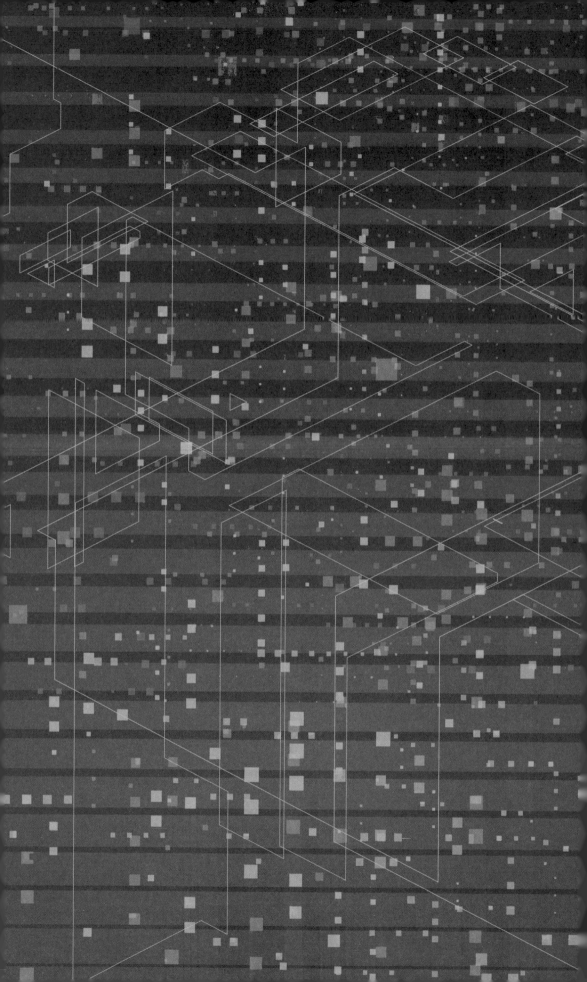